SHACKING UP

HELENA HUNTING

St. Martin's Paperbacks

This is a work of fiction. All of the characters, organizations, and events portrayed in this novel are either products of the author's imagination or are used fictitiously.

SHACKING UP

Copyright © 2017 by Helena Hunting.
Excerpt from *I Flipping Love You* copyright © 2018 by Helena Hunting.

For information address St. Martin's Press, 175 Fifth Avenue, New York, NY 10010.

ISBN: 978-1-250-19966-9

Our books may be purchased in bulk for promotional, educational, or business use. Please contact your local bookseller or the Macmillan Corporate and Premium Sales Department at 1-800-221-7945, ext. 5442, or by e-mail at MacmillanSpecialMarkets@macmillan.com.

Printed in the United States of America

SMP Swerve trade paperback edition / May 2017
St. Martin's Paperbacks edition / December 2018

St. Martin's Paperbacks are published by St. Martin's Press, 175 Fifth Avenue, New York, NY 10010.

10 9 8 7 6 5 4 3 2 1

For my family, whose love and support make this dream of mine possible

CHAPTER 1

KEEP YOUR TONGUE
TO YOURSELF

RUBY

I set the half-full limoncello martini—it's as close to honey and lemon water as I'm going to get right now—on the table, and nab the waiter as he passes. Taking one of the offered napkins, I daintily select a variety of appetizers, oohing over the mushroom blah blah blah canapés. The name of the appetizer doesn't matter as much as how good it is. My taste buds are dancing with joy and so is my stomach. If this engagement party is an indicator of what the wedding will be like, I'm going to smuggle Tupperware in my purse.

My best friend, Amalie—who I refer to as Amie and have since we met in prep school—is marrying an insanely wealthy man, which makes sense since she also comes from an incredibly wealthy family. This union is still a couple of steps up the social ladder for her, so in her family's eyes, she's making a very smart partner choice.

As a product of the same kind of privileged background, I will say this financial partnership dance is one of the less desirable parts of being among the wealthy. Our parents all preach about marrying for love—but really, it's marrying for love of the bank account and maintaining status. Amie's fiancé has a bank account the size of a porn star's dingle—according to her reports, his actual dingle is just average, which is a little sad. But you can't have everything.

I ignore the waiter's disapproving frown as I delicately shove an adorable shrimp tart in my mouth to make room for one more on my cocktail napkin. Plates would be far more effective, but I set mine down somewhere and someone's already been by to clear it away. I'll make do with the napkin.

My current employment status—or unemployment status, to be more accurate—means I've had to resort to a modified eating plan. One that consists of a lot of ramen noodles. I could ask my father for help, more than he already provides, but requesting additional funds will prove, to both of us, that I'm struggling to make it on my own. That is *not* an option. The minute I do that, he'll have me moving back to Rhode Island so I can sit behind a desk and become another one of his corporate drones. That definitely ranks low on my list of awesome things to do with my life.

I wait until the waiter has moved on to the next group of people, make sure no one's paying attention to me, then pretend I'm looking for something in my purse—which, in reality, I am. I stealthily open the plastic baggie, fold up the napkin with the shrimp tart, and slide it inside.

This is the third time I've done this tonight. I've racked up quite an array of snacks for the next couple of days. They'll make nice sides for my Raman noodle dinners. And lunches.

Between appetizer thieving sessions, I've been busy scoping out the hotties since I'm without a date. I suppose I could've invited someone, but an engagement party is the kind of event that indicates interest in further dates. Currently there's no one I'm that interested in. Besides, I have an audition tomorrow and I can't be up late. This negates any potential for post-date make-out sessions, so it's better that I came alone anyway.

Instead of wallowing in self-pity over my datelessness, I'm ranking the eligible bachelors on their hair and shoes. Hair says a lot about a man. I know who has plugs and who doesn't. Plugs indicate self-consciousness and excessive vanity.

Shoes also tell me a lot about the type of man I'm interacting with. If the shoes are pointier than mine, the man is usually too high maintenance and by that I mean that his expectation of women is outside of anything that I'd ever be willing to comply with. Plugs and pointy shoes are the worst of the worst. Those men are the ones most likely to insist on boob jobs and liposuction—whatever it takes to make their wives look as close to Barbie as possible. I refuse to be someone's silent arm candy.

"Ruby? Everything okay?" Amie puts her hand on my shoulder.

"What? Oh, yeah. Everything's fine. I have to get going, unfortunately." I should've left half an hour ago, but the food is incredible.

She side hugs me. "I'm glad you could come for a little while."

"I honestly wish I could stay longer. I feel bad about having to leave so early." And without even one phone number. Although, in fairness, I've been distracted with appetizer thieving.

She waves a dismissive hand. "I'm sure there will be

plenty more parties before the wedding. I know you must be nervous about the audition, and excited."

"I'm crossing everything that it goes well tomorrow. I'd even cross my vagina lips if they hung low enough."

Amie coughs and glances around to make sure the pickle-up-the-ass trust-fund boys missed my inappropriate vagina talk.

"Sorry." I only sort of mean it. I don't want to embarrass my friend, but it's only since a massive three-carat-diamond-toting man came into her life that she's adopted this somewhat snooty, upper-crust attitude. Vagina jokes used to be our thing. At least in college they were.

She flutters a hand around in the air, the one with the rock, and smiles. "It's fine. I shouldn't even care, but Armstrong's mother will end up with a case of the vapors if she hears anyone say anything pertaining to who-has."

That my best friend is referring to girl parts as "who-ha" is more reason to worry about this engagement. Never have we traded dirty sex-part names for highbrow, approved ones until now.

"Amalie! There you are. I've been looking for you everywhere. I need you for photographs."

Amie turns to address the woman who's approaching. "Oh! I'm so sorry. I didn't realize they were scheduled now."

She looks as if she's probably somewhere in her late fifties, although extensive surgeries keep her skin baby-bottom smooth, at least the skin on her face. Her neck tells another story. I take in the rest of her. She's wearing a black dress that says funeral more than engagement party and around her neck is some kind of animal. "Is that alive?" I reach out, as if I'm about to give her pet a pat, but her recoil has me mirroring her.

"Ha!" she barks out a laugh. "Aren't you a funny one." Her tone seems to imply she doesn't find me funny in the least.

"That's a stole," I say stupidly. "Is that a fox?"

She strokes the dead animal wrapped around her neck, her lip peeling back in distaste. "It's a mink."

At least it's not a baby seal. Who in the world wears fur stoles in this century unless they've been abandoned in the wilderness and need it for survival? And it's May. "Let's hope PETA isn't waiting outside with a bucket of paint, huh?"

She blinks at me.

"Gwendolyn, this is my best friend and maid of honor, Ruby Scott. Ruby, this is Armstrong's mother."

Shit. I've just insulted my best friend's soon-to-be mother-in-law. This is not a good start.

Gwendolyn holds out a hand as if she's expecting me to kiss it. I shake it instead. "Oh, yes. Amalie's told me about your family. Scott Pharmaceuticals, isn't that right?" She tilts her head and arches a brow, or at least I think that's what she's doing. It's hard to tell since very little of her face seems to move.

"Uh, yes." I hate this part. The way people look at me differently the moment they know who my family is and that I come from money. Then there's the judgment that I don't quite belong because I'm "new" money, unlike Amie. I'm third-generation trust fund, but in this circle, that's considered new.

"Your father's new medical laboratory has made some groundbreaking discoveries, hasn't it?" She sounds like she disapproves. Maybe her husband has discovered the wonders of the artificial, never-ending hard-on and her dried out vagina is angry with me.

My father's team created the newest erectile dysfunction medication. It's a real porn-star legacy. I nod and smile, even though my father had absolutely nothing to do with the actual development of the medication. He just struts around making people think he did.

"Ruby is just on her way out. I'll be along in a moment and then we can take some pictures."

"Of course, of course." Gwendolyn waves us off as Amie takes my arm and guides me away. Gwendolyn is already striking up a conversation with someone else.

"I'm sorry about the stole comment," I mutter as we cross the room.

"It's fine. She's drunk, so she probably won't remember anyway."

She seems like a real piece of work. It also explains a lot about Armstrong. I'm still trying to figure out his allure. He seems to walk around with an entire jar of pickles rammed up his ass at all times. I'm also wary about how fast things have moved. They've only been together for a few months, but Amie seems convinced they're a match made in heaven. I guess the scandalous option of divorce down the line is there if necessary.

Not that I'm predicting divorce or anything.

I'm just rather familiar with the way these men trade in wives like cars when the model gets a dent—or the Botox stops erasing the wrinkles. My own father is on wife number three. His current wife is all of twenty-eight. She used to be his secretary—so cliché.

Amie fingers my hair when we reach the door to the ballroom. I used a curling iron to no avail, it's already straightened itself out for me. Amie has this incredible wavy, sandy blond hair, the opposite of mine in color and body. "Should I give you a wake-up call in the morning? Just to make sure you don't sleep through your alarm?"

"You don't have to do that. You'll be exhausted tomorrow morning after this. You should sleep in for once."

"I have to work tomorrow. I'll be up early."

I don't really understand why anyone would plan an engagement party on a Monday night, but apparently Armstrong's mother was highly influential. Even if it had been on a weekend, there's a good chance Amie would be up early anyway. It doesn't matter what time she goes to bed at, her internal alarm is set for 5:45 a.m.

"Sounds good. Maybe you can come by my place for lunch or something later?" I'm sure I can manage to scrounge up enough money to buy the necessary items to make sandwiches.

She makes her scrunchy no-no face. "I'm having lunch with Armstrong's mother to discuss wedding plans."

I mirror her displeased expression. "Have fun with that."

"We can do dinner later in the week. My treat."

"You don't have to buy." In all honesty, I can't afford to go out for dinner with Amie unless we do the dollar menu at the burger place down the street from my apartment, but my pride won't let me admit that. Sadly, Amie swears that place gave her food poisoning, so she refuses to entertain eating there. Being in between jobs sucks.

"I'll take you out to celebrate your audition."

"If you insist." I would love to eat something that isn't from a cellophane package.

"I do." She smiles, as if it's not a big deal. I'm already reviewing the menus at various restaurants and picking the most reasonable, filling dinner options.

Amie's unaware of how dire my financial situation currently is. I honestly didn't realize how bad it was until

I checked my account yesterday. The one my father doesn't know about. The one that's very close to zero. Until three weeks ago, I had a steady paycheck and a role in a successful production that had been running for five months. I'd known something was up when the last two paychecks were late, and then bounced entirely. The production company had gone bankrupt, and I suddenly found myself with no income.

To make matters even worse, less than a week later, my agent decided to take early retirement with no warning. She dumped her entire client list, leaving us all scrambling for representation. So far I'm not having much luck securing a new agent, or a new role.

I need this role, otherwise I'm going to have to bite the bullet and get a part-time gig making overpriced coffee for the over-pampered dicks in this room. Which I'm not opposed to. It just sucks, given that I graduated with a Triple-Threat Award from Randolph almost two years ago. I naively assumed my ability to sing, dance, and act would mean an automatic ticket to Broadway. Boy was I ever wrong about that. So far, I've managed two small parts in Off-Off Broadway productions. Hopefully tomorrow pans out and I'm back on the payroll. I don't really want to entertain the alternatives, so I'm thinking positive and hoping for the best.

I give her a hug, drain my martini, set the glass on the table, and tell her to have fun . . . As much as she can, considering the crowd she's managing. The massive chandeliers hanging from the ceiling have been dimmed, so the lighting isn't great. Or maybe it's the effects of the martini impacting the clarity of my vision.

I've never been a big drinker. In college when my friends were chugging beer and doing keg stands at frat parties, I'd be the girl nursing the same red plastic cup all night. It didn't help that all they usually had was beer, which I've never developed a taste for. So even though I've been sipping the same martini since I arrived, downing the back half of it hits me like I've chugged an entire bottle of vodka straight without eating . . . For at least two days. The feeling won't last long, but it's discombobulating regardless.

I step through the doors and decide before I jump on the subway I should use one of the nice, swanky bathrooms. I'm not sure my bladder will be able to make the trip home and the walk to my apartment. Only a few people mill around in the open foyer, talking on cell phones. I spot the restroom sign and head in that direction, attempting to maintain poise.

The lighting in this hall is even worse, with only a few accent lamps illuminating the way. It's kind of creepy. The actual bathroom is lovely, with a couch in the corner and a primping mirror. Some woman with ridiculously high heels, abnormally long legs, and a super short, tight dress is currently taking up residence in front of the mirror with half her purse contents strewn over the counter. She's also talking on her phone, speaker style. She might be on video chat, actually, based on the way she has her phone propped up.

She pauses for a moment, her gaze shifting to me for a quick glance. I don't even have half a second to form a polite, potentially fake smile before she pulls a face as if she's smelling garbage and looks away.

I push through the first door to find a plugged toilet. Holding back a gag I move on to the next one and find it's clean. Once I'm locked safely in my stall, the modelesque bitchy chick resumes her conversation, as if closing the door somehow makes it impossible for me to hear what she says.

I drape my shawl over the hook, along with my purse, and hike up my skirt, tucking it into the front of my dress to prevent it from getting wet and pull a hover squat. I don't care how nice these bathrooms are, I don't want my skin touching the seat if I can avoid it.

"Ugh," the woman preening moans. "Do you think this dress makes me look fat?"

I make a face at the door and hold in a snort. She's rail thin.

"You look amazing. I bet you look better than Armstrong's fiancée. I don't know why he's even marrying her. Her family doesn't have nearly as much money as his."

"But they're old money, and you know what that means."

Her friend makes a disapproving sound. "Still."

"Her dress is so last year. Anyway, I think my date with Banny is going really well."

"Now that he's not doing that soccer thing anymore and he's taking a role in his family business, he's definitely more appealing."

"He played rugby, not soccer, and I totally agree."

I roll my eyes at their conversation. These girls are the exact reason I rebel against the entire room of people out there and everyone associated with them. So shallow.

"Do you think you'll get an invite back to his place?" her friend asks.

"I really hope so. That would be ideal, but I don't know, he's been sick or something. He's been taking cold medication all night. Not that it matters. Do you think I should have sex with him if he does invite me back, or should I play it coy? I need another date out of this, so I don't want to come across as too easy."

"Maybe just a blow job, then?"

"That's a good idea."

"And don't let him take your clothes off."

"Of course not. I did send him that picture of me suck-ing on a lollipop a few minutes ago. You don't think that was too forward, do you?"

"He used to be a professional athlete, I'm sure he's used to forward."

Wow. This is a seriously classy conversation. I finish my business and avoid eye contact as I head for the sink and turn on the water, hoping to drown out their conver-sation.

There are little bottles of lotion, packaged mints, and, ironically, lollipops arranged by the disposable hand towels. I select a grape one, unwrap it, and pop it in my mouth. I also take a package of mints. If I was alone, I might have hocked everything in that little basket.

I drape my shawl over my hand so I don't have to touch the handle, or anything really.

As I'm passing the men's room the door swings open and a huge suited-up guy steps out. He's a tank of a man, his shoulders so broad he has to turn a bit to get through the door. He's staring at the phone in his hand and nearly walks into me. I have the self-preservation required to at-tempt to get out of his way, lest he mow me over. But my grace has taken a vacation and I stumble into him instead of away, while simultaneously trying to get the lollipop out of my mouth so I don't appear completely trashy.

"Hey!" His voice is a low, deep rasp. Like sex dragged over smooth stones.

I grab the lapels of his suit jacket to stop from toppling over and he wraps an arm around my waist, to keep me upright I suppose.

I barely get a glimpse of his face before he's right in mine. "You're a bit forward, aren't you?" His nose brushes my cheek as he speaks, warm breath caressing my lips. Warm breath that smells like booze.

"I don't think—" My attempt at a protest doesn't have the desired effect since he takes the parting of my lips as an invitation for his tongue to enter.

The first thing I notice is how much he tastes like scotch. What's worse is that I can probably name the brand if I think about it hard enough.

He groans into my mouth and his arm tightens around my waist. Obviously this guy's made a mistake, but as shocked as I am, I have to admit, he's a great kisser.

Aside from the boozy taste, his lips are full and soft, and he does this sweep thing with his tongue that makes my knees forget their purpose—which is to keep me upright or knee him in the nuts for attacking me with his mouth. All the right parts of my body start to warm and tingle as our tongues dance—that's right, I said our, because I'm definitely kissing him back, even though I'm not the intended tongue target.

My eyes are wide as a result of the unexpected, although not unwelcome, assault, so I can see his long, pretty lashes resting against his cheek and the straight slope of his nose. I think in addition to being huge, he might also be hot.

I flatten my hands on his chest with the intention of pushing him away, because that's what I should do instead of allowing the continued tongue gymnastic routine. I note first, the solid wall of muscle underneath, followed by the softness of the fabric. Instead of creating space between us, I accidentally smooth my hands over the lapels, up past the collar where I'm met with warm skin. His hand shifts from my hip to my ass. Suddenly, I can feel a whole lot of something going on behind his fly. At my gasp he makes another low noise in his throat.

Before I can decide whether I should still shove him away or keep making out with him, a shrill, familiar voice cuts through Awesome Kisser's rumbling groan. It's close. Like right in my ear. "Ban—What are you doing?"

His tongue retracts from my mouth and his hand from my ass. Turning his head toward the horrific noise, his confused gaze flips between me and the bathroom selfie girl, and then he coughs, right in my face.

I make a gagging sound and use my shawl to wipe his spit from my cheek while Awesome Kisser apologizes— to whom I'm uncertain. He searches his pocket for something—a tissue maybe?

Bathroom girl gives me a look of revulsion and turns her angry gaze on Awesome Kisser. "This"—she sweeps a hand down, gesturing to her ultra-fit body wrapped in her tight dress—"could've been yours tonight." She spins on her eleven-inch heels, her hair fanning out impressively as she sashays past us down the hall.

"Brittany, stop! I thought she was you!"

Of course her name is Brittany. It's a common money name, like Tiffany and Stephanie and all the other names that end with an *ie* or *any*. Not that mine is any better. How I ended up with a name like Ruby, I'll never know. I'm not even born in July, so it has nothing to do with my birthstone.

The only similarity between Brittany and me is that we're female, with hair on our heads. Hers is close to the same color as mine in this awful lighting, but it's about eight inches shorter. We're also both wearing dresses. They're both dark, mine a deep wine color and hers black. Mine hits a few inches above my knee, hers barely skims the bottom of her ass.

Brittany spins dramatically to face her could've-been-bed-partner, her expression incredulous. She gestures a perfectly manicured hand at me. "How drunk are you? You think this bargain-basement-wearing slut looks like me?"

I huff. "Seriously? If your dress was half an inch shorter your vagina would be showing, and you're calling me a slut?" Mostly I'm jealous of how good she looks in it, but she's the one who started with the insults. Besides, I'm not at fault here. It's the amazing kisser who stuck his talented tongue in my mouth and subsequently ruined the hotness by coughing in my face.

Awesome Kisser steps between us, his wide shoulders almost blocking out my view of the angry skankatron. "Whoa, ladies, it's a simple misunderstanding, let's not get nasty." I note the barely imperceptible slur at the end, extending the *s*. He reaches out and puts a hand against the wall, as if he's barring a potential attack, except then I realize it's to steady himself. He's definitely drunk. Which would explain the accidental tongue-nastics.

"I don't know why I'm wasting my breath," Brittany sneers. "I'm going home. Delete my number."

He runs a frustrated hand through his thick, wavy, luxurious hair. And this man does not have plugs either, all that sexy is his. "Fuck." He turns and gives me a quick once-over. I take a quick look down and notice his shoes are black and polished, with no pointy toe. Confident and low maintenance.

I note a few important details while he assesses me, the error that cost him the hot sure-thing. First of all, his eyes are bloodshot and his focus is divided, which could very well explain his inability to discern me from the dark-haired Barbie doll storming away. His nose is a little red and he seems pale. His brow is also glistening just a smidge. I also note the very obvious lump jacking up the front of his dress pants. I feel some satisfaction that my kissing skills are decent enough to give him a woody.

Finally, and most important, this brick house of a man is smokin' hot, even if he is sick, based on Brittany's bathroom reports. Like on a scale of one to ten he's a seven million.

He clears his throat. "I'm really sorry I sexually harassed you and coughed on you. I've been popping cold meds like candy tonight and I think I had one too many scotches. I honestly thought you were her, even though clearly you're not."

Well that's rude.

He gestures to my body and then my face as he expels a quick breath. "I mean, you're, wow, just—hot."

Or maybe he's not that rude.

"Anyway, she's a friend of the family, so I have to fix this. I need to go. You might want to take some vitamin C or something when you get home."

With that unnecessary, but somewhat appreciated, explanation he turns around and jogs down the hall.

I guess I should be flattered that he mistook me for a supermodel, even if he is hammered and drugged.

CHAPTER 2

THE IMPACT OF FLU MEDICATION AND ALCOHOL

BANCROFT

I take one last look at the woman I accidentally molested before I follow Brittany's swishing hair and swaying ass down the hall and through the foyer. If Brittany wasn't my date, and I hadn't promised my mother I'd give going out with her an honest shot, I'd be inclined to go back and get that girl's number. She's got a nice mouth. In the very short time I kissed her, I imagined putting things other than my tongue in it. Not very refined of me, but honest nonetheless.

I don't call after Brittany once I'm in the foyer. I know too many people and I think, based on her recent reaction, she's likely to throw a fit, drawing attention I don't need. What I should've done was canceled tonight, on account of being sick as a dog this past week. But I didn't want to upset my mother by canceling the date, or piss Armstrong off by missing the engagement party, so I loaded up on a variety of drugs and bit the bullet. Now I'd have to smooth things over with Brittany.

Pretty much the second I picked Brittany up, she alluded to coming back to my place later.

I've heard some rumors about her and her mouth—and not just about her penchant for gossip, which I'm also familiar with, since I've known Brittany most of my life.

The selfie of her sucking on the lollipop was a pretty solid indicator that a nightcap would not just involve talking. When I ran into that woman in the hall, I assumed it was Brittany making her move and figured I might as well get it over with. I should've known better than to jump on that opportunity, since it would likely cause more unnecessary issues, but the cold meds and the drinks tonight are messing with my ability to make rational, well-thought-out decisions, hence my making out with some random woman in the hall.

Besides, bringing Brittany was a favor, orchestrated by my mother. Apparently Brittany's date ditched her at the last minute and my mother thought it would be the perfect opportunity to swoop in and play matchmaker. Normally, I don't bend to my mother's whims when it comes to my dating life, but, a little over a year ago, the importance of family was pretty much thrown in my face all at once. She had a health scare, one that resulted in a battery of tests and lot of anxiety. It was during the middle of the championships, so I couldn't come home at all while she was in and out of the hospital. To make matters worse, not long after that, my grandmother passed away. She was an incredible woman; her loss shook us all. She'd been very much the glue in our family. So, ever since I moved back to New York, my mother has been on me about dating and settling down. I have a lot of guilt about not being there for her when she needed me so I caved when she suggested the date with Brittany.

It also got me out of the charity bachelor auction that she was going to volunteer me for, but I had to agree to a second date. According to her, Brittany comes from "good breeding," which in the world I was raised in, is more important than it should be.

I understand that my mother's views on relationships aren't uncommon based on her upbringing, and there may have been a time when I would've probably shared her ideals. But I've spent the last seven years playing professional rugby, and it's changed my views on a lot of things. Relationships, and how they function, or rather dysfunction, being one of them.

I don't make eye contact with anyone as I maintain a brisk, but casual stroll toward the elevators. It's taking more effort than I expected to stay on a straight path. People kept handing me scotch tonight, it was hard to say no, especially in this crowd.

Brittany's too-high shoes prevent her from making a speedy escape. She walks like she's on the runway no matter where she goes. It's a little ridiculous. She reaches the elevator just as the doors open, so I have to pick up my pace. She keeps jamming the button, but I shove my arm in before the doors can close all the way and step inside.

"Thanks for holding the elevator for me." I should rein in the attitude, but I'm annoyed at the negative turn in my evening. And the cold meds I took a few hours ago are already wearing off. I feel like garbage.

She makes a disgruntled sound, crosses her arms over her chest and stares straight ahead.

I don't feel like dealing with this. I could manage when she was being flirty and alluding to things she wanted to do later. Now she's being an overdramatic princess, and I don't do overdramatic princesses. Although,

I can understand her current discontent even if the hissy fit seems unnecessary. Mistake or not, I did stick my tongue in someone else's mouth when I'm supposed to be her date.

I lean against the opposite wall as the elevator descends. "I'm sorry about that other girl. I thought it was you."

"I'm not going home with you tonight," she huffs.

I shove my hands in my pockets. If she still wanted to come back to my place, I'd have more concerns than I already do about her. There's no fucking way I'd sleep with her anyway, because I like my balls where they are and I'm not interested in losing them to her father if he found out I screwed his daughter the first time I took her out. "That's probably a good idea. I'm still not feeling a hundred percent."

I have a business trip coming up in a few days and a meeting tomorrow morning. I don't have time for this. I'm still in recovery mode from this cold and flu double slam I've been hit with and I can't afford to feel like this when I'm getting on a plane in the near future.

"I can't believe you thought she was me. I'm prettier than her, aren't I?" She lifts her chin and sniffs, her offense clear.

That other woman is ten times hotter, but telling Brittany that would be me digging myself a deeper hole. Honesty isn't always the best choice. I'm in such a bad mood now. "I didn't get a good look at her." It's lame, but I've written off any more fun for tonight. In my head, I'm already in the shower, rubbing one out to the image of the woman I did kiss, not the one pouting in the corner.

Besides, Brittany really isn't my type. She's pretty, but she wears far too much makeup. In the few seconds I had to get a good look at the woman I made out with in the hall—and recognized the very serious error I'd made—I noticed she's definitely gorgeous. Dark hair and green eyes, not too petite with curves in all the right places and a natural beauty that makes my nuts ache. And that's saying something with all the medication I'm on. I've only had to rub one out twice this week. I'm *that* sick.

"Why're you looking at me like that? I already told you, I'm not coming home with you." Brittany huffs and glances at her reflection in the mirror, fixing out of place hairs.

I shake my head, coming out of my haze. I must've spaced out while she was talking. God, I feel like garbage. "I'm still going to make sure you get home safely." Despite my frustration over the situation, I'm not going to leave her to find her own ride.

"I know how to hail a cab."

I give up on talking and mentally review my checklist for the next few days. My suit is already laid out for my morning meeting—this Monday night engagement party isn't helping me get the sleep I need. I have to be out of the house first thing, and then I need to get on organizing paperwork for my trip. Five weeks overseas is a long time, and I can't afford to forget essential files. This trip is important. It's my test to see if I can manage things without my father breathing down my neck.

The elevator dings and Brittany struts past me, flipping her hair over her shoulder, smacking me in the face. I let her walk on ahead. I've forgotten to call my driver, so I have to spend a few extra, awkward minutes with a pouting Brittany.

Finally the car comes and Ralph, my driver, exits the vehicle, apologizing for the delay. I'm sure he can tell by the look on my face, and Brittany's sour expression, that neither of us is excited about having to wait.

I open the door for her and extend a hand, which she ignores.

"We'll just head to Ms. Thorton's, 'kay Ralph?" I pat him on the shoulder and he lifts a brow, but remains silent as I slide in beside my annoyed date.

She shifts away from me until she's in the corner. I lean my head against the backrest and wait, because this can't be the end of her words. I'm so tired. And then I remember that my mother made me agree to two dates. I'm beginning to wonder if the bachelor auction would have been better than this. My mother will make sure I follow through on my promise. She's determined to have me settled down since my older brother, Lexington, whose former girlfriend ended things several months ago, has shown no interest in returning to the dating pool, unless it's for a hookup.

Seven years of being on the road, of constant travel, has made any kind of lasting relationship impossible. I've learned that long-distance relationships rarely ever work. When I agreed to come work with my father I assumed I'd finally be able to put down some roots. And with that, I might actually be able to find someone I could have a relationship with. It's been a long time since I've had something stable, or significant. Except now he's making me travel again and the distance thing just isn't something I want to contend with.

"I don't look anything like that slut."

Brittany pulls me out of my internal musings. "Nope." Arguing seems pointless. "Although I'm not sure I'd classify her as a slut."

"Do you know her? Have you gone out with her before? Did you know she was going to be at the party? I can't believe you'd do that to me in front of all those people!"

I slowly turn my head to look at her. This is an awful lot of drama for a first date. "No, I don't know her. No, I haven't gone out with her before. No, I didn't know she'd be at the party, and what do you mean all those people? We were the only ones in that hallway."

"She was kissing you back! I saw tongue! Hers! In your mouth." She points an accusing finger at me. "And yours was in hers."

This is true. Despite me being a complete stranger, my mystery girl did indeed kiss me back. That's something to ponder later. "Look Brittany, I already told you, it was a mistake. And I get that she doesn't look like you, but the hallway was poorly lit. I saw long hair and a dark dress and I reacted. I've been sick all week and on cold medication all day. I didn't want to cancel our date, so I took more than I should've tonight. I know it's not an excuse, but it's the truth." I avert my gaze and close my eyes trying not to picture the woman I ended up kissing tonight.

"You're right, it isn't an excuse at all. I thought we were having a nice time." She's pulling out the whiny voice now. "I hope kissing that skank was worth it."

It's a good thing my eyes are closed, otherwise she'd see me roll them.

The car comes to a stop and Ralph buzzes me through the intercom to let us know we've arrived. He won't lower the privacy window or open a door until I buzz him back.

"This is you," I say.

Brittany makes a pouty face. "Too bad we didn't have more fun."

I buzz Ralph to thank him. I may be annoyed by my date, but I still have manners. "I'll walk you to your door."

"You don't need to do that."

I open the door and step onto the sidewalk to wait for her. She rearranges her skirt and takes my offered hand. As she steps out, she flashes me. She's not wearing panties, so I get a glimpse of what I'll be missing out on tonight. I'm sure she's done this on purpose. I assume it's to taunt me. Considering my current state, I'm likely to pass out on her at any minute.

Over the years a lot of women have pulled this move on me. It worked the first few times, but it's a little boring when there's no chase. It's always better when I have to work for it.

I walk her to her door and apologize for what happened, again, even though I'm not sure how sorry I really am anymore. Her theatrics are a little much to handle.

Apparently my courteous actions seem to have flipped yet another one of her switches. After she unlocks the door she turns to me, looking me over as she licks her lips. "You know"—she adjusts my tie, which was perfectly straight before she touched it—"if you really wanted to, you could show me how sorry you are."

As drugged up as I am, I'm almost positive this is a proposition. "Oh? And how would I do that?"

"By coming up for a nightcap."

I turn my head and cough into the crook in my elbow. I can't believe she's still interested after the shitshow tonight has turned out to be.

"I should probably take a raincheck on that, considering I'm not feeling well. I wouldn't want to make you sick, too."

"There are other places you can kiss me besides my mouth."

I have to resist the urge to sit her down and lecture her

on self-respect. I can't believe she's propositioning me after I kissed someone else, accidentally or not.

"That's usually where I start and it seems like a poor idea with how I'm feeling. Wouldn't you agree?"

She sighs and runs her hands over my chest. "I guess. Are you free next week? I'm sure you'll be feeling better by then."

"I'm leaving on a business trip later this week, but can I call you when I get back?" I cringe internally and hope the emotion doesn't make it to my face.

"Okay!" she says enthusiastically.

I let her hug me and give her my cheek when she goes in for a kiss.

I wait until she goes inside before I head back to the waiting car, mystified by her continued interest in me.

As I settle in for the ride home, I think about the woman I did kiss. I definitely need to find out who she is so I can send her flowers and maybe a bottle of vitamin C capsules for my accidental manhandling.

CHAPTER 3

SCREW YOU, AWESOME KISSER

RUBY

I eat an entire Listerine PocketPak on the subway ride home to kill any lingering germs in my mouth from Awesome Kisser. I'm annoyed by the whole thing, but at least he apologized and seemed sincere about the accidental tongue invasion. Too bad the hotness of the memory is marred by raging Brittany and the hack in the face.

After getting home, I rinse with mouthwash, down six vitamin C capsules and some anti-flu holistic stuff, and then I go ahead and make myself my customary before-bed, pre-audition nighttime drink of hot honey-lemon water, and pray I've done a good enough job of ridding myself of cough germs.

I climb into bed, note my sheets lack a fresh scent, question when I last washed them, then I set my alarm and close my eyes. Behind my lids appears the hottie—whose name is apparently Banny, or maybe I misheard and it's Danny. It's not really a hot guy name. I'm going to stick with Awesome Kisser.

Now that I'm past the shock-and-awe factor I can fully

appreciate that man's hotness in the shouty caps sense of the word. It's unfortunate he dates vapid, self-absorbed model-y types and not starving artists. I have a feeling "date" isn't the appropriate word anyway. It's also unfortunate that he has poor coughing manners.

I consider that he was likely a guest at the engagement party and he very well may be a guest at the wedding as well. If I'm still dateless by then he could make an excellent potential dance partner, depending of course on how tight he is with Armstrong. If they're close friends I don't think it's advisable to get involved in any semi-unclothed dancing outside of the wedding celebrations, no matter how hot he is. I don't want to run the risk of encountering him again should things not go as well as one hopes.

Eventually I stop fantasizing about what's under his suit and pass out.

I'm about to find out exactly what's in Awesome Kisser's designer pants when a repetitive, annoying sound distracts me. I pause just before I smooth a hand over the amazingly prominent bulge while he tilts my head back, his soft lips brushing mine, his hot tongue sweeping . . .

The wisps of the dream fade and I crack a lid. The fantasy breaks with the obnoxious sunlight screaming its wake-up call, along with my stupid phone. Sometimes I'm slutty in my dreams.

I reach for the phone, remembering that Amie promised me a morning call, just in case I messed up my alarm, which has happened in the past. I was on the ball last night, though. I set three alarms, all within five minutes of each other so I wouldn't have an opportunity to fall back asleep.

"Rise and shine, Ruby! I'm your wake-up call!" How

she manages to sound so damn chipper at seven-thirty in the morning after her engagement party is beyond me.

A seal-like bark comes out when I attempt to grumble hello and tell her off for interrupting my dream.

"Ruby? Are you there?"

I make a second attempt at speaking but all I manage is another bark.

"Do you have a bad connection? I told you not to go with the cheap provider. You know how terrible the reception is."

I clear my throat and immediately regret it, as it feels like knives are traveling up my esophagus.

"Ruby?" Amie asks again and then sighs. "I'm hanging up and trying again."

Once the line goes dead I immediately hit the video call. Amie picks up right away. She's wearing a white robe with her wavy hair pulled up into a ponytail, looking as fresh as baked bread out of the oven. I on the other hand, look like yesterday's garbage based on the small image in the corner of my phone.

"Oh my God. Are you okay?"

I motion to my throat and shake my head. I give speaking another shot, just in case my inability to make more than random, audible sounds is a result of waking up. I usually don't have to use words until after my morning coffee. All I get is another one of those squeaky moans and more sharp pain in my throat.

Amie sucks in a gasp and slaps her hand over her mouth. "You have no voice!"

I nod.

"How are you going to audition?"

The final dregs of sleep slip away. I mouth *oh God*. A mime is the only part I can audition for with no voice, or one of the dancer roles with no lines. They don't make nearly as much money as central, or even secondary character, roles—which is what I'm hoping to score. The pay scale for that is far higher than for a lineless role. It definitely won't cover the basics, like rent and food, let alone the minimum payments on my credit card. I've been banking on this audition to get me out of the hole I've dug for myself over the past few weeks.

The phone conversation is pointless since Amie can't read lips and I can't respond. She tells me she's coming over. I try to tell her not to bother, but again, with the lack of words it's impossible to convey. I wait until she hangs up and text her to tell her it's not necessary. Besides, this thing I have is clearly contagious since I must've gotten it from Awesome Kisser, and I don't want to pass it on to her. Damn Awesome Kisser—ruining the already questionable state of my life.

I roll out of bed, the full-body ache hitting me with the movement. I must be dying. And I'm not just being dramatic. Every cell in my body hurts. I drag myself to the kitchen and fill the kettle. Maybe a lemon-honey hot water toddy will help restore my voice. Based on my recent unlucky streak, I have my doubts.

I shuffle to the bathroom, turn on the shower, and root around in the medicine cabinet for some decent drugs. All I have is regular-strength Tylenol, so it'll have to do. I climb into the shower without checking the temperature first—it takes forever to heat up and then fluctuates between lukewarm and scalding. I step under the spray during a scalding phase and huddle in the corner until it's bearable.

I'd like to say the shower helps me feel better. It does not. The warm water also does little to help my voice. Although I'm past just squeaking to barely audible one-word phrases, such as "ow." I'm praying to the voice-miracle gods that the honey-lemon combo will further improve my ability to speak.

Once out of the shower I doctor up my water, adding extra lemon and honey. Not only do I burn the crap out of my tongue, it feels like serrated blades coated in acid sliding down my throat. Still, I get dressed in basic black tights and a black tank with a loose, gauzy gray shirt over top. I dry my hair and put on makeup in hopes that appearing put together will make it so. I have to double up on powder when the effort to prepare my face causes me to sweat.

I take a second hot lemon-honey toddy with me on the subway and arrive for my audition half an hour early. Not that my promptness matters. I'm still unable to speak above a whisper. My despair balloons like a marshmallow in the microwave at the mass of people performing voice warm-up exercises around me.

I make an attempt to do the same, but the hoarse, croaklike sound is drowned out by the crystal clear voice of the perfectly gorgeous woman standing next to me. As I listen to the sound of a thousand soaring angels spew out of her mouth, I shiver with what I fear is the beginning of a fever. Sweat breaks out across the back of my neck and travels down my spine, along with a violent shiver. As if today could be any worse than it already is, my stomach does this weird, knotting thing.

"Ruby Scott."

I glance at the director, who's thankfully still looking fresh, and not beaten down by hundreds of craptastic auditions. Those are yet to come. I shoulder my bag and follow him to the theater.

"You're auditioning for the role of Emma today, correct?" He doesn't give me a chance to confirm. "I'd like you to start with the song at the beginning of act two."

"Okay," I croak feebly, cringing at the raspy sound. At least I can speak, even if I sound like a prepubescent boy with his nuts caught in his zipper.

The director looks up from his clipboard, his frown an omen.

"I seem to have lost my voice." He has to strain to hear me.

He heaves a frustrated sigh. "You can't audition if you don't have a voice."

"I didn't want to miss it. Maybe I could audition for a dancer part?" Fewer words are better.

He purses his lips. "Auditions for dancer roles aren't until later in the week."

"I understand, but I'm here and if you can't hear me sing, at least you could see me dance?" I fight the gag reflex as another wave of nausea hits me.

He sighs and relents, gesturing to the stage. I thank him, then drop my bag at the edge of the stage and get into first position. My brain is foggy and my body aches horribly, but I can't pass up this opportunity for a modest, yet steady income for a few months. I can't afford to rack up additional credit card debt, and I don't want to ask my father for more money, because that will make him aware of how much of a struggle this is. Then he'll make his case for me to come work for him, as is his master plan. I know I can do this.

The music cues up, and as I start to move my stomach does that rolling-heave thing again. There isn't any food in it, but all of a sudden the honey-lemon water I consumed this morning decides to stage a revolt. I'm in the middle of a spin—not the best idea when nauseous—and the next wave hits me; violent and unrelenting.

I attempt to keep my mouth closed, but the intensity of the spasm forces it open. I spray the stage with par-

tially digested honey-lemon water, and what appears to
be last night's shrimp tarts and mushroom canapé appetizer dinner—in an *Exorcist*-like dramatic flair.

And thus ends my audition.

It appears I should've come back later in the week for the
dancer role auditions. No amount of apologizing can
make up for my spray vomit. It doesn't help that I've managed to hit the director with my impressive reach. I almost slip on my own puke spray in my haste to find the
nearest bathroom, because a second wave is coming. I
manage to make it to the hall, and a potted plant, before
it hits. By round three I'm in the bathroom. Sadly, it's a
public stall, and based on the odor, the cleanliness is
highly questionable. I wonder if it's reflective of the suc-
cess of this particular theater's productions.

I spend a good hour in there, moaning and crying until
all I can do is dry heave.

The worst part is that in my rush to find a bathroom
to destroy, I forgot my purse in the theater. I'll have to
wait for a break in the auditions before I can sneak back
in and retrieve it.

Thankfully, it's still at the edge of the stage, so I creep
in, grab it, and haul ass—which is really a very slow and
uncoordinated hobble-run—before the director has a
chance to see me again, or I him.

The subway ride home is perilous. People keep their
distance, likely because I have the cold sweats and smell
awful.

Once home, I spend an uncountable number of hours
on the bathroom floor, curled up with a towel as a blanket and a roll of cheap, rough toilet paper as a pillow.

A knock on my door the following morning—I only
know it's morning based on the light pouring through my

bathroom window—is the reason I pry myself away from my makeshift tile-floor bed.

My body hurts, a lot. So does my head and every other part of me. I'm still dressed in my audition clothes. I smell like day-old vomit. Based on the stains on my gray shirt, I didn't have the best aim yesterday. I rinse my mouth with water, and then mouthwash, but it burns, so I spit it out after a quick swish.

I shuffle to the door and check the peephole before I open it. Occasionally solicitors manage to get into the building. I have no interest in someone trying to sway my political leaning or in adopting a new religion today. Although with the way I look I have my doubts anyone would want me to join their organization.

It's not a solicitor, it's Amie. She never stops by unannounced. I've left the chain lock off, apparently unconcerned for my own safety, so I flip the deadbolt and open it.

"Ruby Aster Scott, what is the meaning of this!" She holds a piece of paper in front of my face, too close for me to read.

She drops her hand before I have a chance to take it from her. Also, my reflexes are slow.

Her angry face becomes a shocked one. "Oh my God! What happened to you?" She pushes her way inside, almost knocking me over. Although I'm pretty unsteady on my feet, so I can't blame it completely on her.

Amie covers her mouth with her sleeve. "What's the smell? Why haven't you answered my calls? I was going to call the police!"

"I think I have the flu," I croak. I have more of a voice today than I did yesterday. Sort of.

"I've been trying to get a hold of you for the past

twenty-four hours. You can't do that to me. Really? *What* is that smell?"

"It's probably me."

She drops her arm and sniffs. Her nose wrinkles. "You need a shower. Or a bath." She surveys my apartment and her frown deepens.

I'm admittedly not the best housekeeper. Until a few months ago, I had someone come in every other week to keep it manageable for me. When my father threatened to cut off his financial assistance a few months ago I cut back on unnecessary expenses, which included Ursula. But, I'll blame the current disorder on my illness.

Amie's expensive heels click across the floor as she heads for the bathroom. She gags her displeasure at the smell in there, which I assume is a more concentrated version of me.

A pair of rubber gloves, some bathroom cleaner, a lot of complaining, and fifteen minutes of vigorous scrubbing, and my bathroom no longer smells like the Vomitron. Amie runs a bath in my freshly cleaned tub, pushes me inside, and closes the door.

"Don't come out for at least twenty minutes," she yells from the other side.

I've been friends with Amie since freshman year in prep school. We moved to NYC together five years ago for college. Of the two of us, she's definitely the more successful. Although there is a big difference between a dual degree in business management and public relations and one in theater.

In the two years since we've graduated she's managed to turn her final internship at one of the most popular fashion magazines into a full-time job and she's already been promoted once. On top of Amie's fabulous job with its excellent paycheck, Amie has also managed to meet the man of her dreams—at least that's what she claims—while I routinely manage a handful of dates before I tap out, or until they do when I don't put out. Or I'm kissed by germ-infested strangers with an angry date. I wonder if this is karma's way of trying to tell me something. And if so, what exactly is the message? Don't use the bathroom? Don't suck on lollipops? Be sluttier?

I must fall asleep in the tub, because I startle at the knock on the door. "Ruby? It's been more than half an hour. Are you still alive?"

"I'll be out in five!" I call in my broken, craggy voice.

The water has cooled and I shiver as I rush through washing my hair and my body. I feel a lot more human and a lot less barfy after I'm clean. Exiting the bathroom I find Amie has tidied my apartment.

The garbage and dirty dishes that were stacked in the sink and on the counter have either been thrown out or washed. My sheets have been changed, and the pile of clothes on the floor is now crammed into my laundry basket.

"You didn't have to clean my apartment."

"Well you sure don't seem capable of it. You look like hell. I'm taking it the audition didn't go well."

"Not unless I was trying out for a part in *The Exorcist*." I flop down on my bed, the energy it's taken to bathe requires me to be prone again.

"What do you mean? What happened?" She hands me a steaming mug with a slice of lemon in it. I set it on the nightstand, unsure if I can stomach the last thing I hurled.

I give her the abridged version of the events, including the worst parts, like the projectile vomiting.

"Oh lord."

"Yeah. I don't think I'll be getting another audition with that director unless I officially change my name."

"Do you think it was food poisoning? Oh God. Is this *my* fault?" She claps one hand over her mouth in horror and grips the arm of the chair with the other.

The well-worn chair is one of the few items in this apartment I actually own. I've had it since freshman year of college. I bought it from a thrift store in a show of rebellion against my father, who disapproved fully of my plan to pursue a career in theater. He still footed the bill for what my scholarships didn't cover in tuition. And he dropped money in my bank account that I obviously used along the way—just not for furniture.

"It's not food poisoning. Some random guy mistook me for someone else and jammed his tongue down my throat when I was leaving the party. Then he coughed in my face and his date accused me of being a slut."

"Pardon?" She drops her hand and gives me a disbelieving look.

I can understand why it sounds crazy—and realistically, the whole situation definitely is. Again, I have to wonder if karma is responsible for this. I explain the entire thing from the beginning.

"So this *is* my fault."

"How are you responsible for some random guy mistaking me for his date in a semi-dark hallway?"

"They were probably my guests."

"It's still not your fault." I close my eyes for a few seconds and consider whether or not I can tolerate food yet. The thought of chewing exhausts me.

After a long pause Amie asks, "When was the last time you asked your dad for money?"

It's an odd lead-in question considering my current

state. "Not in a while. Why?" Amie knows how much it burns my ass that I'm still reliant on him at all. For the past five years he's been taking care of my rent, and some of my other expenses. When he threatened to cut me off a while back I opened another account, including an additional credit card and a small line of credit.

My plan was to be able to put away some money on my own and not use his so I could show him, once and for all, that I'm capable of surviving without his bank account. Unfortunately, with the recent lack of paychecks, I've had to use my credit card more than I'd like. And my line of credit.

"Are you by chance planning to move, but forgot to tell me?"

"If I was moving out of this craphole you'd be the first person I'd tell." I have no idea why she's asking me this.

"I was afraid you'd say that." Amie sighs and pushes up, crossing over to my desk—which she didn't bother to clean—and picks up a piece of paper. I live in a studio apartment that's about 350 square feet so it doesn't take much for her to retrieve it. "I hate to bring this up right now, unfortunately, it's kind of a big issue that needs to be managed."

Huge, block letters spell out LEASE TERMINATION NOTICE at the top of the page, followed by a bunch of legal jargon outlining the parameters of my lease agreement and the date by which I have to be out of my apartment, which is five days from now.

I read the blah-blah-blah between the TERMINATION and the date of my lease's expiry. The last three checks have bounced.

"This doesn't make any sense." My father's new secretary—the one he's not married to—puts money in that account every month to cover the rent.

"Maybe you should call your dad."

I drop down on the edge of the mattress. There has to be a reasonable explanation for this. "I'm going to call his secretary." I pull up my contact list and scroll down to Yvette. She's only been working for my father for the past six months or so. I preferred his previous secretary, unfortunately I have a feeling my stepmother may not have appreciated her youth or her bubbly personality. Yvette is significantly older.

Yvette answers on the third ring. "Scott Pharmaceuticals, Yvette speaking, please hold."

"Hi, Yve—" I'm cut off by the elevator music, followed by an advertisement for my father's penis drugs. I roll my eyes and put my phone on speaker while I wait.

Five minutes later she finally clicks back over. "Thank you for holding. Yvette speaking, how may I help you today?"

"Hi, Yvette, it's Ruby."

"Hello. How may I direct your call, Ruby?"

Amie and I exchange a look.

"It's Harrison's daughter."

"Oh! Ruby, of course. How silly of me. Would you like to speak with Harrison? I believe he may be in a meeting, however you can leave a voice mail for him and I'm sure he'll return your call as soon as he can."

"Actually, I think you may be able to help me. I've just received a notice regarding the termination of the lease on my apartment. Apparently the last three checks have bounced. Do you happen to know if there's been an accounting error?" I clench my fists to avoid chewing on my fingernails.

"Oh, hmm. Let me have a look," she says in her high-pitched, lilting voice.

"Thanks so much, Yvette."

"Of course. It's no trouble." Clicking on the other end of the line tells me she looking at my financial files. "Oh, yes! Now I remember! Your father stopped direct deposits to this account about three months ago."

"Why would he do that without telling me?"

"I sent you an email from him with the details. Let me just bring it up." There's more clicking on her end of the line. "Ah! I found it. Oh. Oh, no. It appears it's still in draft form. I'll just send it now. Bloop! There you go! Would you like me to read it to you?"

My phone pings with the email alert. "It's fine. I can open it now."

"I'll just wait while you read it, then." She hums pleasantly while I open the email and scroll. The roll in my stomach grows progressively worse as I absorb the contents. My father stopped his financial assistance three months ago and had his incompetent secretary send me an email notification. Apparently it was up to me to renew my lease and continue the payments. In case I've forgotten his plan, he ends the email with a note that a job would be available should I need to return to Rhode Island. And my whore-mother is looking forward to working with me.

Once my father married whore-mother, he moved her to another department—because God forbid there was a conflict of interest happening. Not only is her paygrade exceptionally higher than before, she was also given a sweet promotion which means my father wants me to work under her. I scrub a palm over my face. I'm not sure if I feel more like crying or vomiting again. It's a real toss-up.

I must groan, or make some kind of noise, because Yvette speaks again. If her chipper voice had a face I'd

want to punch it. "I apologize for the delay in communication."

"It would've been good to have this information
months ago." Not that it would've helped that much. The
rent still would've been a stretch to pay, let alone afford-
ing anything beyond the ramen noodles I've been eating
for the past three weeks. I could've started my new meal
plan that much sooner, I suppose.

"Would you like me to put you through to your father?
I'm not sure when his meeting will be done, but you
can leave him a message, or I can take one down and
give it to him as soon as he comes available." She sounds
nervous now.

Talking to my father isn't going to solve this problem.
It's likely only going to make things worse. "No. No,
thank you Yvette. I need to go. Thank you for your time."
I end the call before she can say anything else.

Amie's staring at me with wide eyes and her mouth
agape. "Why aren't you going to talk to your father? He
can fix this."

"I need to think." I rub my temples. "I have to call my
landlord." So I do. Not that it helps. Turns out my apartment is already rented and I still owe three months of
overdue rent. I'm embarrassed that I didn't even notice
I'd missed it. I imagine it's my father who would've gotten the notification instead of me, because he's the one
who's been paying the rent.

"You have to call your dad and ask him to fix this."

"He can't fix this now."

"He can at least help you out with the rent."

"And then what? I'm still not going to have a place to
live."

About six months ago, just after I scored my last role,

my father and I had had a heated conversation about my career path. He's made his disapproval clear, but he tolerated my choices because of my mother's influence, and her guilt trip. His money still came with a price tag, and in this case it was shame. He'd said I'd finished my program, so I should be employable. If I couldn't manage on my own, I'd be coming home to work for him.

I've heard that lecture so many time I can recite it in my sleep. Until now I thought he was blowing smoke up my rear end. It was after that conversation that I opened my own bank account, secured my own Visa, and the small line of credit. When my paycheck stopped coming in, I opted to raise my credit limit by a few thousand dollars instead of going to him.

If I call him now, I'll have to admit defeat. And I feel as though he may be setting me up for this to happen. It's as if he wants me to fail. If he finds out what's happened, and how I have no other options, he'll definitely send someone for me. Well, he might not send someone. He's more likely to put me on a plane because driving that far isn't on his priority list.

Home is not where I want to be. Home is Rhode Island. Home means I've failed. Home means my dream is dead and my dad was right all along: I'm not good enough for a career on Broadway. Or Off-Broadway. Or anywhere near Broadway.

Admitting failure isn't the worst part. Going home means working for my father's pharmaceutical empire where he deals in penis-hardening drugs. He'll turn me into a corporate drone. I'll have to sit behind a desk and type letters and stamp things and make sure meetings are scheduled in the right rooms. All my creativity will end up in the shredder bin, along with my dignity.

I know there are people out there struggling for a job,

any job, and I should be grateful. And while the idea of working at my father's company is not my idea of fun, it's not the end of the world. Working under his new wife would be it's own special kind of hell. I completely disagree with my father that it would be a good way for us to get to know each other and bond. I told him it's a good way for me to end up in prison for murder. He did not appreciate my humor.

"He's the reason you don't have a place to live, you don't think he'll feel bad and try and make it right?"

"You heard my landlord, the place is already rented. You know as well as I do he's been waiting for this to happen. He wants me to fail."

"He doesn't want you to fail." I give her a look and she sighs again. "What about your line of credit? Can you pay off some of the rent with that?"

I pull up my account details on my phone. Even if I could raise it by a few more thousand, I can't cover three missed months. I shake my head.

"What about a cash advance on your credit card?"

"There's not a lot of room." I have maybe three hundred dollars left before I hit my max. It's a low max, but adding to my credit card debt seems like a bad idea, especially considering my current circumstances.

"Oh God."

"Yeah."

"I could lend you—"

"Nope. No way." I cut her off before she can finish. "I won't borrow money from you."

"You have to let me do something. I'm not going to let you be homeless. You won't do well in an alley. Cardboard boxes aren't your thing."

She's trying to be funny, but the reality of my situation finally slaps me in the face like a three-day-old dead fish. Amie's right. Unless I can find a new place to live and a decent job that can cover more than just rent I'm going to end up homeless or forced to move back home. Worse, I'll have to live in my dad's house with his horrible slutty wife who's four years older than I am and probably screwing the gardener. Or the pool boy. Or both.

Moving to Alaska, where my mother currently lives, is an absolute no-go. New York winters are long enough. Besides, her cabin in the woods and little to no contact with the outside world is a bit on the extreme side for me. I'm fine to live in a crappy apartment in Harlem, but sub-zero temperatures and no neighbors is far outside of my comfort zone.

"I'll get a part-time job."

Amie gives me one of her mothering looks. "Okay, sure, but what about a place to live? You're still going to need to save up at least first and last month, right? And pay back what you owe here. That's a lot of money to come up with on your own."

She makes another good point. "I don't have an alternative, Amie. Not unless I want to move back to Rhode Island, which is the absolute last thing I want."

"I can't believe your dad did this. There has to be a way to make this work. What if you stay with me?"

I give Amie a look. "Where would I sleep? Your couch isn't even a pullout."

Amie purses her lips, considering this. I have a point. Her place is small. Her bedroom is tiny, her queen taking up a good portion of the room. Her living room can't accommodate a full-sized couch because it, too, is small.

"I'll call Armstrong. I'm sure I can stay with him, and then you can have my place while you sort things out." She calls her fiancé and holds up a finger to silence me before I can argue against this plan. "Hi, Armstrong, I have a bit of a favor to ask—" She pauses for a few seconds before she continues. "Do you think it would be possible for me to stay with you for a little while . . . a week or two?" She gives me a questioning look. I shrug and then nod. I doubt two weeks will be enough, but it's better than nothing. "But I—it would just be for . . . right . . . but—" She rolls her eyes and taps her foot.

I don't need to hear the conversation to know what's being said. I mouth *just forget it.*

"I understand. Never mind. I don't want it to be an inconvience for you. We'll figure something else out." Her sarcasm isn't lost on me. She ends the call. "I probably caught him at a bad time. I can try again later."

"You don't have to do that."

"He's just particular. He needs time to warm up to the idea."

I think it's about more than being particular, but I don't know that a week or two will be enough time to get me out of my current hole. My dire situation is far worse than I originally thought. My choices are beyond limited. I've never been good with failure. Especially not this kind. I don't want to be a pampered rich bitch. I want to prove I can survive on my own, without my father's handouts, but I'm worried I might not have an option now.

"Oh my God." Amie's eyes light up. "I might have a solution."

"What's that?"

"Army's cousin, Bane, is going out of town this week."

"What does that have to do with my being homeless?" I'm already deciding which alley would be the best location to set up my box. I still have my gym membership. I think it's valid for another few months. I can use the showers there. "Wait, he has a friend named Bane? Does he look like Tom Hardy?"

"Um, no? His real name is Bancroft," she explains.

"Ah. Another last-name-for-a-first-name trust-fund boy?"

"Mmm. He comes from a line of last names for first names, but he's actually quite nice. Anyway, he asked me to stop by his place and take care of his pets while he's away. He'll be gone for five weeks, maybe you could take care of them instead."

"He doesn't even know me, why would he be okay with a stranger taking care of his pets? And that doesn't really solve my homeless situation."

"You're my best friend. If I trust you, he'll trust you. Besides, he has a rabbit, or a guinea pig, or something like that. He inherited her I think. Maybe we could suggest you stay there while he's gone."

"To take care of his guinea pig?"

"Why not? He said she needs lots of care and play time. And you know how I have allergies. It's worth a shot isn't it? Five weeks should be enough time for you to get a job and save some money to secure a new apartment, right?"

"It should be enough time." I'm not actually sure it will be unless I get a pretty major role, but temporary accommodations will buy me some time to sort that out and it's better than crashing on Amie's loveseat. "When will you ask him?"

"We're going out for dinner with him tonight. Think you can stomach a meal?"

"I can try."

Amie smiles. "Perfect."

"Totally." Fingers crossed this works out. I could really use some good karma. And a home that isn't a box.

CHAPTER 4

DINNER PLANS

RUBY

Upon deciding my new life mission is to become a squatter/pet sitter for the next five weeks, which is slightly more dignified than living in a box in an alley, Amie raided my closet for an introduction-appropriate outfit.

Over the past several years I've traded in my pretentious, ultra-expensive and often uncomfortable clothes for a wardrobe of black, inexpensive pieces with a few colorful items for those days when I want to rebel against New York's mourning-inspired fashion rules. The recent lack of money flow also impedes my ability to buy unnecessarily expensive items to add to my ever-shrinking, unimpressive wardrobe.

"How long have you had this dress?" Amie holds up a little red number.

I shrug. "Awhile."

"Didn't you wear this to high school prom?"

I ponder that for a moment. It's totally possible. I grab the hanger from her and check the tag. It's a Vera Wang, so it had to have cost quite a bit of money. I wouldn't have thought anything about dropping that much on a dress a few years ago. Now I'm considering how much I can get for it if I put it on eBay.

At my prolonged lack of response Amie says, "I'm almost positive you wore this to prom. It's a classic, though, so you could get away with it tonight." She thrusts it at me. "Try it on."

I pull on a pair of panties before I drop my robe. I have no shame, and Amie's seen me in some questionable states, so underwear isn't a big deal. I root around for a clean bra which takes far more effort to put on than it should, then I shimmy into the dress and pull up the side zipper. It's a bit on the snug side in the chest and the hips, but otherwise it's fine. Unfortunately, there's a grease stain on the skirt right over my crotch.

I motion to the spot highlighting my vagina. "Unless I'm looking to draw attention to my pleasure center, I think I'm going to have to pick another option."

"It wouldn't hurt. Bancroft is hot, and from what I've heard he has an excellent skill set in the bedroom."

"The fact that there are rumors about his skill set is not really a selling feature. Besides, I'm not trying to bed him, I'm trying to get access to a bed in his condo. Do you even know if his place has more than one bedroom?"

"He lives in a penthouse in Tribeca. It has more than one bedroom. And the rumors aren't bad. I don't think he's a manwhore, I've just heard he's very . . . equipped."

"So he has a big dick? Whoop-dee-do. His dick is not my primary concern."

Despite my lack of excitement over Bancroft's hotness and his potentially large assets or his skills in the bedroom, I try on another six dresses before Amie approves my dinner outfit. I have to lie down for a while after that.

She spends the rest of the day attempting to nurse me

back to some sort of reasonable health, by feeding me drugs and alternating Gatorade, chicken broth, and a few saltines. At least I can keep liquids and crackers down. When it's time to get ready for dinner, Amie takes care of my hair and makeup because I lack the energy to make it happen. I'd ask why it matters how good I look, but since we're meeting up with Armstrong and this Bancroft guy, I have to assume we're going to some highbrow restaurant where they serve things like skate and Green Elder Rubbed Elk, which begs the question, did a group of unfortunate and senile geriatrics in green jogging suits rub themselves on a herd of elk before they were slaughtered for the upper class's benefit?

At five, we leave my soon-to-be-vacated apartment and take an Uber to the restaurant—Amie's treat since I can't afford anything right now. By this point, I could really use a five-hour nap and another shower. I'm not so sure I'm completely over whatever it is Awesome Kisser passed on to me. I naively assumed it was some kind of twenty-four-hour bug, but the trickle of sweat that slides down my spine concerns me. As does the mild roll in my stomach. It's nothing like the full-stomach seizures that ruined yesterday, but it's still not right in there.

I manage the Uber ride okay, but I'm so clammy even with the windows rolled down that I'm wishing I brought deodorant with me. If I'd planned ahead I could rub it all over my body to solve the sweat issue.

Amie shifts so she's facing me. "So let's review the story one more time just to make sure we have all the details down."

"Okay." This is not an uncommon conversation for us. As teenagers we used to cover for each other often. Well, me for Amie more than her for me, but still, covering happened. There's a reason her nickname was Anarachy

Amie when we were growing up. She was far more likely to use staying at my place as a ruse to go make out with whatever boy she was seeing at the time. Who would've thought that same girl would be marrying someone named Armstrong?

This is a little different because there's a lot more at stake than just being grounded for getting caught in a lie. This is a potential place to live and buying me some time to find an actual job that pays real money again. Enough to help pay my debt down without my father's help. Enough to save me from working with his whore of a wife. Without his financial assistance, I'm finally seeing exactly how easy life has been for me up until now. I know I should be grateful that if I really needed help, he'd be there for me, but the truth is, I wanted to prove, more to myself than anyone else, that I could do this.

"Why don't you have a place to live?" Amie asks, patting my hand reassuringly at my cringe.

"My lease was up and instead of renewing I planned to move into an apartment closer to the theater district, but the new lease agreement fell through."

"Excellent. And why did that happen?"

"Is this really necessary? I doubt it's going to be an inquisition."

"It's better to have a full story outlined with lots of details than something half-assed."

"I can improv."

"I'd agree, except you're sick and I'm not sure your improv skills are all that amazing right now."

"Can you refrain from saying that word aloud right now?" Even that's enough to make me queasy again.

Amie's right, though, my ability to do anything other than breathe and stay upright are severely compromised. I sigh anyway, because we went over this three times before we left my apartment. "The lease fell through because there were problems with the pipes in the apartment above mine. They have to gut the apartment. It could take months to renovate." I give Amie a wide-eyed, sad look, indicating I'm distressed by the unfortunate circumstances I find myself in. And I honestly am.

"Perfect." Amie nods her approval at either my recollection of our fabricated scenario, my superb acting skills, or both. "And why can't you stay in your current apartment?"

"It's already been rented out and the new tenant takes over the lease in five days," I continue rambling, "The only unit available in my complex is scheduled to be rented out mid-month, so I'd be moving my stuff only to move it again two weeks later." Dabbing the back of my neck with a tissue I say, "I still don't think this needs to be so elaborate. Can't we just say there were issues with my new apartment?"

Amie gives me a withering look. "Didn't you learn anything from high school? We want the story to be plausible, the more details the better. What about your job situation?"

"I'm between roles right now, but I have several auditions lined up." This comes out monotone, mostly because yesterday's audition was the last one I had scheduled with my now-retired agent. I'm on my own until I find someone new.

She squeezes my arm. "You'll get something, Ruby, you're too talented not to."

I'd like to believe this, and honestly, a few months ago I did, but my inability to find a new agent and my small Off-Broadway roles make it hard to keep the faith.

"Here we are." Amie smiles as the Uber pulls into the valet and the attendant opens the door. Before we head inside Amie smooths out my hair. "Okay. So when Armstrong or Bancroft brings up the trip I'll be the one to mention the pet-sitting and you can get excited about his guinea pig or whatever it is."

"Sounds good."

"Okay. Let's get you a place to live."

I nod, take a deep breath, and let her link arms with me as the doorman hurries to allow us entrance. Tonight's restaurant choice is exactly as I predicted. Over-Botoxed women in their sixties cling to the arm of their balding, paunchy husbands with wandering eyes. Excessive jewelry tells me the wandering eye has probably extended to a wandering hand, and likely their dick.

I'm familiar with this particular scenario considering it's exactly what my dad did to my mom. Although she was never really one for baubles, so I'm guessing my father found other ways to apologize for his indiscretions. At least until she got tired of the philandering and left.

My mother is gorgeous, but she refused to play by the same rules as so many of the other women in this environment seem to. She wouldn't get the surgery, the facelifts, whatever tucks and nips to keep her looking like the twenty-three-year-old my father married. So he upgraded to a newer model, and test-drove a lot of them along the way.

It's why I'm a little jaded when it comes to the trust-fund boys. Like father like son is usually how it tends to go, and I haven't met many fathers who aren't looking at their daughters' friends like they're the next toy they want to play with. It's disgusting really.

Armstrong is already at our table drinking scotch, or bourbon, or some kind of amber alcohol, sans his cousin Bancroft. The waitress at the table has her back to us, her tray balanced on one palm, her other hand perched on her jutting hip. She laughs at something he says and flips her long dark ponytail over her shoulder.

I glance at Amie, who's stiffened, her grip on my arm tightening just a little. I want to believe this match is a good one, but I'm not sure I do. On the outside, Armstrong appears to be ideal husband material. But I worry that this whirlwind romance is clouding her judgment, as is her parents' approval of this match.

Despite being a bit of a wild child, Amie is also an approval seeker. Anarchy Amie used to like to get up to no good, but she'd suffer serious remorse if she got caught in her acts of defiance. On the rare occasions our cover story didn't work, she would spend the next month attempting to be the perfect daughter to atone. It's an interesting dichotomy. She wants to do the right thing, but she also likes to push the boundaries.

Even her degree was more about making her parents happy than actually doing what she wants with her life. Although, she seems reasonably satisfied with her job—and she has one, so there's an upside to all her pleasing of other people. Maybe if I suffered from that affliction I'd also be gainfully employed. With my own fiancé.

Armstrong's smile dips for a second when he notices our approach, and then widens to reveal his perfectly white, perfectly straight teeth. He nods to the waitress and slides out of his seat, smoothing a hand over his tie as he gives Amie a heated once over. She's wearing the same simple black dress she had on when she showed up at my apartment. It's cinched at the waist with a pencil style skirt that highlights her curvy hips and an ass shaped by hours of Pilates and uncountable squats.

"My gorgeous fiancée." The waitress moves aside and Armstrong takes Amie's hand, pressing a kiss to each one of her knuckles.

Amie giggles and blushes when he pulls her in close to whisper something in her ear. I'm assuming it's in relation to activities taking place later in the evening based on how red her face goes.

It's short-lived anyway. Armstrong steps back and turns his charming smile to me. "Ruby, I'm so pleased Amalie extended the invitation for dinner tonight. I trust you enjoyed yourself at the engagement party."

"Thanks. I had a lovely time. The food was exceptional." At least until the morning after. It seems best to leave that part out.

"Excellent, excellent." He sweeps a hand out to the chair on the other side of the table, where a host is waiting for me to take a seat so he can tuck me in like a five-year-old. "I'm looking forward to getting to know you better. I haven't had much of an opportunity to meet many of Amalie's close friends, especially not ones who have known her for as long as you have."

"Yes, well, it's been quite the whirlwind, hasn't it?" I smooth my hand down the back of my skirt as the host moves the chair under my butt. I fall into the habits I've spent the last several years shedding like an old coat, nodding at him with a polite smile and a quiet thank you.

Armstrong waits until the host has moved on before he gives me what seems to be his signature, pickle-up-the-ass smile. "When you know, you know. I'm sure you'll understand once you find your soul mate." He turns to gaze lovingly at my best friend.

I hold back both the snicker and the gag—although the latter had more to do with the return of the roll in my stomach than the actual cheesiness of his response. Instead I smile and nod my agreement. "I'm sure when that day comes I'll be just as excited as both of you. Maybe

I'll even want to elope." I glance down at my drink menu so he can't read the disingenuousness on my face.

"I wouldn't suggest elopement, it makes it seem like you have something to hide," Armstrong says with an air of snoot. Although almost everything he says comes across as pretentious.

Any potentially sarcastic response is thwarted by the sudden arrival of Armstrong's last-name-first cousin whose home I'm hoping to move into for the next five weeks.

"Sorry I'm late. I got caught up at work."

"Don't you ever rest?" Armstrong asks.

"Last-minute trip details," he replies.

I look up from my drink menu as the chair opposite mine slides across the carpeted floor. The hand doing the chair dragging isn't a manicured one. The nails are imperfect and scars litter his knuckles. And the hand is huge. Like it belongs to some behemoth Neanderthal.

As I lift my eyes to further judge this cousin of Armstrong's I realize the abnormally large hand is attached to one hell of a forearm and that is attached to a rippling bicep. Up, up, up I go until I reach the thickly corded muscles that make up his neck, and the incredibly cut jaw with the perfect amount of five o'clock shadow. As with any finely crafted physical specimen, I'm definitely intrigued to see whether the face does the body justice. I'm met with a plush set of lips that currently have a tongue dragging across them, making the bottom one glisten in the expensive chandelier lighting.

His nose is mostly straight, but there's something a little off there. I can't figure out why, though. My gaze reaches his eyes, his dark blue eyes. They're stunning. Just unreal. And he has these perfect arching eyebrows to complete the perfection of his face. Amie wasn't lying. This man is seriously f'ing hot. And I haven't even checked to see if he has all his hair yet.

As I put together all the individual components of his rugged, sexy face, I also come to realize that beyond his being hot, he's also terribly familiar. In my somewhat lust-induced haze of stupidity, combined with the still-hanging-on fever, it takes me a few more seconds to come up with a reason as to why this man is so familiar.

I break the rules of etiquette that were bitch slapped into me my entire life by pointing at him and saying, "You!" Thankfully, my voice is still hoarse so it's a lot quieter than it may have been otherwise.

His smile, his pretty, white-toothed smile falters and he cocks his head to the side. His expression registers a flicker of recognition, although there's also confusion. "Do I know you?"

"Do you know me?" I parrot.

"You look incredibly familiar." He drops into the chair across from me, those eyes of his could be burning holes in my damn dress they're so hot. Jesus. This man is like a nuclear bomb of sexy, just waiting to go off. I'm honestly surprised women aren't super-gluing themselves to his body like in one of those men's spray deodorant commercials. He may actually need women repellent. "I feel like I should know your name already."

His now lopsided grin is making my panties reevaluate their importance in my life.

I recall him telling me he'd been popping cold medication like candy. Maybe his memory is fuzzy. Sadly, I remember every second of that accidental kiss, and the unfortunate aftermath.

I gawk for a few extra seconds before I finally remember how to put words together. "Well, you have had your tongue in my mouth." Not really the best words, or the most appropriate ones, unfortunately.

"Do you know each other?" Amie's smile is tight and her voice is high.

I wave a hand in his direction. "That's Awesome Kisser."

"I'm sorry, what?" Now she looks concerned, and she may have a right to wear that expression, because I'm about to go off.

"This is the guy who kissed me and then coughed in my face."

There's one of those lulls in conversation at the tables near us, so a few people stop to stare for a second or two before resuming their fake conversations.

Awesome Kisser whose name I now know is Bancroft, looks horrified. As he should. I lost the part in the play because of him. Well, that's also assuming I would've given the best performance out of all 175 people who tried out for the lead and supporting roles. But, with my background I should've at least been offered some part, even if it wasn't a major one.

"What?" Armstrong looks from Bancroft to me and then to Amie, apparently not in the know.

"Oh shit." Bancroft's distress is real. At first, I think it's embarrassment, until he continues, sounding remorseful, "I really am so sorry about that. I probably shouldn't have attended the engagement party in the first place, but Armstrong's my cousin and I couldn't miss it. Too much scotch and cold medication makes for a terrible combination."

"Apparently. Your date certainly wasn't pleased."

"Does someone want to fill me in here?" Armstrong looks super confused. And annoyed. I can't decide if this is a good or a bad thing, because it means the incident

isn't something Bancroft's shared—out of mortification
or tact, I'm not sure yet, since I don't have much of a
gauge on his personality. My knowledge of him is limited to the way his mouth feels and his tongue tastes.

I turn to Armstrong and smile. "Just a misunderstanding. It isn't a big deal."

The waitress comes by to take drink orders. Based on
the turn in events, I consider a glass of Prosecco, but ul-
timately decide to go with sparkling water, hopeful the
bubbles will settle my stomach, although maybe the alcohol would help kill whatever bugs are floating around
in there.

Armstrong does a good job of dominating the conversation and Bancroft's references to his business trip
are quickly turned into another jumping-off point for
Armstrong to talk about himself and his family's media
empire. Maybe he's a nervous talker. Or a pompous ass.
Either is possible, though the latter seems more likely.

Appetizers arrive. Apparently Armstrong took the lib-
erty of ordering for us prior to our arrival. A selection of
tapas is placed on the table, including smoked salmon
and sautéed calamari. Usually I'm a fan of seafood, but
my recent unintentional fasting makes anything with
actual flavor seem rather unappealing. I go with the saf-
est option: baked pita chips, skip the hummus, and I order
pasta primavera; the plainer the better.

"You must be looking forward to getting your feet wet
on this trip," Armstrong says to Bancroft before popping
an oyster—he decided they were a necessity—much
to my stomach and my gag reflex's dismay.

Bancroft lifts a shoulder. "It is what it is. Now that my
rugby career is over, I don't have much of an option but
to immerse myself in the family business."

I stop making patterns in the pool of olive oil on my

plate with my pita triangle and check him out again. Now his size makes sense, as do the scars and the slightly imperfect nose. "You played professional rugby?"

He turns his attention to me, a half-smile pulling up the corner of his mouth. "I did. For seven years."

"And you quit to take over your family's business?"

"No. I blew out my knee."

"You can't recover from that?"

"I can, but if I have another accident like that there's a good chance I won't ever walk without assistance. I didn't think it was worth the risk, and the agreement was, when my rugby career ended, I'd work with my father." He doesn't seem particularly excited about that. I completely understand his lack of enthusiasm—it's the reason I'm still sitting here, trying to figure out how to get this man to let me move into his house despite how embarrassing this is.

"Rugby's a pretty violent sport." Wow. What an excellent conversationalist I am today.

"I prefer the term *aggressive*. Do you watch?"

"I don't have a favorite team or anything, but I went to a couple of games when I visited Scotland a few years ago. I guess that aggression would work well if it translates from the field into the business world." This is my way of finding out what kind of business Bancroft's family runs.

"Hopefully I can find the same level of passion for hotel management as I did for rugby," he says with some disdain.

"I'm sure it won't be difficult to transfer your Harvard MBA skill set to the Mills empire." Armstrong pats him on the back.

Mills? Holy crap. "The luxury hotel chain?" I ask.

"That's the one." He gives me a tight smile.

Mills hotels are legendary for their spas and extensive services. They're not just a place to sleep, they're an experience. At least that's what the commercials say. I don't even want to think about what his family is worth, although it wouldn't take much to find out.

Armstrong shuts down the opportunity to segue into Bancroft's trip by offering up information about my family legacy. "Ruby's father is Harrison Scott, of Scott Pharmaceuticals."

Bancroft regards me curiously. "Oh? That sounds familiar."

"He specializes in erectile dysfunction medication," I mutter.

"Is that right? Well, here's hoping I won't need those for a lot of years, if ever," Bancroft replies.

Armstrong laughs.

Thankfully, dinner arrives, putting an end to that potentially embarrassing conversation. The men start talking business, and Armstrong goes into a serious monologue about his first year learning how to manage staff at the leading media conglomerate in the country. Amie hangs off every word as if he's some cult leader looking to recruit her as his sacrificial virgin.

I pick at my dinner, my stomach continuing to do that unfortunate roll thing, even with the minimal amount of food I'm putting in it.

It doesn't help that everything Armstrong ordered has a pungent aroma and is slightly disgusting to look at. Or maybe my current state of mind and body is the issue. When the gurgle becomes audible I excuse myself, praying I avoid further humiliation, except in a public restaurant rather than during an audition. Although I suppose this is an audition of sorts.

I lock myself in the end stall and take a few deep breaths, hoping I can manage to get my stomach to settle. These bathrooms are actually quite nice, but butts that aren't mine have sat on them and left behind five-star-dinner remains or the aftermath of expensive champagne. I also feel bad about destroying a bathroom in a place as nice as this.

I push aside those unpleasant thoughts and concentrate on breathing. It takes a few minutes, but my stomach finally settles enough that I think I can manage sitting through the rest of dinner, as long as I don't eat anything else substantial.

I check myself out in the mirror prior to vacating the bathroom. I need to get myself under control and fast if I want to secure a place to live. No one in their right mind would willingly let me stay in their home and care for their pets in my current state. I wish I'd had the good sense to stay the hell home tonight. I seriously look strung out, like someone coming off of a meth binge. Not that I actually know what that looks like outside of those intervention shows on TV.

I shakily pat my face with a wet paper towel—the thick kind that doesn't disintegrate when they're soaked with water. After eating a Listerine strip, reapplying lipstick, and dusting my cheeks with powder, I step out into the hall only to run into the same man I did the last time I exited a public bathroom.

I grab Bancroft's shirt as I careen into him—unintentionally. Again. He isn't wearing a suit jacket like the last time, so it's easier to both see and feel all those hard packed muscles. Despite my recent near conversation with the toilet bowl, my vagina still notices how nice his body is.

"Are you okay?"

His voice has that deep, resonating baritone that juices me right up, quite literally.

"I'm fine. It's fine." It's still more raspy croak than it is actual words.

"I don't believe you."

Sweet lord, this man is seriously intense. The way he's looking at me makes me wish I had a breath mint, or another one of those mouthwash strips for good measure, just in case he accidentally kisses me again. Oh God. He better not kiss me again.

"If you're thinking about molesting my mouth with your tongue again, you might want to reconsider your timing. I'm pretty sure my breath is horrible right now." I wish my brain wasn't as sick and stupid as my body.

"I really am sorry about that." He skims my forehead with his fingertips, brushing away the stray hairs hanging in my eyes. He follows with the back of his hand. "Jesus. Do you have a fever?"

"I'm just a little warm."

"A *little* warm? I could cook steak on your forehead."

"That's a super-sexy image."

He frowns. "Is this really my fault?"

My first instinct is to tell him no, mostly because my upbringing wants me to take the blame for him. Also he's hot and I don't want him to feel bad, but in this case he's absolutely at fault, and I'd really like a place to live, so if guilt helps make that happen, I'm all for it. "It really is."

"I feel awful about this. I can't believe I sexually assaulted you and made you sick."

"And you ruined my audition." For some reason he still has his arm around me. Not that I'm complaining. I'm feeling rather weak, so it's nice to have someone supporting some of my weight.

"I did what?"

"I had an audition for a play the next morning, but I projectile vomited all over the director. It ruined my chances of ever working with him again, I'm probably blacklisted everywhere. I'll never get another role in this city." Okay, the last part is likely untrue, but if he feels bad enough, maybe he'll agree to me pet sitting/squatting in his pad for the next five weeks.

"Are you serious?" He looks absolutely horrified. Maybe I've taken it a touch too far.

"I don't know about not working in the city ever again, but I definitely won't get a part if that director is involved."

He releases me and runs his hand through his full, luscious, slightly curly hair and expels a long, slow breath. "I really screwed you, didn't I?"

Well, you sure did screw my mouth. At first I think those words are in my head, until I watch his eyebrows rise.

"I screwed your mouth?"

"Uh. With your tongue. When you kissed me, with tongue. You screwed—" *Oh God, Ruby, stop talking.* "My mouth. With your tongue." And he did it, very, very well. My lady parts agree with this assessment, based on the way they're tingling. I must be on the mend if I have tingles. Or maybe I'm sicker than I thought.

He crosses his arms over his chest. A half-smirk tugs up the left corner of his mouth. "You kissed me back."

I blink a couple of times. I guess he noticed that. I'm not going to admit it, though. "You caught me off-guard and I'd been drinking."

"Drinking? Really? How do I know you weren't just hungover and that's why you hurled all over that director?"

Even the word *hurl* makes my stomach feel like it wants to stage another revolt. "I had one drink! And I'm still—" I make gestures instead of saying the word.

"You can't have it both ways, sweetheart."

"Both ways? What are you even talking about?"

"I'm talking about you coming up with bogus excuses to explain away why you kissed me back when you didn't even know me."

My mouth drops open. I clamp it shut, just in case, and glare at him. "I have a very low alcohol tolerance. I had one martini." I hold my finger up in front of his face. "It hit me a lot harder than I expected."

"Right." His smirk is infuriating. I want to suck it right off his gorgeous face, with my lips, either set.

"You cocky f—" I bite back the nasty expletive and narrow my eyes. I'm so sweaty right now, and I don't think it's just the sickness. "You know, regardless of your perception of what happened the other night, considering how drunk and doped up you were, you are the reason I'm jobless, and now I'm about to be homeless, too. So I hope you're well entertained by my misfortune."

"Homeless?" That wipes that godforsaken gorgeous smile off his face.

I shouldn't have said that part. "Never mind." I turn around. I'm not sure what my plan is, whether I'm going to bolt, although the idea of leaving behind three quarters of a perfectly delicious, edible meal when I'm down to my last six packages of ramen noodles seems rather wasteful. I might not be able to finish it tonight, but I can certainly save it for another day. Primavera will last at least a few days in the fridge. I should be better by then.

"Whoa, whoa!" Bancroft grabs my arm, not hard, gently but firmly. "You can't say something like that and just walk away."

"It's not like it affects you," I bite out, embarrassed. I can't believe I've gotten myself into this kind of situation.

"Right now it affects me, especially if I'm responsible for your predicament. I need you to explain the homeless part."

I wave my hand around in the air while I debate whether I want to tell him the fabricated story Amie and I concocted or some version of the truth. I'm excessively flaily tonight. "There was a problem with my lease renewal. The rent was doable and nothing else out there is, especially without this job, so I'm screwed." That's not quite a hundred percent true, because even with that role, I wouldn't have had the money to pay down the overdue rent and my place is already rented out, so either way I was going to end up homeless. But he looks like he's feeling some guilt over this, and I need a place to live. I'm not above manipulation. Or girl tears. Plus he's gorgeous.

"And you don't have anyone who can help you out? What about your family?"

"My father's not exactly supportive of my career choice, so asking him isn't an option." Here I go again, giving him far too much information. It's like his voice is truth serum.

There's that frown and that furrowed brow again. I've never seen such a sexy furrow. "You don't think he would help you?"

"He's made it very clear he won't help me."

"Why not?"

"Because he thinks I should be done playing make-believe and come home to work for the family like my brother and sister." Before my dad married my mother he had another, shorter marriage that lasted only a few years. Long enough to give me two older siblings who lived mostly with their mother apart from summer holidays until they were old enough to be involved in the pharmaceutical company.

Bancroft's jaw clenches. I can't tell whether that's a good or a bad thing. And I don't have a chance to find out, because Amie comes around the corner.

"There you are. I was getting worried." Her eyes dart back and forth between us. "Is everything okay?"

I step back, realizing just how close we are to each other, and smooth the front of my dress, putting on what I hope looks like a natural smile. "Just fine. We were on our way back to the table."

"I'll be right there," Bancroft mutters and turns away, heading for the men's room. It might be a figment of my imagination, but I swear he shakes out his left leg a little.

"Are you okay? What did he say to you?" Amie whisper hisses in my ear.

"I'm fine. He accused me of kissing him back."

"He did *what*?" Amie stops walking, but her arm is linked with mine, so I'm jerked to a halt. "Sorry, sorry!"

"Well first he accused me of kissing him back and then he apologized."

"I'm glad he apologized." She looks relieved. "Why would he accuse you of kissing him back though?"

I get busy picking at imaginary lint on my dress.

"Ruby?"

I mutter something unintelligible.

"Did you kiss him back?"

I shrug.

"You didn't even know who he was!"

"I was caught off guard. He's a good kisser. And have you seen him? That man could revive a corpse with his hotness."

"Sometimes you're very creepy, you know that?"

Amie looks over her shoulder and then sighs. "I'm so sorry about this, I didn't realize Bancroft was the mystery kisser. I'll figure something out. I won't let you be homeless." Her eyes light up, all devious-like.

It makes me nervous—it's the same expression she used to wear when we were younger and she wanted to do something we could get grounded for.

"Actually, this might be perfect."

"Perfectly humiliating?" I ask.

"Let me work my magic."

"Your magic is exactly what I'm afraid of."

CHAPTER 5

HOMES FOR THE HOMELESS

RUBY

We return to the table. Armstrong looks a little put out that he's been left alone. I assume it's because dinner plates don't act riveted by his engaging conversation.

I sit down and notice my meal is gone. "Did you have my pasta packed up?"

"Packed up?" Armstrong's nose twitches, as if he's trying to mask his disgust. I'm sure leftovers are only for the dog in his house. And the dog would be hypoallergenic and never bark.

"To take home?" I have to work hard to speak normally, and not like I'm addressing a toddler.

"Why would you want to do that?"

"Because I hardly touched it."

"I thought that was because you didn't enjoy it." He gives me a strained smile, his gaze moving from me to Amie, as if he's uncertain whether he's done something wrong or not.

"It's not a big deal." I smooth my napkin across my lap so I have somewhere to focus. This night is turning to crap. Not only is what little I've eaten not sitting all that well, now I can't even enjoy the leftovers when my stomach finally settles. And the only things in my fridge are lemons and maybe some salad dressing and random condiments. If I wasn't already highly embarrassed, I might want to cry.

"Why don't we order dessert?" Amie suggests.

"Are you sure you want to do that?" Armstrong asks.

If he's implying that Amie needs to watch what she eats he needs a slap across the face, or maybe a punch, with brass knuckles, below the belt. Amie is stunning, with a fabulous body that she maintains with regular visits to the gym. Unlike me. I rely solely on my unfortunate dietary restrictions to maintain my current supermodel like figure. Which isn't really all that supermodel-y, but my clothes have been a little bit looser lately.

"I don't know about anyone else, but I'm really looking forward to checking out their dessert selection." Bancroft slides smoothly into the chair across from me.

Maybe they have sorbet or something that would be easy on my testy stomach.

When the waitress comes back, Amie orders some elaborate chocolate lava dessert, even though Armstrong makes comments about it not being gluten-free. She also orders a latte, but makes it nonfat. Bancroft orders apple pie with ice cream and a boozy cinnamon coffee and I opt for mint tea and watermelon gelato, because it seems like I might actually be able to eat it without irritating my sensitive tummy. Armstrong orders espresso. Black. No sugar. Of course.

"So Bancroft, you fly out this weekend, right?" Amie asks.

Here we go. I can tell by her expression that she's planning her attack. Armstrong hasn't been with her long enough yet to fully appreciate her mischievous and devious side.

"I do. You're still okay to come by and take care of Francesca and Tiny while I'm gone?"

"I just have to feed them, right?"

"And change Francesca's litter a couple of times a week," Bancroft says.

Amie makes a face, like the idea of changing litter is a repulsive task. She grew up with a dog, but I don't thinks she was responsible for taking care of his lawn deposits.

"Oh. Okay. I guess I can do that."

"I have a list of instructions that should help make it easy for you." He adjusts his tie, looking a little nervous. I'm assuming it's directly related to her look of distaste. "I'm sorry I'm asking you to do this but I can't really use a professional pet sitting service. I don't have time to fully vet one and I just need someone I can trust."

It made sense, even though Amie's experience with pets has been fairly limited. Their family poodle, Queenie, was as high strung as her mother. Caring for Queenie consisted of the occasional pet and maybe a walk once in a while. That dog probably got more attention from me than her entire family combined. It's not Amie's fault. Her mother wouldn't let her near the dog because she has allergies, even though Queenie was hypoallergenic as far as dogs go. She didn't even shed.

"And I just need to stop in a few times a week, right?"

"Uh . . . well, Francesca needs some attention, so—"

"What kind of attention? I should take allergy pills before I go, shouldn't I?" She turns to me. "Maybe you could come with me? In case I have a reaction and need help."

I shrug. "If you want." Amie half-wasted her potential.

She could easily have become an actress with the performance she's currently putting on.

Amie turns a bright smile on Bancroft. "Ruby's great with animals. She probably could've been a vet."

That's untrue. I discovered in high school biology that I'm not good with strong smells and cutting open small, helpless animals. Even if they're dead and embalmed.

Bancroft studies me for a moment as he folds his napkin and places it neatly on the table. Oh, yes, this man is definitely from good breeding. Which is a horrible thing to notice. I hate that it's ingrained in my DNA.

"Have you ever owned pets?"

"Not since I moved to New York. But I grew up with two dogs and a cat, and for a while my mother had a raven."

Bancroft's raises an eyebrow. "A raven?"

"It kind of adopted my mother." Until some stupid kid with a BB gun shot it.

Bancroft looks around and drops his voice. "Have you ever taken care of a ferret?"

"You have a ferret? I thought you said it was a bunny or a guinea pig," I say to Amie.

Amie shrugs. "They're both furry and they live in cages, right?"

My opinion of Bancroft shifts slightly. Ferrets are atypical pets. I became a little obsessed with them as a teenager thanks to my time spent working in an animal sanctuary. I'd wanted to adopt one who ended up there, but I wasn't allowed—for a barrage of reasons. First of all, they're stinky until they have the gland business taken care of, a fact I hadn't been aware of. They also have to be caged because they're small and can get into very tight spaces. And my dog probably would have eaten it.

"I also have a tarantula." Bancroft taps on the table, awaiting my response.

I try to keep my voice from going too high. "Oh wow. That's, um . . . unusual."

"Are you afraid of spiders?" he asks.

"Not really, no." I don't particularly love spiders, but I'm not the kind of person who will get up on a chair and scream like a banshee if I see one. I'm also more likely to usher them outside rather than stomp on them if they happen to be sharing my space.

"She's pretty harmless if you know how to handle her."

"I've never held a tarantula."

"Well we'll have to change that, won't we?" Bancroft gives me a warm smile that makes me all melty and blushy—beyond the fever I'm still rocking, anyway.

"So you're okay with—" Armstrong makes hands gestures to go with his pinched expression. "—odd animals," he finally finishes.

"I wouldn't call them odd, they're just a little unconventional. I volunteered at an animal sanctuary when I was in high school."

"Really? How would that benefit your résumé?" Armstrong asks.

"It didn't. I volunteered because I wanted to." And also so I wouldn't have to spend my weekends and afternoons at my father's office, filing papers or editing the pamphlet for his penis-inflating prescriptions.

Bancroft taps the table and leans in closer. "Ruby, how would you feel about taking care of Francesca and Tiny?"

"Francesca's the ferret, isn't she?" I can feel my nose wrinkle with my smile. I try to tone it down. My father always told me it makes me look childish and silly.

Bancroft's cheeks turn pink and he returns my grin.

"She is. However I regret to inform you that I did not have the pleasure of naming her, as fitting as it may be."

"I can't wait to meet her." I'm not saying this just to suck up, I'm genuinely enthusiastic about it, although I'm sure it's helping my case.

Bancroft looks from me to Amie and back. He smooths out the napkin on the table again. I wonder if it's an unconscious reaction. Like when I'm concentrating really hard sometimes my tongue peeks out of the corner of my mouth. It's a little embarrassing. When I got caught doing it as a kid my dad would use bitters to make me retract it. It worked until I started to like the taste.

"You know, it might be nice to have someone around for Francesca on a more regular basis," Bancroft says.

"I can alternate days with Amie if you think that would be better for Francesca. She'll need quite a bit of care, won't she?"

"She will." Bancroft is still playing with his napkin. "But I was thinking about something a little more . . . involved."

"Involved?" Amie's plan might just be working.

"Well, you need a place to stay and I need someone to take care of my pets. It would be much better for Francesca to have someone there all the time; that way I'm guaranteed she'll have playtime."

The way he says *playtime* does interesting things below the waist. Now I'm hot not just because of the fever, but because I'm imagining what playtime might look like with him. Which I probably should stop doing if this conversation is going in the direction I think it is. Lusting after my potential employer/temporary landlord is not recommended.

"What a great idea!" Amie claps her hands. "Isn't that a great idea?"

"You want Ruby to move into your apartment to take care of your pets?" Armstrong's expression reflects his confusion.

"Would that work for you?" Bancroft asks me.

Score. I blink innocently. "If you think it would be helpful."

"Immensely." He smiles again. It's a little nervous, which is understandable. He doesn't know me and he's about to let me move into his place and take care of his pets for more than a month. But, lord almighty, that smile is killer.

"I'll be gone for five weeks. Is that reasonable for you? It should help with the apartment issue?"

"Definitely."

"Excellent. It's settled then." He leans back in his chair, still grinning. "You'll move in."

Mission Don't End Up Living in a Box complete.

CHAPTER 6
MOVIN' ON UP

RUBY

Two days later my belongings are packed into a pitifully small pile of boxes and carted down to the lobby—thank God the elevator is working today—where Armstrong and Bancroft are waiting to load them into the truck.

That's right. Bancroft drives a truck. It's so not high-brow at all. It makes him even sexier. And it's not even a rental, which is practically unheard of in New York. It's a nice truck, one of those limited edition ones with all the upgrades, but it's still a truck and very un–trust fund of him. I can understand why he wouldn't want to get rid of it, however impractical it may be.

What's also sexy is the way the muscles in his arms flex every time he picks up another one of the boxes and carries it out the door. He's wearing a Harvard T-shirt and a pair of shorts. The only thing that sort of ruins the sexy a bit are his socks. They're white and reach his shins. If he could just take them off, or maybe trade them for a pair of ankle socks, then he'd be perfect.

It's hot, stiflingly so outside, and it's even worse in my

apartment since I don't have air. Thankfully, there's not much left in my apartment. I'm assuming Bancroft lives in some swanky place since it's in Tribeca. With central air.

Bancroft insisted we take all of my things to his place rather than renting a storage unit since I don't have a lot in the way of worldly possessions. I felt weird about it at first, until he said he has three bedrooms, two of which are rarely used. I also don't have the money to rent a storage unit, so that settled that argument pretty quickly.

The elevator doors open and Amie comes out toting my luggage, which is filled with the contents of my dresser and my closet. Once upon a time those bags would've been full to bursting. Not so much anymore.

"That's the last of it!" she says brightly. "Why don't you do one last check and then we can get out of here."

How she can still be so chipper and perfectly put together after spending the past hour riding up and down in an elevator is beyond me. I appreciate it, though, because I'm looking the part of a wilted flower. This flu bug thing Bancroft gave me is a real hanger-on-er.

"Sure thing." Once I get up there I go through all the cupboards, checking to make sure I didn't leave anything behind by accident. I stand in the middle of my tiny apartment, a little sad to be leaving it behind. Even if it isn't the nicest place, it was mine.

I grab my purse and toss the six-pack of water bottles into it. As I'm about to close the door on this chapter of my life, quite literally, I scan the apartment one last time, taking in the bare mattress with the orange stain in the center where I spilled butternut squash soup last year.

My gaze lands on my lounge chair. The one piece of furniture that didn't come with this apartment. There's no way I'm leaving it here. It's too heavy for me to carry, so I have to slide it across the floor. Then I have to jimmy it through the doorway. I'm sweating by the time I get it down the hall to the elevator. More than I was in the first place, anyway.

I shimmy it in there, hit the lobby button, and drop into the chair, out of breath from the exertion. The doors slide open when I reach the ground floor and I have to maneuver the chair back out.

"Want some help with that?" Bancroft's deep, baritone comes from behind me.

"I'm good. I've got it." The chair isn't in the best shape. It's pretty old. When I recline in it, it lists a little to the right. But it's mine. So I want to take it with me, even if it should be destined for the dump. The elevator doors try to close on me as I'm dragging it out.

Bancroft chuckles. "Here." He taps my hip. It feels like a lightning bolt just shot out of his fingertip and zapped me in the vagina. I'm instantly tingly down there. I jump out of the way and he graces me with that damn pretty smile. Then he picks up the entire eight-million-pound chair. "You want this on the sidewalk, or . . ."

I give him a dirty look. "It's coming with me."

One eyebrow arches and that grin of his grows wider. "You're the boss."

I watch his incredibly toned rear end as he carries it through the open door. I follow him outside. It's hot and sticky. Like my panties. And the rest of me. Armstrong looks grossed out as Bancroft lifts the chair high enough to clear the tailgate.

"Doesn't that belong on the curb?" Armstrong motions to my chair. "That thing looks like it has fleas. Are you dropping it off at the dump on the way back to your place?"

"Army," Amie chastises.

"Amalie, how many times have I told you, I don't like that nickname in public," Armstrong snaps.

Amie's referred to Armstrong by that nickname more than once, but never in his presence. I suppose now I know why.

"I love my chair," I say defensively.

"Who else has loved that chair?" Armstrong mutters.

"Anything left up there?" Bancroft grabs the hem of his shirt using it to wipe the sweat trickling down his neck. His treasure trail appears first, followed by his navel—it's an innie—and then he reveals a tight, defined six-pack I would happily lick every inch of, even in his totally disgusting sweaty state right now. Okay, maybe I wouldn't go that far, but if he jumped in a shower I'd be totally game.

It'd be really great if he just took the shirt off right about now.

"Pardon?" he asks.

Did I say that out loud? I'm pretty sure it was an in-my-head thought. I clear my throat. "That's everything." It still comes out a little pitchy and breathless.

"Thank God. This heat is stifling. Amalie, let's call the car and go home. I need a shower," Armstrong says.

Amie frowns. "Aren't we going back to Bancroft's?"

"You've got this from here, right, Bane? Besides, we have dinner with my parents tonight."

"That isn't for hours, though."

"But you'll need the time to get ready," Armstrong argues.

Amie has never been a primper. She can go from yoga to ballroom ready in less than twenty minutes.

"We're good. Ruby doesn't have much stuff. It'll all fit into the service elevator in one trip," Bancroft replies.

"See?" Armstrong flips a set of keys around his finger. "Have a safe trip."

Amie gives me a quick hug. "Sorry about Armstrong, he doesn't deal well with this kind of heat. Are you sure you're going to be okay?"

"Why wouldn't I be okay?" I ask.

"I don't know. The move, everything being new."

"I'm fine. Really." Maybe a little nervous, but relieved I have a place to live.

"Call me later."

"Will do."

Bancroft opens the passenger door for me, as a gentleman would, and I climb in. It smells like him. There's a massive console in the center and a huge backseat, which is where my luggage is currently stored.

This should be more awkward than it is, but I'm surprisingly comfortable around this man I hardly even know. Apart from how good he is at kissing, his penchant for unusual pets and willingness to take in strangers makes me like him even more.

He climbs in the driver's side and turns the engine over. Hot air blasts through the vents, cooling quickly.

"I need to stop and get something to drink," Bancroft says.

"Oh! I have water!" I spread my legs so I can get to my purse on the floor between my feet. I pull one out and hand it to him.

"You're a goddess." He twists off the cap and tosses it on the dash. Tipping his head back he opens his lovely, luscious mouth and basically pours the contents of the bottle down his throat in thirty seconds. It's impressive.

"You want another one?"

"You have more?"

I produce the rest of the six-pack from my purse.

"What else do you have down there between your legs?"

I fight back a cough. "Should I assume you're asking about the contents of my purse and not what's in my shorts?"

"You can assume whatever you'd like, but if you're hiding a water bottle in your shorts, I gotta say, I'd be curious to see how you managed that."

"Oh my God. You did not just say that!"

He makes a face. "Too far?"

"Ya think?" Although, in truth I wouldn't mind showing him what's in my shorts. After I've had a shower. Dammit. I need to get a handle on where my head keeps going around this man.

"I'm blaming it on the dehydration." He huffs a laugh and frees another bottle, twists off the cap and repeats the entire sequence, which I watch, raptly.

"I probably smell like a locker room right now. Can I get you to open the glove box for me?"

I hit the button and it drops open. He reaches over, his fingers brushing my knee as he grabs a stick of deodorant and a balled-up shirt.

Oh man. He's going to change his shirt. In front of me. In an enclosed space. I wonder if I have enough time to grab my phone and snap a couple of pictures as he pulls the Harvard tee over his head.

Some men have nice faces and great bodies. Other men have great faces and okay bodies. This man has both. On a scale of one to smokin', he's on fire. And he has a tattoo. A big one on his right shoulder that travels along his biceps and ends above his elbow. Oh God. That's so hot.

He's quick to pull the fresh shirt over his head, covering his inky deviance. He follows with the deodorant, tosses it back in the glove box, and gives me a sheepish grin. "I feel better. I hope I smell a little better now, too."

"You smelled fine to me. I'm pretty sure that was just an excuse to show me your abs."

His smile grows a little. "You don't think I was just trying to be courteous? That maybe I didn't want to offend your delicate senses?"

"Do you see where I lived?" I motion to the building. It's old and run down. Not a bad place to live, but definitely not Tribeca. "At least once a week someone set off the fire alarm and the whole building smelled like burned toast. I can endure man sweat."

"But should you have to? That is the real question."

He shifts the truck into gear, puts on his signal, and pulls into traffic.

"So, uh, how long have you lived in that apartment?" Bancroft asks. Now that we're on the way back to his place, with all my things, he seems a little nervous. I wonder if he's having regrets.

"Five years. I'm not sure I'm going to miss it all that much. Having my own place has been nice, but half of the appliances didn't work all that well."

"Right. Gotcha." He taps the steering wheel. "So how'd you end up living in Harlem?"

"Amie's parents had already bought a place for her by the time I accepted the placement at Randolph, where I went to college, but it was a one bedroom, so I needed to find my own place. My father was against me coming to the city to begin with so he set a small budget for rent, thinking that I'd go back home when I realized what it cost for an apartment in the city. But I wanted to be here and this was reasonable, plus it was furnished, and it came with no roommates."

"Not a fan of roommates?" Bancroft asks.

"It's not that. It's just . . . living with someone else is tricky, right? We all have routines and quirks. If I was going to live with anyone it would've been Amie, so I thought it would be best to live on my own. What about you, ever had a roommate before?"

"Only when we were touring for games and tournaments. I like my space." He does that finger tapping thing.

"Yeah. Me, too. Well, what little of it I had. At least it was mine, though, right? I could only bitch at myself if there were dishes left in the sink for days."

"Are you a dishes-in-the-sink-for-days kind of woman?"

"Last week I was." I don't tell him I was also that woman the week before, and the month before that. He's not going to be around to witness my poor housekeeping skills, thankfully.

It takes a little more than half an hour to get to his place in Tribeca. No traffic.

The building he lives in is exclusive and gorgeous. All windows and mirrored glass. With the help of two men who work in the building—who address Bancroft as Mr. Mills—we get all of my belongings into the service elevator. When I attempt to follow things, Bancroft puts a hand on my shoulder. My nipples react immediately. They're so slutty when a hot guy is around.

"They'll bring everything up, we'll take the other elevator," he says.

The other elevator has a black marble floor and mirrored walls, which allows me an incredible view of Bancroft from all angles. The socks are still really distracting.

When we reach the penthouse floor Bancroft ushers me out. The hallway is wide, walls painted champagne, and more black marble leads us down the hall. The doors are spread far apart and I assume it's because these condos are much larger than my little apartment.

At the end of the hall Bancroft keys in a code, opens the door with a somewhat nervous smile, and ushers me inside.

I step past him into the foyer and come to a halt. My apartment could fit into this space ten times over. Bancroft crashes into me from behind. I stumble forward and his arm, his thick, well-defined, muscular arm, wraps around my waist, preventing me from face planting into the gorgeous, gleaming hardwood floors.

His hard chest presses against my back for a few brief seconds. I'm almost positive I can feel the ridges in his abs. Too bad this didn't happen when he had his shirt off. It's also too bad my shirt is on, along with the rest of our clothes. Sadly, he's quick to set me back on my feet. "Whoa. Sorry about that."

"My fault." I take a few more steps inside. "This is really nice."

"It's all right," he mumbles.

"I think it's a little better than all right."

Bancroft's condo is huge. This is the kind of place I should be accustomed to, but having lived in my apartment for the past five years, I've grown used to small spaces and crappy appliances that don't work well.

To the left is a kitchen. A big, beautiful kitchen full of shiny, stainless steel and granite countertops. To the right is a hallway with a set of double doors at the end. Directly in front of me are floor-to-ceiling windows providing a gorgeous view of the East River, rather than a view of a brick wall—which was what I had.

The living room boasts a huge leather couch and a massive chair covered in a funky pattern that doesn't seem to match Bancroft's personality at all. Although I don't really know him well enough to make an astute, informed opinion yet.

I kick off my shoes and head straight for that chair, flopping down in it. The space is so open. It's not particularly warm or welcoming. There aren't any knick-knacks or little things that tell me anything about who Bancroft is as a person.

Across from the chair I've thrown myself in is a floor-to-ceiling wall unit, and that's really saying something since it appears I'm looking at twelve-foot ceilings. A gigantic TV takes up the middle of the wall unit. Square shelves hold a variety of neatly stacked books. A rugby-playing reader, now that's sexy.

I glance past the wall unit. "Holy crap! Do you have a home gym?" I bounce out of the chair and rush across the open space, barely containing the urge to do a few spins on the way, because I have the room.

On the other side of the wall unit are a series of workout machines. There's a treadmill, a recumbent bike, a Pilates machine, and a variety of weights, as well as a bench for lifting.

"Wow, no wonder you look like this." I motion to his athletic form, then to the elaborate home gym setup. "Do you use this every day?"

He runs a palm over his chest. "I try to."

"This is fantastic." My gym is probably a half an hour from here and that's on a good day when the subways are running properly. It's a busy gym, so sometimes it's hard to access the equipment I want. Bancroft's treadmill is set up so it overlooks the river as well. The view is spectacular.

Opposite the gym is an office, a very neat office with a very nice desktop computer and a monitor large enough to watch movies on. To the left of the office, against the wall is a terrarium. "Oh! Is this where Tiny lives?"

"It is."

I tiptoe over, I'm not sure exactly why. It's not as if I'm going to frighten her and she's going to come flying out of her glass enclosure. I drop down into a crouch so I'm at eye level with the terrarium. Long, fuzzy legs appear over a small stone as she comes into view. "Holy crap. She's huge," I whisper.

Bancroft's reflection appears in the glass. My stomach tightens as he drops down in a crouch behind me, his chest brushing my shoulder. My gaze locks onto his mouth, which moves in close to my ear. His breath is warm when it breaks across my neck. For a second I think maybe I'm going to get to feel those lips on my skin again.

Until he whispers, "She can smell your fear." Then he makes this weird noise that reminds me of horror movies. I shudder and he laughs, pushing up to stand. "Relax. She's really harmless." Bancroft lifts the lid off the tank.

If I turn my head to the left I'll be looking at his junk. It's a real challenge not to follow through on that. Instead I stay where I am as he slips his hand in and taps Tiny on the butt, making her scamper forward.

She's a gigantic spider, her legs spanning Bancroft's massive palm. God, his hands are *huge*. I wonder if the rest of his assets match.

I give in and side eye him. He's wearing basketball shorts, which are loose, so I'm unable to confirm or deny whether his unit size is directly related to his hand size. And he's still wearing those damn socks.

"Would you like to hold her?" Bancroft asks.

"What? Oh. I don't know about that." I scramble back a bit and land on my ass.

"You'll be fine. I'll be right here to save you from her if she gets aggressive." He lowers himself to the floor and crosses his legs, like we're getting ready for storytime in kindergarten. Except it's not storytime. He's holding a giant spider. After a few seconds of hesitation, I mirror his pose.

He crooks his free finger. "Come a little closer."

God. Why am I turning everything he says into something dirty? If he wasn't holding that spider, the thought of climbing into his lap, right after I take off all my clothes, would seem rather appealing. God. I really need to get a handle on where my mind keeps going whenever I'm close enough to touch him.

I scoot a couple of inches closer. He rolls his eyes and slides forward until his knees hit mine. Well, my knees actually hit the middle of his shin, but now our bodies are touching. Not particularly exciting parts, but my nipples don't seem to understand that with the way they've perked right up.

Of course, then he has to go and hold up his spider hand and all the perking is overshadowed by the fuzzy, eight-legged beast staring at me with all eight of her eyes. "Give me your hand."

At my reluctance, he grabs my right hand, which I immediately ball into a fist. "She's not going to launch herself at you and even if she bit you, she's not poisonous. How are you going to take care of her if you can't even touch her?"

He has a point. I unfurl my fingers and his thumb smooths over my palm. For someone as big as he is, he sure is gentle. And all my important, sensitive parts are responding to that touch as if they're going to be on the receiving end of it as well. I mentally tell my hormones to back off, which isn't all that difficult when he scoots Tiny from his palm onto mine.

I shiver at the feel of her legs, then giggle. "It tickles."

"You'll get used to it." His hand is still cupping mine.

"What do I do?"

"Just hold her, no sudden movements, that kind of thing. They're actually pretty fragile, so you don't want to drop her."

I hold her for a minute. She's actually not at all scary now that I'm touching her. "How do you feed her? What do you feed her?"

"I feed her crickets, or grubs, depending."

"Live ones?" I glance up.

"Yes. Live ones."

"How often? Every day?"

"No, only once or twice a week. You'll need to change her water daily, though. Are you going to be okay with that?" His expression turns serious for a moment.

I nod. "I can do that. Do I just stick my hand in the cage? Will she attack me?"

"Just put a pen in front of her first so she doesn't think you're food and you can easily change out the water. I'll show you how to do that later. And I can even show you how to feed her, although she might not be hungry right now, she fed a few days ago."

"Okay."

I let her explore my forearm, her fuzzy legs tickling my skin. The sound of the doorbell startles all three of us. "That's your things." Bancroft scoops her up gently before she can skitter off and puts her back in her terrarium while I run to get the door.

My luggage and boxes are neatly piled in the hall. It takes the servicemen all of five minutes to bring my belongings into the foyer. My chair is the last thing to arrive. It's rather pathetic in this particular environment.

I grimace and look to Bancroft. "Maybe I really should consider getting rid of that."

"Why?" he asks as the servicemen close the door behind them. They leave the dolly, though, so we can move the boxes to my room, I suppose. Or the room I'll be staying in while I'm here. I guess I'm glad I don't have a lot of stuff, otherwise the unpacking part would be unpleasant.

"Well, look at it." I motion to the dilapidated chair. "It doesn't really fit with the décor."

"I didn't choose the décor in this place, so you're welcome to put your touch on whatever you want while you're here."

I can think of a few parts of him I'd like to put my touch on, starting with losing those damn socks. And the rest of his clothes. Permanently. Maybe I can just burn his entire wardrobe. Or shrink it in the dryer while he's away.

I wag my eyebrows as I look him over. "You might regret giving me free rein like that." One side of his mouth quirks up, as if he knows where my mind has gone. I look away and gesture to the boxes. "I guess I should get these out of the way?"

Bancroft gives his head a small shake. "Right. I'm not being a very good host. I should probably show you where you'll be staying, shouldn't I?" I get a sense that he's a little apprehensive, as am I. This is a fairly unconventional situation, and we don't really know each other, apart from dinner and an accidental kiss. I guess now that I'm in his space the awkwardness is finally starting to set in.

He loads a few boxes on the dolly and I grab the

handles on my wheelie suitcases and follow him down
the hall to the second door on the right.

"I have two spare rooms, this is the bigger of the two.
If you'd prefer, we can keep your boxes in the other room,
but it's really up to you." He pushes the door open and
moves aside.

"Oh wow." This room is pretty much the size of my
entire apartment. And the bed is a queen, which is a serious upgrade from the double I've been sleeping on for
the past five years.

"It's pretty plain, but like I said, it's yours to do with
while you're here. You can look at the other room as well,
if you'd like."

"No, no. This is perfect. I love this room." The walls
are a pale, icy blue-gray. The comforter is off white, the
bedframe the same creamy color. It's pretty without being overly feminine. I wonder who did the decorating if
it wasn't him.

"There's a bathroom through there, and a walk-in
closet. I can store the boxes in there if you want them out
of your way."

"Just against the wall is good. I can move the ones I
don't need into the closet later."

"Sure." Bancroft wheels the dolly across the room and
props the boxes against the far wall.

I cross over to the bathroom. It's five-star fabulous.
There's a deep tub I could probably do laps in, and a sep-
arate stand-up shower with a huge rainfall showerhead.
There's even a double-sink vanity.

I have a moment in which emotions swirl to the surface, the kind that make me want to cry a little. It's been
so long since I've had nice things. I mean, of course when
I go home to visit my father I have nice things, but I'm
usually only there for a day or two before I come back to

the city, back to the worn-down little apartment I'd been in for the past five years. I've always treated the visits home like a stay in a hotel: temporary luxury.

And for the next five weeks this level of luxury is going to be mine. Moving back into a shitty apartment is going to suck. And that's assuming I'm going to be able to land a job that will allow me to rent more than a room in some frat house. I better enjoy this blip while I can.

After we move all the boxes and luggage into my room Bancroft stands at the doorway with his hands shoved into the pockets of his basketball shorts looking a little uncertain.

"I can, uh, give you some time to unpack? Then maybe we can order dinner and I can go over feeding schedules and all the other stuff."

I don't know what other stuff he's talking about, but dinner definitely sounds good. "Sure. But can I meet Francesca first?"

He laughs a little. "Right. Yeah, of course. That's why you're here. Come with me." He steps out into the hall and motions for me to follow him to the door at the end. "Usually I keep her out in the living room area, but I didn't want all the noise and moving your stuff in to freak her out, so I put her in my room."

He opens the door. For half a second I imagine that the accidental kiss he laid on me turned into something else. A one-night stand, or possibly a marriage proposal.

His bedroom is a cave. Not literally. It's not fashioned out of stone. But it's incredibly large. And the bed. Don't get me started on the bed. I think I'm becoming obsessed with beds. Big ones. And it is huge.

This is 100 percent a man's room. More than that, it's an athletic man's room. Gym shorts hang off the end of the footboard and a pair of running shoes sits below them, along with discarded socks. The same kind of socks he's currently wearing right now. Ones that hit his shins and ruin my view of his nice, muscular legs with seriously defined calves.

The walls are a paler version of the room I'm staying in and the comforter is dark blue. Someone, a woman I'm guessing—maybe his mom or a sister, if he has one—has decorated his bed with a couple of throw pillows.

I'm choosing to avoid the possibility of a past girl-friend's involvement, or even a current one considering his recent date with Brittany. I'm hoping his accidental behavior has put an end to that budding love story. Any-way, the throw pillows are tossed on the comforter like they're a pain in his ass, as throw pillows often are.

On the massive bed is an open suitcase and three suit bags, unzipped. It's a good thing. If they weren't there I might have succumbed to the urge to ask how he feels about naked pillow fights. As it is, I'm having a hard time not imagining one.

"Sorry about the mess." He rushes over and picks up the few discarded items from the end of the bed, crosses the room, and tosses them in the closet.

While he worries about tidying up, I glance around the room, and finally notice Francesca's cage. It's a wonder that I missed it until now, as it's the second most promi-nent item in the room. Like the rest of condo, it's a lux-ury setup with clear tubes and several levels, giving her lots of room to run around while she's caged during the day.

"Hi there, pretty," I say softly when she peeks her head out of a tube. Her pink nose twitches, her sable head lift-ing, the black swatch fur making her look like a masked bandit as she regards me curiously. She slides out of the tube, her long, brown body dropping to the wood chips.

She does a little roll, showing us her pale belly. She is so flipping adorable.

"There's my girl," Bancroft says from behind me. The affection in his voice makes all my sexy parts excited. More excited than they already were. Men who love animals are so hot. So that takes Bancroft to volcanic levels.

He opens the cage and gently lifts her out. As soon as she's in his arms she scales his chest and wraps herself around his shoulders, nipping at his jaw, then grooming his stubble. I want to do exactly the same thing. Except after he showers.

He coos at her and lets her snuggle into him. She's so cute, and so is he, being all sweet with her. I think my ovaries are melting, or crying, or calling for his sperm.

After a minute of cuddles he asks. "Would you like to hold her?"

"Of course!"

"You can either take her by the scruff"—he gently grabs the loose skin at the back of her neck, holding her up—"or hold her under the front and back paws."

I choose the latter because it would mean I would also come into physical contact with Bancroft. Having started off at a seven million on the hotness scales, he moved up several notches to off-the-charts with all his sweetness, patience, and consideration. Especially with how awkward this entire situation could be. How is this man not taken already? Maybe he has some weird quirks, beyond the socks.

Francesca is adorable and full of mischief, which is the allure of owning a ferret. As soon as I have her in my arms I remember exactly what it was like when I worked at the rescue sanctuary and why I'd wanted to adopt the one that ended up there. I'm in love with her within five minutes.

I put her down on the floor with Bancroft's permission and she takes off, bounding for the door. She's down the hall and into the living room in seconds.

"She's fast," I observe.

"She is. The condo's pretty much ferret-proof, though, so it's safe. All the wires are hidden and covered so she can't get to them." He gestures to the wall where the cords that would normally be visible coming out of sockets are not.

"That must've been a lot of work."

"I had a professional come in and do it for me. It took a bit of getting used to, but she's worth the effort. I always wanted a dog as a kid, but my mom's allergic, and my dad traveled too much, and I played competitive rugby, so there were a lot of away games. It wouldn't have been fair to do that to a dog."

"So why did you decide on a ferret instead of getting your own dog?"

"It was accidental. Someone snuck a ferret into one of my father's New York hotels a while ago. They're uh . . . illegal to have as pets in some states, and she was at risk of being exterminated, so I brought her home instead." He looks nervous as he waits for my reaction.

"Really? It's illegal in some states?" I had no idea.

"Just a few."

"But not New York, right?"

He purses his lips but stays silent.

I lean around him and smooth my hand across his back, between his shoulder blades. The muscles flex and he draws in a sharp breath.

"What're you doing?"

"Checking for your angel wings."

He laughs and then motions to Francesca whose head is peeking out from under the couch. She bounds across the living room and skids into the kitchen. "Look at her. How could I let them do that?"

"Exactly. That's really great that you decided to keep her. And your secret is safe with me. I won't tell anyone you're harboring a fugitive ferret."

"I appreciate your discretion. I didn't realize quite how involved the whole process would be, but she's proved to be worth it. I also wasn't expecting to do a lot of traveling, so I thought it wouldn't be an issue. I'm hoping that part will only last a short while."

Francesca finds a ball with a bell in it, the same kind you'd give a cat, and rolls it across the floor. I snatch it up before she can get to it. "Wanna play, little lady?" I toss it across the room and she races after it.

Once she catches it, she brings it right back to me. I look over my shoulder at Bancroft who's watching me with an amused expression.

"She plays fetch!"

"It's her favorite. She also loves snuggles while we watch TV."

"I'm in love with her already."

He mutters something I don't catch. "If you're all right with her, do you mind if I have a quick shower? Or I can put her back in her cage and you can have one, too."

For half a second I take that completely the wrong way. Probably because the second he said *shower* I started picturing him naked and wet. "Why don't you go now and I'll have one when you're finished."

"Sure. Great. Then I'll order dinner?"

"Um, you don't have to order in. I'll eat pretty much anything." Except for everything Armstrong ordered the other day. And I can't really afford to splurge on expensive takeout.

"My fridge isn't well stocked. It'll be my treat."

I feel some guilt over accepting more handouts from him, but I'm hungry enough to agree. "Okay. Sure."

"Excellent. I won't be long." I smile and turn back to Francesca when she nudges my hand, the ball already at my feet.

I toss it and watch her bounce across the floor. She really is the cutest little thing. The next time she comes back she has a new toy. It's a mouse, so I dangle it and she jumps for it. When Bancroft returns from the shower I'm lying on my back on the floor with one mouse dangling from the tail between my toes, and jingling the bell ball in my hand.

His feet show up in my field of vision first. His socked feet. What the fuck? Maybe he's got a thing about bare feet. Maybe he hates feet. Maybe he really loves socks. At least these are ankle socks and not the ones that cover up his amazing calves. I look up, past his knees to the cargo shorts, the black belt that cinches at his waist, and the half-unzipped fly. I get a very brief glimpse of red as he stuffs his hands in his pockets. Too bad he's not commando. Not that I'd be able to do anything about it if he was, but I'd have five weeks of self-pleasure fodder.

I remember, rather vividly, what it felt like when what he's hiding behind his fly was pressed up against my stomach during our accidental kiss. I keep going, up, up, up that very mountainous body. He's wearing a red T-shirt. That's rather disappointing. No shirt would be greatly appreciated. Maybe I should make a sign while he's away, one that says No Socks, No Shirts Required or something. He seems like the kind of guy who might find that funny. And who might accommodate me by taking it seriously.

"Want to take a break from entertaining Francesca?" he asks.

"Sure." I toss him the ball, which he catches under-hand with a quick step to the side thanks to my poor aim.

Francesca scampers over to him and tries to scale his leg. Instead of throwing the ball, he scoops her up. "I can order dinner while you're getting cleaned up, then we can go over the house rules."

"House rules?" I raise a brow. "You mean like no boys in my room after nine?"

Bancroft frowns. "Do you have a boyfriend?"

"Not at the moment." But I'd sure like to be friends with whatever's hiding behind the fly of those cargo shorts he's wearing. I do a half bridge and roll up to a stand. "Does this mean I have to cancel the kegger I was planning for tomorrow night?"

Bancroft's eyebrow lifts.

"I'll just remove that post I put up a couple hours ago. I think only, like, two hundred people responded."

He cracks a grin. "Only two hundred?"

"Tomorrow I was planning to take an ad out in the *Times*, pass out a few thousand fliers, that kind of thing, but I guess I'll just cancel those. I was thinking to charge like twenty dollars a person, but now I'll just have to settle for cable TV and chilling with Franny and Tiny." I brush past Bancroft on my way to my temporary room, enjoying his wide-eyed uncertainty.

"You are kidding, right?" he calls after me.

I just laugh and close the door, leaving him to wonder.

Once I'm in my room I survey the boxes, glad I had Amie's help packing, otherwise I'd have no idea where anything is. Thankfully the box labeled *bathroom* is close to the top of the stack, so it's easy enough to get to. I carry it into the bathroom and then realize I have no idea how the shower works. There are seven-hundred buttons and levers and I don't know what belongs to what.

I make a guess and press one of the buttons in the middle. Cold water shoots out of a jet in the wall at face level. I scream and try to hit it again, but I manage to hit the wrong one, activating yet another jet. So of course, I scream again. The water goes from freezing to scalding in a matter of seconds. I back away from the jets, into the corner, instead of out the open shower door. Now they're alternating scalding spray from all six jets. It's like a very hot game of Whack-A-Mole, except no one's hitting me over the head with a mallet, I'm being blasted with fiery sprays of water.

There's a knock in the middle of my yelps. It sounds like it's outside my door. Bancroft's muffled voice follows. "Ruby? You okay in there?"

"I think I need some help!" I call back.

"Is it okay if I come in, then?"

"Please!"

"Ruby?" Bancroft's voice is closer now, inside my room but outside the bathroom.

"I'm in here! I'm trapped in the shower!" I call out.

"Trapped?" Worry makes his voice a little deeper.

"The jets are shooting scalding water at me." I yell back. "I can't get past them."

"Can't you just turn them off?" Now it sounds like he's trying to stifle a laugh.

"I did try!"

"Are you—" there's a brief moment of hesitation, followed by the clearing of his throat. "—decent?"

"I'm being cooked in your shower and you're worried about my state of dress?"

The door opens slowly and Bancroft's dark hair appears, followed by his eyes, which dart toward the shower.

His brows come down and then pop up. Crinkles appear in the corners of his eyes. He pushes the door wide. "How'd you end up in the shower fully dressed?"

"Don't sound so disappointed. It was an accident," I snap.

"Geez, there's water all over the floor. Hold on. I'll be right back."

"Where are you going? Don't leave me in here!"

"I'm putting Francesca in her cage so I can save you. Give me a second." He disappears, but he's back again quickly.

It takes him all of three seconds to figure out the timing of the intermittent jet spray before he reaches in and hits three buttons. The water stops. The only part of him that's wet is his forearm. I, on the other hand, am soaked head to foot.

My tank top, which is pale blue, sticks to my skin, and its soaked state renders it transparent. Which means Bancroft can see the darker blue bra underneath. My shorts are drenched as well, showing off my panty-line. There isn't much of one since I'm sporting a thong.

Bancroft's gaze seems to get stuck on my chest.

"Can I have a towel, please?" Now that I'm no longer being pelted with scalding water the air-conditioning is doing its job, making my skin pebble, among other body parts. My nipples are particularly obvious thanks to the lack of padding in my bra.

"Right. Yeah." He grabs one from the rack and hands it to me as I step out of the shower.

"Thank you." Since the danger of being burned by water has passed, I'm now appropriately embarrassed. As I should be. Especially with the way Bancroft looks like he's trying to hold back his smile. "Do not laugh at me."

He holds up his hands in mock surrender, his cheek

ticking. "I guess it's a good thing you didn't wait until tomorrow to shower or you would've been stuck in there until the hot water ran out."

"It was like being blasted by a volcano."

"It's not that hot. There's a sensor that won't let the temperature get too high. I'm not sure why you didn't just run past the jets and save yourself, but I'll take white knight status."

"I have sensitive skin and I panicked," I reply.

"Too bad you didn't panic after you were naked. I didn't even get to see anything good."

My mouth drops. "So much for being a white knight."

His grins widens. "I still saved you from my molten lava shower."

"Only because you thought you were going to see me naked, apparently."

His eyes drop again, slowly perusing my body until he reaches my feet, where a puddle has formed. "I can be a white knight with a dirty mind, can't I?"

"You know what would be really nice?" I pull the towel tighter around me.

"What's that?" It takes a while before his gaze finally reaches mine. There's heat in it. The kind that makes me want to drop my towel and strip out of my clothes. The kind that begs the question, what kind of dirty happens in that mind of his? I'd capitalize on that hungry look he's wearing—if I wasn't relying on this man for a place to live while I sort out my messed-up life.

I clear my throat and try to come across as affronted, rather than turned on. "It'd be nice if you'd stop making fun of me and show me how to use your space-age shower."

"You're a little high strung, aren't you?" He's still smiling. It's as sexy as it is infuriating.

I just give him a look, more because I'm worried about what might come out of my mouth right now if I don't keep it shut.

Bancroft shows me what each button is for. It turns out I can actually set the temperature. This is a crazy high-tech shower. He adjusts the spray to rainfall and I tell him when it's the right temperature for me.

"Seriously?" he asks, feeling the tepid water.

"I told you my skin was sensitive."

"This is lukewarm."

"So? It's not like you're getting in there with me. What's it matter to you?"

His eyebrow dip, along with his eyes. "You wouldn't need hot water if I was getting in there with you." He smirks at my semi-fake outraged gasp. "I'll leave you to it."

I watch his ass leave the bathroom—and the rest of him, but it's his finely sculpted rear view that's my focus. And his fucking ankle socks. I don't know why they bother me so much.

Once I hear the door to my room close—my very nice, large room—I strip out of my wet clothes and step under the spray. It's a little on the cool side, but I'd rather that than the inferno water. Also, I could use a little cooling down after that.

The rain showerhead is so nice, the water pressure far superior to that in my old apartment. After a few minutes, I bump up the temperature a degree or two, because Bancroft is right, it's pretty cool, and now that he's not heating up the room with his comments and his hotness, I can make up for it with water temperature.

Once I'm done it takes me another five minutes to find a reasonable outfit. Everything I own is a wrinkly mess since it's been packed in suitcases for the past two days, but there's not much I can do about that. I can't even find a pair of decent underwear, so I'm forced to go commando, and all I can locate in the bottoms department that's even remotely reasonable is a pair of running shorts, a cami with a built-in bra, and a loose tank to throw over it.

It's not like I'm trying to impress Bancroft. Or seduce him with my sexy outfits. Not while I'm depending on him for a roof over my head. That could make things messy. But that doesn't mean I can't flirt.

Bancroft is stretched out on the couch watching sports with Francesca curled up in his lap. Right on top of his penis. What a whore. I wish I was her.

He glances over. "Looks like you recovered from the shower trauma."

"Ha ha." My lounger has been moved into the living room alongside the funky oversized chair. It looks even more dilapidated beside his nice furniture. "Did you pick this chair?"

"No. My mother did. She likes furniture a lot. She thinks this place doesn't have enough"—he flops his hand around—"personality or whatever."

"Ah. Do you agree with her?"

Bancroft shrugs. "She was excited that I was moving back to New York and I was recovering from knee surgery, so interior decorating wasn't high on my list of priorities. She's always been involved in that part of the hotels so I let her do her thing here because it makes her happy."

"That's sweet. It doesn't really seem like your style."

"What's my style?" he asks.

"Hmm. Good question." I tap my lip. "Maybe you should replace it with a throne. You know, to go with your white knight status."

He makes a snicker-y, snortish kind of noise.

Instead of taking a seat, I step into the gap between the couch and the coffee table. Bancroft gives me a questioning look as I lean over and give Francesca a pet.

"Uh, what're you doing?"

If I'm not mistaken, I hear a hint of excitement in his voice.

"What does it look like? Petting your ferret."

Francesca opens her eyes, blinking sleepily. I give her one long, full body stroke, considering the other thing underneath her that I wouldn't mind giving a stroke.

CHAPTER 7

FIRECRACKERS
IN MY PANTS

BANCROFT

Holy fuck. Ruby Scott is going to kill me. My dick is incredibly excited about what's happening right now. He seems to be taking the wheel a lot these days, especially in relation to the woman currently stroking my pet ferret, who has picked a rather inconvenient location to have a nap.

For the past two days I've been second-guessing my decision to let Ruby move in here while I'm away. Reneging would make me an asshole, but the last time I had someone pet sit for me Francesca almost escaped. And all of Tiny's crickets ended up getting free. They were all over the condo. It was disgusting.

Asking Amalie to take care of Tiny and Francesca hadn't been ideal, but I needed someone reliable and trustworthy. With Francesca being a fugitive because of her illegal status, I like to have a friend look after her while I'm away, but it's usually for much shorter time spans. Lex had a girlfriend a while back who would do it, but she's out of the picture, so I can't ask her anymore. Amalie was someone I knew personally, and she seemed to have a good head on her shoulders. But stopping by every couple of days isn't enough, not for five weeks. So out of desperation, and some guilt, and with some internal convincing that Ruby wasn't going to lose my ferret in one of the heating vents, I stuck to the plan. So here she is, stroking my ferret.

As Ruby's long, dark hair tickles my arm and her shirt gapes, giving me an excellent view of her cleavage, I can admit—to myself—that my dick is one-hundred percent in control of all decision making where Ruby is concerned at this moment, and that he was partially responsible for allowing her to move in here.

She's still petting Francesca. Which would be fine, except her favorite place to curl up happens to be right on top of my decision-making cock. And his awareness of how close Ruby's hand is is causing an unfortunate reaction, because he would like the same treatment.

Which isn't going to happen. Not tonight anyway. Not when I'm leaving her in my condo for the next five weeks. I barely know her. She could be one of those women who automatically assume sex equals a relationship. And since she's taking care of my pets, I can't have additional complications getting in the way of that. Maybe once I'm back and her living situation is taken care of it could be a possibility. Unfortunately, getting my head below the waist to acknowledge the downside of getting into her shorts tonight seems rather impossible.

Shit. I need to get my head under control. Both of them. Under any other circumstances I'd relocate Francesca, because I recognize her preferred napping location is a little odd. Usually there's no one else here to witness it. Unfortunately, I'm starting to get hard, and she's the only thing hiding what will definitely become a full-blown problem if Ruby keeps petting her.

I'd like to attribute the blame, in part, to the shorts Ruby is wearing. They barely cover her ass. In fact, they *just* cover her fine, sculpted ass. I'm currently fighting with my hands to stay tucked behind my neck rather than reaching out and copping a feel. As an athlete—or a former athlete—I can appreciate how much time and effort goes into an ass as tight as Ruby's.

I'm not being a pig. Not intentionally. But she's freshly showered and, based on her casual attire and her complete lack of makeup, she's not concerned about impressing me. I like it. A lot. She's different from the women I'm typically subjected to, especially with my mother's recent interference in my dating life.

I drag my eyes up, away from the perfect globe of her ass, hugged by tiny shorts, to the curve of her waist, up over her cleavage, along her neck to the line of her jaw. I get caught at her mouth. Her tongue peeks out just a little, a tongue I've had in my mouth before. The memory is a little fuzzy thanks to the cold meds and scotch combo, but I still have it—and I'd like to see what else that smart, sassy mouth of her can get up to.

But not tonight.

This is my new mantra. I'm sure I can keep my hands and my mouth to myself long enough to get my ass on that plane tomorrow morning. Normally I'm pretty decent with self-control. For as many years as I spent playing professional rugby where female fans will happily shed their clothes with little more encouragement than a smile, I didn't take advantage of opportunities for endless hookups. I mean, obviously, I took part in hookups, but I was discreet, and I didn't leave a trail of fucked fans across the globe.

First and foremost, it wouldn't have reflected well on my family. I've seen enough scandal to understand the ripple effect it can have. I've watched the way my parents are with each other, and while there may not be an overwhelming amount of affection, my father has enough respect for my mother to keep his wandering eye to a minimum. That's not always the case in their circle. I don't ever want to be the kind of person who believes that status or money absolves me of morality.

But there's something about Ruby Scott that makes me want to behave badly. Very badly. Which is why I'm imagining yanking those shorts down and bending that sweet, tight ass over her ugly chair and fucking her until it breaks.

I check the clock. It's only seven. I have ten hours to manage myself. I just have to make it to the morning when I'm on a plane with an ocean between us to make it easier to keep my dick in check. It really shouldn't be as difficult as it seems.

Ruby gives Francesca a couple more strokes before she prances over to her chair—which I moved so she could sit in it if she wanted. She flops down, sprawling out over the ugly lounger. She's a gorgeous picture. Her long, toned legs hang over the arm. Her toes are naked, not painted. She's not manicured or primped at all. It's refreshing. That's what Ruby is: refreshing.

Pretension is almost ingrained in my family's DNA. Although it seemed to pass me by, it's what I've been raised to endure and expect. Ruby's the same, at least based on her last name and who her father is, but like me, she seems to be missing that awful genetic component. The chair she's sitting in tells me that. Where she was living tells me that as well. The whole shower fiasco tells me she's been out of the circuit for a while, and I want to know exactly how she got where she is, and why she's made the choices she has to get here.

Unfortunately I don't have time for that tonight. My goal this evening is to make sure she's going to take care of my pets and not ruin my condo while I'm gone. Based on what I've seen so far, I have a feeling I'm dealing with a bit of a live wire when it comes to the lovely Miss Ruby Scott. For now I'm trying to figure her out.

"I ordered Italian for dinner, I hope that's okay."

Her eyes go wide. "Pizza?"

"Um, no."

Her face falls a bit.

"Authentic Italian. Spaghetti Bolognese, chicken Parmesan, bruschetta, meatballs, pasta primavera, that kind of thing. I didn't want to disturb you once you were in the shower and not being attacked by the jets, so I just got a bit of everything."

"Ha ha. All of that sounds amazing." She pats her stomach. "I hope I can handle it."

"How're you feeling? Have you been able to eat?" The flu bug I'd had lasted for days. Enough days that I worried I wouldn't be able to get on the plane tomorrow. But I'm fine now. Although I'm down a good ten pounds still. Ruby's small. She's compact and tight, all muscle and lean lines. I'd like to see how she feels under me. Or on top of me. Shit. This woman makes my imagination want to go on a detour to the land of perversion.

"I'm okay. A steady diet of Gatorade and saltines seems to have gotten me through the worst of it."

"I'm sorry I did that to you." *I'm also sorry that I'm currently imagining all the things I'd like to do to you.*

Ruby shrugs and motions to the condo and the chair she's sitting in. "You're more than making up for it now. I really appreciate this."

"It benefits us both, right? You have a place to stay until you find a new apartment and I have someone to take care of Francesca and Tiny."

Ruby smiles. She has a pretty smile, with white, straight teeth, except for one eyetooth, which is turned just a touch. I like the small imperfection. After years of playing professional rugby, I have a lot of those.

The buzzer goes off, signaling the food has arrived and someone will be on their way up shortly. "That must be the food." I sit up and Francesca makes a snuffling noise as I lift her from my lap, turning away from Ruby so she can't see the adjustments I make.

"I should probably learn all the codes and stuff, shouldn't I?" Ruby leaps out of the chair, landing soundlessly on the hardwood. She's incredibly graceful. I imagine that must translate nicely into bedroom activities.

I manage to pull my head out of the gutter long enough to give Ruby a rundown on the entry system. "Any deliveries are intercepted by front desk security."

"Don't you have to go down and get it?"

"Generally, whoever is working the security desk will bring deliveries to the door unless otherwise requested."

"That's so awesome. I used to have to wait for the stupid elevator or run down four flights of stairs if it was taking too long, or out of order, which was often."

"I don't think you'll find that to be an issue here. Since we're on the penthouse level we have a dedicated elevator, so waiting is rare."

"You could totally be a hermit living here, couldn't you?" she asks.

"If I didn't like people, I suppose I could."

Ruby cocks her head to the side, and her smile holds a hint of devious curiosity. "Do you like people?"

"It depends on the people."

"But you like me." She makes a face, as if she's embarrassed by her own statement.

"What I know of you so far, yes." I smile at the flush that creeps into her cheeks. "While I'm gone I'll give you access to services I use so you'll be able to get what you need."

Her tone hardens a little, as if she's offended by the courtesy. "You don't have to do that."

"You're staying here, there will be things you require, both for yourself and Francesca and Tiny. I won't have you spending your own money taking care of my animals."

Her gaze drops to her feet. "I guess that makes sense when you put it that way."

I have to wonder a little about her financial situation. She comes from money; however, that reveal at the restaurant is another reason I caved and offered her a place to stay. At least my family was supportive of my decision to pursue rugby as a career. It doesn't seem as though she has even that.

"I have groceries delivered every Friday, although the order is tailored to my taste. I was going to cancel it, but since you're here . . ." I trail off. "I'll show you how to make changes after dinner."

"Sure. Okay." Ruby wears an unreadable expression. I'm unsure what to make of it, and I don't get to ask because there's a knock at the door.

Which reminds me that Francesca needs to go back in her cage. "Would you be able to put her in my room while I get this?"

"Of course." Ruby flits over to the couch, scoops up Francesca, and carries her down the hall.

I wait until she slips into my bedroom before I open the door, accept the takeout, provide a generous tip, and

lock up. If I'm being honest, I'm a little nervous about
leaving Francesca. Especially since ferrets are illegal in
New York, which is part of the reason I ended up with
her in the first place. Someone brought her to one of my
father's hotels without fully understanding the implica-
tions. Or maybe they had, since they'd smuggled her in.
She was improperly caged, so she got loose, chewed
through wiring, caused all kinds of damage, and disappeared into a vent. Her owners just left her. She's
lucky she's alive.

My father's plan was to give her to Animal Control,
which probably would have terminated her. I told him I'd
take care of it. And I did. Just not the way he expected
me to.

Within twenty-four hours I'd had a cage delivered to
the condo and I'd set up a habitat for her. The few people
who have access to my condo are aware of the delicate
situation and are compensated for their silence. It sounds
far more mafia than it is.

When I took her in as a refugee I hadn't expected to
be traveling. I've been fighting my dad on this trip for
weeks now, but there's no getting out of it. I know how
he works. If I have a hope in hell of getting what I want
in the future, I have to give him what he wants now,
which is weeks of travel and research so I can learn the
company ropes and be another cog in his machine.

I unpack all the containers. It's the best Italian takeout in this city as far as I'm concerned. Their pizza is also
amazing, but I thought it was safe to order something I
knew Ruby would like, hence the pasta primavera.

I pull a bottle of white from my wine fridge and a
bottle of red as well, in case she prefers one over the
other. She mentioned liking martinis, but I'm not adept
at making those, so wine will have to do. I'm also not

sure how fully she's recovered from her illness. I know it took me more than a week to recover.

I debate whether I want to set the table, or the island. The table is a bit too formal, I think. Casual is better. I pour sparkling water and set places for both of us. Then I wait for her to return. For some reason I'm nervous. As if this were a date, not two people reviewing pet care instructions.

A giggle filters down the hall. A very pretty, feminine giggle. I follow the sound, which gets louder the closer I get to my bedroom. What the hell is she doing in there? A million and one highly inappropriate scenarios blow through my mind.

I push the door open and what I find isn't really all that far from what I was imagining. Just with more clothing. Not much more, though, considering Ruby's outfit.

My suits have been moved from my bed to the dresser and my suitcase lies open on the floor. She's in the middle of my bed—my unmade bed—on her knees. Her shorts have ridden up, one side higher than the other, exposing some cheek. A lump moves around under the sheet and she follows it around, giggling every time Francesca bolts in a new direction. It's a game I play with her sometimes. It's a game I'd like to play with Ruby. Naked.

"Dinner's ready." My voice comes out a little gravelly.

Ruby's head snaps around mid-giggle. "She loves playing under—"

I wonder what my expression must be for the words to die on her tongue like that.

"The sheets." I finish for her, my voice still too low. "I know."

She looks around and then down, maybe realizing where she is. Her eyes go comically wide and she pulls the sheet back, scooping up Francesca and scrambling off the bed. "I'm sorry. That wasn't—" She gestures to my bed. "I didn't mean to. I put her down so I could manage the cage latch and then we started playing."

I let her ramble for a couple more seconds before I crack a smile. "It's fine. You're good. It's one of her favorite places to hide."

"Well it's such a big bed, and there's so much room to play."

I'm not sure if she means it the way my brain interprets it. Ruby carries Francesca over to the cage, her shorts still riding high on one side. Half of her left ass cheek is on display. It's a very nice ass cheek. I'd like to get my hands on it or sink my teeth into it. I really need to get a handle on myself. And I plan to. Later. When I'm alone in this room and she's locked away in hers.

I follow Ruby to the cage and watch as she latches it to make sure it's done properly. There have been a couple of occasions in which I've mistakenly thought I'd locked it, but hadn't. Francesca likes warm, cozy places. Something else she and my dick have in common. The difference being, if she escapes from her cage, she's likely to find a hiding place I can't easily retrieve her from.

"There we go," Ruby says softly as she lowers Francesca into the cage. "Do you ever let her sleep with you?"

"Not typically. Sometimes she's hard to find in the morning, and I can't have her roaming while I'm at work." She's ended up under the covers with me in the middle of the night because I've fallen asleep while watching TV. She has a few choice places she likes to sleep, and since I'm not a big fan of boxers, it was a bit of a shock the first time it happened. Since then, I've taken to wearing boxers if I let her sleep with me since she seems to have a bit of a fascination with things that dangle.

"I imagine that wouldn't be very good."

"It's okay because of the ferret-proofing I've done, but I still don't want to invite mischief if it's unnecessary."

"No one likes mischief." Ruby gives me a wide smile that says exactly the opposite. "I'm starving. Let's see if I can keep food down!"

And off she goes, practically dancing her way down the hall. She doesn't wait for me to make it back to the kitchen—I check the latch one more time, just to be safe. When I get there, all the containers are open and she already has a fork in one. She twirls it, gathering noodles. It's a massive amount. She tips her head back, opens wide, and shoves the entire thing in her mouth, making sounds that I would definitely not isolate to food enjoyment.

She groans and turns to me, puts her hand up in front of her mouth, and says, "Dis ib so gub."

"So you like it then?" I grab a fork and load up a plate, handing her one so she doesn't feel compelled to eat out of the box.

She takes it, her cheeks coloring pink as she continues to chew the huge mouthful. She loads her plate. I'm surprised by the amount of food she piles on, considering her size, but I don't say anything. I like a woman with a healthy appetite.

Once we're loaded up with food she slides into the chair beside me.

"Wine?" I gesture to the open bottles on the counter.

"Oh. Uh, white, maybe?" She looks uncertain.

"Don't feel obligated."

"I don't." When I raise a brow, she brings her fingers up, Girl Scout style. "Promise. No obligations. I just haven't had any alcohol since I became the Vomitron last week."

"Vomitron?"

"It's my superhero name. Not very badass, but rather fitting, all things considered."

We eat in silence for a few minutes. I'm starving. I haven't had anything to eat since breakfast, so I could probably plow through two or three entrees no problem, but I try to scale it back so I don't come across as uncivilized.

Ruby makes an uncomfortable noise. "I think I took too much."

"Your eyes are bigger than your stomach," I observe. She's only managed to get through half the contents on her plate.

She pats her stomach. "It appears that way."

When her shirt was sticking to her skin in the shower I noted the definition there. She's in very, very good shape. I drag my eyes back up, which means I'm looking at her chest for a second before I meet her eyes. "Did you leave room for dessert?"

It comes out heavy sounding, and a little raspy.

Ruby's eyes flare and then her lids lower, so does her voice. "Dessert?"

"I always order dessert when I get takeout from this place. It's in the fridge."

"Oh. Right. I might need a little time for my stomach to settle before I can put anything else in there." She rubs it a few times for emphasis.

I try to keep my eyes in safe zones, away from her chest.

She clears her throat. "Now that we're cleaned and fed should we go through the house rules?"

"Right. Of course. Hold on." I push away from the table and cross the kitchen to retrieve the binder I put together. Since I'm away for such an extended period I wanted to make sure I cover all possible scenarios.

"Wow. You have a binder?" Ruby looks like she's trying not to laugh.

"There are a lot of things that need to be covered."

"Uh huh."

"Your tone implies you think this is excessive."

She takes the binder from me and opens it. "How many pages is this? More than a hundred?"

"It's ninety-eight. Francesca and Tiny have very specific needs."

"Ninety-eight pages of needs." She leafs through it and mutters, "I wish someone was this in tune to *my* needs."

I bite my tongue and say nothing about how I'm sure I could attend to every single damn one of them if she'd like to go back to my bedroom and play "hide and seek" in my sheets with me. "It's not *all* about Tiny and Francesca. It also contains codes, passwords, fire safety, where to locate things, how to use various technological equipment, public transit information, areas to avoid, that kind of thing."

"Is there a section on how to make the bed? Do you have a diagram for hospital corners?"

"I trust in your ability to make your bed however you see fit."

She stops flipping, jabbing her finger at the page. "You have instructions on how to use the washer and dryer."

"This is coming from someone who got stuck in the shower because she couldn't figure out how to adjust the temperature or work the jets. Besides, they can be difficult to figure out." It took me three loads to get what was going on at first.

"I'm more of a visual learner. Why don't you show me all this stuff? Do you have a checklist? Maybe a star chart? I can have dessert when I earn five stars." Her eyes

light up with the same mischief I caught a glimpse of
when she was playing with Francesca on my bed.

I spend the next hour going over everything in the
house, from where to dispose of the garbage to how to
use the TV remote, to where to find Francesca and Tiny's food. Ruby appears as if she's paying close attention.
When she has a question she puts her hand on my arm
and looks up at me with wide, inquisitive eyes.

I'm in the middle of showing her where to find the pots
and pans should she want to cook when she walks away
from me.

"Um, what is this?" She taps the table across from
Tiny's terrarium.

"It's an answering machine."

"What year is it from? Nineteen-eighty?"

She's probably pretty close.

"It even has the mini-cassette tape!" She appears flab-
bergasted. "You have a cell phone, don't you?"

"I do."

"Then why do you have this?" Ruby picks it up and it
takes everything in me not to freak out and tear it out of
her hands.

Instead I gently pry the machine away from her and
set it carefully back on the table, brushing away any dust
or fingerprints. "It's nostalgic."

"Because you were born at the end of the decade?"
She's sort of poking fun, but her voice is soft, and she
seems more curious now than anything.

"It was my grandmother's. She'd had it forever. The
tapes were so hard to find so I figured I would try to teach
her how to use a cell phone. She kept saying no, and I
kept trying to persuade her."

"Did you?"

I nod. "I told her we could play poker against each other all the time and she was sold."

Ruby laughs. "She's a card shark?"

"She was."

"It sounds like you're close."

"We were. She passed away last year." I'd been away at the time and almost missed the funeral, much like I'd missed a lot of things relating to my family. That's why I'm glad to be back in New York.

"I'm so sorry." Ruby reaches out and puts her hand on my arm, giving it a soft squeeze.

"Me, too. She was a great woman. She was the mastermind behind the whole hotel empire, although my grandfather took all the glory for that. Anyway, when we were cleaning out her place I found the answering machine and took it. It was one of those things . . . I should probably get rid of it, but . . ."

"I think it's sweet."

"Hardly anyone calls me on that line. My mother sometimes does. There's a manual in here if you run into issues." I tap her hip and she shifts to the side. I open the drawer and show her the dog-eared manual in the Ziploc bag.

Her nose crinkles. "Maybe I'll just leave this one alone."

I lean against the counter behind me. "That's probably best, and if there are any real issues you can always call, text, or email."

"It might be easier than going through this." She pats the binder tucked under her arm. "Unless there's an appendix and a quick reference guide."

When I say nothing, she moves to stand beside me, her arm brushing mine as she sets the binder on the counter and flips to the back page, where there is, indeed, a quick reference guide, but only for the most major of potential issues, such as Francesca getting ill or the fire alarm going off in my condo, both of which I sincerely hope don't happen.

"Wow. You're uh . . . super organized, aren't you?"

I shrug. "I just like to be prepared."

She shifts, angling her body toward me. I'm quite a bit taller than she is, so I get a nice peek at her cleavage. "Were you a Boy Scout?"

"I spent a few years in Cadets."

"Ah. So you're very disciplined, then?"

"I guess." I suppose in some ways I am. As an athlete, I had to constantly push myself, especially when I was injured.

"Does that mean in addition to being organized, you're a rule follower?"

"It depends, I suppose."

"On what?"

"Whether I like the rule or not."

She laughs. "So you just like to enforce them? Not follow?"

"Something like that."

Ruby pinches the sleeve of my T-shirt between two fingers and lifts it until she reaches the edge of my tattoo. "This seems pretty anti-rule to me."

"It's hardly anti-rule anymore. Everyone has tattoos these days."

"I don't."

"I bet you've thought about getting one, though." I imagine it would be something small. Not like mine.

Ruby shrugs. "If I did it would have to be somewhere I could hide it."

"Like your hip?" I tap the spot with a finger, then quickly retract my hand when she jumps a little.

"I guess, and then what's the point of wearing art if no one else gets to see it?"

"You'd see it every day, and I'm sure someone would get to see it, eventually."

"But only when I'm wearing a bikini, or maybe not even then."

"Or when you're naked," I supply.

Ruby leans in a little closer, until her chest is an inch from mine. She has to tip her chin up in order to maintain eye contact. If I didn't have a better handle on my hormones I might be tempted to lean down and kiss her. But my dick is not in control of my brain right now. Mostly.

Her voice comes out low and sultry. "You realize this is the second time you've referenced me being naked since I've been here."

"Are you keeping track?"

She fingers the strap of her tank. "I'm just noting your apparent obsession with me being naked."

"I'm just providing helpful suggestions; you're the one making it about nudity."

She scoffs and backs up a step, which is unfortunate, I could've sworn I felt her nipples brush my chest a second ago. Or maybe that's wishful thinking on my part. It's not as if I'm going to say no to her if she happens to make a move. I just don't think I should be the one to make the move being that I assaulted her in a hallway and just moved her into my condo.

"You're putting an awful lot of thought into a tattoo I'm never going to get."

"Never say never."

"I hate needles and I have no interest in letting someone I don't know put their hands that close to my . . . my . . ."

"Your?" I prompt.

She ducks her head and mumbles, "My special place."

I laugh. "Your special place?"

"Shut it." She pushes on my chest and I grab her hand.

"You can do better than that." I should really stop, because this is its own special brand of torment for my cock, but I really want to hear her say something dirty.

"You mean like my who-ha? Lady garden? Love tunnel, Precious flower? Or do you mean slit." She drags out the *s,* then runs her tongue across her bottom lip. "No, not slit, you're probably more of a *pussy* lover, aren't you?"

"Fuckin' right I am." Maybe I don't give a shit about complications. I'm still holding her wrist, and she's not making a move to get away. I bow my head, inches away from that sexy, naughty mouth. Her eyes lift to mine and her lips part. She wants this. Fuck it.

I'm about to take it when my goddamn phone rings. It's enough to break the tension. Ruby steps back, eyes darting away, head dropping, as I mutter a curse and check the contact. It's my father. "I have to take this."

"Of course." Her hand flutters to her throat and she gives me a nervous smile. I answer the call and walk across the room, to the office, adjusting my hard-on, which has returned with a vengeance. I rubbed one out in the shower, but it looks like I'm going to have to do that again after I go to bed.

My conversation with my father is brief and unnecessary as far as I'm concerned. When I return to the living room I half expect her to have disappeared into her room for the night on account of my behavior. She hasn't. Instead she's reclining in her dilapidated lounger balancing a cup of Tiramisu on her stomach. A second dessert sits on the coffee table in front of the couch. I assume it's for me.

"I figured I earned all my stars so I was allowed to have dessert. But I waited for you, just to make sure."

I get another one of her impish grins, which is a relief. I could've made things awkward if I'd let my dick take control again. "You probably deserve both of these." I drop my phone on the coffee table, beside my dessert and flop down on the couch. "Sorry about that. Last minute pre-trip conversations."

"Everything okay?" she asks.

"Yeah. My father likes to micromanage."

"That seems to be a pretty common father trait," Ruby says.

"Sounds like you're familiar with that."

"There's a reason I'm here and he lives in Rhode Island. Well, one of the reasons, anyway." She smiles and drops her gaze. "So you and Armstrong are pretty close?"

It's an abrupt change of topic, clearly talking about her father is as unpleasant for her as is talking about mine right now. "We went to the same prep school. Our parents spent a lot of time with each other, so it sort of forced us together, if that makes sense." Armstrong and I are close in some respects, but he does a lot of things that irk me. If I had to work with him I'd probably punch him in the face. Often. He's an overbearing prick at the best of times.

Ruby cocks her head to the side, like she's seeking the deeper meaning in my tone. "Are you in the wedding party?"

"I am. So are you, aren't you?"

"I'm Amie's maid of honor. I'm surprised I didn't meet

you at the engagement party, before the uh . . . bathroom run-in."

"I was tucked away in a corner, not feeling all that well most of the evening. I guess we'll be spending a lot of time together when the wedding plans get underway."

"Mmm. That we will."

Now it's my turn to assess her tone. "You don't seem all that excited."

"About the wedding?" Ruby lifts one shoulder. "It's just really fast. I mean, I guess when you know, you know, but Amie has never been one to jump into things, well not this kind of thing, so this feels a little . . . rushed."

Armstrong is an intense person. When he sees something he wants, he goes after it, not always considering the rashness of his actions. In the past it's created some conflict, particularly with my brother Lexington, as they often seem to have an affinity for the same type of women. My other brother, Griffin, is the only one of the three of us with a stable relationship history. But then he's the oldest, so that makes sense, I suppose. "You've told Amalie this?"

Her expression becomes incredulous. "Of course not. I'm not going to rain on her parade. I'm probably just being overprotective. We've been friends for a long time. I just want her to be happy."

"And you think she is?"

"She seems that way."

"But—" I prompt.

"But nothing, I guess. I'll support her no matter what, even if dealing with Armstrong's mother is going to give me an ulcer."

I laugh. "Gwendolyn can be challenging."

"Any tips you might have would be greatly appreciated."

"Don't let her smell your fear."

Ruby snorts. "Awesome. Thanks. So she's exactly like a tarantula."

She dips her spoon into her dessert and daintily brings it to her mouth, full lips parting. She moans her appreciation. "This is ridiculously delicious."

"They have the best desserts."

"I'd forgo the actual dinner part and just order six of these next time." She digs her spoon in and takes a much larger, more decadent bite. Her head falls back and her eyes drift close. "Seriously, Bancroft. This is amazing."

I'm a big fan of the way my name sounds coming out of her mouth. Apparently so is my dick, since he's trying to give her a wave from inside my shorts. That reprieve didn't last very long. "I'll leave the takeout menu for you."

"I may eat nothing else for the next five weeks if you do that."

When she's halfway through her dessert, she sighs and lifts her gaze.

I haven't been eating my own, more than entertained watching her. "So you said no boyfriend, right? You're not even casually dating anyone?"

She stops with her spoon halfway to her mouth. "What?"

Shit. That's not a random question I can just throw out there without having a reason for asking it. I flounder for a second, trying to come up with something that makes sense. "Or friends you plan to entertain while you're here?"

"Oh, uh . . . just Amie I guess. And of course the two hundred people I invited to the kegger tomorrow." She wags her eyebrows.

I tap my spoon on the edge of my dessert and give her a rueful smile in return. "Right. Can't forget that."

She regards me speculatively. "Would you prefer it if I don't have guests?"

If they're male, yes, I definitely prefer she doesn't have them here, but I'm not about to say that aloud. That makes me sounds like a territorial asshole, which I have no right to be. "No, no. It's fine, but I'd prefer you don't give out the entry code."

"Of course not. I won't leave any strays unattended." Her grin is impish. "Is there anyone who has the code who might pop by, other than the cleaning lady?"

"Just my brothers and immediate family, but they don't have a reason to stop by if I'm not here."

She taps the arm of her chair and regards me for a few seconds. "So . . . that woman you were with at the engagement party, I'm guessing she's not your girlfriend or anything? I don't need to worry about her freaking out because another woman is living in your condo?"

"You mean Brittany? Uh, no. She's definitely not my girlfriend."

"Good to know."

"With all the travel a girlfriend hasn't been all that practical."

She cocks her head. "What do you mean?"

"When I played professional rugby I was on the road a lot. And now it seems like I'll be on the road more than I anticipated. At least for a while. It makes it difficult to get involved."

"Ah. I understand. Theater is challenging like that, too. The hours are odd since performances are typically in the evenings and on the weekends. Unless you're dating another actor it's not very practical." She dips her spoon in her dessert again. "So that Brittany chick was just meant to be a hookup then?"

I'm sure Brittany would've been good with the hookup

part, but I don't mention that to Ruby. "I went out with her as a favor."

She grimaces. "Wow, that's some favor."

"She's not that bad." I'm not sure why I'm defending Brittany, other than it seems to irritate Ruby.

"She called me a slut!"

"Well, you were kissing me, so . . ." I have to bite back the smile at her incredulity.

She points her spoon at me, her annoyance clear. "*You* kissed *me*."

I shift an arm behind my head. "You didn't put up much of a fight."

Her mouth drops open and snaps shut just as quickly. It's the same reaction I got out of her the other day when I brought the same thing up at the restaurant.

Her eyes narrow into slits. I bet she's a real firecracker when she's angry. I sort of want to push her buttons just to see what happens when she goes off. I bet angry fucking with her would be incredible. I wonder if she's a hair puller, or a biter, or a scratcher. Wow. That got dirty fast.

She narrows her eyes. "We are *not* talking about this."

"About you kissing me back? I wasn't going to bring it up, but now that we're on the subject—"

"Consider it un-brought-up." Her cheeks flush.

I can't help myself. I keep pushing. "No way. You as much as admitted that you kissed me back, right there. You opened the door. I'm walking through it. Why would you kiss a complete stranger?"

"I said I wasn't talking about this." The pink in her cheeks rises to the tips of her ears.

This is way too much fun. She's got one hell of an angry glare going on. "I'm leaving you in my house for more than a month, alone. I need to be certain you have sound judgment."

"I'll have you know my judgment is usually very sound. However, when an incredibly attractive man surprises me with his tongue in my mouth, the most logical response is to kiss back."

"You think I'm incredibly attractive?"

She rolls her eyes. "Of course that's the part you choose to focus on. You see yourself in the mirror every day. You can't tell me you don't know you're nice to look at. I'm just stating a fact."

My ego inflates a little at this. I know I'm not unattractive, but my nose has been broken a couple of times, and there's a bump I can't ever get rid of without plastic surgery. I've had knee surgery and I'm not great under anesthetic, so I'd prefer to avoid that scenario. I also have a few small facial scars from playing rugby all those years, which, in the environment I grew up in, takes me down a few points on the desirability scale. Not that I give a fuck. It's my mother who seems to be worried about it, as she does about every line and gray hair. It's a blessing I don't have any sisters.

"I see. So you're telling me if any incredibly attractive man did what I did, you'd respond the exact same way."

"Now you're generalizing. It's circumstantial."

"What do you mean by circumstantial?"

"Well, I guess I assumed you had to be a guest at the engagement party."

"So that made it okay to kiss a stranger? Because we were attending the same event?"

She pauses with her spoon at her lips. "That's not what I said."

"It sounds like that's what you're implying." That spoons slips into her mouth and she licks it clean before she responds. The entire time I'm thinking increasingly dirty thoughts about that tongue of hers.

She flounders a little. "It's not like I was at some seedy bar with seedy douches. It was an engagement party."

"So that makes me better somehow?"

"Are you always this antagonistic?" She throws up her hands. "You kissed me. You smelled good and you're good with your tongue so I went with it. Stop judging me."

"I'm not judging, I'm just asking. So on top of being incredibly attractive and smelling good I'm also an excellent kisser."

"I never said *excellent,* you added your own adjective. And if you keep talking about how attractive you are you'll go from a ten to a nine pretty fast."

"Oh? So I'm a ten?"

"You were an eleven before you started pushing this angle. That last question puts you at an eight-point-five."

"I guess I should change the subject before I'm in the negative."

"You just earned back half a point."

"Maybe I should stop while I'm ahead, or less behind, anyway."

"Good plan." She leans over and grabs the remote to turn on the TV. I guess that conversation is over. For now.

We finish our dessert in silence. Not uncomfortable silence, but there's weight in it. Every so often I look over at Ruby, thinking I feel her looking at me, but maybe it's just in my head. Or maybe I'm looking for a reason to keep baiting her.

The next time I look over her eyes are closed. Her legs are still hanging off the edge of the chair, but she's slouched down and her head looks like it's at an uncomfortable angle. If she stays like that too long her neck is going to be sore. The tiramisu container is empty and resting against her thighs, right over a different kind of dessert I'd like to try. She's still holding the spoon and there's a smear on her tank. She must be exhausted and still recovering from that flu bug I passed on to her.

"Ruby."

She makes a little noise and shifts around, her brow furrowing as she tries to get comfortable, but can't because of the limited amount of room she has to maneuver.

I turn off the TV aware I need to go to bed, so I can manage my early morning flight. I have hours of work to accomplish on the plane.

I push up from the couch, pluck the empty container from her lap, and slip the spoon out from her fist.

Her hands immediately smooth down her stomach and nestle between her legs as she tries to roll to the side. I'd like to get my hands between her legs, among other parts of my body. Not while she's sleeping, obviously. That would just make me a creepy douche.

I shake her shoulder. "Ruby."

Her eyes pop open and she blinks blearily, confusion knitting her brows together as she looks at me and then at her surroundings.

"You fell asleep."

"Oh." She glances down at her hands, tucked between her legs, and pulls them free.

It takes her a moment to get her bearings. She stretches, arms going over her head, chest pushing out as she stands. Her tank rides up, exposing toned abs, and wait . . . is that a *belly* ring? How did I miss that before now? There's definitely a streak of rebellion in this one.

She shuffles across the floor, a shiver running up her spine and goose bumps break across her arms. Her shorts are askew, half of one butt cheek on display again. She has a tiny mole on the right one, not that I'm looking that closely or anything.

I toss the empty containers in the trash and drop the spoons in the sink. Ruby stands half in, half out of her temporary room. "What time do you leave in the morning?" Her voice is raspy with sleep.

"Early. Before six."

Her nose scrunches up. "Yuck. That's an awful time to be awake."

"It's pretty typical for me."

"Sometimes that's when I go to bed."

"Partying hard?"

"Just a nighthawk. Productions tend to be in the evening, it makes my schedule a little unconventional, when I have a role." She leans her head against the doorjamb. "I don't think sleeping is going to be a problem tonight, though." She stifles a yawn. "Well, I guess I'll see you in five weeks."

"I'll check in once I'm settled."

"Great."

We stare at each other for a few long seconds and then she takes a tentative step forward. "Thanks again for trusting me to take care of your babies." Suddenly her body is flush against mine as her arms come around my waist.

I barely have enough time to return the hug before she releases me and steps away, eyes darting down as her cheeks flush pink.

"I'm glad it worked out for both of us."

"Me, too." She bites her lip, her gaze shifting to me. "Have a safe trip, Bancroft. G'night."

"Night."

She gives me a small smile, slips into her room and closes the door. I head to mine so I can take care of the issue that's been plaguing me all night before I catch a few hours of sleep. And then leave this woman in my home for five weeks while I learn how to manage hotel properties.

CHAPTER 8

BON VOYAGE

RUBY

Noise wakes me at 5:36 in the morning. It takes me a few seconds to orient myself to the unfamiliar surroundings. I'm not used to the mostly quiet, so the footsteps and the sound of a suitcase being wheeled down the hall seem louder than they probably are.

Bancroft must be leaving for the airport. We said good-bye last night, but I'm suddenly very awake, and alert. I won't see him for five weeks. I stare at the ceiling while I listen to him tooling around in the kitchen, trying to decide if I should get up and say good-bye again or stay where I am. My vagina decides for me. She wants a visual hit of Bancroft before he leaves for the next month.

I throw off the covers and tiptoe to the bathroom, blind myself with the light and check myself out in the mirror. My hair's pretty screwed and I have puffy sleep eyes, but otherwise I'm fine. Well, fine-ish. I rinse with mouthwash, and finger-comb my hair so it doesn't look like I'm trying too hard, but I also don't look like a troll, either. I clear my throat and find it doesn't hurt anymore, and my stomach actually rumbles.

Opening my bedroom door a crack, I peek out. Light filters down from the kitchen. I shiver as I walk down the hall, the hardwood floor cool beneath my feet. I'm definitely not accustomed to the air-conditioning. Two black suitcases come into view as I approach the foyer.

And then there's Bancroft. Holy sweet mother of one-hand-clapping material, is this man ever *not* hot? He's standing at the kitchen counter, writing something on a piece of paper, dressed in a black suit, complete with jacket and tie. His broad shoulders and narrow waist make it look absolutely fantastic. His hair is styled, the dark curls tamed with some sort of product. I want to run my fingers through it and mess it up. He's freshly shaven, unlike last night, and completely put together.

"Hey." My voice comes out all gravelly, possibly from sleep, possibly because I'm thinking about how fun it would be to peel that suit off him. With my teeth. And get to all the good stuff underneath.

His head jerks and he glances up to where I'm standing at the edge of the hallway, half in the dark. I step into the foyer and his eyes flare, sweeping over me.

"I didn't mean to wake you." His voice matches mine in rasp. He reaches up and adjusts his tie. His hand smooths over the shock of electric blue fabric. I follow the movement, watching as he fastens the button of his jacket. He was dressed similarly at the engagement party, but I didn't have an opportunity to appreciate it the way I can now.

I've been staring and he's said words. I'm also biting my knuckle. I release it from my teeth. "Don't worry about it. I'm used to hearing traffic, so the silence is going to take some time to get used to."

His eyes keep darting down and then back up to my face. They seem to stay down longer and longer each time.

I follow his gaze trying to figure out what the deal is when I realize that my current attire isn't all that appropriate. I'm wearing a white tank, which isn't a problem, it covers all my important parts—aside from my perky nipples. What I didn't take into consideration was the fact that my bottom half is covered only by a pair of underwear. At least they're full coverage. They also happen to be lacy, since they were the only pair I could find in my semi-sleepy haze last night. I've worn less during dance competitions, but contextually, this isn't awesome. Or maybe it is considering the way he doesn't seem to be able maintain eye contact any better than me.

"Oh." I drop my hands and cover my crotch, as if that's going to help. "Uh. I'll be right back."

Bancroft's eyebrows climb a little, and a half-smile appears as I turn and rush down the hall, with my hands shielding my ass.

"Don't feel compelled to put more clothes on for my benefit," he calls after me.

I grab my kimono from the back of the bathroom door—one of the very few items I unpacked last night before I passed out—and shrug it on. On the plus side, my cheeks now match the color of the flowers decorating my robe, so at least I'm coordinated. I return to the kitchen where Bancroft is now sipping a cup of coffee. He regards me over the rim of his cup, his amusement apparent in the arch of his brow.

"Sorry about that. I've been living alone for a long time."

"No need to apologize. Your wardrobe choices are you own. I'm certainly not going to complain." He's wearing a devilish smirk as he gives me another lingering once-over.

I prop a hip against the counter and cross my arms over my chest. "Hasn't anyone ever told you it's not polite to ogle?"

His gaze lifts to mine and he leans in close, voice dropping to a whisper as if he's about to tell me a secret. "I'm not always polite."

Oh God. I'd like to experience his *not polite* all over this condo. Right here on the kitchen island would be a good place to start. I go with snark rather than offering to be his breakfast. "You're going to drop below a nine again if you keep it up."

That sexy smile of his widens. "I guess it's good that I'm leaving. I'd hate to bring myself down to a lowly eight-point-five again."

I'm first to break the stare down. "What's this?" I motion to the scribbled notes on the counter. There are also a couple of envelopes. The one on top has my name on it, but the notes are first to grab my attention. "Isn't the hundred-page care manual enough?"

He blushes a little. "It's just a few things I forgot to tell you. And we didn't discuss payment."

"Payment? For what?"

"For taking care of Francesca and Tiny."

"You're giving me a place to live and free groceries."

"You'll have other expenses. You need a stipend. Will two a week be enough? I've left a little cash to start." He taps the envelope. "I'll get bank details from you later."

"Sure, that sounds reasonable." Two hundred a week on top of having a place to live and food already taken care of will definitely make things manageable while I look for a job.

I pick up the pages, the writing is nearly illegible. "I'm supposed to be able to read this? What is it, hiero-glyphics?"

"My writing isn't that bad."

"Is that what your mom told you when you were in grade school?"

"I'll just email you later." He tries to grab the notes from me but I hide them behind my back. It pushes my chest out, drawing his attention there.

"It's fine. I'll just do some Internet research later on runes. It'll be like one of those hidden-message puzzles."

He opens his mouth, likely to shoot back another barb at me, but his phone rings. He pats his pockets and locates the device. "I have to get this." He answers the call. "Bancroft Mills speaking." A short pause follows. "I'll be right down." Once he ends the call he pockets his phone again. "It's my car for the airport." He gives me another lingering stare, and it could be in my head, but he looks like he's not all that excited about leaving at the moment.

"Have a safe trip. I promise I'll take great care of Francesca and Tiny while you're gone."

"I'm sure you will. I'll send a message when I land. And I'll check in later in the week."

"Okay." We stand there for a few seconds, staring at each other, neither one of us making any kind of move. I'm half a second away from making a colossally bad de-cision by grabbing him by the lapels of his suit jacket and dragging those luscious lips of his down to mine when he looks away and clears his throat. It's enough to break me out of my fantasizing.

"Okay. I have to go." He's said that already. He brings a hand up to his hair, but drops it. Pats his pockets, then crosses to his bags.

"I'll get the door for you." I rush ahead of him, flip the lock, and hold it open.

He pauses at the threshold. He looks like he wants to say something.

"I promise they'll be fine with me. We can always video chat if you miss them."

"Yeah. Okay. That might be good."

I'm a hugger. I've always been a hugger. Usually in my world you're allowed to do the air-kiss, back-pat, so it's on impulse, and maybe a small hormonal component, that I lean in toward him. I realize too late that my reflexive action isn't the best idea. And that I've shocked him.

"Oh. Okay," he mumbles as my face hits his chest and my arm comes around his waist. I'm about to release him when he returns the embrace, his thick arms wrapping around me. God, he's solid. And he smells incredible. Like warm laundry with a hint of cologne. His arms tighten and his head drops, his freshly shaved cheek brushes against my temple.

The press of his palm against my low back has me tilting my pelvis just the tiniest little bit. I both hear and feel his heavy exhalation against my cheek, and then his other hand is smoothing up my back, between my shoulder blades, under my hair. It makes me want to follow through on the lapel-grabbing and lip-locking.

I stop breathing when his fingertips brush over the back of my neck and his lips touch my ear. I suck in a gasping breath when the hand pressed against the dip in my spine eases just a bit lower. "I was managing just fine before the fucking lace panties," he murmurs.

The sound of another door opening and the yippy bark of a dog has us awkwardly shoving away from each other.

"Bancroft!" The heavy accent belongs to a woman

wearing more makeup than a circus clown. I have no idea how old she is, or whether she's related to humans or aliens based on the amount of cosmetic surgery she's likely had to achieve the false youthful look she's sporting. A tiny dog jumps around her feet, yipping and nipping. It tries to make a run for Bancroft's door, but Clown Woman yanks on the leash. "No, Precious! Sit!"

Precious doesn't sit, in fact, Precious growls and snaps at Bancroft. The woman snatches Precious up into her arms, chastising and then cooing.

"Hello, Ms. Blackwood. Hello, Precious. You're up early today." Bancroft's smile is as tight as Clown Woman's skin as he takes a small, but obvious step away from me, creating more distance. He also shoves his hands in his pockets, possibly doing some rearranging. I bite the inside of my lip to keep from smiling too wide.

"I'm off for a week at the spa." The Spa must be a highbrow code for a visit to the plastic surgeon, or rehab. I'm guessing it's the former rather than the latter. Ms. Blackwood's gaze travels over Bancroft—her ogling is quite obvious—and then slides to me. "Who is this you're hiding?"

Bancroft's cheek tics, as if he's trying to keep his smile from dropping. He looks just as annoyed as I feel. "This is Ruby Scott. She'll be taking care of my place while I'm away on business."

"Oh?" She gives me a speculative look. "Is she a friend of yours, then?"

"She is."

"Mmm. Well, isn't that nice. Welcome to the building, Miss Scott, is it?"

She holds out her wrinkly old hand, the one that in no way matches the stretched wrinkleless skin on her face.

I hold the top of my robe closed with one hand and

take her offered palm with the other. "It's nice to meet you, Ms. Blackwood."

"Yes. Of course. Are you enjoying the accommodations so far?"

If she wasn't pushing eighty I'd be worried about the look she's giving Bancroft.

I'm not sure what's going on here, but there seems to be some kind of weird tension between them. "Oh yes." I turn a warm smile on Bancroft and bat my lashes. "Bancroft is an incredibly accommodating, attentive host."

The tic in his cheek is back, except this time he's working to keep his smile from growing too wide. There's got to be a story with Ms. Blackwood.

"All right! Enjoy your time at the spa." I fake a yawn and smile brightly at Bancroft. "Have a great trip. I think I'll just go back to bed since you kept me up so late and woke me up so early. Call when you're all settled." I drop a quick kiss on his cheek and step out of reach.

Ms. Blackwood looks scandalized and Bancroft looks like he wants to rip my kimono off and maybe spank me. Okay, the last part is just me fantasizing. I'm going to take that back to bed with me.

I give them both a jaunty wave. "Bye Bancroft, bye Ms. Blackwood." I close the door on her horrified face and lock it, then peek through the peephole. Bancroft looks over his shoulder once before disappear down the hall to the elevators.

Five weeks of phone flirting with Bancroft might just kill me, and if it does, it's going to be the sweetest death.

CHAPTER 9
PHONE CALLS

RUBY

I go back to bed, give myself an orgasm while thinking about Bancroft, and promptly fall back to sleep. I don't get up until two in the afternoon. And the only reason I roll my lazy butt out of bed is because my bladder forces me to. That mattress is like sleeping on a cloud.

Once I've taken care of my bathroom needs, I make a trip down the hall to Bancroft's room. The door is ajar. His bed is made this time, although it's clear it was a hastily done job. The covers are wrinkly and uneven. I have the urge to smooth them out. While I've never been the best at keeping things organized and tidy, I've always made my bed. Even as a child when there was a housekeeper to take care of that kind of thing I was the one who made it. There's just something comforting about slipping into a neatly made bed.

"Hi, Franny!" I say when she peeks her head out of a tube. She makes a little noise and runs back and forth across the cage as I undo the latch. She stretches up on her hind legs, eager to be free as I open the hatch.

I pet her head and lift her out. She cuddles into me for a few seconds, then pushes away, clearly wanting the freedom to roam. My stomach growls as I wander down the hall after her. I think I might actually be able to handle coffee for the first time since Bancroft made me sick.

I find all the components for coffee and reheat some of the leftovers from last night, watching them whirl around in Bancroft's space-age microwave. Like everything else in Bancroft's condo, all of his appliances are top of the line, which means they have seven million functions and buttons to press.

After I scarf down my food I take a coffee and Francesca to my room, closing the door so I can keep an eye on her while I go through the boxes. I'm grateful that Amie helped, because she labels everything. The only stuff I really need while I'm here is clothing and toiletries.

I check to make sure Francesca hasn't burrowed under the covers before I set my massive, heavy suitcase on the bed and begin the process of transferring items into the dresser.

Francesca climbs into the drawer and sticks her head through a pair of underwear. Her nails get caught in the lace waistband so she frolics around in there, getting herself tangled up. I grab my phone and snap a picture, then send it to Bancroft without really thinking about what exactly she's gotten herself tangled in.

I don't hear back from him right away—I assume he may still be traveling since he's headed to the UK—so I get to stew in my own idiocy while I put away the rest of my clothes and move on to my toiletries. At least they're my nice undies. I'm careful about making sure all the chemical products are well out of the way and that anything with a cord is behind a closed door.

Once I'm done the bulk of my unpacking I return Francesca to Bancroft's room, play a little hide and seek with her under the covers, making a mess of his hastily made bed until she tires out and wants to nap. She curls into a ball, puts her little head down, and falls asleep while I pet her. I can totally understand why he couldn't bear to let Animal Control have her. She's adorable.

At that point I return her to her cage so I can snoop around Bancroft's bedroom. His bathroom is amazing with a huge soaker tub and a shower twice as big as the one in my room with twice as many jets. As far as man bathrooms are concerned, it's not too disgusting. The toilet seat is down, which is a bonus. There's a blue towel half hanging out of the laundry hamper and another draped haphazardly over the towel rack.

I leave his room for another, more detailed tour of Bancroft's condo. Last night I was mostly paying attention to his biceps, and his butt, and all the other nice parts of him.

On my way to get a better look at the home gym I stop to check on Tiny. She's sitting right beside her water dish, which I need to change. I follow the instructions in the binder and refill the dish. Since she's eaten recently, I won't need to feed her a cricket for several more days. She's definitely going to be the easier of the two pets to take care of.

One detail I missed about his gym—and I'm not actually sure how—is the life-sized photograph of Bancroft hanging from the wall. Apparently he was the poster boy for the Rugby Championship a few years ago. The picture is an action shot of him mid-kick.

Holy sweet thighs. Holy sweet everything. The only thing that would make the picture better would be if he were shirtless. His face glistens with sweat, which should be unattractive but isn't. His hair curls around his neck and sticks to his forehead. Every muscle in his body seems to be flexed with exertion. I wonder if I can take this off the wall and bring it into my bedroom. I check the edges and pull on the corner of the frame, but it doesn't budge. Too bad.

My phone rings from somewhere in the condo, three bars of the same catchy tune repeating as I search for the location of the noise. The nice thing about living in a studio apartment is not having a lot of ground to cover when things go missing. Bancroft's condo has to be somewhere around two thousand sprawling feet of living space, which means there are significantly more potential locations for items to get lost in. I'm notorious for leaving my phone in strange places. Like the fridge. The sound isn't muffled enough for it to be there, though.

I miss the call, but find my phone in Bancroft's room, on his bed. Excitement makes my toes tingle at the possibility that it might be him checking in. I have no idea how long his flight was, although I think that information might be in the binder.

I have a message, but it's not from Bancroft, it's from Amie. I call her back without listening to the message. I'm sent directly to voice mail though, so I try again, but the same thing happens.

I text her, telling her to stop calling so I can call her. Half a second later she sends me the same message. I laugh and wait for two minutes, wondering when the standoff will end. I get a question mark, so I cave and call.

"I've been thinking about you all day," Amie says by way of greeting.

I flop down on Bancroft's bed. "Does Armstrong know you're fantasizing about me? I won't tell him if you don't."

She snorts—delicately. "Obviously you're feeling better if you're making dirty jokes again."

"Much, actually. I slept forever last night. Bancroft has the comfiest bed." I fluff the pillow behind my head, settling in.

"What? You *slept* with Bane?" Amie's voice is so shrill it sounds like a fire alarm.

I realize the error and bark out a laugh. "I mean the bed in his spare room. Not his bed."

"Oh. I was going to say, it's not really like you to just fall into bed with someone. Except that one time—"

"And we're never, ever going to speak of that again."

"I saw Drew recently."

"Did you miss the part about never again?" I briefly dated Drew McMaster in the second year of college. And by briefly I mean that we went on one damn date. He was an excellent flirt, and after several weeks of persistence on his part, I agreed to go out with him. I mistakenly fell for all of his lines and ended up in his bed. It was a lackluster experience at best. He spent the entire two minutes thrusting like a jackhammer was attached to his hips. At least he came, I didn't even get close. And his penis was incredibly subpar. I don't even think it was average.

That was the last date I went on with him. After that I made sure not to get naked, or even close to naked, with someone on the first date. If a guy is worth it, he can wait to experience the wonders inside my panties. That way I have a sufficient number of dates in which to engage in some make-out sessions. Foreplay is an art. If a guy sucks at that, he's probably going to suck in the sack. Although if I had met Bancroft, and wasn't dependent on him, I wouldn't say no to climbing into his bed, regardless of the rule. I bet he's incredible between the sheets, especially with those powerful thighs of his.

"Well I wouldn't have brought it up because I know it gives you nightmares, but I thought you might like to know that he's started balding."

"He's only twenty-six."

"Exactly."

"It's horrible how happy this makes me," I reply.

"It's not horrible, it's justified. He was a jerk."

"He really was." Speaking of jerks . . . "How was dinner with Armstrong's parents?"

"It was fine. Good. It was good."

The way her voice raises to a pitch reserved for birdcalls tells me she's lying. "Amie."

"His mother's a bit cold."

That's an understatement. She's about as warm as a freezer, at least from what I experienced at the engagement party. "I'm sure she'll warm up to you. Everyone loves you. How about his dad? Is he any better?" I met him only in passing, a handshake and a brief introduction.

"Fredrick is lovely. He's been so pleasant with me. I don't actually understand how someone so nice can be married to such an ice queen."

"Maybe she lets him in the back door."

"Ruby!" Her shock turns to laughter.

"Men will tolerate a lot for anal."

Amie snickers. "I think she already has something stuck up there. There probably isn't room for anything else."

This is the Amie I know. The one I love who can have dirty conversations with me, not the one who has to look over her shoulder when the word *vagina* is spoken.

"Okay. Let's not talk about my future mother-in-law's sexual habits anymore. I have to see her for lunch this week and I don't want to be thinking about where Fredrick puts what. How are you settling in? How was Bane last night?"

"I'm settling in fine. He seems really nice. Very organized." I don't tell her about the shower incident, or hugging him both last night and this morning and how it got a little awkward there with his neighbor, or how it seemed as if he was going to kiss me this morning before Ms. Blackwood interrupted.

"Armstrong said he can be a little . . . intense. He's always been nice to me, but then I've only met him a few times. Armstrong says he's a bit rough around the edges."

I imagine his career as a rugby player might make him less pickle-up-the-ass than what Armstrong is used to.

I remember his comment from this morning, when he said he wasn't always polite. That, combined with the ass grab and the bit about my lace panties, sends the ghost of a shiver down my spine. I'd like his rough edges to rub all over mine. Especially the rough edge of his stubbly jaw, on my vagina. I need to back the horny bus up, at least until I'm off the phone with Amie.

"He was well enough mannered for me, which is almost unfortunate since I already know he's an amazing kisser."

My phone buzzes against my cheek and I check the screen, which means I don't hear most of Amie's reply. I have a new text. From Bancroft. Speak of the kissable devil. I put Amie on speakerphone so I can check the message.

"—meet Armstrong's friends."

"Sorry. I missed that. Who am I meeting?"

"There's a party next Friday night, you should come.

I can introduce you to some of Armstrong's friends you didn't get to meet at the engagement party. It'll be casual."

"Yeah. I don't know about that. Is it going to be all coupley? You're not going to try and set me up with one of those guys, are you?" Amie sometimes like to play matchmaker. She was especially fond of setting me up with her boyfriend's friends in high school. It was rarely successful.

"No setup. I promise. Although he does have a few cute friends."

"I'll go, but cute or not, I'm not dating anyone in your new inner circle." As much as I love spending time with Amie, whenever I go to one of her parties I feel like I'm interviewing for the position of a stand-in wife or a mistress. The older men—the ones who have already succumbed to male-pattern baldness—have a tendency to tout their bankroll stats between conversations about their sports cars and their property acquisitions or their stock market investments.

The younger ones talk about their next big promotion in blah, blah, blah company and how much they love blow jobs in the bathrooms. That last part I'm making up, but none of them would say no if it was offered, not even the married ones.

I finally manage to get Bancroft's message up:

Bancroft: At the hotel. Time for a call?
Ruby: On the phone with Amie. Give me 2.

I interrupt Amie, who's still talking about the party next weekend to let her know Bancroft has arrived at his destination and wants to call.

"Oh! Okay. Tell him I said hello. We'll talk tomorrow. Let's figure out when we can see each other this week."

"'Kay. Sounds good. Thanks for all your help yesterday."

We end the call and a minute later my phone rings again, Bancroft's number appearing on the screen. I answer the call, my stomach flipping a little with excitement. "Hello?"

The connection is full of static for a few seconds before the line clears. "Hello? Ruby?"

Some men have great phone voices. The kind of voice that makes all the parts below the waist heat up. Bancroft Mills has that kind of voice. And he's only uttered two words.

"Hey. How was the flight?" I sound all kinds of breathless, for absolutely no reason other than his voice makes me want to have multiple orgasms.

"It was long but good. Am I catching you at a bad time?"

I turn my face into his pillow and clear my throat before I answer. "No. Not at all."

"Did you have a good day? How's everything going?"

Obviously, he's checking up on me to make sure I didn't kill his pets in the twelve hours he's been gone. I consider telling him I lost Francesca and that Tiny's escaped her habitat, but I don't think he'll find the humor in that. "We had a great day. Francesca partied herself out this afternoon and Tiny's in super-chill mode."

"Super-chill mode?"

"Mmm-hmm. She was having none of the partying. Francesca's a bit of a naughty girl, trying on all my thongs, taking naked selfies." Oh my God. *What the hell am I saying?*

I expect at least five seconds of silence and an *okaaaay,* instead I get a deep rumble of a laugh that ping-pongs around until it lands in my clit. "It's a good thing you weren't wearing those ones when you came out to say good morning."

"Why's that?" I press my thighs together and wait.

"Because my flight was already painful enough."

"I'm not seeing how my choice of panties would impact your flight." Jesus. Is he saying what I think he's saying?

"Do you have any idea how amazing your ass is? Or how long seven hours would've felt with that image burned into my brain and no way to alleviate the issue?"

I'm pretty sure Bancroft just told me he wants to whack off to images of me wearing a thong. Or maybe he just has.

He clears his throat, but it doesn't do away with the gravelly sound, or the pinging still going on in my clit. "Sorry. That was probably too much information. Francesca's second favorite place to hang out is my underwear drawer, so I'm not surprised she took a liking to yours, too."

"I'm sure mine are a lot more exciting than yours."

"From what I saw that's definitely true."

Okay. I need to move this conversation away from my underwear before I need to change them, or succumb to the urge to send him pictures of my panties. While I'm wearing them. "What time is it in England?"

"Two in the morning. I need to think about getting some sleep, but I'm not sure it's going to happen. I have a meeting at nine and I'm not the least bit tired."

"When I can't sleep I read the dictionary or fifteenth-century literature."

"Why would you do that?"

"Because it's so boring it puts me to sleep."

I get another laugh out of him. "Well that's an idea." It sounds like things are being shuffled around in the background. "What're your plans for the evening?"

"Well I have that party starting in about an hour, so that should keep me busy tonight. I managed to cut the guest list down to a hundred, which is manageable, don't you think?"

"Much more manageable than the two hundred you originally planned for."

"I thought so, too."

"You have the fire department on call?"

"The entire guest list is comprised of firefighters, so you don't have to worry about that."

I get another laugh, although it's a little nervous-sounding.

"So what's the meeting for tomorrow?"

"I'm supposed to review the plans to upgrade some of the London hotels. We have five hotels here and all but one are set to undergo some form of renovations. I'm here to oversee the projects with one of my older brothers."

"You don't sound too excited about it."

"Well, we're a lot alike in some ways, so it can be difficult to work with him, and I have to deal with him every day for the next five weeks, so there's that."

"That sounds . . . unpleasant?"

"Lexington likes to be in control of things, and he believes he knows everything."

"Is that a family trait?" I bit my lip to keep from laughing at his unimpressed noise.

"Lex is far worse than me. If my father had sent Griffin along, this trip would be a lot easier."

"So they both work for your father as well?"

"Straight out of college and into the hotel business."

"Do you all look alike?" Clones of Bancroft strolling the streets of Manhattan might be more hotness than this city could handle.

"Not really."

"That's unfortunate." I need to have a look around for family photos.

"Lex doesn't have a great track record with dating and Griffin has a girlfriend. I'm fairly certain he plans to propose this fall, so don't get any ideas over there."

There's a hint of genuine irritation in his voice, as if he doesn't appreciate my line of questioning. "Calm down, I'm just playing with you."

"Sorry. I'm snappy because I'm jetlagged and I'd rather be home, not spending the next five weeks here."

"I understand where you're coming from. Being pushed into something you don't really want because you're out of other options, I mean."

"Yes. Well, my rugby career wasn't going to last forever, so this was inevitable. Anyway, I'm being whiny. I need to stop that before I lose more points. I was down to eight-point-five this morning, wasn't I?"

"Mmm. It might take a while for you to earn that half point back."

"That means I'll have to be on my best behavior then, doesn't it?"

"Well I'm sure it's a lot easier to behave yourself from across the ocean."

"You'd be surprised," he mutters. "Hold on, room service is here with my dinner."

I'm surprised they serve food at two in the morning, but then maybe because his family owns the hotel he gets whatever he wants, whenever he wants.

I hear his muffled voice in the background and then he's back again. "I don't know why I'm making you stay on the phone with me, I'm sure you have better things to do than listen to me eat."

"Actually, I haven't eaten dinner yet, so I could heat something up and we could eat together."

"Isn't it nine there?"

"I slept in a little and had a late lunch." I don't mention getting up at two in the afternoon. Not when he's been traveling all day.

I put him on speakerphone while I prepare a plate of leftovers and stick it in the microwave.

"What are you having?" he asks.

"I'm on to the chicken parm and spaghetti. I ate all the primavera this afternoon. What about you?"

"A burger and fries. It was pretty much the only option at this hour."

Once my meal is reheated I take it over to the counter, grab a bottle of Perrier from the fridge, and drop onto a stool.

"So this traveling you're doing now, will you have to keep it up?" I twirl noodles onto my fork.

"Probably for a while, at least until my father thinks I have the basics down."

"I guess it's good that you're used to it then?"

"I don't mind the travel but I feel like I've done enough of it over the last seven years. It can be"—he pauses for a few seconds, searching for the right word—"lonely, I guess. I missed so many birthdays and holidays with my family. I was looking forward to being able to spend more time with them, put down some more roots I guess, but it seems like that will be delayed again."

"You're close to your family then?"

"They're important to me. My mother was sick a while back and I wasn't there for that, because of my job. I'd like to be around more. There are some New York projects I'd like to be involved in, but it really depends on how quickly I pick things up whether or not I'll get to work on them." He sounds a little despondent.

"Is it a steep learning curve?" I have no idea what the hotel business entails.

"I have all the theory from school, but I haven't been actively using any of the things I learned in college for this purpose. It's a new application, if that makes any sense."

"It does. So after you have the basics down, then you'll get to work out of New York?"

"Not strictly, but my hope is that I'll have the opportunity to manage some of the properties in the US, and travel will be limited."

"And that's what you'd prefer?"

"I think so, yes. It's just a big transition. It'll take time to get used to suits instead of cleats."

"Mmm. That is a big change." I lean back, holding on to the edge of the island until I can see the giant, sweaty poster of him on the wall. "If it's any consolation, you look just as good in a suit as you do in cleats."

"Nine out of ten good?"

"It would've been if you hadn't asked that question."

He laughs. "So how does a Scott end up in New York, looking to get on Broadway? I thought you were all born with your times tables memorized."

I snort. "Ah, that's typically the way it goes. I'm the rogue, unfortunately. My passion has always been in theater. My father only let me come to New York out of guilt. And possibly to get rid of me for a few years so I wouldn't ruin his extended honeymoon phase."

"I'm not following."

"My mother waited until I was done with high school to hand my father the divorce papers. Then she moved to Alaska. I'd applied to Randolph before that happened and my mother had been a big supporter. My father not so much. Of course he found it in his heart to support my decision when he brought his new girlfriend home to meet me two weeks after my mother left."

"Ouch."

"She was his secretary at Scott Pharmaceuticals. She'd been working under my dad for two years. I'm fairly certain he'd been dipping his quill in the company inkwell for a long while. So he let me go to New York."

"How convenient for him." Bancroft's derision makes me happy.

Obviously, my father was smart enough to draw up a prenup, so he wasn't just letting his penis guide his actions.

He'd done the same with my mother, but the money had never been the thing for her. I'd been her glue; and when I was all grown up and ready to make my own way, she'd finally walked away. It had been so difficult to lose her like that at first. I'd been angry, until I realized what she'd sacrificed and that my father was just another privileged asshole.

"Oh it gets better. As soon as the divorce was final he married her. And my whore-mother is four years older than me."

"Pardon?" I'm pleased by how horrified Bancroft sounds.

"I mean my stepmother. She's twenty-eight and I'm twenty-four."

"That's just—"

"Gross? Sadly typical? At least she's older than me. She's actually five years *younger* than my half-sister and seven years *younger* than my half-brother."

"That's just wrong."

"On so many levels. And they all work together. She's moved to a different department so she's not directly under him anymore."

"So many tasteless jokes there," Bancroft says derisively.

"Right? But he's still her boss and she's still the employee he screwed his wife and family over for. I think it's rather ironic that he deals in erectile dysfunction medications. Of course he needs a trophy wife to parade around so everyone knows he can still get it up. It's embarrassing."

"I can see why New York would've been alluring, and still is."

"Honestly, I probably would have murdered her had I stayed in Rhode Island, so moving was really the only viable option."

"Very practical, and far less complicated than murder," Bancroft says. I almost wish we were on video chat so I could see his smile.

"Exactly. I don't think I'm designed for murder. I mean, I love watching horror movies, but I can barely manage preparing meat, so I think I probably would've sucked at getting rid of the body."

Bancroft laughs. Then yawns.

"Am I boring you with my tales of murder?"

"I'm so sorry. I think the carbs and the jet lag are finally hitting me."

"I'll let you go so you can get a few hours of sleep before you have to be up for meetings."

"It's probably a good idea. I'll touch base later in the week, okay?"

"Okay. Bye, Bancroft."

"You know, you can call me Bane."

"Like the bane of my existence?"

That gets me another sleepy, gravelly sounding laugh. "Is that what I am?"

"Not even a little. You're my white knight in shining armor, saving me from living in a box on the corner, singing on the subway to earn a living." As much as it's supposed to be a joke, he really is the only thing keeping me from having to move back to Rhode Island for at least the next month.

"I'm not so sure I deserve that title, considering my role in sabotaging your last audition," he says ruefully.

"I'm confident this makes up for it."

"That eases my guilty conscious more than you can know. Night, Ruby." The warmth in his voice wraps around me like a hug.

"Night, Bane."

CHAPTER 10
LUCKLESS

RUBY

I don't hear from Bancroft for the next two days apart from a few text messages asking how things are going. So he'll know they're alive, I send him pictures of Francesca and Tiny, with little thought bubbles proclaiming their love for me. Bancroft thinks it's funny.

After that the phone calls come almost nightly. Bancroft has taken to calling me around dinnertime—well, dinnertime for me, but since he's across the ocean it's more like bedtime for him. Which I don't mind in the least. Especially since, two nights ago, he video called instead of voice called because he missed seeing Francesca. If I put him on speakerphone while she's in the room she goes nuts, and I wanted him to see how cute she is.

Both times we've video chatted he's been wearing a white undershirt that hugs the muscles in his chest and outlines the incredible abs hidden underneath the thin fabric. I don't get to see what he's wearing from the waist down since we're clearly not staring at each other's

crotches while we talk, but I like to picture him in boxer
briefs that also hug all the good parts and outline his
package nicely.

Dinner conversation usually starts with Bancroft asking about Francesca and Tiny, then I ask him how his
day was, he tells me all about things his brother does to
drive him insane and I point out he does a lot of the same
things.

When he asks how the job hunt is going for me I tell
him it's great. I've managed to line up two auditions for
next week, but both of the roles are small, and not likely
to be enough for me to come up with a down payment
for any kind of apartment, let alone allow me to start paying down my debts.

Two days ago I secured part-time employment in a bar
serving drinks. I had reservations about the place, partly
because the manager hired me on the spot with barely a
glance at my résumé. Apparently my "bad plan" radar
was accurate.

I lasted all of one shift. Not because I'm incapable of
serving drinks and bar food, but because being proposi-
tioned by the manager during my first shift did not bode
well for the long term. I pocketed the $120 in tips and
walked.

I'm trying to stay positive. I have the auditions. I still
have time. At least that's what I keep telling myself.

Over the next week, I take the job-hunting business seriously. When I'm not playing with Francesca, or letting
Tiny crawl up and down my arm, I spend most of my
days scouring the Internet for potential auditions and
seeking agent representation or passing out my résumé
at every damn place I can think of.

I bomb the first audition. Just choke. Like literally. I'm

in the middle of my audition, singing my heart out when all of a sudden I'm choking on something. I double over coughing and spit out a giant housefly, covered in my saliva. It's everything I can do not to throw up on stage again.

The night before my second audition I get nervous. For good reason. I feel like I'm jinxed. I've been practicing my dance routine all afternoon and I have it down perfectly. I know every step, every word to the song. I can perform it in my sleep. I don't take any chances with food. I eat Cup-a-Soup and drink hot lemon water. Bancroft tells me to break a leg. It's supposed to be good luck. But I go to sleep feeling uneasy anyway.

I wake up in the middle of night screaming bloody murder because I have a nightmare that I left the lid off Tiny's terrarium and she escaped her habitat. In my dream I felt something crawling on me and I jumped out of bed stepping on something warm and squishy. In reality I do jump out of bed, but the warm and squishy thing is a wet washcloth I left on the floor after I'd given myself my nightly pre-bed Bancroft-inspired orgasm. In my haste to get away from the terrifying washcloth I slipped on the floor and landed on my ass.

I should've known from the lack of sleep, the bad dream, and the bruised bottom that the audition was going to be a failure.

The next day I nearly do break a leg, just like Bancroft told me to. The dance routine I know so well goes sideways when I faceplant on the stage in the middle the routine thanks to a rogue puddle of water. I go home— or back to the condo—feeling doomed. It's as if karma is giving me the middle finger.

When I get home from my epically terrible day where I not only embarrass myself on stage, but also get turned down for not one, but three cashier positions—word to the wise: a Triple-Threat Award does not make one universally employable—all I want to do is curl up in bed and forget this day ever happened.

Bancroft will be back in little more than three weeks and I'm still minus a job. It's not good. The envelope of cash—which contained the full five weeks' worth of my stipend, well, double it, but it's not my fault if his math is off—helps a lot, but I need to pay down my bills and save for an apartment. I have another audition lined up in two days, but with the way things are going, I'm worried I'll bomb this one, too. The only thing I seem to be good at is taking care of Francesca and Tiny.

I almost caved when I spoke to my father earlier in the week. He asked how things were going and if I'd sorted out my apartment situation. I played dumb and asked him what he meant. Apparently, his brainless secretary told him I'd called about my bank account even though I'd said she didn't need to. There was no way I was going to admit to not being able to take care of the situation on my own. I'm not at point critical quite yet. It's close though.

I kick off my shoes and cross over to Francesca's cage. A few days after Bane left I moved it to the main living area, which is where it stays for the most part. She's already scaling the bars, jumping around and doing tricks for me.

"Hi, pretty girl," I coo. "Did you miss me today? I missed you!" I unlatch the cage and lift her out. She cuddles into me, nuzzling into my cleavage like she's looking for snacks. It's her signature move every time I pick her up, as if she thinks I'll have lost food down there. She's a bright light in my otherwise shitty day.

I carry her down the hall, exhausted and defeated, looking for anything that will brighten my spirits. I grab my phone on the way, in case we end up chilling out and watching movies. It's probably one of my favorite things to do, especially after a long, crappy day. Francesca loves nature documentaries and she's great company when I watch horror movies.

I pass my own bedroom and keep going. In the past two weeks, I've only slept in my room once. That was the first night I stayed here. Half of my boxes still line the wall, unpacked. A constant reminder that I need a job, any job, and soon.

I push open the door to his room. The bed is made, because it's so much more fun to mess it up when it's already perfect. Last week I relented and changed the sheets, because they were smelling less than fresh, but I sprayed them with Bancroft's cologne so they still smelled like him. It's not authentic, but it's kind of the same. I refuse to acknowledge that it's a little creepy, this behavior of mine, but I tell myself it's for the benefit of Francesca so she doesn't think he's abandoned her.

I put her down on Bancroft's bed and she does her little nose twitch-sniffle thing, bouncing around, waiting for me to start the game. I'm tired and grumpy, but this at least will put me in a semi-better mood. I pull the sheet up over her and she makes this little noise of excitement. We play for a good fifteen or twenty minutes, until she's had enough and all she wants to do is cuddle.

It's just after six, but I didn't sleep well last night and the failed audition and unsuccessful attempts to secure employment exhausts me, so I turn off all the lights and find a good horror movie. Sometimes torture and fear are a good way to remind me my life isn't so bad.

I don't even have the energy to consider making dinner. Francesca wriggles her way under my shirt and peeks her head out through the neckline. She likes be-

ing close to my boobs, right in the valley. I let her snuggle in and close my eyes. I just need a few minutes to
manage the disappointment.

Digital ringing pulls me from sleep. I blink a bunch
of times, trying to throw off the haze. I realize the sound
is coming from my phone. I check the clock. It's 8:03.
At night. Shit. Bancroft said he'd call at seven and he's
prompt with phone calls, which means he's been trying
to reach me for the past hour.

I fumble around and hit the answer button, my uncoordinated fingers struggling to grab hold of the device.

"Ruby? Are you there? Ruby?" Bancroft's concern is
clear in his tone.

"Here." I rasp. "Fell asleep. Sorry. Here now."

"Is the connection bad? I can't see anything."

The room is dark. I didn't even manage to start the
movie, apparently. "Hold on." I reach across for the lamp
on the side table and flick it on. The brightness blinds me
and I drop my phone on the bed, rubbing my eyes for a
second. I glance around, looking for Francesca, but I
don't see her right away.

"Ruby?"

"Right here. I'm so sorry, did you have to call a bunch
of times?"

"Uh . . . just a few. Is everything okay? Are you feeling all right?"

"I'm good. Fine. Just a long day. How are you?" I finally focus on the screen, not my surroundings. Bancroft
is in a bed. Shirtless. In a bed. His hair is wet, like he's
fresh out of the shower. Did I mention he's in bed. Shirtless?

I can see myself in the tiny screen in the corner. I look
like a bag of dog poop. My hair is all over the place. I
have crease lines in my face from the pillow.

Bancroft's brows come down. "Where are you?"

"Huh?" I ask, because the answer to that question isn't exactly one I want to give or explain.

He tilts his head to the side. "Are you in my bedroom?"

"What?" Panic flares for a second as I struggle to come up with a reason for my being in here.

"You're in my bed."

Oh Jesus. Is he mad? His eyes are dark. Although the room he's in is not well lit, so that could totally account for the whole darkness aspect.

"I, uh . . . I was cleaning and I moved Francesca in here and then we were playing hide in the sheets and I must've fallen asleep and I'm sorry about that. I'll wash your sheets."

A smile quirks the corner of his mouth. "You don't have to apologize for playing with Francesca. How's my girl?"

For a very brief moment I think he's referring to me as his girl, but then I realize he's asking about his pet, who is nowhere to be found. "She's good. We were cuddling and I fell asleep."

"Where is she now?"

"Um, hold on." I put the phone down so all he gets is a view of the ceiling. Then I hop off the bed and call Francesca's name a couple of times. I look under it, because that's a logical place for her to be.

"Ruby?"

"We were cuddling when I fell asleep!" I call out. All the horror stories I've heard come back to haunt me. She better not have escaped. It's what ferrets are known for.

I glance at the bedroom door. It's closed, so she has to be in here with me.

I cross over to the bathroom. Sometimes she likes to hide in the discarded towels, because in addition to sleep-

ing in Bancroft's bed I've also taken to using his shower.
It's even nicer than the one in my room, and slightly more
complicated, but I managed to figure it out without scalding myself.

She's not in the bathroom, though.

"Ruby?"

"She's in here somewhere!" I glance at the bed and
note movement near the pillows. A little brown head
peeks out from inside the case. "There she is." I return
to the bed and scoop her up, then prop my phone against
the headboard so I can hold her and talk with free hands.

"You scared me," I coo at her, my voice cracking a
little. "Daddy wants to see you." I'm so relieved that I
haven't lost her, tears spring to my eyes. I blink them back
as I hold Francesca in front of my face and wave one of
her little paws at Bancroft.

"Are you coming down with something?" he asks.

"No, no. I'm fine," I assure him, even though I'm not.
I almost think I have things under control and then he
asks the one question designed to put me over the edge.

"How'd the audition go today?"

I open my mouth to speak, but all that comes out is a
squeak. And those stupid tears leak out of the corners of
my eyes.

"Ruby?"

Francesca squirms out of my grasp when I wave a
hand around in the air. I'm trying to breathe, but I can't
seem to manage it without making horrible high-pitched
sounds.

"Babe, what's wrong?"

I try to get myself under control. At least a little. I
stammer out, "I-I b-bombed the audition."

"I'm sure it wasn't that bad."

"I fell on my face in the middle of my dance routine.

I have a bruise on my cheek." I lean in closer so he can see the slight bluish tint to my cheek. It's tender to the touch.

Bancroft purses his lips. "I'm so sorry."

"What if I can't do this? What if I end up having to go back to Rhode Island to live with my father and whore-mother? What if I have to go work for my father? What if his skank wife really is my boss?" The panic is starting to set in again. I don't want to have an emotional breakdown on Bancroft. I don't want him to think I'm some loopy, unstable nutter. I want to have my life sorted out, like Amie does.

I need to get my shit together before Bancroft comes home. Because the more I talk to him, the more I want to do more than talk to him. At this point I want to do more than just get naked with him, but I definitely still want to do that, and sometimes it feels like maybe he wants the same thing. But he's not going to want anything to do with an unemployed, homeless crybaby with more than ten thousand dollars in credit card and loan debt.

My internal pep talk isn't helping with the tears.

"Maybe my dad's right. Maybe I can't hack it. I just wanted to prove him wrong." My voice is still pitchy.

"Take a breath, Ruby." Bancroft's voice is soft, lilting.

I do as he says and suck in a deep breath.

"That's it, babe, good girl. Take another one for me."

I take another slower, deeper breath.

He nods his approval. "And another."

I keep taking deep breaths until the panic subsides. "I'm so embarrassed," I mutter when I get myself under control again.

"Don't be. You've had a rough day, it knocks you down a little. You have to get back up and brush it off."

I let out a soft laugh.

"I have complete confidence that you'll get a role, you're too talented not to."

He's never seen me act or dance. He's heard me sing, because I do it unconsciously sometimes. He'll put on music while we're talking just to make me hum. "I wish I had the confidence in me that you seem to."

"You know what I'd do if I was there with you?" His voice is so soothing. I want to know what that sounds like in my ear with his body covering mine and no clothes getting in the way.

"What's that?" I sound less pitchy and more breathy.

"I'd get you drunk."

"And then take advantage of me?" I mean it to be sarcastic, not hopeful. How mortifying.

His expression turns serious. "I'd hope I wouldn't have to resort to such tactics to get you into bed with me."

"Well, I'm already in your bed, so we're halfway there aren't we?"

Bancroft's tongue sweeps out to wet his bottom lip. "I think you should pour yourself a glass of wine. I have a bottle here. We can drink together."

"Did you have a bad day, too?"

"I've had better."

I grab my phone and carry it to the kitchen so I can raid his wine fridge. I decide on a crisp white. Also, his sheets aren't dark enough for me to consider drinking red.

Once I've poured myself a glass I return to the bedroom. Francesca is curled up on top of the comforter. As soon as I'm half lying down, she pulls her favorite move and wriggles her way under my shirt, peeking her head out through the neckline, between my boobs.

I show Bancroft, who seems to appreciate her choice
of location. He tells me about his day, about a multimil-
lion dollar mistake someone on his team made, and about
the phone call from his father. His troubles don't necessarily make me feel better, but they certainly put my own
into perspective. At least one small error isn't going to
cost me millions.

CHAPTER 11
PARTY TIME

RUBY

On account of my bombing my audition Amie forces me into accompanying her to the party I was intent on avoiding. She thinks I need to get out and have some fun. I think a pint of Ben and Jerry's sounds like a better time than spending my evening with a bunch of stuck-up snobs, but I haven't seen much of Amie since moving into Bancroft's condo, so I relent.

When Amie said "party" I stupidly assumed it meant there would be lots of people to mingle with. I could put on my "Ruby Snob" face, impart the occasional witty response, and rotate through the guests, air kissing and smiling. I also assumed it would be in a hall, or a ballroom of some kind, as is typical.

What I don't expect is to end up at some last-name-first mansion with eleven other guests as the only single female in the room. Did I mention that there's only one single man in the room, as well? This is possibly the worst and least subtle attempt at matchmaking ever. I don't need to be set up with anyone. I have bigger things to worry about.

I'm holding a glass of prosecco, there seems to be no non-alcoholic option available at this point, and I'm thirsty. I spent an hour on Bane's treadmill, staring at the life-sized portrait of him reflected in the window over-looking the river. Working out would be way easier if I could look at him all day, every day.

The impulse to pull a Ziploc baggie from my purse is strong as the server makes the rounds with a tray of appetizers. I'm slowly conditioning out that behavior. Thanks to Bane's grocery delivery service, I finally know what it feels like to be full again. On real food that doesn't come in a cellophane package. I'm actually starting to fill out this dress. It's too bad my hips are the first to expand and my boobs are the last.

Last-Name-First #11, the single guy in the room, is droning on and on about his Ivy League education and how people assume the high-level position he has at Douchebags & Douchenozzles was handed to him, but that's untrue, he worked hard to get where he is. I call bullshit. Not out loud. Just in my head. I know for a fact that Wentworth Williams's—his name is even alliterated—father is a fifty-percent shareholder in the company, and that means if he wants his Ivy League–educated douche of a son to work there, all he has to do is send over a résumé and, poof, a new job title is created.

My father does not work this way. Not for me, any-way. I know I'll be starting at the bottom rung. And that wouldn't bother me so much if my siblings hadn't been given corner offices and nice titles from the moment they started working for him. Not like I want to even work for him at all, but fair is fair. If I'm going to partake in nepotism, I should get what I can out of it.

Wentworth is still talking. I'm still nodding and smiling politely, asking the occasional question to appear interested when I tune into what he's saying long enough to know he's still going on about himself. It's as if he's sharing his entire résumé with me. Dating in the upper class is weird. People parade themselves around like show ponies, waiting for someone to pin them with first prize.

While he takes another truffle-steak-tartar-blah-blah and some goose liver paté on a blah-blah cracker I do a furtive check around the room. I've been standing for the last twenty minutes. I'm wearing heels and they're becoming uncomfortable. My calves are seizing because of the hour spent on the treadmill.

Amie is halfway across the room. Armstrong has his arm around her waist. Actually, I'm pretty sure he keeps goosing her while she talks to one of the other fiancées based on the way her eyes go suddenly wide and his grin becomes pervy for a moment.

When her gaze meets mine from across the room she gives me one of her apologetic smiles. I just glare. She does the eye-widening, pleading thing. There's no way she would try to set me up with the guy on purpose. I bet it was Armstrong's doing. Asshole.

"Armstrong says you're in theater." Wentworth forces me to stop shooting death-ray lasers from my eyeballs and brings my attention back to him. It's not exactly a question, but it's the first thing he's said that isn't about him.

"I am."

"But isn't your family in pharmaceuticals?" He tilts

his head a little, blinking a few times, a small smile pulling up one corner of his mouth. It's an expression of fake attentiveness. His eyes keep dropping below my neck. I'm not surprised, my cleavage is epic. That I'm not currently following in my family footsteps makes me seem like a bit of a wildcard. Which admittedly I am. For some of these douchebags it means I'm something to tame.

"My father is, yes."

"But not your mother?"

"They're divorced. My mother's an artist." I'm hoping the divorce revelation will turn him off. It doesn't.

"Ah. So that's where you get your creative side from, then?" He leans in closer and fingers a lock of my hair. It's pretty close to my boob, so a finger graze also happens. "Is that where your beauty comes from as well?"

I'm sure he thinks he's smooth. I'm also sure many women would simper, put a hand on his forearm and giggle. I don't do any of those things. Instead I ask a question I probably shouldn't considering present company and Amalie's future role in this unfortunate social circle. "Why? Are you into MILFs?"

His eyes go wide, because I'm being so scandalous, and then a questioning, somewhat uncertain smile spreads across his face. I suppose he's attractive. He's tall, more than six feet, but he's lanky. He's athletic enough, but it's clear he spends more time and energy behind his desk than he does working out.

Normally that wouldn't even factor into someone's date-ability for me, but my standards seem to have shifted, in Bancroft's direction.

Wentworth leans in even closer, so his mouth is next to my ear. He's been drinking hard liquor, some expensive brand of scotch based on the peat moss scent, so his breath is sharp. "I'd like to get into you."

I take a small step back. There are several possible in-
terpretations for that horrible line. Based on his tone
and his facial expression I have a feeling he means it in
the naked horizontal sense. I decide to play it stupid. "I'm
sorry?"

He blinks a couple of times, assessing my reaction. I'm
feigning idiocy, although my distaste is actually real. He
covers his dirty comment with another smile. "I'd like
to get to know you."

"Isn't that what we're doing?" I take a sip of my prosecco. My glass is almost empty.

"It'd be nice if we had a little more privacy, don't you
think?" He makes a small gesture to the rest of the party
attendees. Most of them are engaged in a group conversation. It's only me who's been cornered. And Amie
seems to be tethered to Armstrong.

I don't have a chance to respond to that, because the
chef appears from the kitchen to inform us that dinner
is ready to be served. I try to sit beside Amie, but my
attempt is thwarted by Wentworth. He puts himself between the two of us, which isolates me at the end of the
table.

And then the real flirting begins. I get the knee brush
about twenty times. Then he decides he's worried about
my hair ending up in my food, so he brushes it over my
shoulder. By the time they bring out the main course,
which is filet mignon and lobster tails, I'm about ready
to stab him with my steak knife.

I'm also on my second glass of prosecco, or maybe it's
my third. One of the servers keeps topping it off when
I'm not looking, so it stays at the same level of fullness
consistently. My face is feeling rather warm, so now
would be a good time to switch to water.

Just as they set my plate in front of me, my phone

buzzes in my purse. I have it on vibrate, but I can feel it against my leg. I ignore it, I'm not expecting a call from Bancroft tonight because it's a travel day. He has a flight to Amsterdam and I don't think I'm supposed to hear from him until sometime tomorrow. Although with the time difference, it can get confusing.

The buzzing in my purse stops for a few seconds before it starts again. The third time my foot starts to vibrate I excuse myself to the bathroom.

I rummage through my purse on the way, hoping to locate my phone before it stops ringing. It's Bancroft. He's trying to video call me. My stomach does one of those little flippy things. I don't even consider how rude it is that I'm taking a call in the middle of dinner. My excuse is that I'm staying in this man's house, taking care of his pets, so if he contacts me it must be important. Mostly I'm just dying to talk to him as it's been more than twenty-four hours since the last call.

I hit the answer button as I step into the powder room and close the door behind me. "Hey! Hi!" I have to slap around in the semi-dark to find the light switch.

"Ruby? Is everything okay?"

"Just fine." The words come out whispery and a little breathless. I want to keep my voice down because, well, I'm on the phone in the bathroom in the middle of dinner, and also, Bancroft is reclined on a couch in a white undershirt. His hair is freshly washed but he's sporting a serious five o'clock shadow. He looks exhausted. And sexy. And exhausted. But so, so hot.

His brow furrows. It's also sexy. "Are you in a bathroom?"

"What?" I look around, like I'm unsure, even though I chose to lock myself in here. "Oh. Yes. I'm in a bathroom." I think the prosecco is hitting me now.

"You're not at home?" The way he says home sends a shiver down my spine, and a shot of warmth between my legs. I can imagine him stretched out on his couch back in the condo, me acting as his blanket. "Ruby? Where are you?"

"I'm at a party."

"A party?" he parrots. He shifts in his chair, setting down his mug, the furrow in his brow growing deeper. "What party? Who're you with?"

Now I don't usually appreciate it when a guy pulls the territorial business. Mostly I'm very much a twenty-first-century woman and I feel like I have the right to do what I want, when I want, without having to answer for it. Obviously if I'm in a committed relationship I'm fully committed. I don't play games or mess around. But there's something about the way he's asking, as if there's a hint of panic, that warms all the parts below the waist. Well, warms them more than they already were, which means my panties are thinking about lighting themselves on fire.

"Ruby? Is the connection bad?"

"Oh! Sorry. You froze there for a second," I lie. "Amie forced me to come out to this party. I didn't ask enough questions, obviously, because it's not at some huge event hall, it's at some Richie Rich's house. Well, *house* isn't a very good descriptor, actually. I'm pretty sure this qualifies as a mansion seeing as this powder room is the size of my old apartment."

"Who's throwing the party? Is it one of Armstrong's friends?" Bancroft voice is suddenly low and even.

"I assume so. Or maybe a colleague?" I'm distracted by the way Bancroft's jaw is working. "Except me and him, everyone here is either engaged or married. I guess someone wanted to play matchmaker."

"Amalie's trying to set you up with someone?" Now he sounds incredulous.

I might not be the most civilized, refined woman out there, but I don't think I'm a bad catch. Maybe a little untamed, but that's not necessarily a bad thing.

"Not Amie, Armstrong apparently, and I shouldn't have to sit at home alone every night," I say defensively.

"You're not alone. You have Tiny and Francesca and me." The incredulity is replaced with irritation. "Who's he trying to set you up with?"

"Wentworth something or other." I'm trying to figure Bancroft out. The flirting and the sometimes overly sexual comments have become commonplace in our conversations and, frankly, something I look forward to. But earlier this week he called me babe, and now he says things like this, and he's acting rather jealous. For all the distance currently between us, we've been spending an awful lot of time together. It's blurring the lines I've made in my head a little.

"Wentworth Williams?" The incredulity turns to something like anger.

"That's it. Yes."

"Oh, fuck no. You can't date him."

"Pardon me?" I set the phone down on the vanity and start rummaging around in my purse for my lipstick. I hate being told what to do.

"He's an elitist fuckhead cocksucker. He's not allowed in my condo. Ever. You can't date him. I forbid it."

"You *forbid* it?"

"Yes."

"Really?" I prop a hand on my hip, then realize Bancroft's current view is of my purse, not me. I move it aside. Now he has a very good view of my dress, which I'm filling out nicely these days. The angle is actually rather flattering and it makes my boobs look amazing.

Bancroft runs a rough hand through his hair. It's an absolute mess. He's all furrowed brow and ticking jaw. Goddamn it. Why does he have to look so hot when he's being a jerk?

"What're you wearing?" he snaps.

"A dress. What does it look like?" I think I look nice.

"I see cleavage. You have cleavage. Don't you have a shawl? Can't you cover up?"

"Excuse me?" I look down at my chest and cup my boobs, making sure I'm not flashing anyone anything they shouldn't see. Everything is right where it should be. "My cleavage looks fantastic, and it's modest, not excessive."

"I just—you can't. Wentworth is an asshole. He dated my friend's sister's cousin last year and she found out he was cheating on her, with three other women, and one of them was a damn escort." He's not sitting down anymore. I think he might be pacing with how unsteady the phone is.

"Escort? Isn't that just a nice term for prostitute?"

"Yes."

"That's dirty."

"Yes, it is. So you understand why I forbid you to date him."

The *forbid* makes me bristle. It's a word my father used to toss around all the time. While I have zero intention of pursuing anything with Wentworth, I don't think it hurts to keep Bancroft on the edge a little, especially since I hate that word and he's being bossy. "I don't think he's interested in dating me."

"With you dressed the way you are, I'm pretty sure you're wrong about that."

And now he's insulting my outfit. "I think he's more interested in a hookup."

Bancroft's jaw clenches. His nostrils flare. His eyes narrow and darken. Dear God, it's hot. Hotter than it should be. "Ruby." The word is a grave warning.

I smile sweetly at him and purposely adjust my dress so I'm showing more cleavage instead of less. "Don't worry, Bane, I would never bring a hookup back to your condo. I have to go. We're in the middle of dinner and I've been gone longer than is appropriate."

"Ruby, don't hang u—" I end the call and power down my phone before he can get the rest out. My stomach is doing all kinds of acrobatics. A bead of sweat trickles down my spine. Bancroft is acting like a jealous ass. And he's being territorial. Over me and my cleavage. It makes me giddy.

I don't have rules for this particular tennis match. I like Bancroft. If he wasn't across an ocean and I wasn't relying on him for my current, modest income and a place to live, I would definitely want to find myself under him, in his bed, or on his couch, or floor, or anywhere really, but current circumstances prevent that. So, for the time being, I'm going to let him stew for acting the part of a Neanderthal, even if I find it sexy. He doesn't need to know that.

CHAPTER 12

MINE

BANCROFT

She did not just hang up on me. I stare at the blank screen for a couple of seconds before I hit redial. It goes straight to voice mail. I try again and get the same thing.

Somewhere in my head, beyond the white noise, I recognize I'm being irrational. I don't honestly think Ruby is going to hook up with Wentworth. She has better taste than that. All conversations up to this point indicate she does. I think. I hope.

The image of that jackoff in my condo, in my spare bedroom with her, naked and under him, makes me want to get on a plane and go home right the fuck now. Which again, is highly irrational. Unless I can wrap things up here faster, I still have a few weeks before I'm home. I'll need a miracle to make that happen at the rate we're going.

Beyond the possible hookup with Wentworth—which I know is unlikely—I'm actually not all that excited about the idea that Ruby might be interested in dating anyone. In the time she's been staying in my place, the part of the day I've been looking forward to the most is our almost daily video chats.

After endless meetings and hours spent dealing with a room full of Type-A personalities and the fine details of project management, Ruby is a breath of fresh air. She's the person I want to come home to the most. Which is kind of a problem I suppose, because I'm not her boyfriend and she's supposed to move out when I get back.

I have no idea if she's been dating anyone, casually or otherwise, while I've been away. I certainly haven't had time for that. Well, I suppose that's not 100 percent true. There have been a few women who have expressed interest in spending time with me, but my schedule doesn't accommodate dates. Not when I have calls with Ruby scheduled in the evening. Although while I've been in Amsterdam I started calling first thing in the morning instead since I'm an early riser and she seems to be a nighthawk. Her bedwear is my favorite. Little tanks with shorts. Sometimes I can see her nipples through the fabric.

But it's not just about nipple visuals. It's far more than that. Ruby is a vibrant, gorgeous woman with a mind of her own. She has fire and sass. I like her. A lot. She's funny and witty and sweet. We seem to share the same views on how frustrating family expectations can be. I like talking to her and hearing her perspective is always refreshing. She doesn't just say things to bolster my ego. It's a nice change from some of the women I've dated in the past. She'd be a great plus-one at some of these terrible, stuck-up parties I'm forced to attend. I want to take her out. I want to take her to bed. My bed. The one she's always lying on with Francesca.

None of that is going to happen though if she starts seeing someone else in the time I'm gone. It could happen. Beyond how lovely she is to look at, her father's bankroll is desirable. That alone would be reason enough for many of the single guys in Armstrong's circle to be interested. It would make her doubly alluring for an asshole like Wentworth.

I try calling again, but I get tossed into voice mail. She must've turned her phone off. That's fine. I have other ways to get in touch with her. I call Armstrong's phone, but unfortunately I get his voice mail, too. So I call again. And a third time.

"Hello?" He sounds annoyed.

"Hey, Armstrong."

"Bane! How are you?"

"I'm fine. Good."

He murmurs something and I hear the sound of a chair moving across the floor and voices in the background.

"That's great. I hear the projects are going well. How's Amsterdam? Have you been taking advantage of some of the perks over there?"

Of course that's his first question. "If you're referring to the weed cafés, the answer is no." I'm sure Lex is out partaking. He's been off for the last few weeks and I can't figure it out. Regardless, one of us needs to be able to pay attention at the morning meetings.

"I was thinking along other lines."

"I'm not risking the health of my dick for a trip to the red-light district." It's definitely something I could see Armstrong doing, prior to Amalie.

"I'm disappointed in you, Bane. You can't even be bothered to enjoy yourself while you're in a country where prostitution is legal."

"Too bad it's me here and not you, huh?"

"I'd certainly be taking full advantage of the perks."

I snort. "Except you're engaged."

"It's another time zone. It doesn't count."

I don't laugh at his joke. "Listen, Ruby mentioned that she was going out for dinner tonight with you and Amalie, is she available? I've tried to call her, but maybe she has her phone on silent."

"She's here. We're in the middle of dinner, though. Can I have her call you back?"

"It's a bit of an emergency. It would be better if I spoke with her now." The lie sits uncomfortably in my throat. Even I'm questioning what I'm doing right now.

"I'll get her." His voice is muffled as he covers the receiver.

I hear Ruby's confused voice, also still muffled.

"He said it's an emergency." That's Armstrong.

"Oh? Okay."

The phone must change hands. I hear the muted clip of heels and a door opening and closing, followed by Ruby's muttered, "Emergency, my ass." A second later her annoyed voice is right in my ear. "Are you fucking kidding me with this, Bancroft?"

I love it when she says my name. I love that she rarely shortens it and when she does it always sounds a little breathless. I also love that she's pissed off at me and swearing. I have a problem. I know.

"Did you turn your phone off?" I don't know why this is my leading question.

"Yes."

"You can't do that."

Her heavy exhalation of breath does amazing things to my dick. I adjust my semi and smile.

"I can when you're acting like an asshole," she snaps.

"I'm concerned."

"About what? I told you I wouldn't hook up with Douchey McHornball. What more do you want?"

"That's not what you said at all."

"That's exactly what I said."

I wish I could see her right now. I imagine her with a hand propped on her hip, chin tipped up in defiance. "No. You said you wouldn't bring him back to my condo. You left that wide open for interpretation and other possibilities."

"What are you even talking about?" She falters a little. It's all I need. "And I think you did it on purpose."

"You're not making sense," her voice wavers. "Is there a purpose to this phone call, or are you just looking to start a fight over perceived context?"

"It's not perceived context."

"You're infuriating. What exactly is the issue here?"

"I already told you, I'm concerned."

"Because?"

"You're under the influence and you're susceptible to making bad decisions when you've been drinking."

"Oh my God. You are seriously pissing me off right now."

"You kissed a perfect stranger after one drink in the past. You don't think that's a poor decision?" I'm pushing her buttons. It's a bad idea, but I can't stop myself. I don't want someone like Wentworth to get her intoxicated and take advantage of her. I want to be the one to do that, repeatedly. Okay, that sounded bad in my head. I'd like her to be sober and willing when I get her naked.

"This is your emergency? You're going to shame me over kissing you back, for what purpose? To ensure I don't sleep with some jerkoff friend of Armstrong's? I assure you, I'm not the least bit interested in Wentworth. He's the exact opposite of my type, but if you call again tonight and try and pull more of this bullshit on me I'm going to sleep with him out of spite."

"You will not."

"Are you *still* trying to tell me what to do?"

I'm pretty sure she would reach through the phone right now if she could and throttle me. "There's no way you would sleep with someone just to spite me."

"Are you sure about that, Bane?" Her voice is suddenly soft, menacing even. "Are you willing to test that theory?"

There's no right answer to that, I realize, as I open and close my mouth and no words find their magical way out. I'm not totally sure. I think I'm right. I hope I'm right. I get the sense that Ruby is a bit more traditional than she likes to let on, or at least she's more selective.

Her embarrassment over kissing me back tells me this. I also think she's far more liable to make rash, poorly thought-out decisions when she's been drinking—hence her kissing me back in the first place. Which I don't regret in the slightest. What I do regret, maybe just a little, is not staking some kind of claim prior to leaving her in my condo. Although, at the time, I had only known her for two days. That might've been a little weird and preemptive.

All it would've taken was a few words. If Ms. Blackwood hadn't interrupted our good-bye I would've followed through on that kiss and maybe we wouldn't be having this argument.

I take a deep breath and go with honesty. "Ruby Scott, I know better than to think I can tell you what to do, but the very last thing I want is for someone as dickish as Wentworth to get his hands on you, especially if it's solely for the purpose of spite."

I get breathing for several seconds. Deep breathing. The kind I'm not opposed to. The kind I'd like to hear as a result of my abilities to make her feel extraordinary. In a very sexual way.

"I'm going to hang up now, Bane, and you're not going to call me back tonight, because I don't think you want to see how far you can push before you reach my limit."

I don't get another word out before the dial tone happens. As much as I want to call her back right away, I know it's a bad idea. A very bad idea. So I keep it together and leave things alone. It's late. I should go to bed. But I can't, because all I can think about now is that fuck Wentworth and how one man can put things in perspective and screw everything up for me at the same time.

It's been forty-eight hours. I tried to call Ruby yesterday. The only response I received were pictures of Tiny and Francesca, like they're ransom notes in image form. Tiny was on the back of her hand. Francesca was hiding under my sheets. My messed-up sheets. A reminder that she has my pets and she has access to all my things, including my bed.

I may not have reacted well to the Wentworth situation. I called Armstrong the next day and ripped him a new asshole. Except he seemed to think my reaction was hilarious and uncalled for. Then he went on to tell me I had nothing to worry about because Ruby was a frigid bitch as far as he could tell, and he doubted she opened her legs or her mouth for anyone. I ripped him an additional asshole for that comment.

I also know that's untrue. She opened her mouth for me. And I'm hoping her legs will, eventually, follow.

A full fifty-seven hours later she finally picks up

when I called her via video chat. I had apology flowers delivered this morning hoping it would defrost her a little. "Hey," I say by way of greeting.

She glares at me through the two-dimensional screen. If I was in my condo with her, there are so many ways I could wipe that glare off her face. But I'm an ocean away, so all I have are words.

"I'm sorry."

The side of her mouth twitches, just a little. It's barely a tic. She's eating pasta. She dips her fork into the bowl and lifts it, twirling the noodles slowly, keeping her eyes fixed on her food. Ruby opens her mouth. Her luscious-looking mouth. The one I've had my tongue in. The one I'd like to have wrapped around my . . . the fork slides between her lips.

A noise startles her. And then I realize it's me. Groaning.

The fork slides out from between her lips. She's eating pasta primavera. The sauce is oil and garlic based. Her breath would be horrible right now, but her lips are glistening and I have no control over my head or where it goes—or how hard the one in my pants gets.

She has the upper hand. She knows it. She raises a brow and chews slowly. It takes forever before she speaks. "You're sorry?"

"Yes." It comes out low and raspy. Goddamn it. I need to get a handle on myself. Not a real handle, well, at least not while I'm talking to her . . . afterward maybe. Why is she so sexy? Why do I like that she refuses to let me get away with the shit I pulled the other night? Why am I looking so forward to her wrath?

"What exactly are you sorry for? Being an asshole?"

"The flowers came?" I sort of expected them to smooth things over for me a little better than they have.

"They did. They're beautiful. But I'd still like to know what exactly you're sorry enough for that you'd send flowers."

That's a great question. It's also legitimate. The card didn't exactly allow for an extended inscription, so I went with *Sorry for being an asshole*. I need to word my explanation in a way that isn't going to get me into more trouble. "For questioning your character." When all I get is more staring, I continue. "I'm well aware that you're an intelligent woman who is more than capable of making sound decisions. My concern wasn't your ability to make decisions, but Wentworth's propensity for taking advantage when he sees opportunity."

Her silence is long. Her chewing is slow. She sets her fork down and dabs daintily at her mouth with a napkin. "Well, I suppose your concern is warranted. Wentworth is a massive douche and I did kiss a random stranger under the influence of a single martini. But in my defense, it was rather unexpected and he was incredibly attractive."

Now I'm silent. "Was?"

"Mmm."

"But isn't incredibly attractive anymore?"

"Recent behavior has taken him down a few points."

"A few?"

"I'm sure with some good behavior he'll be able to recover most of them."

"How many points did I lose?"

"You think I'm talking about you?" The lightness in her tone drops as she continues, and her focus moves away from me to her pasta. "How do you know I haven't kissed any other random strangers under the influence of a single martini while you've been off enjoying the extracurriculars in Amsterdam?"

"Extracurriculars?"

She lifts her fork, twisting the noodles, but they slip off, along with what appears to be false bravado. "Come on, Bane, you're in the country where narcotics are legal and so is prostitution. I'm sure it's not all work and no play."

"You think I'd pay for sex just because it's legal?"

She lifts a shoulder in a careless shrug, but her body language is stiff. In the time I've been away I've become fairly good at reading her. She's expressive—hand gestures, the look on her face, her posture all tell me things her thorny words do not. The idea of this bothers her. And that makes me happy, because I feel like we are on a level playing field now.

"Honestly, Ruby?" It comes out with real bite.

Her gaze shifts my way. I see the thing I want: worry.

"I'm offended," I say. "You should know me better than that by now, don't you think?"

She scoffs.

"What's that sound supposed to mean?"

This time when her gaze drops, so does her voice. "Armstrong implied you were enjoying the perks."

Fucking Armstrong. The next time I play golf with him I'm going to Charlie horse him with a nine iron. "Armstrong can be an asshole."

She fiddles with her napkin, twisting it until it tears. "So you're not enjoying the perks? You haven't even gone to a café and smoked a hookah?"

"Is that an approved activity or will it cost me more points?"

A hint of a smile tugs at the corner of her mouth. "You might even earn some back if you send me a picture."

I wish I could reach through the screen and touch her. "You could use it for blackmail purposes."

She bats her lashes. "You think I would stoop to such low tactics?"

"I don't know. You did lead me to believe you intended to sleep with Wentworth. My faith is shaken a little."

"You were trying to tell me what to do!"

"You were drunk and at risk of poor decision making!" I counter.

She leans in closer, eyes narrowed, her fire having returned. "I was not drunk."

I arch a brow.

She tips her head to the side and concedes, "Okay. I was a little drunk."

"And there was cleavage. Excessive cleavage."

"It wasn't excessive. It was a perfectly tasteful amount of cleavage. You used the word *forbid*. At this point, you should know that words like *can't* and *forbid* make me want to do exactly the opposite. You know what happened the last time someone forbid me to do something?"

"I hope it wasn't sleep with an asshole." I have so many inappropriate thoughts going through my head. I'd like to test out her response to the word *forbid* in a variety of scenarios.

Ruby shoots me a dirty look, as if she can read my mind. "No. I moved to New York and pursued my dream." She mutters something else that I don't quite catch. "Anyway. If you still have enough time to do something fun that doesn't include prostitutes, I highly recommend enjoying a few hours in a café with a hookah, it might calm you down a little."

I run a hand through my hair. "I'm usually very calm."

"Unless cleavage and Wentworth are involved."

"I'm fine with the cleavage, as long as it's not combined with Wentworth."

"But any other time the cleavage is acceptable."

"I'm not answering that. I'm working my way into a points deficit and this feels like a trap."

She points the fork at the screen and smiles deviously. "You're learning."

"How are my other two girls?" I ask, intent on changing the topic so I don't get myself into more trouble.

Ruby blinks a few times, as if I've shocked her. "*Other* two girls?"

"Tiny and Francesca?" I like her in green.

"Oh. Right." She shakes her head a little. "Do you want to see them?"

"When you're finished eating. Don't let your food get cold."

"I'm full. It's fine." She takes me over to the terrarium first where Tiny is resting on her rock. Then she goes over to Francesca's cage and takes her out, walking down the hall to my bedroom. "Sorry. Your bed's not made, we were in here earlier."

There's some rustling around. I hear a few things hit the floor and then she sets the device up against the pillows and climbs up onto the bed. My bed. She's wearing those tiny little shorts of hers again. And a tank. Her legs are incredible. I want her ankles resting on my shoulders and the very limited amount of clothing she's wearing to be gone when that happens. Not that I've been thinking about this scenario a lot or anything.

Francesca runs around on the bed, playing hide and seek under the covers until she gets tired. Then she crawls onto Ruby's lap and sticks her head under her shirt.

"What's going on there?"

"She likes to hide out between my boobs." Francesca peeks her head out of the neckline.

"Smart girl," I reply.

I can't wait to go home. Actually, I'm hoping to be back sooner than I originally planned. I only have a few more things to do in Amsterdam and then it's back to London. Lexington is going before me to tie up some loose ends there, which is great because he's driving me batshit nuts with all of his micromanaging. I also think his inability to lay off of the perks here is interfering with work. Normally he's pretty good at moderation, but it doesn't seem that way right now. He needs to dry out for a few days.

I've done all the sightseeing I want to. Home is where I want to be most. In my own bed, eating my own food, prepared in my own kitchen. I want dinner with Ruby. Except she's likely going to be moving out when I get back. Which I'm not all that excited about. I like my time with her.

"How's the job hunt going?"

Ruby bites her lip and her gaze shifts away. "It's okay. I have another audition later this week. I have a couple of interviews for some part-time work outside of theater, just for something a bit more steady."

"Oh. That's good news then?" Her tone makes me think it's the opposite. That she's looking for something outside of acting must mean she's having difficulty finding a role and that seems like a real travesty. She's a born actress from the stories she's told me. From the moment she could talk, she's been performing, school Christmas concerts, drama classes, lead roles in every high school production. Even her first kiss was on a stage. She said it was awful because the lead had eaten a burger with raw onions on it before they rehearsed the scene. She sounds exactly like I was with rugby, except she's just starting and I've already been down that road.

"Oh, yeah. Definitely. Things are looking up."

"And what about apartment hunting? How's that going? Have you found anything suitable yet?" It's another reason I want to come home early. I'd at least like a little time with Ruby before she moves out.

"Oh, um, well . . . I'm still looking, but I have a few friends I can stay with once you're back." Her fingernails are at her lips. She's not biting, but I think she'd like to be.

"That seems like a lot of unnecessary work."

"What does?"

"Moving your stuff again."

"Well, I don't have much to move, right?"

"Still. It seems pointless. To move out when I get back, I mean. You might as well stay until you find something that works. If you want."

"That's very kind of you to offer, Bancroft, but I don't want to impose. You've already done more than enough for me."

"It's not an imposition, Ruby. I have the space and Francesca loves you. I'd hate for you to have to move all your things just to do it all over again. And there's no point in rushing, I don't want you to end up in some dive just because you feel like you're imposing when you're not."

Ruby props her cheek on her fist. Francesca is still snuggled up in her cleavage with her head poking out. "You're sure it's okay?"

"Positive. I have lots of space."

"Obviously, I'll pay rent and help out with groceries."

"We can negotiate that later. I'm not particularly worried about it."

"I don't want a free ride."

I'd be more than happy to give Ruby all the free rides

she wants, but I keep that to myself. "We'll figure it out when I'm back."

"Okay. Thanks Bancroft. You're being awfully good to me, especially considering I gave you the silent treatment for two days."

"I'm trying to earn back some points. Where am I now?"

She smiles and ducks her head, then scratches under Francesca's chin, which is conveniently located very close to her boobs. I've never been so jealous of a ferret as I am now. It gives me a legitimate reason to stare. Her eyes lift and a small smile appears. "A solid nine-point-five now. You're almost back where you started."

"Excellent." Letting her stay is a curveball I've thrown myself, but I don't plan to allow it to get in the way of my ultimate goal.

CHAPTER 13

JOBS FOR THE JOBLESS

RUBY

My living situation is ironed out for the time being, which is good because I was about to go into panic mode with Bancroft coming home soon. I really wish time would slow down.

"Okay. So you have a place to live for now. That's good." Amie sounds reassured.

I nod, although I'm not sure I can call the situation good.

Bancroft is going to let me stay in his apartment until I can find a new place. It's highly preferable to the alternative. Until now I've been relatively positive about things, but the closer we get to Bancroft's return, the more worried I become about having to return to Rhode Island to work with the whore-mother.

Beyond that, the excessive flirting and banter with Bancroft felt more acceptable when there was an end date to my stay at his condo. When I was just his temporary pet sitter it seemed harmless to engage. Now that I'm going to be his roommate for a while I'm not sure how acceptable it is anymore. It could get messy—especially if things don't work out and I'm still living there.

"And you're on top of the job thing. You have an audition tomorrow, right? Everything is working out just fine." Now Amie sounds like me.

"And I have a couple of interviews for regular jobs." I'm glad one of us is optimistic.

She sips her cleansing tea. She's on some sort of healthy-eating program. It sounds a lot like a diet. Which is absolutely ridiculous. Amie is tiny. She's never had to work to be that way, she's just naturally built like a model. She's never been worried about her weight. Until recently. I'm attributing it to Armstrong's constant, unnecessary commentary. I'm liking him less and less the more I get to know him. "What kind of interviews do you have?"

"One is at a restaurant, the other is a café. I just need some quick money to help get me by." I've avoided nightclubs so far. I don't want to end up dealing with the same situation as I did in the last place.

"Oh." Amie makes a face that looks disapproving. "What if I talk to Armstrong about getting you something temporary?"

"Thanks, but I'd rather you not." If I take a job from Armstrong it'll get back to my father. I don't want that.

"Come on, Ruby. It would just be until you get the role you deserve."

I sip my coffee. I need all the liquid energy I can get. After this I'm back to handing out résumés and filling out applications. To places I should've worked when I was in college, not after it.

"What happens when Bancroft comes back? I know I can stay for a little while longer, but eventually I'm going to have to find a place to live that isn't his spare bedroom." Like his actual bedroom.

"You'll have a place to live."

I'm not so sure that's true, but I don't want to put this on Amie. It's my fault I'm in this predicament. She's done enough by getting me a place to stay while I try to sort out my life. It'd be great if I could actually make some headway on that front.

"Do you smell that?" Amie's nose wrinkles as I pull my phone out of my purse.

I sniff and get a whiff of something disgustingly rancid. I put my hand over my mouth to stop from breathing it in again. "What is that?" I look around the café, curious to whether there's a garbage truck nearby.

"I don't know. We should go. That smells toxic."

I gather my things. I have job-hunting to do anyway. Coffee dates are for people who are actually taking a break from being productive.

For some reason, the horrible smell from the café seems to stick with me all day. I keep wondering if it's seared into my olfactory senses. People seem to be giving me a wide berth.

I check the bottom of my shoes for carcass remnants, or dog poop, but all I have are a couple of stones stuck between the treads. It's weird.

By the end of the day I'm pretty sure I'm on the verge of some kind of emotional breakdown. I resorted to begging at one café. It was rather embarrassing since the manager looked to be about seventeen based on his inability to grow even a basic, fuzzy mustache.

Today has been a failure on all counts. All I want is a job. It doesn't matter what it is, as long as I can make some consistent money. I've been careful with what Bancroft left for me, but I don't want to rely on that. Especially since I'm going to need to pay him rent soon.

Calling my father isn't an option since he's made it clear what I'm in for if I go back to Rhode Island. I need some perspective, so I get on the subway and head to Central Park.

It's another travel day for Bancroft, back to London to finish off his trip around Europe, so I don't expect to hear from him until much later, or maybe not even until tomorrow. The steady rocking of the subway soothes me. I close my eyes, tired from worry and the stress of knowing Bancroft is going to be back and I still have nothing to show for the weeks of pounding the pavement.

I'm jolted awake by the jerk of the subway. Apparently I've been out for a while, because I don't recognize the station. I exit the nearly empty subway and head for the platform, disoriented and confused.

Late afternoon has turned into evening while I've been passed out on the subway. I must've been really freaking tired. I'm also in a sketchy, unfamiliar part of the city. And I have to pee like nobody's business.

I find what looks to be a bar called EsQue. It's open, so I go inside. The hallway is painted deep burgundy, and a steep set of stairs lead to a glowing sign with one of those flashing arrows. Drunk people must break a lot of limbs here. The need to pee supersedes the need to find an alternate location.

I rush down the stairs only to get stopped by a bouncer. "ID, please." He holds out his hands.

I shuffle from foot to foot, kegeling to prevent an accident as I root through my bag for my wallet. I'm hit with a horribly pungent, revolting smell. The same revolting smell that's been following me all day. It's like a rodent crawled in there and died. I gag when I skim something mushy and drop my purse. I shove my face into the crook of my arm to prevent the smell from invading my nostrils more than it already has as I crouch down.

Bouncer man makes an unimpressed noise but doesn't offer to help as I hover at crotch level—his, not mine—and try to navigate my purse without touching whatever is creating the offensive odor, while still trying to make sure I don't pee myself. Opening it only serves to magnify the smell.

He ushers three men in suits around me without carding them, although they're all silver foxes, so that might explain it.

"You got ID or not?" Bouncer man asks, irritated.

"Do you have a flashlight? I can't see a thing!"

He blinds me with the flashlight on his phone before aiming it at my purse.

Surrounded by lipstick tubes, a few pens, a couple of pads, and a wad of napkins, I spot my wallet. And three Ziploc bags.

It's then that I remember the appetizers I hoarded at Amie's engagement party all those weeks ago. Following the flu episode, I'd forgotten all about them. I haven't touched this purse since. They've been marinating in here for weeks. The contents appear to have liquefied during their rotting period. One of the bags glistens, and it seems to be the main source of the putrid smell. I manage to retrieve my wallet without disturbing the bags and flash the bouncer my ID.

"Cover's twenty bucks."

"I just need to use the bathroom."

"Cover's twenty bucks," he says again, his expression remaining neutral.

My situation has become dire. I don't have time to find another bathroom. I grudgingly part with twenty dollars, then rush through the bar toward the bathroom sign. I'm fortunate there's no line for the women's room. I take the most amazing pee of my entire life. It's the physical manifestation of the word *relief.* So worth the twenty dollars.

When I'm done I carefully remove the appetizer bomb baggies from my purse and leave them in the trash. Then I wash my hands four times. The smell seems to be stuck in my nose and a leak in one of the bags has left a small stain in the bottom of my purse. I use paper towels to clean that up, aware I'm very fortunate that none of the baggies burst while rolling around in there, especially since I have things like tweezers and emergency scissors. Sadly, I have a feeling I'm probably going to have to throw out my purse, which is a bit tragic, since it's nice and I can't afford to replace it.

On my way out of the bathroom I nearly collide with another woman. I step aside, and mumble an apology. Her expression morphs into disgust as she passes me, her hand coming up to cover her mouth.

"It's horrible, isn't it?" I don't want her to think it was me who destroyed the bathroom, even though it was. Since I'm already in the bar, and I've paid the cover to get in, I might as well get something to drink while I figure out the best route home.

The lack of line for the ladies' room should've tipped me off that this is not a normal bar, but it's also not that late, so I just assumed I'd beaten the crowd. Also, the urgency of my overfilled bladder prevented me from taking in my surroundings. The room is full of mostly men with only a handful of women scattered throughout.

At first I think I'm in a strip club, but the women dancing on the stage aren't getting naked. Well, not totally. They're scantily clad, but they're clearly costumes. The distinct lack of poles is another tipoff.

It takes me a few more seconds to put together that I'm at a burlesque-style show. Not true burlesque, but a modernized variation. These women aren't up on stage getting naked. Sure, their costumes are extravagant and skimpy, but it's more about sensuality. There's no pole to hump or swing from. I tried out for a role in a burlesque play recently. That was the time I fell on my face. Part of me wondered if karma was trying to do me a favor, but sitting here now, I know that it really was just karma giving me the middle finger.

I take a seat at the bar and order soda water because a real drink will cost too much and I'll be tempted to drain it in one gulp. The show is actually fairly classy, classier than the play I auditioned for. Any loss of costume pieces is strategic, and at no point does it become bawdy or pornographic. The dancers know what they're doing, most of them, anyway. They appear to be professionally trained, but something is off about the routine. It looks like maybe they're missing someone.

I sip my soda water, but I'm thirsty, so it doesn't last very long. The bartender comes over and asks me if I want another one. I check my phone, pretending I'm not sure if I have the time to drink more non-alcoholic beverages in a bar.

She drops another drink in front of me without waiting for an answer. I open my purse, but she waves me off. "That one's on me."

"Thanks?" I give her a questioning look and she just shrugs. "I must look pretty pathetic."

She tips a half grin as she wipes down the bar in front of me. "I saw what happened at the door. Figured you didn't mean to end up in here. And yeah, pathetically sweet seems to be your deal."

I laugh, then sigh and take a sip before looking back at the stage. "They're all trained, aren't they?"

"Most of them. Two of the leads went to burlesque school, the other girls have a dance background."

I watch the girl in the center. Her form is incredible. "What do the dancers make here?"

"Depends on the girl, how many shifts they work, the crowd they draw."

"It's not just an hourly wage?"

"They can make a lot in tips on their solo numbers. Why? You looking for a job?"

I glance her way. Her expression tells me she means it as a joke.

I focus on the stage again. I have the training and the skill to learn those moves. They're not outside of my repertoire. I probably watched *Burlesque* three million times. My father would have a heart attack if he found out I ended up having to take a job in a burlesque-style show because I don't have money or alternative job prospects. Which might not be a terrible thing. If I can shame him enough, it's possible he won't *allow* me to work for him.

I realize I've yet to answer her question. "Do you know if the manager's hiring?"

The bartender sizes me up, her gaze shrewd and assessing. "What kind of experience do you have?"

I keep it vague. "I'm professionally trained."

She looks skeptical. "What kind of professional training?"

"I took dance, voice, and acting in college." I spin the glass between my palms.

"Oh, yeah? Which college?"

"A little arts college outside of the city." If she asks

me to get more specific there's no way she'll offer me any kind of audition, let alone a job so I ramble on, "I gradu- ated two years ago, but theater's a tough market to break into unless you know someone. I managed to get a couple of small parts, but it's not steady. We all have big-city dreams, right?"

"We sure do." Her gaze drops to my purse; thankfully the brand name is hidden. "Come back tomorrow at noon if you're serious."

I sit up a little straighter. "Really?"

"I'm not promising anything." She drops her card on the bar, and I snatch it up like it's a hundred-dollar bill. "But they need a new girl, and you might just be a good fit. If you know how to move."

I don't hang around the bar. I leave a tip for the soda waters—not so much that it looks like I'm trying to buy myself a job—then head back to the street and program the address of the bar into my phone. I'm a seriously long way from home. Actually, I'm pretty close to my old neighborhood. The job is less than ideal, but it's a job, it might be fun for a while to do something a little risqué, or risky, as it were, apart from my attempt to succeed in one of the most unstable careers in the city.

It'll just be temporary. Until an audition opportunity comes along and I can get my debt under control.

It takes more than an hour to get home. I read articles on burlesque on the subway ride. The level of bawdiness varies greatly, but this club seems to lean to the more conservative, classy side, which is good. I don't want a job that makes me feel like I'm on the verge of a career in stripping. That's not a line I can cross. I'm jazz trained, so I should be able to handle whatever routines they throw at me. I treat it like I would any other audition.

When I get home I put on my music videos and practice the one burlesque routine I've memorized since I saw the movie *Burlesque*.

I set four alarms and plan my subway route for the morning. Then I go to bed and say a prayer to the financial stability Gods that I get this job.

The next morning I receive a text from Bancroft minutes before I have to leave. I let him know I'm on my way to an audition and I get four leaf clovers and a good luck horseshoe in response.

At eleven forty-five I'm standing outside the bar wearing what I hope is a reasonable audition outfit. Under a shift dress I'm wearing a black strappy camisole and a pair of black dance shorts. It's simple and hopefully revealing enough. My shoes are in my bag. I brought both heels and flats, because all the women were wearing heels last night.

The bar looks a lot seedier in the light of day than it does at night. I try the door, but it's locked. Maybe there's some secret back entrance I don't know about. I root around in my purse until I find the card the bartender gave me. I changed bags this morning before I left. I'm still mourning the loss of the purse that I fear will forever smell of rotten appetizers, but I dumped a container of baking soda in there and sprayed it with some of Bancroft's cologne, so I'm hoping to salvage it.

Before I can find the card, the door opens. The bartender from last night greets me, except she's wearing a suit, not jeans and a corset top. "Wow. I'm surprised you showed. You must be pretty desperate for a job."

"I'm just keen to have steady employment." I maintain what I hope is an even smile. What else am I going to stay to that?

She laughs and rolls her eyes, opening the door wide

to let me in. The bar looks a lot different with the lights
up than it did last night. The dark walls need fresh paint
and the tables are chipped at the corners. I remind myself again that this is temporary as the bartender, who
still hasn't introduced herself, takes a seat and gestures
to the stage. There are a few other employees milling
around, a man lugging boxes, a woman carrying a notepad, but they don't acknowledge me.

"Is there a song you want?" she asks.

I dig around in my bag and retrieve my portable
speaker. "I brought music, just in case."

She arches a brow, but she flashes a hint of a smile.
"Aren't you prepared?"

I have a feeling she's being condescending, but I
need a paycheck, and I've had to deal with my father
for the past twenty-four years, so I'm used to being pa-
tronized.

I drop my bag on a table, shed my sheath dress, and
set up the speaker. I cue the music and take position.

I spent the entire trip here giving myself a mental pep-
talk. I'm pretending like it's practice for the audition I'm
supposed to have early next week, just prior to Bancroft's
return. If I can manage to get that role, I might not need
this job anyway.

I don't look at the bartender while I perform the routine. I can't, because I'm terrified of screwing this up.
And if I see her look at me with disdain I know that's
exactly what I'll do. When the song ends I finally look
her way again.

Her hands are steepled under her chin, her expression
pensive. "Where'd you say you went to college?"

"I didn't."

Her serious expression drops and she laughs. "That's
some pretty sophisticated training you've had."

I clasp my hands to stop from fidgeting. "I've been dancing since I was a kid."

"The routines are different than what you're probably used to."

"I'm good with that." Oh God, is she telling me I have a job?

I cross my fingers behind my back while she taps her lip with a painted nail. She pushes out of her chair and crosses over to me. "Show me your arms."

"What?"

"Your arms. I need to see them. Palm up."

I hold them out and she grabs my wrists inspecting my forearms. It takes me a few seconds to understand that she's looking for track marks. Jesus. What am I getting myself into? "I don't do drugs."

"You can never be too careful." She drops my arms. "All right. You got yourself a job. I'll give you some paperwork to fill out and a couple of videos to watch. You can move, but you'll need to step it up if you want to make real money."

She sashays down the hall and disappears through a door. I pack my things back in my purse. This is the weirdest audition ever.

She returns a minute later with three sheets of paper and a stack of videos. "Watch these and bring this back filled out tomorrow, same time. If you can handle working with my lead dancer, and she thinks you can hack it, the job is yours."

"When can we talk about wages?" I call after her retreating form.

"When my girls tell me if you're workable."

The bartender, Dottie, is actually the owner of the bar. She isn't the one who greets me the next morning. Instead it's Diva, the lead dancer. I can't tell if everyone's names are fake or real or somewhere in between. She was the one who came into the bathroom post–baggie bombs. I sincerely hope she doesn't realize I'm the one responsible for that.

I pass the test, which consists of four hours of dancing in heels, lots of yelling, and several references to me being similar to a floundering walrus.

I'm five-five and all muscle. There's nothing walrus-like about me. Diva is harsh. She's also an incredible dancer so I take the insults. It feels almost like a hazing. Like if I can take the bitchiness I get to be part of the cool crowd. What I really need to know is what kind of money is attached to this job. If it's enough to get me out of the hole I managed to dig myself, I can deal with Diva for as long as it takes.

Before I leave I'm set up with a schedule. For the rest of the week I rehearse daily from three to five and then I'm on stage for the first and second sets only, from eight until nine and then nine-thirty to ten-thirty. The third and fourth sets are eleven to twelve and twelve-thirty to one-thirty. Apparently that's when all the best tippers are here.

I won't get to dance the late shifts until I prove myself, according to Diva. However, they are short a girl, so proving myself may not take all that long. Base wage isn't great, but with tips I should be okay—better than my current two hundred a week stipend from Bancroft, at any rate. It's a start, and that's what I need.

"How long do you think it will take for me to get on the third set?" I ask.

Diva shrugs. "Depends on how long it takes before you stop screwing up the routines."

I should be happy as I get on the subway and head

home—back to my temporary accommodations. But it's just that—temporary, like everything seems to be in my life right now.

I have another audition coming up, though. Maybe my luck has finally changed. Maybe I'll be on to even better things sooner rather than later.

CHAPTER 14

DANCING SHOES

RUBY

Being employed is very good for one's ego, even if the employment is of a questionable nature. I'm choosing to look at it as a fringe role in a fringe-type production in order to make myself feel reasonably okay about the whole thing. I have a job. That's the most important part.

The potentially scandalous nature of the employment is secondary to the actual income I'm about to generate. And it won't be provided by Bancroft. It means when he comes back I won't be reliant on him for money. That brings me one step closer to self-sufficiency. I'd really like to see whether all this flirting will turn into something else, but not when it feels like I'm being bought or kept.

That's exactly what it's felt like with my father; he paid for my education and my life, but it came with an expiration date and huge side of shame. It's also how my mother seemed to exist for a long time. He bought her complacency in their marriage until she decided it wasn't worth the price anymore. Moving to Alaska was an extreme measure, but I understand it better now that I'm getting out from under his bricks of money, and I never want to end up in that kind of situation ever again.

When Bancroft calls later I'm all smiles. Until I realize I'm going to have to fudge my job title. Theater is one thing, burlesque isn't quite on par with what's acceptable employment in my world, and if it gets back to my father it won't be good. I also don't want Bancroft to know. He went batshit when he thought I was showing cleavage to one of Armstrong's friends. He'd probably have a coronary if he saw what I was going to wear on a daily basis at work. I don't need to deal with that at the moment.

"You're in a good mood," he observes.

I'm lying on his bed with Francesca, who's playing in my hair. My feet are killing me, but I don't care. I have a job.

"I'm gainfully employed."

"That's fantastic, Ruby. You had an audition? Or was it a job interview? Either way we should celebrate. I'll order some champagne and you can open a bottle on your end."

"We're not having champagne. It's not that kind of job."

"It's a job, that's all that matters. Go get yourself a drink."

"You're a little bossy, aren't you?" I don't argue, though. I wouldn't mind a drink, and sometimes it's important to celebrate, even if it's the little things. I pour myself a glass while he orders room service. I'm halfway through glass number one by the time his bottle arrives. Bancroft insists I top my glass up, so I do.

"So tell me about this job of yours," he says, as I make my way back to his bedroom, where I've left Francesca.

If I'd gotten a role in an actual play it wouldn't be an

issue. But this is not quite the same. "It's like . . . dinner theater." They serve food there, so it counts. Sort of.

"That's good, isn't it?"

"It's a start and a paycheck."

"Both good things."

"Exactly. How about you? How're things in London?" I settle back on his bed.

"Running smoothly now. I'm looking forward to coming home. It'll be nice to sleep in my own bed again."

"I bet. It's a nice bed. You must miss it."

"I do. Especially right now."

"Why right now?"

"Because you're in it."

I prop the phone up against a pillow and rest my chin on my fist. I'm trying not to take that the way I want to. I lower my voice to a sultry whisper. "Are you jealous?"

He gives me the evil eye. "Maybe a little."

"Just a little?" I stretch my arms and legs out, starfishing on top of the comforter. "Look at how much room I have." I make a big production of rolling back and forth across the king-size bed. "It's so firm," I groan and roll to one side, then roll back the other way until I'm in front of the screen again on my stomach. "And it's so big," I draw out the word *big* and flutter my lashes, biting my lip through a grin.

Bancroft's tongue peeks out and then disappears. "You know, I'm going to be home soon and I'll be able to get you back for all this tormenting."

"You think I'm tormenting you?"

"Are you trying to tell you're not, with the way you're moaning, rolling around on my bed, dressed the way you are." He gestures to me from his side of the screen.

I push up on my arms. My tank gapes at the chest as I sit back on my heels. It's one of those ones with the built-in bra. I run a hand over my camisole. "What's wrong with the way I'm dressed?"

"Are you fucking shitting me with that question, Ruby?"

"I'm ready for bed."

"I can see your nipples."

I cup my breasts. "It's cold. The air-conditioning is always on full blast in here."

"Are you even wearing a bra?" Bancroft's arm unfurls, the hand tucked behind his head is suddenly on the move, down his chest and then out of sight.

I lean in, as if it's going to change my view. "What're you doing?"

"Aren't you going to answer my question?"

His bicep is flexing. What the hell is he doing?

"Ruby?"

I shift my gaze up. "Huh?"

"My question? Are you going to answer it or not?"

I'm too busy trying to figure out where his hand has gone to pay attention to questions. "Um . . . what was it again?"

"You're not wearing a bra, are you?"

"No." His bicep keeps flexing, it's mesmerizing.

"What about panties?"

Dear lord. When his voice drops like that it makes me want to take off all my clothes.

"You should just do that."

"What?"

"Take off all your clothes."

Shit. I must have said that aloud. "You want me to roll around on your bed naked?"

"Yes."

"While you watch?" I can't tell if he's serious or joking.

"Fuck yes. Or maybe just in your panties if you're feeling shy."

Sweet baby Jesus. I'm pretty sure we're crossing every platonic line there is tonight. I also think Bancroft might be a bit of a dirty boy, which is fine by me. "What if I'm not wearing panties?" I rise up on my knees which means only my chest to mid-thigh is visible to him.

"Even better."

I ease my hands down my sides until I reach the waistband of my shorts. As far as shorts go, they don't really cover much, and half the time they double as underwear, which is pretty much their function right now. I hook a thumb in each side of the waistband and drag it down over my hips.

"Oh shit," Bancroft groans.

I keep pulling them lower, but I stop before I give him a real peek at the goods. Then I trail the fingers of one hand back up. Catching the hem of my cami I start lifting, up over my navel.

"Tell me about the belly ring," Bancroft says.

"This?" I look to where his eyes have gone and circle the little jewel dangling from the barbell with a fingertip.

"When'd you get that?"

"When I was a teenager. My father forbade it, obviously." I give him a cheeky grin. "See how well that worked."

"Of course you didn't listen."

I shake my head and lift my tank higher, past my ribs.

"Such a naughty girl, aren't you?" Bancroft asks, eyes following the increasingly visible skin.

I pause when I graze the underside of my breast and

let out a little moan. It's not fake. Bancroft's full lips are parted, his stare is rather intense. I imagine if we were in the same room I'd already be naked and under him. And I still have no idea what's going on with his hand that's disappeared. And that's when I realize what I'm doing probably isn't a great idea. What exactly am I going to do if I follow through on getting naked? He's not here to help me out and there's no way I'm going to masturbate for him on video chat. We're not exactly at that stage in our relationship. We're not even in a relationship.

I let the tank drop.

"Wait. What the fuck."

My shorts snap back into place.

Bancroft's expression is the most comical thing I've ever seen. "No, no, no. Babe, what're you doing?" He reaches out and snatches up the phone, as if he can climb through it. "Why're you stopping?"

"It's after midnight. I need to go bed and you need to go to work."

"Fuck work. You need to get naked like you said you would."

"I never said I'd get naked, you just suggested it." I pick up the phone and roll onto my back, I pucker up and give him an air smooch. "Have a great day. I'll talk to you later."

"Wait, wait!" His eyes are wide and darting around. "I—I forbid you to take your clothes off." His smile screams of victory.

I laugh. "That's not how it works, Bane."

"Come on, Ruby, that's not nice."

"I'm not always nice." And then I hang up and put my phone on airplane mode.

I spend the next twenty minutes making myself feel good. I have the best damn dreams ever.

* * *

Over the next few days Bancroft and I play phone and message tag. He makes no mention of what went down the other night, or what didn't, and neither do I. Conversation timing shifts again. Instead of talking while he's getting ready for work, we talk while he's eating dinner, usually at a desk with a noisy background that makes real conversation impossible. It's lunchtime for me, which means I'm stocking up on carbs so I can manage to make it through hours of dancing in heels.

As the weekend approaches I become increasingly anxious and giddy. Anxious because Sunday night I'm being given my first shot at the third set. Sunday is the quietest of the weekend nights, but it still pulls in a decent crowd.

I'm giddy because Bancroft is scheduled to return at the end of next week. I have his flight times marked on the calendar. I've made sure to schedule the cleaning lady early and order groceries so his fridge is stocked for his return.

My job at EsQue is going well. As I gain more hours the tips get better and better. If I can keep making this kind of money consistently for the next few weeks I might actually be able to get a down payment for an apartment together. So, when I'm offered a small part in an Off-Off-Broadway production, I have to seriously weigh what I'll make against what I'm pulling in at EsQue. It's not comparable, so I end up turning it down.

On Monday I get up at a reasonable hour and make a quick trip to the mini-grocer down the street. I woke with a hankering for s'mores. Not the best in terms of breakfast food, but since I'm burning a lot of energy at my new job, I can afford the sugar consumption.

I'm juggling my purse, and three bags of groceries,

while stuffing marshmallows in my face as I walk down the hall. I adore marshmallows in a terribly irrational way. I splurged on the name-brand graham crackers and I have a jar of Nutella waiting to be cracked. My plan is to make microwave s'mores because I'm starving and impatient.

I shove two marshmallows in my mouth while I punch in the code to the condo. As soon as I'm inside, the phone starts ringing. Not my cell, which is stuffed in the back pocket of my jeans, but the real phone attached to the vintage answering machine at the far end of the kitchen.

It's the first time I've heard the thing ring. There are a couple of messages on there, but I haven't bothered to check as per Bancroft's instructions. I allow it to ring since it isn't going to be for me.

After five rings a beep sounds and Bancroft's deep, masculine, panty-dissolving voice booms through the condo. Okay, maybe not booms, but it sounds like he's somewhere on the other side of the room.

"You've reached the voice mail of Bancroft Mills. I'm unable to take your call, but if you leave your name, number, and a message at the tone, I'll get back to you as soon as I can."

It's pretty standard as far as messages go, but I'd listen to it on repeat just to hear his voice. I drop the bags on the counter, apart from the marshmallows, which I keep shoving into my mouth, and walk over to the answering machine. I stare down at the little tape, waiting for it to start whirling. I don't know why I'm so fascinated. I think it's sweet that Bancroft misses his grandma enough to keep this ancient thing around. It's so out of

place in his condo, much like my horribly ugly lounger—
which I haven't sat in once since Bancroft left.

I'm disappointed when no one leaves a message.
Shrugging I give some attention to Francesca, who's skittering around her cage. Flipping the latch, I pick her up
and give her a snuggle. "Did you have a good snooze,
pretty girl?" She makes her little happy noises then jumps
out of my arms and bounds across the room to the answering machine, pawing at the leg of the table. I should
probably do some organizing over there. I've been dump-
ing Bancroft's mail on the table and the pile is heaping
and messy.

"Did you hear Bancroft? I bet you miss him like
crazy."

I go back to my groceries and unload my glorious
booty. I locate the graham crackers and tear open the
box. Arranging four on a plate, I top each with a marshmallow and put it in the microwave. I hit the start button
just as the phone rings again. I pause in my quest for a
s'more breakfast to listen to Bancroft's sexy voice again.

I think he's supposed to call soon, but I can't remember exactly what time we agreed upon today. He was
wearing a suit with the tie hanging loose when we talked
yesterday, speaking words and all I heard in my head was
*Take off all your clothes, Ruby, and I'll let you take off
mine.* I'm pretty sure he made no mention of clothing re-
moval this time, but my imagination has been working
overtime since the night I was rolling around in his bed,
in a camie and shorts.

The message plays again, and in my mind, I change
the words to something more along the lines of:

You've reached the voice mail of Bancroft Mills.
I'm too busy orally pleasuring the gorgeous woman

living in my condo, so don't bother leaving a message because I won't be able to get back to you for at least another week, maybe two.

My daydreaming is brought to an abrupt end when a high, nasally female voice cuts in:

"Hi, Banny! It's Brittany. I know you're away on business, but since you'll be back soon I wanted you to know that I've been thinking about you while you've been gone and I'm really hoping we can go out on another date when you're back in town."

"Date?" I scoff. "Like Bancroft wants to date *you*." I pick up the jar of Nutella with the intention of throwing it at the machine, but then I consider the vintage-ness of it, and its sentimental value, along with the probability that replacing it will either be expensive or impossible.

Brittany rambles on about how it's so nice to spend time with someone so grounded and in control of their career and how she really hopes next time he'll be feeling better so they can find out if their chemistry's compatible.

"Bancroft is *not* interested in your chemistry!" I fire a marshmallow at the machine, then another and another. It's not nearly as satisfying as the Nutella jar would've been.

A huge pop startles me and I drop the bag of marshmallows on the floor. "Oh shit!"

The ones in the microwave have exploded like the Stay Puft marshmallow man in Ghostbusters. It appears I set the time for two minutes instead of twenty seconds. I hit end but it's too late. Marshmallow coats the window of the microwave. That's going to be one hell of a mess to clean up.

". . . Okay. Well, I'll talk to you soon, Banny. Byeee!"

"His name is Bancroft, you stupid cow," I grumble.

I give the microwave a few seconds to cool down before I open the door to check the damage. Oh, yeah. It's marshmallow carnage in there. I swipe a finger across the plate and yelp because it's burning hot.

As if there isn't enough going on, my cell rings. Except it's not a phone call. It's a video chat. And it's Bancroft. I don't know why I don't let it keep ringing. It's a lot smarter than what I do, which is answer the call.

"Hey! Hi! Hello!" I've covered every possible greeting.

"Hey. Did I catch you at a bad time?" He's wearing a white dress shirt and a black tie. It's pulled loose and his hair is a little messy, like he's run his hand through it recently. He's yummier than s'mores.

"Oh no. Not a bad time. I'm just making breakfast and having some play time with Francesca."

"How's my girl? Where is she? Can I see her?" The *my girl* part makes me all swoony. I think it's adorable how much he loves his ferret. And that's not even a euphemism.

"Of course you can. Hold on and let me get her." I leave the phone on the counter and call for her. I find her over by the answering machine, nibbling on a marshmallow. "Oh, no, Franny! Those aren't for you!"

She jumps off the table, scattering mail all over the floor as I confiscate the treat. An envelope opens and a pile of twenty dollar bills flutters across the tile floor. I don't have time to manage the sudden money storm because Francesca is going after another marshmallow.

"Is everything okay over there? Did she get into something she shouldn't have?"

"It's fine! I just dropped a couple of marshmallows on the floor when I was unpacking groceries." I scoop up the marshmallow bombs before Francesca can get her paws on another one. They're a little goopy, as if she's tried to taste them all. I dump them in the garbage so she can't get to them. I carry a slightly disgruntled Francesca over to the phone, wiping marshmallow bits off her whiskers on the way.

"Here we are!" I pick the phone up while awkwardly trying to hold a squirming Francesca. She's not having it, though. She wants to explore the grocery bags I've yet to unpack.

"Let me set this up better." I rearrange the phone on a bunch of bananas so I don't have to hold it and reclaim Francesca. "Say hi to Daddy!" I wave her little paw at him and mumble a high pitched "Hi, Daddy."

The smile that breaks across Bancroft's face could light all the panties in the world on fire.

"Is she making mischief on you?"

"Nothing I can't handle."

"I figured. How's Tiny?"

"She's good. Ate a big fat cricket yesterday for dinner and she's been chilling out ever since."

Bancroft laughs. It's probably one of my favorite sounds ever. "What about you? How are you?"

"I'm good." I glance at the bills scattered over the floor. Now that I'm not so discombobulated and marshmallows aren't exploding in the microwave, and slutty Brittany isn't whining into his answering machine, I can see that it's not just twenties. There are fifties and hundreds on the floor as well. Who sends that much cash in the mail? "So . . . I have a question for you."

"Oh?" His eyebrows rise. "What kind of question?"

"Not a dirty one, if that's what you're thinking."

"Mmm. That's unfortunate. Is everything okay?"

"I think so, but I was moving the mail around and there's a pile of cash on the floor. Can you explain that?"

He frowns. "A pile of cash?"

"Yeah. Francesca knocked the mail on the floor and all of a sudden it was raining large bills. I thought you might want to know, just in case some crazy drug dealer shows up here looking for his brick or what have you."

"Can you show me?"

"Sure." I hold the phone over the pile of mail and money.

"Can you find the envelope it fell out of?"

"Give me a second." I prop the phone against the answering machine, drop to the floor, and gather the letters and cash. All the envelopes are sealed, apart from one, which has my name and #2 scrawled on it in what looks like Bancroft's writing. It's not sealed, and there are a few lingering twenties still inside. I hold it up so he can see it. "Why does this have my name on it?"

Bancroft's brow furrows. I don't know how a brow furrow can be so sexy, but it really is. "Shit. Because I left it for you. It was in the notes from the morning I flew out."

It takes me a moment to understand what he's referring to. "You mean your hieroglyphics?"

"My writing really isn't that bad."

"That's debatable. I still don't understand why you left me another envelope of cash, there was already too much in the first one." I filter the bills out from the mail. There are a lot of them.

"It seemed better than a check."

"A check for what?" I sort them by denomination. I can't count and listen at the same time.

"For taking care of Francesca and Tiny. It's the weekly stipend we agreed upon."

I pause to meet his two-dimensional gaze. I have the urge to mock him when he uses words like *stipend* and phrases like *agreed upon*. "But the first envelope you left already had double the amount we agreed upon for the entire time I'm here."

"No, it didn't."

"Yes, it did."

"There was two thousand dollars in there," I argue.

"Exactly. Two thousand a week for five weeks."

"*Two thousand a week?* For taking care of your pets? That's insane. I thought you meant two hundred."

Bancroft's expression is intense as he adjusts his tie. His gaze shifts away and then back again. "It's not insane, it's reasonable. You're taking care of the things I love while I can't, so I, in turn, will take care of you."

All the sensitive parts of my body feel like they're being stroked by his words. Normally the whole *I'll take care of you* line would get my back up, but the way he frames it makes it sound sexy instead of douchey.

"You don't have to do that."

"Yes, I do. And I still owe you for the last two weeks. If you give me your bank account number I can wire more."

"That's unnecessary. More is unnecessary. This is already too much." I could actually make a real dent in my credit card debt with this, if I planned to take it, but I don't. The first two-thousand is more than enough.

"How have you been surviving if you don't have an income, Ruby? Please tell me you didn't stick to the two hundred dollars a week."

"I didn't have to pay for groceries, so it was totally manageable, and you left the first envelope, remember?"

"Did you use it though?"

"Some of it." I focus on unpacking the groceries so I don't have to look at him. This conversation makes me uncomfortable for reasons I don't quite understand.

Bancroft huffs. "Look at the money like a salary."

"Two thousand dollars a week for pet care is not a reasonable salary." That Bancroft doesn't even bat an eyelid at parting with two thousand a week reminds me of how vastly different our financial situations are. The minimum scale on Broadway isn't even that high.

"I disagree."

"You're welcome to your opinion, however wrong it may be."

"Ruby."

"Bane." I walk away from the phone so I can put away the boxes of sugary cereal I splurged on.

"You're not going to use the money, are you?" He sounds frustrated.

"No." I'm being unreasonable about this. I should take some of the money. It would go a long way in helping me manage some of the debt I've gotten myself into, but the amount is excessive for five weeks of pet sitting, especially since it comes with a bedroom in a luxury condo and a meal plan.

Part of me is also reluctant to grow accustomed to having money again. The idea is actually somewhat terrifying. I'm also tired of handouts. Accepting them from a man I'd like to get naked with feels wrong.

"You know I'll find a way to get it to you."

"Not without my account number, you won't."

"And you don't think I can get that?"

I turn around to face him again, propping a hand on my hip. Oooh. He looks annoyed. This must be the uptight side of him Armstrong was talking about. I think

I might approve of it. "What are you? A professional hacker on the side?"

"I don't know why you're so intent on fighting me on this, but rest assured, I'll find a way to make it happen."

"Good luck with that."

"You do realize you're being difficult, babe." He taps on the table, drawing my gaze to his restless fingers.

"I'm being reasonable. You're trying to give me too much money for doing not enough." I check the time. It's already after one. I need to clean the microwave and get myself together so I can be at work on time. "I have to go. Work calls."

I reach across to end the call.

"Wait!" Bancroft says.

"I really do have to go."

"Are you angry with me?" he asks.

I sigh. I'm not angry with him at all. I'm embarrassed to be in such a predicament that the money he's offering seems massive. It's an important lesson to learn. To know what it's like to struggle, and not just have things dropped in my palm because I hold it out.

"No. I'm not angry. Your generosity is overwhelming. It's making you a ten-point-five, and it's too much for me to handle."

"Ten-point-five." His serious expression grows even sexier with his smirk.

"You're down to a ten again. Bye, Bancroft."

"Bye, Ruby."

I'm in the middle of scrubbing marshmallow out of the microwave when the phone rings again. The one attached to the answering machine. It's Brittany. Again. Apparently she wants to make sure Bancroft hasn't lost her number.

I erase the message. And the other one she left for him.
I don't even feel an ounce of guilt either.

Two days later I pop by the bank to make a deposit on
my credit card and my line of credit thanks to my great
tips. I discover my account is no longer hovering in the
low hundreds any longer. Not even close.

As soon as I get home I video call Bancroft. "You lost
six points," I say by way of greeting.

"Six? What could I possibly have done to dig myself
that kind of hole?"

"How did you even get my bank account information?
Isn't that fraud?"

"It's only fraudulent if I try to take money out of the
account, not if I put it in there."

"That was sneaky."

"I told you I'd get the money to you one way or another. I wasn't lying or being sneaky. I was being totally
upfront about it."

I make an angry sound.

"You can't be angry with me, Ruby."

"Are you telling me how to feel?" Goddammit. I
shouldn't be so upset about this. It's really not rational.
It shouldn't bother me this much that he wants to compensate me, beyond giving me a place to live, even if the
amount is exorbitant.

"Please don't be upset with me. I feel responsible for
you losing out on that audition. I cost you months of potential income, Ruby. Let me do what I can to make up
for giving you that horrible flu bug."

"So this is guilt-induced?"

Bancroft sighs. "I feel like you're baiting me and nothing I say is going to be right here. I just don't want you
to be angry with me for doing what *I* think is right."

Suddenly I realize why the money thing is bothering me. Over these past weeks I've stopped looking at Bancroft as my pseudo-employer. I don't think I ever really looked at him as my employer in the first place, if I'm honest with myself. Giving me a place to stay, food, and access to takeout was one thing, even the modest amount of money I could attribute to incidentals, but actual substantial payment for the pet sitting breaks the illusion that this is more. Or has the potential to be more. And it makes me feel kept, which makes me feel like the situation is no different than with my father. And I definitely don't want this situation to feel *anything* like that.

"I'm sorry. I'm not angry with you. I just want to be able to do this on my own."

"You are doing it on your own."

I motion to my surroundings. "Last time I checked, this wasn't my condo, unless you've decided to transfer ownership into my name."

Bancroft gives me the eyebrow. "You know, it's a damn good thing I'm not there right now."

"Why's that?"

"Because you're being difficult, and if I were there I'd be able to make you stop."

I plant my fist on my hip. "Oh? You think so?"

"I know so."

"And how exactly would you do that?" The way he's looking at me sends a shiver down my spine.

He drags his tongue across his bottom lip, his smile is downright evil. "I don't think I can answer that question honestly without putting the rest of my points at risk."

On Thursday afternoon I get a call from Bancroft. I'm still half asleep from having been up so late. I didn't get

home until after three in the morning, which isn't typical for a Wednesday, but the club was rented out for a big
party. Tips were great. It took a long time to come down
from the high of the evening so I've been out for less than
six. I'm an eight-hour girl.

It's a video call from Bancroft, which is terrible, since
I'm sure I look like hell. I didn't even bother to take off
my makeup last night. I probably look like a well-used
hooker right now.

I answer the call, but leave the screen pointing at the
ceiling.

"Ruby?"

I glance over, but stay out of view. He looks like he's
in a car. "Hey." My voice is raspy from sleep.

"Did I wake you?"

"Yeah, but it's okay. I should probably think about getting up." And then go right back to bed.

"I have some good news!"

"Oh?" I lean over the phone and catch a glimpse of
my messed-up hair. I have to use an ungodly amount of
product to maintain my hairstyle for the duration of my
performance, and I didn't shower before bed. Based on
the quick glimpse, I definitely should've.

"Why can't I see you?"

"Because my face looks awful."

"Your face could never look awful."

"Let's not test that theory right now. What's the good
news?"

"I'm on my way home."

"What?"

"We finished ahead of schedule. I'll be home soon."

I pick up the phone. Then drop it just as fast. Good
lord. I look like a hooker clown on crack. I grab the closest garment, which happens to be a tank top and wrap it

around my head, which makes me look as though I'm wearing a babushka. There's nothing I can do about the makeup still smeared under my eyes, but at least the insanity that is my hair is under cover.

I want to be excited, and I am. I get to see Bancroft after four and a half weeks of constant phone conversations that included incredible amounts of innuendo. But the condo is a mess. And there's little in the way of food in the fridge because I planned for him to be back two days from now.

I pick the phone up.

He barks out a laugh. "What's going on over there Bo Peep?"

I ignore the jab. "My hair looks awful."

"Want to tell me about this?" He motions to my face.

"Performance makeup. So how soon are you going to be home? Tonight?"

"Probably in about an hour, depending on how bad the traffic is."

"An hour?" It's a shriek. A loud, almost ear-piercing noise denoting very clearly my panic. "But you're not supposed to be home for two days. I'm not ready for you!"

Bancroft's smile turns downright lascivious. "All you need to do is wash your face and you're perfectly ready for me, babe."

Sweet mother of vagina tingles. If I wasn't in complete panic mode I might've been able to appreciate the low baritone, and the hot look in his eyes. But I'm 100 percent panicking because his room is a sty and the rest of the condo isn't much better.

I roll off the bed. "I gotta go. I gotta tidy up."

"Hey, are you in my bedroom?"

"Uh—" Fuck. *Fuck*. What do I say to that? The answer is clearly yes. "I fell asleep playing with Franny last night while I was watching TV. See you soon! Safe travels." I hang up. I hope there's so much traffic walking would be faster.

"Oh my God!" I yell to the room. I throw off the tank top wrapped around my head and then run around, trying to figure out where to start. My clothes are all over the floor. I've gotten lazy over the past few days, and the bathroom is loaded with my things. I need a bulldozer to manage this mess. The cleaning lady will be here in a couple of hours, which doesn't help me now.

Okay. Maybe it's not quite that bad, but it's still not good. Cleaning this room is priority number one. I grab one of the empty laundry baskets and get to work on picking up the dirty clothes from the floor. There are a lot of them.

I strip the sheets and pillowcases, cringing at the black smears left from my excessive mascara. I can barely see over the top of the laundry basket it's so full by the time I'm done.

I dump it all in the machine, drop in a detergent tab, and rush back to Bancroft's room with the basket again. I sweep all my crap off his vanity, grab all my things from the shower, including my body poof and all my used towels, and sprint back to my room with it. I'll worry about putting it away later.

I make up Bancroft's bed, clean his vanity as best I can and then rush to the kitchen to tackle the mess there. It's not terrible, but it's definitely not awesome. There are a lot of little things lying around, and from what I witnessed on my first day here he's pretty tidy. I don't want him to come home to a messy house.

I do the best I can with the little time I have. Which turns out to be less than an hour. I'm in the middle of trying to fit the last of the mugs from the sink in the overfilled dishwasher when I hear the ding of the elevator from the hall. I freeze and hold my breath, waiting. The code being punched in spurs me into action.

I still look like a hooker clown. On crack. I leave the dishwasher open and sprint through the kitchen and down the hall. I slide across my bedroom floor, into the bathroom, slamming the door behind me as Bancroft's deep, sexy voice travels through the condo and resonates in my happy clit—along with the rest of me. Oh God. He's home. I am way too excited about this.

I slap all the buttons in the shower, having forgotten how to use it since I've been using Bancroft's for the past four-point-five weeks.

"Ruby?" his muffled voice comes from somewhere in the condo.

"Hey! I'll be out in a few minutes," I yell over the rushing water.

I take the fastest, most violent shower of my life because I can't figure out how to stop the jets until I'm almost done. I scrub the makeup off my face, run a brush through my hair, and step out into my bedroom—with the boxes still lining the walls—wrapped in a towel.

Of course, that's the exact moment Bancroft chooses to pass by. He's carrying Francesca, cooing at her, looking adorable and sexy in his dress shirt and dress pants, and, sweet Lord, I'm mostly naked, and he's here.

Bancroft's gaze starts from my toes and moves up, slowly, all the way to my face. "Hi." It's only one word, but there are a million questions in it.

He's so gorgeous, absently petting Francesca while he stands there, staring. I stare right back, eating up the visual beauty. He's rocking sweet stubble and his shirt is wrinkled. He's a little disheveled. It makes him even sexier.

Anxiety makes my heart race. I want to run across the room and throw myself into his arms. I want him to cross the room, pick me up, and throw me down on the bed. I want his mouth on mine. I want it everywhere. I say and do none of these things. Instead I go with, "Hi."

A month of banter, of conversations spent partially undressed, or in bed, or in pajamas being flirty makes this one of the most awkward situations ever. Also, my being naked doesn't help.

"I see you washed your face."

"And the rest of me."

His eyes dip down and his tongue peeks out, dragging across his lip. "I see that, too."

I tighten my grip on my towel. My fingers would really like to let it drop to the floor just to see what he'll do.

He takes a step forward and so do I. My entire body hums with energy. Francesca wriggles in his arms and he loses his hold. She hops to the floor and skitters across the room, disappearing into the hall. Bancroft doesn't seem to care as he advances on me. Is he going to kiss me? Is that a good idea? I don't know, and I'm not sure I want it to matter.

He's only a foot away when a crash startles us both. He hesitates and glances over his shoulder. It's a second or two before he decides it doesn't matter. In that time, I allow my towel to loosen, exposing the tops of my breasts. If I drop it another inch, he'll see nipple. Just as he turns back to me there's another louder crash. "Fuck," he mutters. "I'll be right back."

He whirls around, hands balled into fists as he stalks down the hall.

I expel a breath and check the time. Dammit. It's already after two. I actually have to leave for work soon, which leaves me no time to enjoy ogling Bancroft or to hear about his trip.

I close my door and rush to get dressed, throwing on a pair of shorts, a sports bra, and a loose shirt, because they're pretty much the only clean things I have in here.

I hastily pack my work bag so I'm ready to go, luckily having never unpacked it from last night. Then I take a few deep, cleansing breaths. We just have to get past the initial awkwardness of seeing each other again for the first time after a month of daily phone conversations and a lot of sexual innuendo. It'll be fine. I don't have to jump him right away. I probably shouldn't, truth be told. I'm so excited to see him, though. Too excited. I need to calm down.

I open the door and step out into the hall. I can hear him in his bedroom. The one I've been sleeping in for weeks. I check my bag, making sure it's zipped up. I haven't even told Amie the truth about where I'm working. I don't want her to accidentally let it slip to Armstrong. He seems like the gossipy type.

Bancroft is visible through the crack in the door. A laundry basket sits at his feet, his suitcase lies open on the bed. He tosses items from the suitcase into the basket, red boxer briefs among them.

I knock on the door and peek my head around the jamb. "Everything okay?"

"Yeah, Francesca got up on the counter and knocked a bunch of stuff over, but it's fine. Nothing broken, or anything. Come on in."

Oh God. His voice is so damn sexy. And deep. Like the ocean. Like . . . I don't know what else. But it sounds even better in real life than it does on the phone, and it does things to my body. Good things. Incredible things.

He stops what he's doing when I peek my head inside,

his eyes moving over me. He glances at the bag hanging from my shoulder and frowns. "Do you have to go somewhere?"

I drop it on the floor outside his room. "I have work."

That frown deepens. "Oh. I thought you wouldn't have to go until later."

"We have rehearsal this afternoon." I glance around his room, making sure I managed to put away all my things. It looks pretty good.

"Will you be home for dinner?"

I shake my head. "I won't be back until late."

"Oh." He misses the laundry basket with a pair of pants and doesn't bend down to pick them up. "What about tomorrow night?"

"I'm working then, too."

He rubs the back of his neck. "Well, that's no good. When are we going to catch up?"

I'm not sure what we have to catch up on, other than his flight, since we've talked pretty much every day, but I don't mind that he wants to spend time with me. I certainly wouldn't mind spending time with him, naked, in his bed, playing hide and seek with his penis in my vagina. Dammit. I really need to get a handle on where my brain keeps going. It was much easier when he was an ocean away.

"I have Monday and Tuesday night off."

"That's four days from now."

"We can catch up in the morning?"

"I have to be up early."

"Hmm. Well, I'm still living here, so it's not like we'll lack opportunities to see each other, right?" Why is this so awkward? I don't want it to be uncomfortable between us. I can't tell if it's me or him or both of us.

"Right. Yeah. Of course." He nods, but he's chewing

his lip, still looking displeased. "I guess I'll probably go into the office in a bit, then."

"But you just got back. Don't you get a day off?"

Bancroft shrugs. "Not much to do around here once I'm unpacked. I have lots of debriefing and meetings in the next few days. I might as well get a head start. Besides, it'll keep me from falling asleep in the middle of the afternoon."

"That's a good idea." I hate how uncomfortable this is right now. "Okay. Well, I should go. Maybe I'll see you in the morning?"

"Sounds good. Break a leg tonight."

I grimace, not because I'm actually worried about breaking anything, aside from my recent, botched auditions. I'm typically graceful, but because it feeds into the lie.

"Is that the wrong thing to say?" Bancroft asks.

I force a smile. "No, not wrong at all. Thanks. Thank you." I'm stumbling over my words, aware I need to leave, but I'm having a hard time not going in for a hug.

It turns out I don't need worry about it. As I step around Bancroft his huge hand wraps around my wrist. The sensation is damn well magical. It's been almost five weeks since he's touched me. Longer than that since he's kissed me—accidentally or not. In that time I've been flirting my ass off with him on the phone. So much flirting. So much self-gratifying once I'm no longer on the phone with him.

And right now he's touching me. I must make some kind of noise, because his gaze locks on mine and he hesitates. It's only for the briefest moment. I don't want to lose this opportunity, so I step toward him. It's enough of a positive signal. He tugs me closer still, and wraps his free arm around me.

Now the contact isn't limited to his hand wrapped around my wrist, it's his entire, massive frame pressed up against mine. He winds an arm around my waist, his palm smoothing over my lower back, pulling me in tighter. I imagine how much different this would've been had it happened when I was still just wearing a towel.

I swear I hear a hum come out of him. And I barely resist the urge to drop my hand to his ass and give it a squeeze.

I'm pretty sure I feel his nose in my hair and his breath on my neck before he lets me go. When he steps back he jams his hands in his pockets.

"I'm glad you're home," I say. "Safely. Home safely," I tack on at the end, although it doesn't help much with the breathless quality of my voice or the fact that every nerve in my body is singing.

"Me, too." Based on the gravelly tone, I'd like to think I'm not alone in this feeling.

"Okay. Well, I should really go now."

"'Kay." He nods a bunch of times.

"See you in the morning." It's only possible if I'm still awake when he gets up.

"Definitely."

I leave the condo before I say or do anything stupid. Now more than ever it's apparent that I need to find a new place. I have feelings for this man, and it's not just about wanting to get naked with him. The feelings have become real over the past several weeks. For me at least.

If I keep socking away the money from my tips, I should have enough for first and last in the next month or so, maybe sooner. The longer I stay here, the more difficult it's going to be to manage the sexual tension between us, if this welcome home is any indicator.

At this point, I'd really like to get out of his space before I get into his bed. Sleeping with him while I'm still dependent on him for a place to live creates an inequity I don't want to deal with. I never want to be in a position where I feel like I'm being kept and that's exactly what this will be for me.

CHAPTER 15

ACCIDENTAL SNUGGLES

RUBY

By the time I get home from work it's almost two in the morning. The condo is quiet. I assume Bancroft is asleep. As I head for bed I nearly bypass my own room and keep going to his. That would be a colossally embarrassing mistake.

For the first time since he left on his trip I sleep in the spare bedroom that's supposed to be mine. It feels really strange.

Bancroft is walking around the apartment in a pair of boxers.

Aside from the boxers he's naked. No shirt. No socks. Just boxers. And for some reason they're all wet and clinging to him. I don't know why he's wet, but I offer to help him out of his soggy underwear, dripping on the floor, making a messy puddle around his feet. I reach for the waistband aware I seem to be going against my own plan not to sleep with him, and watch goose bumps rise along his skin. Just as I pull them over his hips I wake up.

So much sadness.

The dream fades away and all I'm left with is dry mouth and zinging clit. I reach for the glass on the nightstand, but it's empty. It's four in the morning. I've only been asleep for an hour. I don't remember finishing it off before I fell asleep. I do, however, remember rolling my marble while shoving my face in my pillow to thoughts of Bancroft before I passed out. The extra exertion probably didn't help with my thirst issues. I also have a headache, possibly from being underhydrated. Diva told me to drink more water last night, but it must not have been enough.

I throw off the covers and hoist myself out of bed. I grab the bottle of aspirin tucked into my nightstand and my glass and make the trek to the kitchen—the built-in water dispenser in the fridge provides the best, most amazing cold water ever. Which is what I need right now.

I lean my head against the fridge as I wait for the glass to fill, down two aspirin with the water, then fill the glass again before I head back to bed with my eyes half-closed.

I slide under the now cool sheets—which makes me shiver a little—and rest my cheek against the pillow. Closing my eyes, I try to bring back the dream I was having before thirst woke me. I go back to the beginning, where he must have been dressed, because I'm a big fan of taking him from a suit to his birthday suit in my head. I imagine the way Bancroft—*Bane*—looks in his buttondown with his tie hanging loose. Or his snug-fitting undershirt.

As I mentally undress him in my mind I can suddenly smell him. I must be on the verge of dreaming again because it's incredibly vivid. I snuggle deeper into the pillow, willing my mind to go where my body would like to. I hear a groan, low and deep and then the bed shifts and a heavy arm comes thudding down on my hip.

My eyes pop open. *What the hell?* This is definitely not a dream. At least I don't think it is. The bed shifts. Nope. Not a dream. Who the hell is in bed with me? The sheets rustle and the mattress dips as the hand attached to the arm that's resting on my hip starts moving up my body.

"Mmm. This feels nice," comes the mumbled, male voice that belongs to the hand exploring me over the blanket.

Holy shit. Bane is in bed with me. *What is Bane doing in bed with me?*

I'm frozen, sort of. I mean, I'm not really sure what I should do, because as much as I'm enjoying being felt up—even through the covers—I'm still really confused as to why exactly this has happened. Or how.

Suddenly Bane's very fit, very warm chest is pressed against my back. And wait. Oh my God. *Oh my God.* Is that . . . it can't be. *Oh yes.* It is.

Bane is naked. How do I know this? Because I can feel him against my lower back where my sleep tank has ridden up, leaving several inches of skin exposed. And his erection—*his very hard, ample erection*—is pressed right up against me. My theory on big hands is definitely true.

He nuzzles into my hair, burrowing his way through it until his stubbly chin rubs against my neck. I don't think he's actually awake. So I stay still, waiting for him to . . . I don't know . . . stop moving around? I just need him to settle and then I can figure out what I should do. Well, I know what I should do, but I'm enjoying this a little too much at the moment.

He doesn't settle, though. Instead, he adjusts the comforter so the hand that was exploring over the top is now exploring underneath. His arm comes around my waist, and then his warm fingers slide under the hem of my tank and splay across my stomach, moving up. He gets stuck at the elastic-y built-in bra and drags the fabric up.

He cups one of my boobs through several layers of cotton and groans. I barely restrain my own when he rolls his hips.

I open my mouth to say something, like maybe; "Hey, Bane. Why are you in my bed, feeling me up?" Or; "If you wanted to get your freak on with me, there are better, less awkward ways than creeping into my bed in the middle of the night and surprising me." Or even; "Mind if I check out how generous that stick is jabbing into my low back?"

But none of those things come out of my mouth. Instead all I do is whisper-moan *Bancroft*.

It doesn't seem to have an impact on the breast palming. In fact, he's gone from palming to kneading. He makes a second attempt to get under the elastic with a grunt.

I should stop this. My brain registers this thought and immediately wants to dismiss it as unnecessary.

I really should do something apart from lie here, because this shouldn't be happening in the middle of the night without some kind of adult discussion in which we weigh the consequences of me living in his house, being his pet sitter, and getting a little screw in on the side. Especially since he's mentioned he's not interested in getting into a relationship while he's doing all this traveling. But since I've been fantasizing about the exact scenario, I'm a little too willing to let it go on for a little while longer.

This time he makes it under the elastic, his wide, warm palm curving around my breast. And then I feel his hot breath on my neck, followed by his lips on my skin. Oh Jesus, is he going to, oh no . . . oh yes . . . he rolls my nipples between his thumb and finger, his groan vibrating against me as his lips part and his tongue sweeps across my skin.

Okay, at this point I have zero good excuses for not saying something to stop him since he's still obviously not quite conscious. And instead of doing the one thing I should, I arch and press my butt against his erection. It nestles all snug along the cleft of my ass—my underwear are clearly barring the way, although they're not full coverage, so I can feel a lot of skin on skin. With a final, rough nipple twist he abandons my breast and his palm moves heavily down my stomach.

My eyes go wide as I realize he has a destination in mind. I would like to say my next action is a result of my acknowledging that this has gone too far. However, it has more to do with the fact that I think I need to shave my nether regions. I grab his hand just as it passes my navel. "Whoa!" I rasp-yell.

That seems to startle him out of whatever semi-sleep-induced lust-haze he's in. His hand retracts and he rolls over as I jump out of the bed.

And that's when I realize I'm not in my bedroom. I'm in *his*.

"I just—I didn't—I made—" I'm flailing around like an idiot as a very sleep-bleary Bancroft blinks at me with confusion. God he's sexy when he's just woken up. My eyes follow his hand, which is smoothing down his stomach. And that's when I take note that the sheets have abandoned his glorious body. He's so naked. And I can see every inch of him. Well, apart from his right thigh.

Bancroft shirtless is a vision. Bancroft naked is damn well fucking phenomenal.

"Oh God, that is *huge*!" I say when I finally reach the visual destination of Erectiontopia.

It's not completely dark in here, thanks to the night owls of the city who are awake in the buildings across the street. I can see very clearly how ample his erection truly is. And I'm definitely gawking. In my defense, there's quite a lot to gawk at. My mouth is actually watering, it looks that amazing.

Prior to this moment I've never really been all that impressed with a penis. If there were a penis rating system, Bancroft's would be in a class all its own. Now part of this may be due to the amazing shadows cast over his naked body by the ambient lighting. It may in part be due to the entire package framing the penis I'm currently staring at.

I scan his naked body, wishing like hell for a photographic memory, because his body is a gift from the heavens. And that erection is magnificent.

On a scale of one to ten, with one being depressingly inadequate and ten being deity inspiring, his dick is so beautiful it would make angels weep and virgins offer themselves up for sacrifice. Okay, maybe not that last part. But it's a gorgeous penis and I'm really, really turned on.

Now I want to get back under those sheets with him and pretend I didn't just accidentally crawl into his bed and let him feel me up, for quite a lengthy amount of time.

"Ruby?" He pulls a sheet up to cover his junk. "What're you—" He looks me over. His hand is resting on his erection. Cradling it. That could've been me if I'd been smart enough to keep up the ruse.

I try to cover myself, because my choice of sleep outfit doesn't leave all that much to the imagination. Well,
more than Bane's obviously, but it's still pretty skimpy.

"It was an accident! Sorry!" I spin around and sprint
to the door, slamming it behind me. I run all the way
down the hall to my bedroom, being much more careful
about closing the door this time. And of course, I lock it.
My embarrassment is so huge—bigger even than the
cock I was just staring at—and there is no way I can face
Bane right now.

CHAPTER 16

HARD TO CONTROL HARD-ONS

BANCROFT

I'm lying in my bed, staring at my closed door with my hard-on in my hand, wondering what the hell just happened.

Well, I know what just happened, but the question is why was Ruby in my bed and why isn't she in it anymore? Both myself and my erection, who I feel is an independent, although very linear thinker, would like an answer to this question.

I consider getting up and going to see if she's okay, but I'm still achingly hard, so I can't go anywhere right now. Also, based on her rushed exit and her inability to speak in coherent sentences, she seems pretty damn embarrassed about the entire thing. I suppose I can wait until morning, which is only two hours away anyway, and we can deal with it then.

As I lie here, filtering through the foggy event that has just transpired, I consider how much of it was related to my dream and how much was real. Mostly all I recall is some boob grabbing and nipple tweaking, and some cock-to-ass rubbing. I would like to do more of all of those things with her while conscious.

After five more minutes of lying in my bed, thinking about Ruby, I give up on her magically reappearing at my door and rub one out. Alone. This time I have some realish fodder to help me reach the end. The only thing that would be better is if it was the lovely Ruby helping me out, instead of me doing it on my own.

Usually orgasms are a decent sedative, but it doesn't work the way I'd like it to. I can't seem to fall back asleep and ninety minutes later my alarm goes off. I pull on a pair of boxers and shorts before I leave my room— something I'm going to have to get used to doing with Ruby living here. At least until we get past this whole awkward reintroduction phase. When I woke up with my hand almost in her panties I figured we were about to resolve the issue, but then she bolted.

I put coffee on and rifle through the contents of the fridge. It needs to be stocked; pickings are fairly slim. I didn't even think to check the contents before I went to the office yesterday afternoon.

How my arrival was received and my expectations are not at all in line with each other. In my head, Ruby greeted me at the door with high enthusiasm and little in the way of clothing. I got the little in the way of clothing part, but the enthusiasm was replaced with awkwardness. And I hadn't taken into account that she'd have to work, and definitely not for the next four days.

Instead of sitting around in my condo feeling sorry for myself, I went to work. It helped keep my mind occupied. And it gave me a leg up on Lex, who didn't show up until four hours after I did. By that time, I'd already gone through spreadsheets, marketing plans, and development costs with my father. He'd seemed impressed by my dedication to the team and the projects. Having just got off a plane a few hours earlier, he'd fully expected me to take the day. And I would've, if Ruby had been home.

I survey the contents of the fridge, deciding what I'd like to make for breakfast. I have the necessary ingredients for pancakes. I've gotten used to starting or ending my day with Ruby, and I'd like it to continue.

Once the coffee is made I knock on her door. I'm met with silence. I try again, the odd knot forming in my stomach gets tighter. "Ruby," I call out when the second knock produces more silence.

I try the knob, but it's locked. Shit. Did she think I was going to try and get back into bed with her last night? Was this preventative, or born out of embarrassment?

I've talked to her almost every single day since I left, apart from a handful of travel days. There's been an extensive amount of sexual innuendo in those conversations. In a lot of ways, it's felt like long-distance dating. I've had weeks to get to know Ruby, weeks to appreciate her sense of humor. Time to get to know her mannerisms. Time to discover what makes her tick, what her insecurities are, how strong she is, how much she loves my pets, how much I appreciate her choice of bedwear.

I might have been reading things wrong, but my expectation was that when I came home, all that two-dimensional flirting would turn into something three-dimensional. With nudity. That I was so close to that reality last night makes me impatient to get the moment back. Except I have a feeling that's not going to happen right now.

I give it one last try. I have no idea what time she came home, and I fell asleep on the couch last night and didn't wake up until after midnight. She hadn't appeared to be home at that point, although I hadn't checked her room.

Her shoes, a pair of worn flats, sit close to the front door. I don't remember if they were at the door when I relocated from the couch to my bedroom.

I give up on trying to wake Ruby. I take my time getting ready for work, hoping she'll come out before I have to leave. She doesn't.

My entire day is spent in meetings presenting the PowerPoint I created on the flight home while my brother slept. I didn't consult Lex, determined to have my own findings. He's currently stewing in the seat opposite me. Every time he tries to throw me a curveball question I have the right answer, or at least one my father approves of. There's always been competition between us and my approach to this hasn't done anything to make it better. But I don't like being micromanaged and that's how the last five weeks have been with us working together.

My hope is that this trip overseas will be my last for a while and that I'll have done enough to be able to ask to manage a few of the New York properties. We have ten, so it should be doable.

When the meeting is over my father pulls me aside.

I really should be able to ask for what I want. But I'll have to put the feelers out first. My father always has a master plan, and I'm concerned it's one that involves more travel for me.

I take a seat in one of the club chairs in his office and he sits across from me, rather than behind his desk. "Good work in London."

This is high praise from my father. "Thanks. It was a good learning experience. I feel like I'm getting a good handle on the renovation aspect."

"Once you're settled in I think it would be a good idea for you to work with the design team on the new build concepts in Germany."

This is preferable to working with Lex, but if I'm part
of the design team, there's a good chance my father is
going to want me to be part of the groundbreaking team.
That means another stint overseas, which is not what I
want.

"Layla heads that up, doesn't she? You don't think it
would be better for me to work with Griffin instead for a
while?" He's been taking care of some of the Chicago
hotels. That's much closer to home than Germany.

"Are you worried about your ability to focus around
Layla?"

"Pardon?" I smooth my hand over my tie. Layla's been
part of the design team for quite a while. She's incredibly career-driven and focused, so I can't see why he
thinks I won't be able to manage working with her.

My father rolls his eyes. "Oh come on, Bancroft.
You've spent the past seven years with an entourage of
groupies running around after you. I'm just reminding
you that this is the business world, and you'll need to
keep a level, focused head, even around the lookers like
Layla."

"Attractiveness isn't the issue, Dad. I played professional rugby, I didn't do battle in a Spartacus-style
arena. I can handle myself around attractive women.
Besides, Layla isn't my type." Until he mentioned it, I
hadn't even really noticed she was attractive at all. She's
blond and petite. I prefer dark hair and an athletic build,
like Ruby. "What about local renovations? It would be
good to work on some projects directly with you." The
best way to appeal to my father is through his ego.

He smiles and taps his pen on the arm of his chair.
"That will happen in the future, once you've had sufficient training."

"You don't think I would benefit from having your

expertise?" I try to tamp the frustration. I don't want to close doors with him before I've even managed to pick the lock.

"You will always have my expertise. I'll oversee all aspects of the projects you work on. But you need a good year of getting your feet wet and learning the company ropes. I want you to be comfortable with all the top-level employees."

"When does ground break for the project in Germany?"

"Late fall, if things go smoothly. There will be other projects I'll want you to have a hand in, as well. The hotels in California need attention and there's property in Costa Rica that we're interested in."

He's talking more travel, like I knew he would. I don't want more travel. Except more travel would mean I'd need someone to stay and take care of Tiny and Francesca. It's an excuse to have Ruby stick around longer or at least stay at my place periodically. If she still wants to. As soon as this meeting is over I need to talk to her. Hopefully she's awake now.

"What about the New York renovations?"

He's already looking at his phone, pretending to check emails. It's what he does when he's either done with the discussion or he wants to avoid a topic. Unfortunately, I'm his son, and I'm a lot like he is in many regards, so I refuse to take the hint for what it is.

"Aren't there plans to start those in the new year? Isn't Griffin working on the renovation project for the Times Square location? Now that I'm on board he and I could work together. The project would move faster then, wouldn't it? We could start right after New Year's, that way we won't miss out on prime summer tourism and we'll still get the holiday business."

My father stops typing an email to regard me. "You've been thinking about this?"

"Of course. New York has so much opportunity for growth. I'd love to be involved in that project." I bite my tongue before I can say I want to make this my hub.

"It's a ways off. We can talk about it later."

It's not a no. I'll take it.

I'd like to say I see Ruby when I get home. I don't. I send her a message asking how she's doing, then I fall asleep on the couch and drag my ass to my bedroom around one in the morning.

I don't have a response when I wake up the next morning. I debate knocking on her door, but I have no idea what time she got in, and since she hasn't responded to my message I leave it alone, although I don't want to.

My morning is full of meetings again, discussions about the projects in the UK and abroad, and I'm fully immersed in the building, project management side of the company. I understand what my father is doing. He doesn't want me to settle in one area of the business yet, because there are so many sides to it, and if I'm going to run it jointly with my brothers eventually, I need to understand all aspects. And I need to be able to work with both of them, no matter how challenging it is.

By noon I still haven't heard from Ruby. I either need a drink or to punch someone out. Or to talk to Ruby. The latter would be my preference.

I have a decent reason to contact her that will inevitably get a response: Francesca's feeding schedule.

Now that I'm home we need to communicate about that kind of thing so we don't overfeed her. I had a routine, but I'm guessing with Ruby's odd hours it's changed significantly over the past month.

I make sure the first message I send is convoluted enough that she would require an explanation to understand exactly what I was taking about.

It works. Her response comes a few minutes later in the form of several question marks.

I close my office door, turn the lock, and hit the video call button. Ruby answers on the third ring.

"Hey." Her voice is gravelly and low.

I'm not looking at her, though, I'm looking at the ceiling of her bedroom. "Did I wake you?"

"Yeah, but I needed to get up. What's up? That text was worse than your handwriting. It made no sense."

"Sorry about that. I realized with me being back Francesca's feeding schedule might be a little out of whack. I thought it would be easier to talk about it."

I hear a drawer open. It's a little squeaky. "I never thought of that. I've just been feeding her like usual. Should I not? Do you want to be the one to do it?"

"Why don't we keep it the way it is until we have a chance to sit down together?"

"Okay. I can do that."

I'm still looking at the ceiling and I can hear the patter of feet and a rustle. "What're you doing?"

"Getting dressed."

"Did you answer the phone naked?"

There's motion and suddenly I'm looking at Ruby's arched brow. "You're really asking me that?"

I fight the grin that's trying to spread across my face. "It's a legitimate question."

She's propped the phone up on the dresser, based on my view of the room. "You know, you can just call me without the video component now, like normal people do."

"It's a habit. I like seeing you." And feeling you, like I did in my bed the other night, but I'm getting to that.

"I'm so attractive when I'm half asleep."

And she's given me the perfect segue. "Speaking of being half-asleep, do you want to talk about what happened the other night?"

Her gaze shifts away and she busies herself with something outside of my line of view, so I'm only looking at her chin. "I'm sorry, the other night?" Her voice is surprisingly even.

"Are we pretending it didn't happen?"

"Pretending what didn't happen?" She's still not making eye contact.

"You. In my bed."

Her brow furrows. "You mean while you were away? I told you I fell asleep in there a couple of times. I changed the sheets before you came home. If it was a big deal you should've said something."

"I'm talking about you in my bed with me in it."

She blinks a couple of times. She's giving away nothing. A sly smile spreads across her face and her voice drops to a sultry whisper. She drags a finger down the side of her neck. I follow the movement, hoping she'll go lower, to the breast I cupped not that long ago. "Have you been dreaming about me, Bane?"

My eyes snap back up to her face. The answer to that question is yes. For the past several weeks I've been dreaming about her nonstop. "You were in my bed the other night."

She laughs. "Was I now?"

Now it's my turn to frown. There's no way I dreamed that. It was far too visceral. A knock at my office door prevents me from asking more questions and verifying that I'm not losing my mind over this woman. Griffin taps his watch through the glass pane. I check the time. Shit. I have a meeting in five minutes. "I have to go."

"Do I need to feed Francesca?"

"I did it this morning. She just needs playtime."

"I love playtime." Her grin is pure sexual evil right before the screen goes blank.

It looks like the video flirting is still on. I have to do some creative rearranging in my pants before I get out of my chair.

I grab my laptop, notepad, and file folder keeping them at waist level. It's been a long time since I've had to shield an issue in my pants.

I go into the office on Saturday and work from home on Sunday. I get up early, because I'm incapable of sleeping in, and go for a run on the treadmill. By nine I'm show-ered and there's still no sign of life from Ruby's room. The only way I know she's home is because her shoes are by the door.

I settle in at my computer with a coffee and pull up my research files. The past weeks have been exhausting mentally. I'm beginning to grow accustomed to using my brain for this type of analytic purpose, but it's been an adjustment. I'm surrounded by pie charts and graphs. Comparative data analysis was never my favorite part of marketing, but I learned how to be good at it.

It's noon when I hear movement in the kitchen. It's followed by muttering and the sound of the fridge door opening. I stay where I am, eavesdropping.

I debate whether I should make myself known, when I hear a big yawn and the patter of her feet moving across the floor. "Morning Tiny," she says, then follows it with, "Morning hotness."

I think maybe she's talking to me, but when I swivel in my chair I discover she's standing in front of the ostentatious picture on my wall of me scoring a goal for last year's Championship game. That photo was taken about ten minutes before I blew out my knee.

Ruby's staring up at the image. She takes a sip from her glass. "Why aren't you shirtless?"

"If I was shirtless no one would know what number I am," I reply.

Ruby startles with a gasp and the glass slips from her fingers. It hits the floor and shatters at her feet, orange juice and shards forming a dangerous moat around her.

I push out of my chair. "Shit. Sorry. Don't move."

Her face is the color of my rugby jersey in the picture, but she does what I ask and stays where she is. I skirt around the mess on the floor and head for the front door, shoving my feet into the first pair of shoes I can find. I return to where Ruby is still standing, a gorgeous, embarrassed jewel in the middle of a glass and orange juice puddle.

"Let's get you out of the danger zone." I wrap my hands around her waist and lift her up. She grabs my shoulders, and leans into me, her chest pressing against mine.

"I didn't mean to scare you." I set her down, but I'm having difficulty letting go.

"I didn't realize you were here." She can't meet my gaze. Her hands slide down my chest and she pushes back. "Let me get a broom and a mop so I can clean that up."

"I'll get it. You're not walking around without shoes." I finally release her so I can take care of the problem in the middle of the floor. It's a good thing Francesca is sleeping in her cage. Well, she's not sleeping anymore, but at least she's safe.

Ruby seems to realize I'm right and stays put while I grab towels and a garbage can.

"Can you grab my flip-flops, please?"

I pass them to her and we tackle the mess in silence. Once the juice is cleaned up and the bulk of the glass is managed, Ruby gets out the vacuum cleaner, while I get out the mop and fill a bucket with soapy water.

"I'm so sorry about this. I thought I was alone," she mumbles, still embarrassed as she winds the cord of the vacuum cleaner back up.

"I figured as much when you started talking to my poster like it was going to answer you."

She grimaces and gives me a dirty look. "Thanks for just letting that go."

"Would you feel better about my razzing you if I take my shirt off?"

"Ugh. I'm going back to bed." She turns to leave but I grab her wrist, stopping her. I don't know what's happened since I've come back from London, but I don't like the awkwardness between us.

"Wait. Don't. I'll stop. Come have something to eat with me."

"I have to get ready for rehearsal."

"What time do you have to be there? I can drive you. Come sit with me. You have to eat before you go, right? Let's have lunch." Shit. I sound really fucking desperate right now. Maybe because I am. "I haven't seen you since I got back, Ruby. It's like you're avoiding me."

Her eyes drop.

"Are you?"

She fidgets with her fingers. This isn't the Ruby I'm used to. "I've been working and so have you."

"Is it because of what happened the other night? You ending up in my bed?"

"I wasn't really awake."

"So you admit it." Thank fucking Christ. I thought I was losing my damn mind.

That gets me an annoyed glare, which I like a lot better than this sudden insecurity. "Are you serious with this?"

"You had me questioning whether or not I was imagining things. I knew it was way too visceral to be a dream."

Ruby purses her lips. "You're going to get on me about this now, too? It was an accident."

"You're more than welcome to have more accidents like that any time you want."

Ruby's mouth drops open. I want to close the space between us. I want to slip my thumb into her mouth and feel her lips close around it. I want to know if she'll suck or bite, but I have a feeling if I do, I'm going to create more distance rather than less.

"Well it wouldn't have happened if you'd been smart enough to lock your door!" she fires back.

"Like you've been locking yours?"

She blinks. "Why are you trying to get into my room when I'm sleeping?"

"Because you've been avoiding me."

"I have not!"

"Have too."

She plants her fists on her hips. "Is this a kindergarten fight? Are you going to stick your tongue out and say neener-neener?"

I can't and don't want to contain my grin. I can see she's trying to keep a straight face, but is unable to maintain it. Her grin is exactly what I need to see.

"I missed you this week." I take her hand and tug her toward the kitchen. "Come hang out with me before you have to leave."

Her fingers wrap around mine and squeeze for a second. "Okay."

The following Friday, Armstrong, his friend Drew, some guy I've never met before and I'm not sure I like, and my brothers follow me down the hall to my condo. It's been a long time since I've had the guys over to watch a game, and I'm not sure how well it's going to go with the way Lex keeps making snide comments to Armstrong every chance he gets. Those two are competitive, particularly when it comes to women, and I really never understood why.

But tonight, since Ruby's out until who knows what time, I figured it would be good for me to do something other than wait for her to come home. It's starting to be a problem. Well, it's been a problem for a while, but it's getting worse. Ever since the night she ended up in my bed.

I'd like to say I've figured out a way to manage this situation, but I haven't. Ruby's hours are opposite mine, so we're rarely home at the same time and I've been stuck at the office until late almost every day this week so we haven't seen much of each other and when we do she's always skittering away like I make her nervous. Even the innuendo-laden banter has died since my return. I can't corner her long enough to find out what the hell is going on.

Tonight there's no sexual tension to contend with because Ruby's working. I hold my thumb to the censor, waiting for my print to register. There's a brief lull in Armstrong's monologue and the sound of bass registers.

It vibrates through my feet and my hand as I turn the knob. Maybe Ruby left the TV on, or the stereo.

Neither hypothesis is correct, I find, as soon as I open the door.

The sight I'm greeted with is immediately stored in the vault in my head labeled "Jerk It." In the middle of my living room are five women. Five scantily clad women, wearing heels, with their asses facing the door.

I can pick Ruby's out immediately. She's on the far right. Closest to me. She's wearing my favorite fucking shorts.

"Is this a surprise bachelor party? Did you buy me strippers?" Armstrong sounds far too excited about this.

"They're not strippers," I snap.

Except the way these women are moving, the sway of hips and the shaking of booty makes me question whether or not what I've just said is true.

They do some kind of dirty, thrusty spin, until they're facing the door. They're all so caught up in the synchronized routine and following the one in the middle, who is shouting directions, that they fail to notice us right away. My focus is solely on Ruby and the way her leg does this pinwheeling thing, followed by a kick in which she catches her ankle, while it's beside her ear.

That level of flexibility will be fantastic in bed. When I get her back into mine. I would like that to be right now.

"I know the one on the end." Drew points at Ruby.

As she releases her leg she notices me, and the rest of the guys standing in the doorway.

Her perfect, pouty mouth, forms the words *oh shit*, but I can't hear them because the music is so loud. She stumbles a little, her eyes going wide. She runs, in heels that look rather dangerous, across the room and stops the music.

"What're you doing?" The woman in the center yells. "We're in the mid—"

Ruby cuts her off, eyes on me. "I thought you were out tonight."

"I thought you said you were out," I reply. My voice is gravel-truck-rumble low.

"You said you were watching the game with the guys." Ruby's is atypically high.

"I am. You said you had rehearsal."

"I do. We are. I'm so sorry. When you said you were watching the game I thought you meant at a bar, not here." Ruby's a little sweaty, her bangs are damp and sticking to her forehead. There's a sheen to her skin and her cheeks are flushed. It's very similar to how I imagine she might look when I'm making her come, hard and repeatedly.

She's also wearing so little that it's easy to imagine such an event rather vividly. She's paired her tiny shorts with a sports bra. Her abs looks incredible. All of her looks incredible. The bra isn't one of those ones that reduces a chest into a uni-boob state, though. It's strappy and sexy and it looks a little complicated to take off, like something I might accidentally tear in my zeal to get her naked. Which I am very interested in doing right now.

"Ruby?" Drew's voice drags our eyes off each other and over to him.

Her eyes go wide. "Drew?"

"You two know each other?" I ask. Actually, I think it may be more of a growl.

Her gaze flickers back to me and then away again.

"Wow." Drew's eyes slide over her frame in a way that seems entirely too familiar. "It's been a while. You filled out nicely."

Ruby's eyebrow shoots up. "Filled out?"

"How do you two know each other?" I ask again, it's definitely a full-on growl now.

"We went out a couple years ago," Drew says absently, still staring at Ruby. He has this look on his face, the kind that makes me wonder if he knows what she looks like with all of her clothes off.

Based on the color Ruby's cheeks are going, I have a feeling that might actually be the unfortunate reality. "Like once. It wasn't a big deal," she says.

"I should get your number again," Drew suggests.

Ruby's lip curls. "Uh, no thanks. I remember very clearly how the last date ended. I'm pretty sure I'm not interested in a repeat of those three, lackluster minutes."

"Oh, snap!" One of the girls behind Ruby says and the other ones start giggling.

I, on the other hand, want to rip Drew's head off and punt it off the roof of my building.

"I see your winning personality hasn't changed much," Drew shoots back.

"I see your hair hated you enough to start migrating down your body," Ruby retorts.

It's actually a pretty decent insult. Lexington snickers.

Drew runs a self-conscious hand through his hair. "Slutty and bitchy, now I remember why I didn't call you again."

Ruby launches herself at Drew. I catch her around the waist and she kicks out at him, narrowly missing his nuts. I almost wish she would've hit the mark.

I point a finger right in Drew's face. "Watch your fucking mouth if you want your teeth to stay where they are."

"Oh, shit. Is she your girlfriend?" Drew asks.

Ruby puts her hand on my chest and pushes, trying to get free. "Put me down, Tarzan."

"I'm sorry I called her . . . those things." Drew looks

a little ill, possibly because I outweigh him by at least fifty pounds and, unlike him, I'm not afraid to get punched in the face.

I set Ruby down and she gets right up in his face, propping one fist on her hip. "I'm right here, jerkoff, if you're going to apologize to anyone for calling me names, it better damn well be me."

Her shorts are all wonky again, one side riding up so her cheek is on display. It always seems to be the right one. I reach out and slide my finger under the fabric, putting it back in place.

She jumps and bats my hand away. "What're you doing?"

"Just covering you up, babe."

She glares at me. It's a sexy look on her.

"Maybe we should head to a bar, unless . . ." Griffin trails off. His expression reflects his discomfort with the current situation.

"We have to go soon anyway." Ruby turns to face the girls. I don't fail to notice that Drew's eyes, along with everyone else's, including Armstrong's, drop to her ass. "Sorry girls. I'll just grab my things."

"You ladies don't have to rush out of here. We're more than happy to share the space," Lex says.

I fight an eye roll. They all just give him a look as they pull tanks or tight-fitting shirts over their heads, grabbing purses from the couch. The tallest of the girls saunters over, her hips swaying hard as she looks us over. Her gaze falls on me. "You must be Bancroft."

"I am. And you are?"

"Diva. Sorry about the confusion. Thanks for letting us use your space. You boys should come see us later." She looks to Drew. "Except maybe not you." She rummages around in her purse and pulls out a card, handing it to me. "We go on at ten. Ruby has her solo at eleven."

"Thanks, I'll see what I can do." I pocket the card without looking at it. I don't know if I want these guys watching Ruby move like that. Especially not this Drew guy, who's apparently already had the pleasure of getting to know what Ruby feels like from the inside. Fucker.

Ruby appears a few seconds later, an oversized sweat-shirt hanging off one shoulder, almost covering her shorts completely, her bag thrown over her shoulder. The heels are gone, replaced by flats.

"I'm sorry I misunderstood," she says to me, then turns to Drew. "I feel like I need to be totally honest with you. If you had called me again for another hookup"— she makes air quotes—"there's no way in hell I would've considered it based on your highly inadequate perfor-mance the first time. It was like having sex with a jack-hammer." She brushes past him, the rest of the girls follow after, every single one of them giving Drew a dirty look on the way.

The one named Diva winks at Armstrong and he winks back.

The sound of yippy barking has me cringing. Ms. Blackwood is standing in the hallway with Precious cra-dled protectively in her arms. Her eyes are as wide as they can go and her mouth is a flat, red slash. She looks utterly scandalized when the one who calls herself Diva prances up to her and taps Precious on the nose while she snarls.

As the girls traipse down the hall she turns to me. "I didn't realize you'd returned, Bancroft. Are those"—she seems to struggle to find the right word—"friends of yours?"

"I got back last week. They're friends of Ruby's." At her questioning look I prompt, "She was watching my place while I was gone. Remember?"

"Oh. Yes. Of course. But she's still here?"

"She definitely is."

"Well I hope her friends aren't going to cause trouble."

I flash her a smile and wink. "Don't worry, Ms. Blackwood. I know how to handle trouble."

As soon as the door closes Lex lets out a low whistle. "Now I know why you let her move in here. That chick is smokin'."

"I didn't let her move in because she's hot. I needed someone to take care of Francesca and Tiny."

Armstrong snorts.

"I call bullshit on that, brother." Lex points to his crotch. "I'd sure let her play with my ferret."

I get up in his space. "Keep your fucking ferret away from her unless you want to lose it."

He gives me one of his know-it-all grins. "Well, this explains everything."

"What're you talking about?"

"London, you fool. Turning down the offers for room keys when we were in the hotel bar. You always wanting to go back to your room early. All the phone calls you couldn't miss. You gotta be hitting that."

"I hit that," Drew says.

He's almost sneering until I turn around and point a finger in his face. "You seriously need to shut it unless you want to know what a broken nose feels like."

He nods. "Shutting it."

"You are hitting that, right?" Lex asks again. I don't know why he insists on having this information.

I give him a look. "Ruby is not a *that*, and I'm not sleeping with her." Yet.

He gapes at me. "Seriously, Bane, we need to sit down and have a talk. How the hell are you *not* hitting that? Did you see what she can do with her leg? Did you see her ass?" He holds up his hands as if he's grabbing it. His facial expression would be priceless if he wasn't talking about Ruby. His eyes light up. "We're gonna go see their show tonight, right?"

I slide the card out of my back pocket and scan it. The address is at the bottom.

Griffin looks over my shoulder. "I thought you said Ruby was in theater."

"She is."

"But that—"

I elbow him in the ribs. The card isn't advertising dinner theater, it's a burlesque show.

"So . . . you want us to go to my place to watch the game?" Griffin asks.

"That's probably a good idea." There's not a chance in hell anyone but me is going to see Ruby's show.

CHAPTER 17

THE JIG IS UP

RUBY

I'm so embarrassed. And annoyed. And embarrassed. What is Drew doing hanging out with Bane? I mean, I guess it's not that hard to believe considering all the superwealthy people in this city like to stick close to each other. It's like wealth incest.

I'm in a terrible mood as I suit up in my costume. It's beautiful, sheer, gauzy, and flowing. It's on the revealing side, which is not unusual for a burlesque-style show, but having seen the way Drew was looking at me—as if I was meat he'd like to sink his teeth into again—makes me even more aware that the job I have really isn't one I can keep long term.

In the weeks I've been working here I've dropped a lot of inhibitions. It's been good for me in some ways. But the secrecy is eating at me.

Diva's sitting beside me, applying makeup, just like me. She sweeps a generous amount of lip gloss along her bottom lip, then dabs with powder, and follows up with liner. She repeats the process three times. Her lips always look fabulous. I'm learning all the best tricks from these women. My least favorite is the glitter, though. It gets into everything, and I mean *everything*. All the time.

"What do you think the chances are that you can hook me up with a number for one of those guys?"

I stop applying mascara to glance at her. "I don't really know if you want to date any of those guys. Except maybe Bancroft, but he's off limits."

"I don't want to *date* any of them. I want to make them fall in love with my pussy so they'll buy me nice things. And don't you worry, baby girl, it was clear the second that man walked in the door that he's all about you."

"What do you mean?" Things aren't quite the same since he's come back from London. It's my fault it's this way. I'm so conflicted. I want him, but I don't want to feel like one of his pets—another thing he has to take care of. And when I'm near him I have a very hard time remembering that, so I've been avoiding him, which clearly isn't helpful at all.

Diva snorts. "I'm surprised he didn't throw you over his shoulder caveman style and carry you off to his bedroom as soon he walked in. How amazing is he in bed?"

"I have no idea."

Now it's her turn to pause in the makeup application. "I'm sorry. Can you repeat that?"

"We're not sleeping together."

"Well, once he sees you shake your thing, I bet that'll change."

"Maybe I should practice my solo routine while he's watching a game next week." I snort at the idea, then think about how he was looking at me tonight.

"I don't think you'll have to wait that long."

"Why do you say that?"

Diva adjusts her tiara, then pulls out her glitter dust. "I told him and his friends they should come tonight."

"You did what?"

Diva gives me one of her calm-the-fuck-down looks. "Girl, that man is going to crack like an egg when he sees you up there."

I can't tell her Bancroft doesn't know about the reality of my job. I like Diva. I like all the girls I work with. They're far more genuine than a lot of the girls I grew up with or the ones I'm forced to deal with at the hoity-toity upper-crust events and socials. Inviting them to Bancroft's to rehearse was a big deal. I explained that it was just temporary, that he was a friend of a friend who needed a hand, blah, blah, blah. I didn't need an elaborate story, just a plausible one.

The only thing they cared about was the incredible space we could rehearse in that didn't smell like stale beer and horniness.

But now, as I sit here, I have to come to terms with the fact that I've been lying to everyone: These girls who have become my friends in the past few weeks. My best friend, the man whose condo I've been squatting in for more than a month and who has been nothing but generous. The man whose bed I slept in. The man I'd like to sleep with on a regular basis.

Oh God. I want him to be my boyfriend or my friend who also shares his penis with me on a regular basis—daily even. Over these past weeks I've begun to really like him. A lot. More than a lot, even. And now he's going to know I've been lying.

If I didn't come from a family with a buttload of money this probably wouldn't be a big deal. But I do, so it is. More than that I've kept it secret because part of me is ashamed. I shouldn't be. These are good women, who work hard.

And now Bancroft is going to see me up on that stage. And maybe Armstrong. And that inadequately endowed jerkoff, Drew. Unless Bancroft has punched him out. That would be nice.

I grab my phone and fire off a text to Bancroft:

DO NOT COME TONIGHT

It takes less a minute for me to get one back. It's a picture of the club business card, followed by a message:

This doesn't look like dinner theater.

I can almost hear his disapproval. Dammit. I don't need his judgment. I have enough of my own.

Well done, Sherlock.

The next message I get from him is a frowny face. The one after that sends my stomach plummeting to the floor.

See you soon.

"Shit."

"What's wrong?" Diva asks, clearly oblivious to my plight. Because she's just another person I've been withholding the truth from. I'm a terrible person. I'm also freaking out.

"Bancroft is coming tonight."

"Hopefully he won't be the only one." She winks. "You'll be magic out there, Ruby, you always are. You move like a dream."

It's meant to make me feel better. She thinks I'm nervous. And I am, but not for the reasons she assumes.

"Come on, we need to be on stage in ten." She pats me on the shoulder.

I message Bancroft one last time, but he doesn't respond. My stomach is in knots. This is so bad. I need this to not be happening right now. But it is. I'm going to have to deal with it. I'm going to have to deal with a lot of things, it seems.

I finish getting ready and prepare for judgment to rain down on me. Diva has a point, though. I'm really good at this. I've always played pretty tame roles. My dancing has always been more classical jazz-ballet than this contemporary sexy stuff I've had to learn in a short period of time. While this may be a far distant cry from Broadway, it certainly has been an unforgettable experience.

We're halfway through the first set when I spot him. He's impossible to miss. He dwarfs the bouncers carding people at the door. All the tables are already claimed so he props himself up against the wall at the back of the room, arms crossed over his chest. He's so pissed off. And sexy. And angry. Wow, does he ever look angry.

And his anger makes me angry. He doesn't have a right to be mad at me for this job. He can shove his judging eyes right up his stuffy, tight ass. Wait . . . that sounds wrong.

The set ends, I have enough time for a quick costume change. My solo is different. It's a little less in-your-face bawdy and a little more along the classical lines I was trained in. It's still sexy though, thanks to the ridiculously skimpy, yet tasteful and arty outfit I'm currently wearing.

Bancroft is still standing in the same place when I take the stage for my solo. He can't see me, because the stage is dark, but I can see him. He keeps looking to the right, toward the door that leads to the dressing rooms and backstage.

And then the lights come up and his gaze is suddenly trained on me. I can't look at him. I'm so nervous. It feels like the first time I ever performed. I remember the butterflies. I remember puking after the first act, and the second. It feels a little like that now. I better not puke. I need this job.

It's the longest four minutes and thirty-seven seconds of my life. The applause usually makes the smile I wear genuine. I'm staring out into the crowd, and I have a smile plastered on my face, but it's forced.

Bancroft is clapping, slow and steady, but his expression is dark. I don't know what it means. Is he going to be waiting for me when I come out? Is he going to change the code and kick me out? The second thought is fairly fatalist of me. He doesn't really have a reason for such a strong reaction. He can be upset that I lied. He can throw his judgment around at me for my choice, but at least I haven't caved and gone home to daddy. Yet.

Dottie stops me on the way out of the dressing room. "There's some guy out there looking for you, says he's your roommate and he's here to pick you up, but he can't wait long. I just wanted to check to make sure that wasn't a load of bullshit and he isn't some kind of stalker fan."

"Tall, dark hair, bigger than the bouncers, drop-dead gorgeous?"

"That would be the one."

"I'll be out in five. Can he wait for me at the employee entrance?"

"If that's where you want him. He doesn't look happy."

"I imagine. I won't be long." I don't even bother to change out of my costume. I grab my outfits, shove them in my bag, throw on an oversized cardigan, and leave my makeup alone. I'll deal with that when I get home, after I freak out on Bancroft for being a judgmental asshole.

He's standing at the entrance to the club looking uncomfortable. When he sees me, his eyes move over me, but I don't get a smile. All I get is a cold stare. "Ready to go home?"

I don't say anything. Instead I brush past him, holding my head up high as my stomach churns. When I reach the top of the stairs I realize I have no idea where he's parked, so I'm forced to cease my haughty strutting and wait.

Sweet lord. He looks delicious. He's wearing a pair of dark dress pants and a dark button-down shirt. It's open at the collar. He's very Johnny Cash right now, even his expression is angsty. And hot. I wish I wasn't preparing to be angry at him so I could fully appreciate it.

He barely glances at me as he turns left and I follow him down the street. He's walking fast. I didn't change from heels to flats. I'm pretty good in them, but it's dark and I can't see the miniature potholes and cracks in the sidewalk well enough to feel safe at this speed.

"Will you slow down? We're not running a marathon."

Bancroft whirls around and I almost slam right into him. As it is, I have to put out my hands to keep from face planting into his chest. His hands are balled into fists. His nostrils are flared. His chest is heaving. And all I want to do is rip off his clothes and ride him like a rodeo bull. Too bad that's not likely to happen.

His left cheek tics. "You didn't seem to have a problem with those shoes while you were onstage."

"It's a flat, even surface." I gesture to the sidewalk. "This is not."

"Would you like me to carry you?"

"I'm not dressed for a piggyback ride," I snap.

His gaze moves darkly over me. "No, you certainly aren't."

With that he takes a step forward, drops almost to his knee, wraps an arm around the top of my thighs, very high on my thighs—so high his thumb is close to grazing parts of me he probably doesn't want to right now, what with him being so angry.

"What are you doing?"

"Getting you home." And with that he stands.

Now if I wasn't a trained dancer with incredibly strong abs I would probably flop right over, because this is clearly his plan: to carry me away like a caveman. Just like Diva said he wanted to. I wonder if she's psychic.

"Are you kidding me with this?" I snap, irate. I'm perilously close to dropping my bag. I consider hitting him with it, but if he drops me it's a long way down. I can't afford a sprained ankle. And bruises are hard to cover with makeup. I let it slide down my shoulder and bump him on the butt. If I relaxed and let him pull this Cro-Magnon BS on me, my face might actually hit his butt, but then I'd be giving him what he wants, which is . . . well I don't know exactly, other than to get me in his truck. And probably get righteous with me.

I stay upright, putting lots of pressure on his shoulder with the heel of my hand to maintain this unnatural position. We pass half a dozen couples on the way to the car. Bancroft is extra pleasant with them, asking them how their evening is going, wishing them a nice night, commenting on the weather. And the entire time his thumb is disturbingly close to my girl parts, which don't seem to recognize that this situation is likely not going to lead to fun things.

Less than a minute later Bancroft is carrying me

through a parking lot. It's dodgy, as is the rest of this neighborhood, but the lot has an attendant. He stares at us as we pass by. Bancroft lifts his hand in a wave and I just roll my eyes.

I'm a little disturbed by the fact that not one person we've passed has asked if I'm okay. Just because Bancroft is hot and well-dressed doesn't mean he's not kidnapping me. I suppose if I was putting up more of a fight it might help.

He sets me down beside his truck. It beeps and the lights flash, he reaches around me to open the door. I'm facing him so it hits me in the butt.

I cross my arms over my chest. "That was completely unnecessary."

"I disagree. Would you like to get in the truck now, Ruby?"

"Not particularly, no."

Bancroft gives me a tight smile.

"Will you please get in before a group of thugs swarm us and tries to steal you?"

"No one is going to steal me."

He steps in rather close. "If I was a thug, I would steal you."

Well now, that's a little disconcerting. "Why would anyone want to steal me?"

"Will you please just get in the truck?"

I hate it when people answer questions with more questions. Evasiveness is annoying. As if I have a right to complain about evasiveness. "Well, if you'd give me some space maybe I could."

He wraps his arm around my waist, pulling me up tight against him. I huff and then maybe I gasp just a little. I swear I can feel hardness against my stomach, and it's not his belt.

He sets me down quickly though, takes my bag and holds the door open, waiting until I'm in before he closes it—harder than necessary.

His jaw is working and his brow is furrowed as he rounds the hood. He slides into the driver's seat and starts the engine without saying a word. I'm so irritated right now. He pulls onto the street. Still silent. I'm the first to break. "You have no right to judge me."

"I'm not judging you."

I scoff.

He comes to a stop at a red light. The tension is so thick it's like wading through Jell-O. He turns his head slowly so he's looking at me. I glare back. "Why would I judge you?"

"Oh come on, Bancroft. Look at me." I shrug out of my cardigan and gesture to my outfit. My skimpy, gauzy outfit. I've never actually felt sexier than I do when I'm dancing in this, but that's beside the point.

"Oh, I'm looking." The light turns green and he shifts into gear. I never learned how to drive stick—not the car kind anyway.

I huff and fume some more.

"You want to know what I think?"

"I'm sure you're going to tell me regardless of what I say."

"You're the one who's judging you."

I bite the inside of my lip, trying to come up with some kind of sassy, snappy retort. But I don't have one. Because he's right. I am judging myself. I'm so worried about what the other people in my life are going to think about this temporary career move—which would be viewed as a complete and utter downgrade from what I've been attempting to accomplish in the theater industry—that I've labeled myself a failure, and I'm expecting everyone else to do the same. Even though it's actually quite far from the truth.

"Of course I'm judging myself. This isn't the direction I thought my career would go. But that doesn't explain why you're so angry with me."

"You want to know why?" Bancroft sounds incredulous.

I throw my hands up in the air. It's dramatic. "Yes. Why?"

"You lied to me."

"I stretched the truth."

Bancroft expels a long, slow breath. He's gripping the steering wheel tightly. "That is far cry from dinner theater, Ruby."

"What did you want me to say? I got a job dancing half naked on a stage in a burlesque-style show?"

"Yes, Ruby. That's exactly what I want. The truth."

"I don't see why it matters so much to you. I'm just your pet sitter."

Bancroft's jaw tics. I'm pretty sure I can hear his teeth grinding. He mutters something under his breath.

"I'm sorry. What was that?"

"Is that what you really think? That's you're *just* my pet sitter?"

"Aren't I?" My stomach is churning. This is a dangerous conversation to have. I know I'm not just his pet sitter. That this thing between has turned into something else, but I'm so hung up on my fear of being financially dependent on him that I've ignored the real issue. I'm already emotionally dependent on him, which may be even worse.

He skirts the question with more of his own. "You live in my house. I gave you access to all of my things, codes, personal information. I put trust in you and you broke it.

And why? Because you think I won't approve of your choice of employment?"

"Well do you? Approve?"

"If you're my pet sitter why would my approval matter?" He fires back.

"Stop answering questions with more questions," I shout.

He licks his lips, eyes fixed firmly on the road. "I don't like the neighborhood you're working in. I don't like that you have to take the subway home at the end of the night."

I keep my eyes on the dash. "Sometimes I Uber when it's really late."

"Does someone walk out with you every night? Do they make sure you're safe? Or are you on your own?" His tone is hard, angry.

I'm evasive with my answer. "It's not that bad of a neighborhood . . ."

"It's not a great one either." His jaw tics with his frustration.

"My last apartment wasn't exactly in an upscale neighborhood either, and no one ever tried to abduct me."

He motions to my outfit. "Were you dressed like this?"

"Usually I change before I leave. Tonight's an exception."

Bancroft makes a right and pulls into the underground lot. I've never been down here before since the only other time I've been in his vehicle was when we moved me into his apartment. I hope this isn't some kind of omen.

He stops at the valet, but tells the attendant he'll park himself and backs skillfully into a spot. He lets me get out of the car on my own. "Not going to throw me over your shoulder this time?"

He looks me over. Beyond being angry, his gaze is hot. It makes my skin tingle, which is annoying.

"Would you like me to?"

"No."

I follow him to the lobby. He angles his body in such a way that I'm partially eclipsed by his broadness as we pass the security guards.

"Worried someone's going to judge you for being seen with me?" I mutter.

He gives me an icy glare, slides his keycard over the elevator sensor that takes us to the penthouse floor and ushers me inside. It's dedicated, so very few people use it. The elevator ride to his condo is full of more silence and tension.

I'm relieved that we don't run into anyone in the hallway. Particularly Ms. Blackwood. I've seen her a few times coming and going and she's always polite, but in that way rich people are when really they think they're better than you. Which is exactly the reason I've kept this job a secret, because I've grown up in an environment where that's the rule, not the exception.

Bancroft lets the door close with a heavy slam. He throws his keys on the counter and kicks off his shoes, then starts down the hall.

"Where're you going?" I call after him.

"To my room."

I plant a fist on my hip. "That's it?"

He unbuttons the cuffs of his shirt. "I'd like to get changed."

"You came all the way to my work to glare at me and be pissy and drive me home, just to go to bed?"

He strides back down the hall toward me, eyes flashing. Jesus. Why is he so hot when he's pissed off? "No. I came to your work so I could see for myself exactly how involved your lie was. I came to your work because I'm worried about the location and your safety. I came to your work because I wanted to see you perform. Now I would like to get changed and I think you should, too."

"What if I don't want to?" I'm being a combative brat right now. I think it's because I'm scared; of this conversation, that I've ruined any possibility of this being more.

"I don't think I can have this conversation with you while you're dressed like . . . like—" he flails his hands around, gesturing at my outfit.

I jut my chest out. I'm rocking some insane cleavage. This outfit doesn't leave much to the imagination. His eyes drop and have a hard time coming back up to my face.

"Like what?" I bark.

"Like this!" he snaps back.

"And what am I dressed like?" I know the answer to this question, but I want to hear him say it. I want a reason to go off on him because he's a damn hypocrite if he can go out on a date with someone like Brittany who wears skimpy, slutty clothes on purpose, and get his balls all twisted because my costume is revealing. I mean, there is a lot of skin showing and half my butt is on display some of the time, but it's not like I have a full coverage option for this gig. And it's not as if I'd wear it off the stage.

Bancroft's face is red. His eyes close and stay that way for a while before they open again. "Everyone was looking at you!"

I don't get why he never seems to answer a question directly. I throw my hands up. "They're supposed to! I'm performing."

"But why do you have to wear *this*? Why do you have to look so . . . so—" He takes a step closer, hands clenched at his sides.

I lift my chin in defiance, challenging him to say what I know he wants to. "So *what*?"

"So fucking hot!" It's more growl than words.

And not the words I expect. At all. I expected him to say slutty, or like a streetwalker, or a lady of the night. "I'm supposed to look hot. It's how I make money right now. Is this another reason why you're so angry? Because I'm too provocative?"

"Yes. No. You lied. This. You. You're driving me insane. I want—" Bancroft's breath leaves him on a hard pant.

I have no idea what's going on. Two minutes ago he was pissed because I lied and now he's mad because I'm hot. "You want what?" We're almost nose-to-nose, me pushed up on my tiptoes, Bancroft leaning down so his shoulders are hunched.

His hands flex at his sides. "You. *Fuck*. I want."

"Is that supposed to makes sense?" Sweet Christ is he saying what I think he is?

His voice drops to a gravelly whisper. "I want you."

He admitted it. Out loud. Thank God. He doesn't make a move to take me, though, so I push what I hope is his very last button. "So what are you going to do about it?"

"You can't make anything easy, can you?" His hand shoots out, fingers sliding into my hair, twisting into the strands. His grip tightens as he tilts my head back and then his mouth is on mine.

It's nothing like the time he accidentally kissed me at the engagement party. If that kiss was a fizzled-out candle, this one is an entire store of firecrackers going off at once.

Weeks of pent-up tension explode as his tongue pushes past my lips and he groans into my mouth. I latch on to his hair, because there's no way we're stopping this now that it's started.

In the back of my head, reason tells me this is a seriously bad idea. I still live here. He's angry at me for lying to him. I'm angry at myself for caring what everyone thinks, and for getting myself into this kind of situation. We need to have a discussion. One with words and some logic. But logic has gone out the window. Jumped the twenty-plus stories in a free fall.

Sweet button of lust in my panties, this man can do amazing things with his tongue. I bet his talents extend far beyond mouth skills, and I'm pretty sure I'm about to find out if this is true.

Bancroft slides his hand under my skirt. He doesn't actually have to do much work to accomplish that since it's so damn short. He grabs my glitter-panty-covered right ass cheek and pulls me against him. Like the last time I ended up with his tongue in my mouth, I can feel his ample hard-on against my stomach. I can't wait to get my hands on it. Better yet, I can't wait to ride it. Screw worrying about arguments and conversations. Forget worrying about having a place to live.

I have a free hand, so I mimic him and grab his ass like he is mine. His grip tightens, and he shifts his hips, seeking friction. I can totally relate to that need.

He breaks the kiss long enough to say, "I want you in my bed."

I groan around his tongue, which is already in my mouth again.

"If you'd just stayed in my bed that first night I came home we could've done this a whole lot sooner."

"I slept in there every night you were gone."

He holds on to my hair and disengages from my mouth. "You what?"

Oh shit. Maybe I shouldn't be admitting this. "I um . . . I slept in your bed." It comes out as more of a question than a statement.

"What else did you do in my bed, besides sleeping?" His lips hover just above mine. I can't get to them though, because he's still gripping my hair. Not hard, just firmly.

"I played hide and seek with Franny," I whisper, because it's true.

"Anything else?"

"Like what?" I bite my lip.

His nose brushes my cheek, his lips at my ear. "Did you get off in my bed?"

"Yes," I moan.

"Fuck." He bites my earlobe and I gasp. His hand drifts down my side. "How?"

I suck in a breath when his fingers graze the edge of my panties and he follows the fabric to the inside of my thigh.

"I want you to tell me how," he murmurs.

"How I got off?" I ask for clarification because I'm a little distracted by his fingers right now.

"Did you finger-fuck yourself while you thought about me?" His tongue sweeps along the side of my neck.

I make a groaning sound, it's supposed to be yes, but I don't think it comes out as a word.

He cups me through my panties. "Did you?"

I nod as much as I can since he's still fisting my hair with his free hand.

"How often?"

"Every night," I admit.

He slips his hand down the front of my panties. His fingers glide over my clit and then he slides a single finger inside. "Like this?"

I nod vigorously and grab onto his shoulders when my knees threaten to give out. "But harder and more."

"More fingers?" His lips move across my cheek again and he backs up until his eyes are on mine.

This man is combustibly hot. "Yes."

He adds another finger, pumping slowly. God his fingers are long, and thick. A lot longer and thicker than my own. His lips touch mine as he asks, "How's this?"

"Faster, please, and harder."

His smile is absolutely sinister. "Listen to those manners." But he does what I ask, pumping harder and faster.

I cry out, grabbing onto his shirt to keep upright. "Bane." The word comes out tortured.

"I can't wait to hear what that sounds like when you're coming all over my fingers."

"Fuck. Shit. Oh my God, I want your cock." So much for those manners.

Bane chuckles. "There's that naughty mouth I love so much."

He kisses me hard and keeps moving his fingers, picking up speed until I'm trembling as the orgasm rolls through me. And then his hands are gone and I find myself pinned to the wall by Bancroft's hips. He starts grinding and, of course, I do the same.

Yanking his shirt over his head, I run my hands over his chest. It's an amazing chest. So solid. So defined.

"Like what you see?" he asks.

"So much."

"Me, too." He grabs the hem of my dress—if we can even really call it that. Mostly it's scraps of material sewn together—and pulls it over my head. My bra and panties are white and glittery, as is pretty damn typical in burlesque.

Bancroft drops to his knees, face level with my crotch. He looks up and flicks the little jewel at my navel. "I fucking love this." Then he skims lower to my hips and drags my glitter panties down my legs. "Fuckin' yes."

Apparently Bancroft approves of my grooming techniques. I'm still pulsing from the orgasm I just had.

He lifts his head enough to meet my gaze, his tongue sweeping across his bottom lip. "You know what I'm going to do now?"

The anticipation is exhilarating. I have a feeling I know, but I want to hear him say it so I can find out exactly how impolite he can be. Based on his behavior so far, I'm thinking he can be a dirty boy. I shake my head. I might also bite my lip and arch my back so my pretty parts are closer to his lips.

"No?" Bancroft runs his palms heavily down the outside of my thighs. "You don't know?"

I give my head another shake. "Why don't you tell me?"

The grin that curves the right side of his mouth makes me squeeze my legs together. It distracts Bancroft, drawing his gaze down—to the part of my body that will happily take his attention.

He rubs his nose over my pelvis, the softest brush. His eyes lift to mine again. "I'm going to tongue fuck your pretty pussy until you come all over my face." He pauses for a second. "Would you like that?"

"Yes, please."

"So fucking polite." He hooks a thumb behind the back of my leg and lifts it, resting it over his shoulder. And then he starts licking. There is nothing soft and sweet about the way Bancroft eats me. Each stroke is fast and aggressive, and—oh God—is he growling? Oh, yeah, that's definitely a growl. If this is what foreplay is like with him, I can't wait to get to the sex part.

I grab onto his hair, because it seems like a good place to hold. Even with the way he has me spread open for him and pinned against the wall, I need a solid anchor. My dancer background gives me better balance than most, but it's a lot to ask for me to stay upright like this while he tongue fucks an orgasm out of me, especially since my knees are already watery from the first one.

They start to buckle, which isn't much of a surprise with the way he's hoovering my clit. I make a bunch of random noises with his name thrown in there on a groan. And then I'm coming. Again. It's a knock-me-out, steal-my-soul kind of orgasm.

When the white lights of heaven fade out and I can breathe and see again, I realize I'm on the floor, staring up at the hall light—which is blinding me.

And Bancroft is still going. He's a pussy-licking machine. It sends me into overdrive. I can't stop the sensations from overriding every logical thought. Not that there were many left anyway. I think I'm in love with this man's tongue. If he's as talented with his cock as he is with this part of his body, I may actually start a new religion. The Church of Bane Cock.

I laugh, slightly deliriously, and then gasp as the graze of teeth sends me tumbling over the edge with orgasm number three. I didn't even know it was possible to have this many consecutively.

My eyes roll up and my vision disappears into a haze of black and white and stars as I arch, pushing myself against his mouth. When I finally regain some muscle control I crack a lid and realize I'm in the middle of a doorway. Craning my neck, I discover I'm looking at the legs of Bancroft's bed. There are a few items of clothing under it. One of them might be a pair of my underpants. Or some socks. His cleaner obviously doesn't do the best job.

The rough scrape of his stubble against my clit draws my attention back to Bancroft. His hair is a mess. Because my hands have been in it. His lips are swollen, because he's been sucking on my clit. We've managed to make it from one end of the hall to the other, our end point rather convenient; it's like a round of curling cunnilingus.

His grin is full of dirty promises. "At least we made it to the bedroom."

He gets up on his hands and knees, slides one arm under my back and lifts me off the floor. In two fluid steps he crosses to the bed and tosses me on the mattress. I bounce once before he's on top of me, settling between my thighs, which have parted for him like magic. His mouth is on mine again as he swivels his hips. Oh God. I can feel him right there, rubbing on me. This is going to be the best sex of my life. I can tell already. The pre-sex orgasms are a fairly good indicator of that.

He breaks the kiss, his lips moving down my neck, teeth nipping, tongue sweeping. "I can't wait to fuck you," he murmurs in my ear.

"I should suck you first, don't you think?" I suggest.

He stops with the kissing and lifts his head so he can meet my gaze. My cheeks are probably pink.

"Say that again."

I want to say no, but with the way he's looking at me, it's difficult not to follow through. "I should suck you." I draw out the word *suck*, making it sound liquid.

His grin is just as lascivious as my words. "With that pretty, naughty mouth?" He sweeps his thumb along my bottom lip before he slips it just inside.

So of course I suck, because clearly that's what he wants me to do. And it mimics what I'm about to do. I get to see his cock again. Up close and personal this time. I'm pretty damn excited about that.

I give him a little bite.

His expression goes dark. "I hope you're not planning on doing that when it's my cock in that sweet mouth."

I swirl my tongue around the tip of his thumb. "Pretty sure I'm going to have to unhinge my jaw to get my lips around that beast."

His grin is almost a smirk. "You don't think you can handle it?"

"Let's bring it up here and see if it fits."

Bancroft pushes up on his arms, his smile deliciously dark. I raise a brow and lick my lips.

He mutters something unintelligible and shoves his pants over his hips, kicking them off.

I glance down at his body and notice he's still wearing his socks. They're black and pulled halfway up his shins. "You need to take those off first."

"What?"

"Your socks. They need to go."

He gives me a look. "You've already had three orgasms and you're worried about my socks?"

He tries to straddle me, but I put a hand up to stop him. "I'm not putting your cock in my mouth until those socks come off. I'll do it myself if it's too difficult for you."

Before I have a chance to react he flips me over onto my stomach and gives my ass a slap. "I've been waiting for a reason to do that."

I cry out, but it's not in pain, it's surprise. And then I feel the sting of his teeth on the opposite cheek before I'm flipped over again. "And that, as well."

He straddles me so his knees are on either side of my

chest. I chance a peek down, the socks have disappeared.
I grin and then check Bancroft out. Now, I've never given
a blow job like this, but I'm thinking if it works, it'll be
pretty damn hot.

He's hovering over me. His cock fisted in his hand.
Sweet lord. This man makes me want to give the most
amazing blow job of my life. Now here's the problem:
Bancroft is very well endowed. I'm kind of serious about
having to unhinge my jaw. So this angle might actually
be preferable because I don't think it allows for deeper
penetration. But I'm just guessing. Fingers crossed I'm
right about this.

He angles his erection down, so that the tip is close to
my chin. Flecks of glitter decorate the head. Which isn't
a surprise. My glitter panties and bra leave a magical trail
everywhere.

He keeps pushing down until the tip of his cock hits
my bottom lip, as if he's knocking on the door to my
mouth, looking to get in there. Then he rubs it across like
it's lip gloss. Or dick gloss, as it were. I smile, but manage to suppress a giggle.

His expression is intense, his lips parting along with
mine as he shifts his hips forward and the head slides
inside. So far, so good.

He groans when I press my tongue forward to circle
the tip. "I can't even tell you how many times I've thought
about this."

I hum my acknowledgment. I can't actually form
words with his cock in my mouth, and while this certainly is something I've thought about, too, I have my
doubts it's to the same degree as he did. I definitely fan-
tasized about the pussy eating, and the sex we're going
to have as soon as I'm done sucking on his lollipop.

I keep my eyes on his face as he bites his lip and

pushes in a little further. "How much you think you can take?"

That's a great question. One I don't have an answer to since I've never tried to get something this big in my mouth at one time. "Let's find out," I say around the head. It's a little garbled, but he seems to understand.

He eases in another inch and I run my hands up the outside of his incredibly muscular thighs. They're like tree trunks. I move around the back so I can grab his ass. His naked ass. It's so firm. I lift my head as he pushes in farther still, another inch.

He swears when I squeeze his ass and pull him even deeper. The hand that isn't wrapped around his cock slides into my hair. He isn't trying to get me to choke on him, instead he cups the back of my head, helping to hold it up, which is nice of him, since I'd be doing a lot of craning otherwise. I start with some suction, which gets another dirty curse out of him.

"You're fucking gorgeous with my cock in your mouth, you know that?"

His praise makes me want to see exactly how deep I can take him. I open wider, take more until his thumb touches my lip and the head hits the back of my throat. I hold on to his hips and ease him back, then do it again, taking him deeper on the next wet, suctioned stroke. I do it maybe two or three more times before he let's go of my hair.

"That's enough." He wraps his hand around his cock and pulls out of my mouth, covering the head.

For the first time ever, I actually want to keep going. "I was just getting started." I might even be whining.

He brushes my bottom lip with his thumb. "Another time I'd love to finish in that incredible mouth of yours."

He releases his cock and reaches down. Hooking his

hands under my arms, he pulls me up so I'm not face-to-cock with him anymore. He's still straddling my hips as he leans down and kisses me, tongue sweeping my mouth. I wiggle around, trying to get my legs out from between his without causing any potential damage to his delicious dick.

Breaking the kiss, he sits back, running his fingertips over my breasts, circling my nipples before he drags them down my sides. We're getting to the good part, not that all the other parts haven't been good, but this is what I've been waiting for, fantasizing about even, since the first night he accidentally kissed me.

He draws a circle around my navel, then travels a straight path down to the crest of my pelvis. If he would just get in between my legs it would make this a hell of a lot easier. Easing farther back on the bed, he smooths his hands along the outside of my thighs, until he reaches my knees. Hooking his fingers underneath them, he encourages me to bend them, then follows the contour of my calves until he reaches my ankles. "How flexible are you?"

"Um, pretty flexible, why?"

He raises my legs, keeping them pressed together as he rests the soles of my feet against his chest. "I'm just trying to decide what position I want to fuck you in."

Oh good Lord. This man and his mouth. These weeks of flirty banter and mostly civilized behavior seem to be evaporating in the face of orgasms and naked promise.

"Do I have a say in how I'm positioned?" I mean for it to be all snark, but I fail, because it comes out all soft and breathy instead.

"If you want one, sure." Bancroft runs his hands over my shins. When he reaches my knees he reverses the movement, his wide palms wrapping around my ankles again. His gaze lifts to meet mine. "Open for me."

Despite it being an order and not a request, I'm still inclined to oblige him. I mean, he tongue fucked me across the floor. I've already come like my clit is the central location for fireworks on the Fourth of July. If he would like to put that magnificent cock of his to good use by pounding another orgasm out of my *pretty little pussy* I am all for it.

Sometimes it's good to play it coy. Show a little hesitation and uncertainty. I do neither of those things.

I can literally hear Bancroft's teeth grinding together as his gaze drops. I don't know exactly what it is about my grooming habits or the composition of my particular vagina that makes the deep, thick groan come out of him, but whatever it is I'm so, so happy about it right now.

I'm completely on display for him. Bare for him. Vulnerable. But it doesn't create any of the self-consciousness I expect, because the expression on his face is pure, unfiltered desire.

He curves forward, spreading my legs farther apart, hands still wrapped around my ankles. I'm not sure what his plan is until he licks me again, one long slow stroke of his tongue, a fast swirl and a long, hard suck on my clit.

I cry out and arch, but he's still holding my damn ankles, so I can't get away from the intensity of his mouth. He keeps me spread, his mouth on me, getting me close again.

Before I fall over the edge and into the blissful abyss he releases one of my ankles, but only one, and looks up from between my legs. Then he fists his cock. "I'm going to fuck you now, Ruby. Are you ready for that?"

"Oh God. Yes. Please. That would be so amazing." I would love it if I could be a little less eager about the whole thing, but he's left me hanging, and all I can think about is how fantastic it's going to feel when he's filling me.

His smirk tells me he knows exactly what's going on in my head. Or maybe it's my breathy tone and the way I'm attempting to lift my hips off the bed, even though he's still holding my damn ankle.

When he rubs the head of his cock over my clit I jerk and moan. Finally letting go of my ankle, he slips his arm under my knee, pulling it up as he stretches out on top of me.

I can feel him, thick and hard against my pelvis. I try to readjust our position, but I'm not having much luck. "I thought you said you were going to fuck me now." I'm a little snappy.

He might be more smug than necessary. "I'm getting to that. This is an exercise in patience, Ruby."

"I've waited a lot of weeks for this."

"So you can wait a little longer." He eases his hips back and the thick shaft slides over my clit, the head following. He reaches across to the nightstand, fumbling around for a second before he finds the condoms. He's quick about tearing one free and rolling it on. And then he's pushing inside and I'm moaning and he's groaning.

The first few strokes are slow as I adjust. But those are the only ones that fall into the slow and gentle category, because after that, Bancroft's civility ceases to exist. He drills into me, hips slapping against mine, fast and hard. I come. And then come again as he growls dirty things in my ear. Telling me how amazing my pussy is. How it's his now, and no one else can have it but him.

I like it a lot.

After he comes he collapses on top of me—not completely, he braces his weight on his straining, twitching forearms. I don't think I've ever been so sated in my life.

I'm so sweaty. I'm pretty sure there's glitter all over Bancroft's sheets. And Bancroft. I can't actually find it in me to care or do anything about it. Not that there's anything I can reasonably do anyway.

One thing I've noticed with the glitter is that no matter how many times I wash things, it's still hangs around after the fact, shiny reminders of my temporary job.

"Does this mean you're not angry anymore?" I ask when he tucks me into his side.

"For now."

"You have plans to be angry with me later?"

"I'm putting it on hold until morning."

"Same." I snuggle into him, getting comfortable. We can deal with all the unsaid things later. Right now I'm going to bask. And then sleep. And then maybe more sex.

CHAPTER 18
BLISS TO BAD NEWS

BANCROFT

Sex with Ruby is unlike the sex I've had in any other relationship. It's not civilized, but it's not savage either. Ruby is the ideal balance between sweetly docile and confidently naughty, and she knows exactly when one works and the other is necessary. She's fucking perfect.

The biggest problem we seem to have is that our schedules don't match. She goes to bed an hour or two before I get up for my day. By the time I get home from work, she's on her way out the door or already long gone.

Two days after our initial argument, followed by the fuck of the century, I'm woken up twenty minutes before my alarm goes off to a blow job. This time I get to come in Ruby's pretty, perfect mouth.

Monday is one of Ruby's days off. I go into work in the morning but I schedule the afternoon to work from home. I don't plan to do much actual work. I plan to do Ruby. Repeatedly. On any available surface.

I arrive home just after two and find her in the kitchen, humming away, making coffee and microwave s'mores.

Apparently it's her favorite thing. I wrap an arm around her waist and pull her up against me, nuzzling into her hair. "Is this your version of a healthy breakfast?"

She turns around in my arms. "Healthy no. Breakfast yes. Want one?"

"That's not really what I'm hungry for."

"Oh no?"

I shake my head and pick her up, depositing her on the counter. She's wearing her bathrobe. It's white with red flowers and made of some silky material. "I'm more interested in finding out what's under here." I pull the bow at her waist and watch as the sides part, revealing taut muscles and perky nipples. She's naked and glorious. I fuck her on the counter. We spend the rest of the day in my bedroom enjoying each other.

I know the second she crawls into bed with me. It doesn't matter that it's between two and four in the morning. It doesn't matter that I have to get my ass up at five-thirty and work a twelve-hour day. All she has to do is press her body against mine and I'm instantly awake. We'll fuck until my alarm goes off. I stopped bothering with condoms when the second box ran out on day four and she assured me she's on the pill.

Which also happened to be the day she decided to re-hearse the dance to the song that broke me. While naked. We didn't make it past the living room floor. I have bruises on my knees from that.

We don't address any of the important issues, such as how we're going to deal with the fact that she's still living here and we're sleeping together. To be quite honest I don't want to mess with this good thing we have now that we finally have it. Which is a problem. Because there are things we need to figure out. I don't particularly want her to leave, but I also know that staying here indefinitely was never part of her plan. I don't want to freak her out by inviting her to move in permanently, even though it's something I've considered. It's a little premature.

A week is not really enough time to make a highly informed decision regarding shacking up. But I'm really enjoying having Ruby in my bed every night. She gives incredible blow jobs. She has a naughty mouth. She likes it when I talk dirty to her. And that's just the sexual compatibility, which has nothing on how compatible we are beyond the bedroom.

It's been two hours since I left Ruby sleeping in my bed. Four hours since I've been inside her. I already feel as if I'm going through withdrawal.

Hours have never felt more like eternity than they do right now. The more we keep doing this, the more aware I become that we really need to stop dancing around conversations and figure out what this is. There's no timeline on moving out, but I'm well aware that she's been actively seeking a new agent and that she's looking to audition for roles that will take her closer to Broadway.

It's a bit of a messy situation I've gotten myself into. If I'm completely honest, I'm still a little angry at her for lying about her job, although I can understand why she did. It took me a long while to come to terms with the fact that a lot of people in my family's social sphere would never approve of my career in rugby, even though it was completely legitimate and I made an excellent salary. Her situation is admittedly different.

The one thing I'm still having difficulty getting past with this entire situation, is that I assumed I'd earned enough of her trust that she'd be honest with me, and I worry that she's still going to feel compelled to withhold things.

Unfortunately, that conversation isn't going to happen

right now because I'm sitting in my office, waiting for my father to call me into a meeting. I received the call at eight this morning, which is a time I'm usually up, but Ruby and I were pretty busy last night, and it was late by the time I was done fucking all the orgasms out of her sweet, hot pussy. Also, it's a Saturday. So being called into work is a bit of a piss off. Being made to wait is even more infuriating. The office phone rings, so I hit speaker, assuming it's my father, finally calling me into the emergency meeting. It's not. It's my mother.

"Hello, Bancroft, how are you this morning?" Phone conversations with my mother are fairly formal for whatever reason. She's a good person, but sometimes she gets far too caught up in the gossip that circulates in her friend pool. Most discussions include the latest scandal.

"I'm fine. Waiting for my father to call me into this emergency meeting."

"Ah. Yes. He shouldn't be long now. He just left the house."

"He *just* left? He called me two hours ago telling me I needed to be at the office immediately."

"Yes. Well, he was . . . distracted. He's on his way now."

I cringe. *Distracted* has meanings I don't want to think too much about.

"Is that why you called? To tell me he's running late."

"Oh! No. I wanted to make sure you're still able to come for dinner next weekend."

"Of course. It's already marked on the calendar. Do you need me to bring anything?"

"It's being catered."

"Okay." Of course it's being catered. My mom doesn't spend much time in the kitchen unless she's pouring a glass of wine. We always had a chef growing up. And a

nanny or two made it possible for her to go to her fun-
draising meetings while me and my brothers went to
our various lessons. Mine were always of the sports
variety.

"We're having a few friends join us, so it won't just
be family."

"Oh." I tap on the desk with my pen. I wonder who
my mother is inviting, and why. "Is it possible for me to
bring a date, then?" It's on a weekend, so it's unlikely that
Ruby will even be able to attend since she works, so I'm
not sure why I'm asking.

There's silence on the other end of the line for a few
seconds.

"Mimi?" I didn't grow up calling her mom, although
that's how I refer to her when I'm not in her presence.

"It would be best if you didn't."

"Won't Griffin be bringing Imogen?"

"Well, of course, she's his girlfriend."

"So why can't I bring a date?"

"The Thorton's are coming."

I thought I'd managed to evade Brittany and the second date. "Mom."

She makes a disapproving tsking sound.

"I thought we already talked about this," I remind her.

"You were ill last time. Brittany is a lovely girl."

Brittany is pampered and a pain in the ass. I've been
avoiding her calls since I went out with her all those
weeks ago.

"I'm seeing someone." I might as well be upfront
about it, maybe it will help allow me to evade more Brittany interactions.

"Since when?"

"It's recent."

"So it's not serious then? Bringing her to dinner would

make it awkward for Brittany, and I arranged this before you were seeing someone. I can't really change the plans now. And your father has business with her father," she's imploring now.

Of course there's business involved. My father can't do it any other way. I wish I didn't feel the need to cave for my mother, but it's not as though Ruby will be able to join me anyway. "Fine. I'll do this for you, but it's the last time."

"That's all I ask."

It's a dinner, with family and a few friends, so it's not even technically a date. It's still frustrating.

Another call interrupts the one with my mother. I'm hopeful it's my father. I'd like to get this meeting over with so I can get home to Ruby before she has to work tonight.

"I have to go, I have another call."

"Okay. Thank you for making this easy for me. Have a good day. We'll chat soon, Banny."

"Bye, Mom." I hang up before I can get angry with her. She knows how much I hate being called Banny.

It's my father's personal assistant, alerting me that the meeting will begin in five minutes in the conference room. Only two hours and twenty minutes later than I anticipated. I could've been in bed with Ruby this entire time.

I gather my things and head down the hall. My father is already sitting at the head of the table. His assistant sets down a coffee and several folders.

"So. What's the emergency?" I ask as I slide into a chair beside Griffin.

"One of the London properties has an issue."

I'm suddenly uneasy. "One of the ones I was working on?"

He shakes his head and I breathe a sigh of relief. My father hates errors.

"Lex was managing it."

That's a surprise. I had no idea he was managing anything outside of the four hotels we'd been asked to oversee while we were there.

"Which hotel?"

"The Concord."

We'd stopped in there briefly, so I could get acquainted with the building and the managerial staff while we were in the area. It's a well-established hotel, up to date, not in need of any real work as far as I knew. "What's the problem? I didn't think we were working on that hotel."

"We weren't supposed to until next year. It looks like some corners were cut regarding permits."

That's not good. I have to wonder if this was what he was taking care of when he went back to London ahead of me. Lex slips into the boardroom, looking rough.

He drops into the chair beside our father. "Sorry I'm late. What'd I miss?"

My father flips open the file folder and pushes it toward him. "Why don't you have a look for yourself."

Lex's smile drops and he blanches.

Three hours later I'm still sitting in the meeting. The first hour was my dad chewing out Lex. There was nothing I could do to help him, since I didn't know he was working on the project in the first place. The past two hours have been taken up with reviewing the original plans for the minor renovations to the ballroom and the indoor pool at The Concord, which weren't scheduled for another full year. Securing permits for this kind of upgrade shouldn't have been difficult.

The indoor pool is where the problem seems to be. I'm barely listening at this point. It's already early afternoon.

I don't dare send any messages or my father will likely shit a brick. He's in a foul mood. I'd really like some time to talk to Ruby. If I don't get out of here before two, I'm not going to have enough time to get home before she leaves for work.

"Isn't that right, Bancroft?"

I look up from the paper I've been scribbling on. I've managed to draw a circle. With another circle inside it. And another inside that one. It looks remarkably like a breast.

"I'm sorry. Pardon?"

My father looks annoyed. It's not good. I don't want to piss him off more than he already is.

"You'll oversee the acquisition of the new permits."

"I don't have the background on this project."

He taps his pen on the desk three times in succession, then flips it into his palm. It's one of his little quirks. When he's angry or frustrated it comes out through small, controlled body movements. That was definitely the wrong thing to say. "You have the basics from this meeting. I'll send Griffin along with you."

Griffin and I glance at each other. It seems to be as much of a surprise to him as it is to me.

"I can fix this," Lexington says. "I'll go on my own."

Our father turns his angry gaze on Lex. "You'll do nothing of the sort. You'll be here, in the office, reviewing permit code for as long as it takes to get this sorted out."

Lex's mouth flattens into a straight line, but he keeps his mouth shut. None of us dare say anything to contradict our father. At least not here, where there are so many people to witness it.

"You'll leave this evening."

"Today?" Griffin and I ask at the same time.

My father gives us the same hard look we used to get as kids when we'd gotten caught doing something we shouldn't. "This needs to be sorted out immediately and we can't do it remotely. We need the investors to feel confident that we have the situation under control."

"How long are we going to be there?"

"For as long as it takes to iron things out. If you're quick, you could be back by the end of the week."

I grit my teeth. I don't want to go away again. I want to be in my condo with my pets. And Ruby. We need to have a conversation. A real one. A serious one. Unfortunately, it looks like that's still on hold.

CHAPTER 19

I HATE BRITTANY

RUBY

I wake to an empty bed, which isn't much of a surprise since morning has passed and afternoon approaches. My entire body is sore, thanks to the new addition to my workout routine in the form of Bancroft. That man can fuck like nobody's business.

I stretch out, smiling, and call Bancroft's name. I'm greeted with silence. That's odd. It's Saturday, and he didn't say anything about having to go to the office. Throwing off the covers I sit up, the muscle aches amplifying as I get out of bed and pad—naked—down the hall to the kitchen. The French press sits on the counter half-full. I touch the side. The coffee is cool, meaning it must've been made hours ago.

"Bancroft?" I call again. I still get nothing.

Maybe he's in his office wearing headphones. He does that sometimes out of consideration, since my hours are so much later than his. I tiptoe over and peek around the corner. He's not there either. What the heck?

Heading back to the kitchen, I root around in my bag

until I finally find my phone. Maybe he went out to pick us up something to eat. He's considerate like that as well. The only messages I have are from Amie. She's been out of town for the past week on a honeymoon test run. That's right, she and Armstrong have gone away for a week to see if they like the location enough to return for their honeymoon. It's a Mills hotel, so I can't imagine they won't love it. I check the counter, which is where I find one of Bancroft's runelike scrawls.

Emergency meeting. Not sure when I'll be back.
Bane

I frown, disappointed that my nakedness will go to waste and that the start to my day isn't going nearly as well as the end of my night. Scrolling through my phone, I check my messages from Amie.

She returned from her pre-honeymoon test run and we have a lunch date. I check the time. Crapdoodles. I have less than an hour to get ready and meet her in Midtown. A shower is a must, I smell like Bancroft and sex.

Firing a message off to let Amie know I'm on my way, I rush to my room to shower. Twenty minutes later I'm fresh and dressed. My hair is still damp, but it'll dry on the way. I slap on some makeup, grab my purse, and run out the door.

Amie's already at the restaurant when I get there. She's never late for anything. She puts down her phone when I slide into the seat across from her.

"I was just about to text you. How are you? How are things since Bancroft's been back? I feel like we haven't talked in forever." She looks around then leans closer and drops her voice. "Has he walked around the condo shirt-less?"

I feel badly that I've been riding Bancroft's disco stick for a week and my best friend doesn't even know. Although that's not really my fault since she hasn't been around to tell. And I also feel bad that I haven't been honest with her about other things. So I tell her everything. Well, almost everything. We're in a public place so there are things I'm not willing to say aloud for fear of someone overhearing. But I tell her about the job, and Bancroft coming to the club last week and getting angry about my lie.

The waiter brings us our lunches just before I get to the best part. I take a pause while he sets our plates in front of us. I've ordered steak frites, which are just French fries with a fancy name and Amie has ordered a salad.

"They forgot your dressing." I point out.

"I don't need it."

"Without dressing it's just a plate of leaves."

"I like the natural flavors." She waves her fork around. "So Bancroft drove you home, then what happened?"

I drop the salad dressing issue and continue with my story. I censor out all the best parts, like the curling for orgasms and the dirty talk and the awesome blow job I gave and finish with, "And then we had sex." I pop a fry into my mouth and wait.

Amie stares at me for a few long seconds, unmoving. She glances around the restaurant and brings her hand up so no one can see what she says, even though she practically mouths the words, "You slept with him?"

I nod.

"Oh my God." She exhales a breath, eyes wide, and blinking and sets down her fork. "You slept with him a week ago and didn't tell me until now?" She looks hurt, which is not what I want.

I lean in closer and drop my voice, imploring her to

understand. "I haven't had a chance. You were away. This is the first time I've seen you since it happened and I didn't want to tell you over the phone, because, well, it's not over-the-phone kind of news."

She sits back in her chair. "Was it just the once?"

I shake my head.

"How many times?"

I shrug. "I've lost count. A lot."

"It sounds like your week was more exciting than mine," she mutters. "So this is a relationship now?"

I stab a fry with my fork. "I don't know. We haven't talked about that yet."

"You've been getting naked with each other for the past week and you haven't had a relationship conversation, yet?" Amie smooths her napkin out. "You're not really a fling kind of girl. Does he know that? Do you know if he wants a relationship?"

I shrug again. I don't actually have an answer to that. The only conversations we've had about relationships were before he left, and maybe once over the phone when we discussed how difficult it would be to have a relationship when he was traveling all the time. But he's home now, and he hasn't mentioned traveling—although we haven't been doing much in the way of talking this past week outside of moans and orgasms.

I consider how much time I've spent "with" him over the last several weeks. If I'm honest with myself it's felt like a relationship since before he came back from the UK.

"I guess you need to talk to him and figure out if you're both on the same page," Amie says, pulling me out of my head.

I nod.

"Do you think you are?"

"I think so? Maybe? God, I hope casual hookups aren't his thing."

"I'm sure he wants the same thing you want. I guess now you'll really need to find your own apartment. Can you afford that yet?" Amie pats my hand in a consoling gesture. I think I might be starting to panic a little.

"I can't live there anymore." It's not a question. It's just that reality is hitting me, and it's a lot like being smacked in the face with a giant penis. Bancroft's giant penis.

"It might be easier if you have your own place now that you're sleeping together."

I nod dumbly. She's 100 percent accurate on this. I can't live with Bancroft if we're in the beginning stages of dating. If that's even what's going to happen. Beyond that, my relying on him financially creates a power imbalance I'm not too keen on. I don't want to feel like my services are being bought, even if they're as incredible as he tells me they are.

"So?"

"Huh?" I've gapped out again.

She mouths *the sex* and then says, "Is it good?"

I think about last night. About coming in from work at three in the morning and waking him up with a blow job and the two-hour fuck marathon that then took place. Bancroft thoroughly enjoys testing out my flexibility. We've had sex in places and positions I'd never thought possible. And that mouth—sweet lord. "The best."

Her eyebrows shoot up. "Really? What's he like?"

"Intense." I lean in to whisper, "He has a very dirty mouth and excellent stamina. He can go for hours."

Amie bites her lip and looks a little wistful. "Aren't you sore?"

"Only in the best way possible." I'm pretty sure I'm ruined for any other man. I'll have this unreasonable bar to hold all other men to. Bancroft Mills and his dirty mouth, and amazingly large penis are my new minimum standard.

"Is he . . ." she trails off and does a few eyebrow raises.

I raise my own in question.

"Adequately endowed?"

"More than," I reply.

"More than?" She touches the necklace she's wearing. It's a gold chain with diamonds. Amie doesn't like yellow gold, she prefers white. I'm assuming the necklace was a gift from her thoughtful, clueless fiancé.

"So much more."

She swallows her mouthful of lettuce and leans in close. "How much more?"

I have no idea why Amie is so interested in the size of Bancroft's penis. "Are you asking me for approximate dimensions?"

She nods once. I look around the table for things that might be comparable. There's nothing. "Wider than a toilet paper roll and about yay long." I hold my hands apart and then widen the gap a bit until I get it just right.

"Wow," Amie breathes. "Wasn't that . . . uncomfortable?"

"He's incredibly adept at foreplay."

Her cheeks flush pink and she looks down at her salad, pushing the dry leaves around.

"It's never too late to trade in your current model for one with more girth, or length, or both." I spear a fry and bite the end off.

Amie snorts and brings her hand to her mouth, eyes darting around, embarrassed the sound came out of her, maybe. I miss the version of my friend who cared less about what people think. We should've gone to a non-posh restaurant so we wouldn't be forced to have this conversation in embarrassed whispers. I wish I cared less, too.

It's half past two in the afternoon by the time I get home—or back to Bancroft's condo. I'm nervous now. I've been enjoying the sex bubble we've been living in, but Amie has a point, we have to talk, and I have to make a plan to move out. I sincerely hope I haven't read things wrong and that this is about more than sex. I think it is. Our conversations up until now have me hoping it is.

The condo is the same as when I left it, which means Bancroft still isn't home. I should probably wash the sheets after last night's sexcapades. I stop at Francesca's cage first. She's been fed recently, by the look of things. Maybe Bancroft did it before he left for his emergency meeting.

"Hi, pretty girl." I nuzzle her head and carry her down the hall.

When I get to Bancroft's room I notice the bed isn't quite how I left it. It's still unmade, but there are a few items of clothing littering the mattress, namely the components that make up a suit. And his closet door is open.

My stomach does a little flip and I return to the kitchen, rummaging through my purse until I find my phone. I missed a call from him about twenty minutes ago. There's a voice mail.

"Hey. Hi, Ruby. Uh . . . look, I'm at the airport. I have to go back to London, there's an issue I need to take care of. I don't really know when I'm going to be back, but we need to talk and it probably isn't a phone conversation . . ."

There's a brief pause and a sigh.

"We need to make some adjustments with our arrangement. This has all happened a bit faster than I expected. I think maybe . . . Fuck. I'll try to call when I'm in London."

My stomach feels like it's trying to jump out of my throat. This doesn't sound good. I sit down at the island and note the envelope propped up against the bananas. I blush at the memory of what I did with one yesterday afternoon in a bid to distract Bancroft when he was busy with a phone call. It resulted in me being bent over the island, spanked, and then fucked.

The envelope has my name on it in his messy scrawl. I open it and find a wad of cash. Sliding the bills out I count it, twice. Jesus. He's left me five thousand dollars. I try to rationally analyze the exorbitant amount of money, but based on the message it sounds a lot like he's intending to pay me for sex.

I'm still holding Francesca. She's squirming to get out of my arms. I give her a couple of pets and set her on the floor.

Maybe I'm reading into things. Maybe I'm being dramatic. Maybe he's just being preemptive in case he's gone longer than he anticipates.

As I pass Bancroft's retro answering machine I note the flashing red number one. There's a message. I hit play.

"Hi, Banny, it's Brittany! I just heard from Mimi and I couldn't get through on your cell so I thought I'd try this number instead. I'm so sorry you had to go away on business this week. Such a disappointment when you just got back. I really hope you'll be back in time for dinner this weekend. But don't worry if you're not. We can always reschedule our date. Mimi said you're just as excited as I am about being able to spend time together again. I can't wait to pick up where we left off last time. Call me when you can!"

I stare at the machine. Hit rewind and then hit play again, listening to the message a second time. Then I listen to the voice mail from Bancroft.

There's really no guessing anymore. I can't believe he's been screwing me all over his condo all week, telling me my pussy is his, while he's been planning a date with another woman. Brittany of all people.

I listen to the message again, looking for some sign that this isn't what I think it is. Has he been playing me this entire time? I remember our conversation about Brittany back when I moved in here, how he said she wasn't that bad. Did he have sex with her that night after he kissed me? Has he been talking to her the way he's been talking to me while he's been away? It sure as hell seems like it, based on her enthusiasm. And what the hell does she mean picking up where they left off?

Fucking asshole.

Talking to me about trust and honesty and here he is, screwing me and he'll probably be screwing Brittany this weekend.

There really is no question now, I need to find a new place to live. The sooner the better.

CHAPTER 20
NEW DIGS

RUBY

Everything happens for a reason. I hate that saying, even if it's true most of the time. It's something people say to you when crap luck slaps you in the face. It's not their crap luck, so it's easy to throw out a useless, annoying saying in an attempt to make a person feel better. Here's the truth: Telling someone everything happens for a reason doesn't actually make them feel less crappy. In fact, it usually makes them feel worse.

Which is why I'm so glad I have a best friend like Amie. As soon as I stop crying—it takes a good twenty minutes to get myself under control. I might be pissed off, but I'm not angry enough that this doesn't hurt—a lot—I call her and tell her what happened.

"Are you fucking kidding me?" Amie rarely swears these days. Her anger makes me feel so much better.

"I need a new apartment. Like tomorrow."

"Do you want to stay here until you do? I know there isn't much space, but is it better than staying there? Why don't you pack your things and we'll get you out tomorrow."

"What about Armstrong?"

"What about him?"

"What are you going to tell him? He's going to ask why I'm staying with you."

"He won't know. He never comes here. My mattress isn't soft enough and I don't have much space. I'll probably be at his place twice next week—I can even try for more, but he's got this thing about having his space. At least you won't have to sleep on the couch or an air mattress those nights. Do you want me to come get you tonight?"

"No. That's not necessary. He's not even in the country. And he won't be back tonight, or at least for a couple of days, so there's no point. I need to pack, anyway."

"Okay. I have to work in the morning. Do you need me to take time off so I can help you?"

"I have a shift tomorrow night, but I have the day free. I can see about getting an Uber van or something."

She's quiet for a few seconds. "Oh! What about Bancroft's truck? Are the keys there?"

"You're a genius. I don't know why I didn't think of that. I bet I can get the people who work in this building to cart all my stuff down to the truck, too."

"I'm sure you can, and you should."

I'm so angry I don't even think twice about using Bancroft's truck without his permission.

I spend the rest of the afternoon packing. Mostly it's me throwing stuff into suitcases and then crying when I can't get them closed. I'm so stupid. I made this into something it wasn't. I was convinced there was more between us, but obviously I was wrong. I still have to go to work, which sucks. It doesn't matter how long I lie with cucumber slices over my eyes, they're still red and puffy.

I guess Bancroft has turned out to be another Last-Name-First asshole. I should know better than to equate sex with feelings. I sleep like crap, and get up after just a few hours of fitful sleep. No matter, I need to get out of this place. I find Bancroft's truck keys and I call the front desk guy to bring a trolley or something up so I can move my boxes out.

Ms. Blackwood comes out to see what all the noise is about. Precious is tucked under her arms. She snarls at me. It's everything I can do not to snarl back.

"Oh, Renee, are you moving?" She looks past me, into the condo. I take a step back and close the door halfway since Francesca's cage is in the living room.

I don't correct her. She gets my name wrong every time, although she always manages to get the first letter right.

"I am. It was so nice living across the hall from you!" I say with fake enthusiasm, holding out my hand.

She accepts the handshake, although she appears a little uncertain about the contact, which is perfect. Once she disappears into her condo I flip her the bird.

It takes fifteen minutes for Stan—the front desk guy—to load all my boxes onto the trolley. While he takes them down and transfers them to the truck I check on Francesca. Except she's not in her cage. I have a moment of panic, or several moments, as I search the condo for her. I find her tucked into Bancroft's pillow.

I cry tears of relief that I didn't manage to lose her. Of all the things I'm going to miss about living in Bancroft's condo, apart from Bancroft, I'll miss his ferret. Francesca, not the one in his pants. I cry while playing with her in his sheets. I know I'll see her again before

Bancroft returns—but I'm emotional and I'm going to miss her.

After he returns there's no guarantee I'm ever going to see Franny again. It's also sort of symbolic of losing Bane—who I never really had in the first place. I change Tiny's water and feed her a cricket even though I did it two days ago. I'm a puffy-eyed mess by the time I'm ready to claim Bancroft's truck.

Stan looks a little uneasy as I try to navigate the truck while still sniffling. Thankfully it has a backup camera with one of those beeper things that tells me when I'm getting too close to other objects. That seems to happen a lot in this beast. I manage to get out of the underground parking without hitting anything.

Driving a truck in the streets of New York is insane. I have no idea how Bancroft manages this thing. It's huge. And the lanes are narrow. The nice thing about it is that if I want to change lanes and no one is letting me go I can just edge my way in and they really don't have a choice but to let it happen. It helps that I don't really care if the truck ends up with a ding.

I have a key to Amie's apartment, so it's not a big deal getting in once I arrive at her place. Carting all my stuff up to the twelfth floor is a bit of a pain in my ass since it takes five trips, plus my luggage. I line my pitiful pile of boxes against the only available wall. Once I'm done, I park the truck in the underground garage, luckily Amie's building has one as well, and get a pass for it. I use my sex money from Bane to pay for that. I'm not driving it back today. I'll do it tomorrow morning. I can't imagine Bancroft will be back by then.

By the time I'm done I'm sweaty and hungry. I check Amie's fridge for food. I'm sorely disappointed. Her food selection is minimal. There's lettuce, and some fruit, but

I'm used to living with a former rugby player who loves his carbs and meat. Plus I'm working a very active job these days. I need the calories to maintain the booty I'm currently rocking.

Amie lives on the fringe of the theater district, much like Bancroft, so her apartment isn't all that far away. It's a fabulous area, and this apartment costs a mint. But she makes great money where she works, so it's affordable for her. Unless I manage to snag a prime role in a Broadway production, there's no damn way I'll ever be able to afford something like this. And doesn't that just piss me off all over again.

I grab my purse and head to the street. It's early afternoon, and I'm starving. I think I might actually be hangry at this point. I check my phone as I'm walking down the street. I have messages from Amie, but nothing from Bancroft. He must be in London by now. That I haven't heard from him is another kick in the vagina.

I need comfort food. Something greasy and unhealthy. I continue down the street, determined to find something that doesn't require me to sit down. I just want food and then I want to go back to Amie's apartment, shower, and maybe catch a nap before I have to head to work.

As I'm passing one of the small, eclectic theaters on the side streets, I notice a poster for open auditions plastered to the door. It's for today. I check the time. And right now.

Now here is one of those instances in which the "everything happens for a reason" adage is actually reasonable and welcome. I abandon the quest for food. It's an audition for a play I've never heard of. Not that it matters. As long as I can read the script and learn the lines in the time they give me, it's worth a shot. I don't have any food in my stomach, so it's not like I'm going to vomit all over the director. The worst that can happen is not getting a callback.

I enter the theater. It's gorgeous inside, and high ceilings and ornately carved pillars lead my eye to a folding table. Behind it sits a woman wearing horn-rimmed glasses and bloodred lipstick.

I put on my brightest, friendliest smile. "There are open auditions here today?"

Her eyes widen when she sees me. "There are," she says with some hesitation.

I look down at my outfit. I'm a bit of a mess. My shirt is smudged with dirt and my jeans have holes in them. I'm far from put together. Oh well, I'm here now. "Okay. Great. I'd like to audition then."

She gives me a patronizing smile and slides a form over. "Fill this out, please."

I scribble my way through the basic paperwork and pass it back, exchanging it for a script. "They'll call you in shortly. You're the last audition before they break for the afternoon."

"Thank you." Well, that's fortunate. I follow her directions to the theater, scanning the script.

The scene they've chosen is one with high emotion. The female lead is angry, frustrated, and explosive. I'm feeling all of these things. If nothing else, auditioning for this role will be cathartic.

I cry real tears during my audition. Ones born of true frustration, for my own predicament, for the role I want. I may take it a touch too far into melodrama, but it's definitely therapeutic.

I leave the theater feeling less angry and really damn hungry. I find a pizza place and scarf down two slices. Then I return to my new, temporary home, shower, and get ready for work.

Tomorrow I need to find an apartment. I won't put Amie out like this for longer than I have to. More than anything, I just want to be able to manage life on my own, without having to rely on anyone else for support—at least the financial kind. While this situation sucks, at least my current job will afford me money for rent and the basics. I don't need or want luxury if it comes with this kind of emotional price tag.

Work feels different tonight. I keep expecting to see Bancroft standing at the back of the club, looking angry. But he's not, because he's in another country. As angry as I am, I'm also sad. He'd become a friend. Someone who didn't judge me and accepted me for who I was.

In the morning I'm disappointed all over again by the lack of communication from him. I guess that tells me clearly where we stand.

I drive his truck back to his condo and allow the valet to park it. I'm surprised I've managed to return it with no damage, apart from the latte I spilled in the center console. I didn't try very hard to clean it up. I hope by the time he gets back it smells like sour milk in there. It's vindictive, but I'm not feeling all that nice on account of his hypocrisy.

I spend an hour playing with Francesca and make sure Tiny is okay—she won't require feeding until the weekend and I'm assuming Bancroft will be home by then. I hope so. Coming back here just hurts. Leaving Francesca is its own kind of painful.

I rub her belly as she rolls around on the floor. "I'm going to miss you so much."

She curls around my hand and nips at my fingers, then she climbs into my lap, sticking her head under my shirt. Stretching up on her hind legs her head pops out of the neck of my top, between my boobs. I laugh, and then start to cry.

She butts my chin with her nose and rubs her little face on my neck. I cuddle with her, letting my ridiculous tears fall until she gets squirmy and tries to wriggle out of my hold. I never expected to become so attached to her, or Tiny, or Bancroft.

I need a distraction, so my mission for the rest of the day becomes apartment hunting. I don't imagine it's going to be easy to find something reasonably priced and available immediately. I don't want to go back to a diet that consists primarily of ramen noodles, but I will if it means being able to pursue this dream I'm not willing to let die.

I'm almost back to Amie's apartment when I get a call from an unfamiliar number. It's local, so it can't be Bancroft. I answer on the third ring.

"Hello, may I please speak with Ruby Scott?"

It's an unfamiliar male voice. Oh God. I hope it's not a collection agency. I've been really good about paying down my loans and credit card. "That's me."

"This is Jack Russell. You auditioned for me yesterday."

My heart jumps up in my throat. I cross my fingers. "Yes. Yes I did."

"We were all very impressed with your audition."

"Thank you so much."

"Unfortunately, the role you've auditioned for has been filled," he says.

Of course it has. Because I have terrible luck. Because I suck. Because I can't do this on my own. Because I'm destined to be a corporate drone, dealing in penis-hardening stimulants for the rest of my life. Or a prison bitch for murdering my whore-mother when I'm forced to work with her, because that's the direction my life is going in.

I tune back in just in time to hear, "—today to audition for another role."

"I'm sorry, could you please repeat that?"

"It's a slightly more challenging role, but your paperwork indicates you have vocal background. If you're interested, we'd like you to come back and audition this afternoon."

"I can do that. Definitely. I'm interested. What time would you like me to be there?"

"Can you make two o'clock? We have an opening at that time."

"I'll be there. Is it at the same theater?"

"Actually, no, it's down the street. Not too far away." I scribbled down the address and realize he's talking about the New World Stages on West Fiftieth. This is a big deal. Not Broadway big, but Off-Broadway significant. It's a huge step in the right direction. Getting this role, or any role in this production would be amazing for my career.

I call Amie so I have someone to be excited with, but it goes to voice mail. A pang of sadness hits me when I see Bancroft's number not far down the list of recent calls. If this had been a few days ago, he would've been the first person I called. Possibly ahead of Amie. That tells me, in a way I didn't expect, just how attached to him I've become. I shake off the sadness and rush back to Amie's to prepare for my audition.

This time I'm put together and organized. I show up half an hour early, expecting it will give me some time to review the script—I didn't even think to ask what the play or the part was, I was so excited.

Ten minutes after I arrive they call me in, so I barely

have enough time to look over the script or learn the song I'm supposed to sing. I don't even have a chance to get nervous.

And maybe that's exactly why I nail it. It's going to be such a cool production and the acoustics in this theater are outrageous. Once again I'm riding a high as I head back out into the warmth and the sunshine. As I'm passing the little theater where I auditioned yesterday, I notice a flyer in warning-sign-yellow. It's impossible to miss. And it says FOR RENT.

I have no idea how long it's been there, but with my current string of luck, I call the number.

I get voice mail, so I leave a message and take a picture of the address. I don't think it's terribly far from here. It would be amazing if I managed to find a place within walking distance, or a short subway ride, of my best friend. For as long as she's still living in her apartment, anyway.

I need to be at the club around six and it's already approaching four, so I get my gear together and grab something to eat. I need to work a trip to the market into my day. Amie's lettuce selection isn't all that inspiring, or filling.

I'm considering leaving for the club early so I don't have to sit around and think about how a few days ago I could've shared my excitement with Bancroft, and now I can't. I can't exactly share it with the girls at the club either.

If I get this role, I'll have to quit or at least cut back my shifts. Quitting is more likely. And that makes me sad, because as scandalous as my job is, it's been a freeing experience. More than that, it's actually fun—aside from the horrible blisters and the calf cramps. Those I won't miss.

But this role would come with a very decent paycheck. One I can live off of. And the production is anticipated to be long running. This is what I've worked so hard for. It's exactly what I want. I try not to get my hopes up, but it's hard.

Just as I'm shoving my feet into my shoes the phone rings. I recognize it as the number from the rental advertisement. I fully expect the person to sound like Darth Vader, or that the ad is old and the apartment is rented, but I'm shocked to discover it's not. It's a sublet, and it's only available for two months.

That's not necessarily a bad thing. I can handle something short term. It will buy me time to find something permanent. I set up an appointment to see the place tomorrow. For all I know it's located in the basement of a dungeon somewhere.

The next day I take the short subway ride to check out the apartment. It's a beautiful, tiny four-hundred-square-foot apartment, built for function. A sliding panel bisects the room, giving the illusion of a separate space for the bedroom, which boasts a murphy bed.

The entire apartment would fit into my bedroom at Bancroft's. Which is not my bedroom anymore. It never really was. Like this place will be, it was temporary. A stopover until I managed to pull my life back together.

"I know it's small," Belinda says apologetically, as if it's her fault the apartment doesn't have more square footage.

"That's okay. It's just me anyway. What would the rent be for this?" I'm afraid of the number she's going to throw out. I have serious doubts about being able to afford this place.

"I'm asking for eighteen hundred a month, with a five-hundred-dollar deposit that you'll get back as long as everything is in the same condition when I return."

I stare at her, certain she can't be serious. I've seen what these studio apartments go for. Living around here would not be possible for me with my current income, so this is a steal.

It's really a no-brainer. I can stay here for the next two months, get myself sorted out, and then find something more permanent.

CHAPTER 21

WORST

BANCROFT

This is turning out to be the worst trip ever. Even the time I ate bad tacos and was sick the entire nine-hour plane ride home doesn't compare.

First, our flight has connections and they lose my luggage. As if that isn't bad enough, Griffin, who doesn't manage planes well, can't seem to find his damn passport once we land, so it takes us forever to get the fuck out of the airport. Then once we get to the hotel, I realize I forget my goddamn phone and my iPad on the plane.

It's an epic clusterfuck. To add to the barrage of shit, when I finally manage to get a new phone on the second day of the trip I discover I haven't backed up my iCloud, so any of the contacts I've added in the past three months cease to exist. Which includes Ruby. Who I haven't been able to get in touch with. I've left private messages for her on Facebook and Instagram but I've heard nothing in response. It's making me seriously fucking anxious.

I leave a message for Armstrong, but he's terrible

about returning phone calls at the best of times. I don't have much of a chance to worry about that, though, because we have bigger problems—not the least of which is replacing Griffin's passport so we're not stuck here in London for the next week.

The permit issue ends up being a lot bigger than my father let on. Or maybe it's bigger than he realized. We'd been one bad conversation away from a lawsuit. Lex was not in a good headspace for most of the trip. He generally makes sound business decisions, but this time he's really messed up. I've spent more time on the phone with my father over the past twenty-four hours than I have in the past fifteen years.

The only positive to come out of the trip is that we dodged a lawsuit and my father's accolades that we've managed to solve the problem.

When I walk into my condo the following Saturday afternoon, I'm exhausted and stressed. I haven't heard from Ruby at all, which really isn't like her. I expected messages from her but there's been nothing, and Armstrong never managed to get me her number. I drop my suitcases at the door and call out for her, aware that she's likely already left for work.

I pause at Ruby's open door. She usually keeps it closed, so I'm surprised to see it wide open, with the light on. Something looks different. It's tidier than usual, maybe. She's not here, obviously, so I continue on to my bedroom, but there's this feeling in my stomach that's been present for the past few days that seems to be getting worse instead of better. It should be the opposite now that I'm home.

My bed is exactly the way I left it, unmade with my clothes still littering it. That's odd. I would've thought

Ruby would still sleep in here even without me considering it's where she'd slept the entire time I was gone before. Something isn't right.

That sinking feeling hits me again and gets worse as
I turn and head back down the hall to her room. I flip the
light back on and go to the closet, throwing the door
open. The boxes. That's what's missing. They're gone.
Maybe she moved them to the other spare room. But even
as I think it, I know I'm wrong. I rush to her bathroom
and throw open the cabinet doors. They're bare apart
from towels. Everything is gone.

She's gone.

What the fuck happened while I was away?

I need to find her. I need to talk to her. I need her back
in my space.

But I can't do that without her number, which I still
don't have. I have Amalie's somewhere, it's just a matter
of finding it. I can always cave and call Armstrong again,
even though he's been less than helpful.

I cross over to the table where I keep mail, phone numbers, and miscellaneous papers I have yet to sort. I expect it to be more of a mess, because that's where Ruby
tosses all my mail, but it's surprisingly still organized.
My answering machine registers a message, so I hit the
play button while I leaf through the papers, searching for
a number I'm not sure I'll find. Losing my phone has
been a serious pain in the ass.

I shudder at the sound of Brittany's nasally, high-
pitched voice and stop leafing through papers.

"Hi, Banny, it's Brittany! I just heard from Mimi
and I couldn't get through on your cell so I thought
I'd try this number instead. I'm so sorry you had to

go away on business this week. Such a disappointment when you just got back. I really hope you'll
be back in time for dinner this weekend. But don't
worry if you're not. We can always reschedule our
date. Mimi said you're just as excited as I am about
being able to spend time together again. I can't wait
to pick up where we left off last time. Call me when
you can!"

It's the "our date" part that I get stuck on. I haven't
spoken to Brittany since I took her to the engagement
party. Not once. The fact that she's treating a dinner
party—one I'd completely forgotten about, and at which
my entire family will be present—as a date is fairly con-
cerning. The picking up where we left off part is another
concern. Fuck dinner. I'm not going.

I hope Ruby didn't hear this message. The machine is
so old it doesn't register the date or time messages are
left.

I continue the hunt for Amalie's phone number, but
after another fifteen minutes of searching, I abandon the
mission and call Armstrong. I get an answer, finally, but
it's Amalie, not Armstrong.

"Bane." She says my name as if it's profanity. Or like
I really am the epitome of my name.

"I hope I didn't wake you." It doesn't sound like it,
despite the early hour.

"You didn't. Armstrong's still sleeping, though."

"I'm calling to speak with you, actually."

"Is that so." Amalie is generally a pleasant, sweet
woman. Today she's the opposite: cold and snippy.

"I'm looking for Ruby."

"I can't help you."

Something is really off here. "You can't help me or you won't?" At her silence I sigh. "Do you know where she is?"

"I'm not answering that."

"I got in this afternoon and her room is empty, all of her things are gone."

"What a surprise."

What the fuck did I do to deserve this treatment? "Is she okay? Is she safe? Can you tell me that?"

"She's as okay as she can be."

"What does that mean?"

"She's safe."

Well, that puts my mind at ease a little. "I don't suppose you'd be willing to tell me where I might find her?"

"Probably asleep. In her bed. Or someone else's if she's taken my advice."

"What? I—" Dead air follows before I can get another word out.

What the hell is going on? What could've happened in the days between Ruby ending up in my bed and now that she's up and vanished?

Based on the time of day, she's likely already at the club. Which is exactly where I'm going. I don't bother to change out of my wrinkled suit. I drive my truck instead of Ubering, so I don't have to deal with waiting. A woman I recognize as one of the ladies who was in my living room, scuffing up my hardwood with her heels, greets me at the door of the club.

She props a fist on her hip. "If you're looking for Ruby, she's not here."

She always works on Saturday night, and she's usually here by now. "Is she coming in later?"

She gives me a funny look. "She doesn't work here anymore. I need to get ready. We have a new girl and she's just as clueless as Ruby Tuesday was when I trained her."

She closes the door in my face.

What the fuck is going on? Did she get fired? I'm sure Amalie will have the answer to that. If she wasn't going to be at dinner I would bail simply to avoid Brittany. Now I don't seem to have a choice but to go so I can find out what has happened to change things so drastically in the time I've been gone.

As it is, I arrive nearly half an hour late. My mother is irate. I can tell by the tic in her left eye.

"Bancroft. You're late," she hisses as I bend down to receive a kiss on the cheek.

"Sorry, Mimi, traffic."

"Everyone else managed to avoid traffic."

"I must've come a different way."

I'm in too bad a mood to be able to placate my mother, and of course I'm assaulted by Brittany the moment I enter the sitting room. She's standing conveniently close to the foyer, so as soon as I cross the threshold she rushes over and throws her arms around my neck.

"Banny!" Her shrill voice makes a shiver run down my spine. She kisses my cheek, then backs up, giggling as she wipes away the lipstick residue. "I'm so glad you could make it. Mimi said your plane landed just a few hours ago. You're such a trooper."

"I got here as quickly as I could," I lie. I take her by the shoulders and step away in an attempt to make it appear as though I'm appreciating her dress. "You look lovely, as always." This is untrue. Much like the other time I was forced into entertaining her, she was dressed like she was ready for a night at the club. And this time her parents are here to witness it.

I feel a prickle at the back of my neck and look up to

find Amalie glaring at me from over the rim of her martini glass.

When I'm finally able to make it over to her side of
the room, she gives me a tight smile.

"I need to talk to you," I say quietly.

"You have nothing to say that I want to hear," she replies through a plastered on smile and gritted teeth.

My mother calls us to the table. Of course Brittany
manages to snag the seat beside me. Lexington takes the
seat next to her. It's unfortunate my mother didn't try to
set Brittany up with him. I have a feeling he might actually enjoy dealing with her. Or at least what she promises to provide later in the night.

I have to move Brittany's hand off my thigh four times
during dinner. She thinks she's being cute. I think she's
being annoying. Now, if it was Ruby trying to feel me
up under the table, it would be a different story.

At one point she excuses herself to the bathroom. She
gives me a less-than-covert wink as she leaves the table.
I assume it's an invitation of some kind. I ignore it. At
some point she must realize I'm not coming after her
because she returns to the table, pouting.

Amalie is stiff during the entire meal and I keep catching her glaring at me. She pushes her food around her
plate, hardly touching a thing. At the end of the meal she
excuses herself. I give her two minutes' lead time before
I do the same.

I wait outside the powder room, which would be
creepy if the situation was different. She has information
I need right now. I also want to set her straight about Brittany, because it's clear she thinks I'm in on this date
business.

As soon as the bathroom door opens I step forward,
making an escape impossible. "I need to talk to you."

She snorts and crosses her arms over her chest. "I will kick you in the family jewels if you do not get out of my way."

"You know, I might even let you do that if you tell me what the hell is going on."

She stops trying to get around me. Her brow furrows and she gives me a strange look. "You would let me kick you in the balls?"

"If it means that you'll tell me why Ruby hasn't contacted me in a week and why she's not working at that club anymore, I might." I glance down at her feet. "But not while you're wearing those shoes. They're dangerous." She's wearing the same kind of shoes Ruby was wearing when she performed that song on stage. In fact, they look like they might just be the same ones.

I drag my eyes back up to her face. Man, her pissed-off face scares me, maybe because she's usually such a soft, warm person. She's never been sassy with me like Ruby always is. Jesus, I miss her.

Amalie steps in close, eyes alight with a fire I've never seen before. "Ruby told me all about the message you left her and the one Brittany left for you. What kind of person are you, trying to pay her off. It's disgusting."

"Pay her off? For what?"

"For the sex." She says it like I'm the stupidest person on the face of the earth. Because clearly I am.

"Whoa, whoa. Hold on here. Why the hell would she think I was paying her off?"

"Because you left her five thousand dollars and a message about how your arrangement changed, you asshole. And all the while you're setting up dates with whoreface Brittany. Ruby doesn't just sleep with anyone, you know. She really liked you and then you had to go and do this.

And you just up and disappear for a week. What kind of jerkoff are you?"

Oh shit. Now this is all starting to make sense. "Okay, first things first, I wasn't trying to pay Ruby for sex. I had no idea how long I was going to be gone and I needed to leave money because I didn't have time to get supplies for Francesca and Tiny. Secondly, I've known Brittany since I was a kid and she's here because my mother wants me to date her, not because I do. Why wouldn't Ruby call me before she went and moved all her stuff out? And she's not working at the club anymore. Please tell me she didn't go back to Rhode Island." I hadn't even considered that possibility until now. It amps up the panic.

"She moved out because she's protecting her heart." She clamps her mouth shut. "I don't even know why I'm talking to you. I can't trust a damn thing you say."

Amalie tries to brush past me, but I grab her arm. "I just need her number. I just need to call her to explain. Or you could tell me where she is."

"Explain what exactly? That you were screwing her and who knows who else while she was living in your place? You didn't even try to contact her once while you were gone this time. What the hell is she supposed to think?"

"I'm not screwing anyone else and I don't have any intention of doing so either. I lost my phone on the plane and I didn't have my iCloud backed up so I couldn't contact her. And she's either not responding to or not getting the messages I sent her on social media. I just want to talk to her, Amalie. I didn't want her to leave. I want her. I want to be with her. I fucking *miss* her."

Amalie eyes go wide and maybe a little shocked at my language. "Oh, well, that explains the lack of messages, but this whole Brittany thing—"

"I'm not an asshole, Amalie. I've never had any intention of dating Brittany. I think she might actually be delusional. Just tell me where Ruby is, please, so I can try to fix this."

Amalie regards me for a few long moments before she retrieves her phone from her handbag. "She's staying at my place. She had a successful audition last week. It's a really great role. She's moving into her own apartment next week."

"She found her own place already?"

"It was a fluke really. A sublet."

My phone pings in my pocket. I pull it out and add the contact to my short, but growing list. "Can I get directions to your apartment?" My phone pings again.

"I can do better than that." She roots around in her clutch and pulls out a key. "Don't make me regret giving you this. Now go unbreak my best friend's heart, please."

CHAPTER 22
ICE CREAM TASTES LIKE HEARTBREAK

RUBY

I'm on my second pint of Ben and Jerry's. The first one was cookie dough, this one is straight vanilla. Amie's having dinner at Bancroft's parent's house tonight and he's supposed to be there if he's back from his trip. She offered to fake being sick and stay here with me in a show of solidarity, but I wanted her to report back. I also want to know if that whoreface Brittany is there with him. I also may have asked her to put a hefty dose of laxative in her food if she is. Amie refused the last part. I still slipped it in her purse in case she changed her mind.

At seven I get my first message from Amie:

Whoreface is here. Dressed like a whore. Bancroft is not.

Forty-five minutes later I get another one:

Bancroft arrived. Whoreface is whoring all over

him. I found the laxatives in my purse. I might slip them into his coffee.

The ice cream suddenly isn't sitting well. I wait to hear back from her again, but after half an hour I cave and send her one:

Is she his date?

It takes a few minutes for her to reply.

I think so. ☹

I can't believe less than a week ago we were having sex on every damn surface in his condo. I should've stuck to my seven-date rule. Living at his place ruined every-thing.

My phone pings again. It's Amie again.

We were wrong.

When I send one back asking for clarification and get nothing in response I frantically type fifty new one-word messages, hoping the constant string of texts will prompt her to reply in order to shut me up. She replies:

About Bancroft. You'll understand soon.

As if that's helpful. It's just as cryptic. The rest of my messages go unanswered. I think I'm on the verge of a panic attack when there's a knock on the door, followed by the sound of the key turning in the lock. It's not even ten. I'm surprised dinner is over already. Rich-people din-ner parties usually last until midnight, with the business component of the evening taking place after food and drink has been consumed. Which seems rather backward to me. Maybe Amie left early to be with me. Maybe she has news. My stomach flips and I reclaim my ice cream in preparation for food solace.

Except it's not Amie who walks through the door of the apartment. It's Bancroft.

"What the hell are you doing here?" I bark.

Bancroft looks me over. I resist the urge to rush to the bathroom and make myself more presentable. I'm pretty sure I look awful. My hair is pulled into a haphazard ponytail and I'm wearing my comfy pajamas. And no bra.

He crosses the room, looking intense. And hot. Damn him.

"We need to talk."

I clutch the couch cushion so I don't launch an attack. "There's nothing to talk about."

"I'm going to disagree. I think there's actually a lot to talk about."

"What would you like to start with? Your date with Brittany the slutface? How excited she is to pick up where you left off? Were you playing us both the entire time?"

He holds up his hands. "I wasn't playing anyone."

"Oh no? How many times did she call while you were in London? Did you ask her to get naked on video chat? Did you talk to her about her panties?"

"I don't actually think she owns panties," he grumbles.

My mouth drops open and I hurl the closest throwable thing at him, which just happens to be a pillow, so unfortunately it does no damage. "How classless are you that you'd fuck her while I'm living in your goddamn condo?"

"Whoa. Hold on, you're misunderstanding." He runs

a hand through his hair. "I've never had sex with Brittany. I've never even kissed her."

As if this makes me feel any better. "How the hell do you know she doesn't own panties then?"

"Because she flashed me the last time I took her out."

"Why should I even believe you?" I push up off the couch so I can prop a fist on my hip. It would be so much more effective if I didn't look so pathetic. "Besides, what does any of this matter since we need to make 'adjustments to our arrangement'? And maybe we need to talk about the money you left for services rendered."

Bancroft shakes his head. "Services rendered? I don't even kn—"

"I must be in the wrong business if my pussy is worth five grand a week." I motion to my crotch.

Bancroft looks so confused right now.

"What am I supposed to think when you leave an envelope of cash to compensate me for sex? Do you have any idea how degrading that is? You can't buy me, Bane." Oh shit. I think I'm going to cry.

His expression turns remote and he crosses his arms over his chest. "You honestly think I'd pay you for having sex with me?"

"Well what the hell else was it for? Just in case I end up with lockjaw down the line from trying to deep throat your cock?" Okay, that might be taking it a little too far.

"I was worried I might be gone longer than I hoped. I didn't want to leave you without money. I'm not trying to buy you, Ruby. I'm trying to take care of you."

"I don't need to be taken care of. And you said we needed to make adjustments, that it was all too fast. And the first thing you do when you get back is go out with Brittany!" I'm incredibly flaily right now. If I was sitting down I could shove my hands under my thighs to keep them still.

"Fuck. This is why I hate voice mail." Bancroft rubs the space between his eyes as if this conversation is giving him a headache. "I didn't set up a date with Brittany. This was my mother's attempt at matchmaking again. I have no interest in dating Brittany. The only reason I went to dinner at all tonight was so I could find out where you were from Amalie. When I said things were moving faster than I expected it wasn't supposed to be a bad thing. I was flustered at being sent to London again."

"Oh." This is a lot different than what I expected. "But you didn't call me once while you were gone."

"I left my phone on the plane and I hadn't backed up my iCloud so I didn't have your number anymore. I messaged you on social media hoping you would respond, but I got nothing back. Do you have any idea how confused I was when I came home to find you'd moved out?"

I suppose deleting the private messages he sent without reading them was a bit hasty on my part. He must read the guilt in my expression. Based on his loud sigh.

"I knew we needed to talk about things, and I probably should've said something long before I did, but then I had to go back to London and I had no choice but to wait. I honestly didn't intend to get you naked so soon after I came back, but then the club happened and I didn't have the restraint necessary to wait."

I raise my hand to stop him. "You *planned* to sleep with me?"

He takes a step closer until my open palm rests against his chest. "*Planned* sounds devious and calculated."

I don't move away, but I lift my chin so I can see his face. "Were you being devious and calculated?"

Bancroft shrugs. "It was a good thing I was out of the

country at the beginning. That first night you stayed in my condo, before I left, I had a very difficult time not making a bad decision that would have felt, very, very good. I'm sorry I wasn't clear in my intentions and that it took this long for me to express them. I would like to be forgiven. Do you think that's possible?"

I nod. "I'm sorry I didn't give you the benefit of the doubt, but the messages and the money . . ." I swallow hard as he covers my hand with his. It's difficult not to get caught up in the feel of him so close to me. "I'm actually glad we didn't make bad decisions before you left."

He cocks his head, his gaze questioning.

"If I'd slept with you before you left it would've complicated things. I would've felt as if I were being bought."

He picks up my hand, bringing my fingers to his lips. "Which is how I made you feel when I left last week."

"I've been dependent on my father's support for a lot of years. His money always came with a price, and I didn't want that to happen again. Even without the misunderstanding I would've had to move out."

"But I like having you with me." The fingers of his free hand trail down the side of my neck. It's rather distracting.

"I can't, Bane. Because it's yours. Because I need to stand on my own first. I can't live with you if we're dating."

"You already were."

"It was different when I was your pet sitter turned roommate. Everything changes with sex and a label."

"You can at least come back to the condo until your new place is ready."

"It's ready next week and all my things are here."

Bancroft's face falls.

"We can have sleepovers. I can stay at your place a

few nights this week and when I have my place you can stay with me."

"It's not the same."

"No. But I need time to be responsible for my own well-being. I'd like to attempt to be successful at it before I merge my life with someone else's. Let's give ourselves some time to date like regular people do."

"I guess we can do that. If we have to." He's pretty much pouting.

I laugh. "I think it would be a bit more logical than me moving back in with you."

"How long do you have the apartment? Not a year?" The furrow is back.

"Only two months."

"How much is it costing you?"

"It's affordable."

His fingers trail up and down the back of my arm. "Okay. So in two months you can move back into the condo, and if I have to go away you'll stay and take care of Francesca and Tiny? And we can have a minimum of three sleepovers a week while we're doing this dating thing."

"You sound like you're negotiating a business arrangement."

"I'm negotiating your girlfriend status and regular sex." Now his hand is on my waist, moving around to my lower back.

"Regular, mind-blowing sex," I correct.

"It really is that fucking amazing, isn't it?" His palm curves around my right butt cheek.

"It is," I breathe.

"We should do it again. Right now. Especially since we're dating and all."

"I think that's a great idea."

SHACKING UP   335

It takes all of a half a second before Bancroft's mouth is on mine. The kiss is explosive. I fight to unbutton his suit jacket and loosen his tie while his tongue strokes my mouth.

Getting me naked is a matter of pulling my tank over my head and yanking my shorts down my legs. Bancroft runs his hands from my ankles, up the outside of my legs all the way to my ribs, then cups my breasts and goes in for another kiss.

"You don't think Amalie will come back here tonight?" he asks.

"Not likely. It's the weekend—she'll stay at Armstrong's tonight, especially if she knows you're here."

"Excellent. That's what I hoped."

I continue popping buttons as I lead Bancroft to the bedroom. I hesitate for a second when I push open the door. It's not my bed. The sheets are fresh, though. I changed them this morning.

"Maybe we should have sex on the floor." I unclasp the buckle on his belt.

"You don't think her bed can handle me fucking you?" And there it is, that dirty mouth I've been missing.

"I don't really know." It's a metal frame, all pretty and delicate. Bancroft's bed is made of solid wood. It's reinforced like a bunker. He can fuck me straight through the mattress if he wants and the frame will stay firmly intact. I'm not sure Amie's bed is the same, although I was more concerned about having sex on the surface my best friend typically sleeps on.

"Let's see how much it can take." Bancroft turns me around, picks me up by the waist, and drops me on the bed. I lean back on my elbows, watching intently as he undresses. I wish I had music playing, something sexy to make into a striptease.

He's gorgeous, with or without a soundtrack. His pants slide down his legs leaving him in boxers, his hard-on visible through the red fabric. The dim lighting casts shadows on the outline. I bite my lip and hum my appreciation.

He tugs at the waistband and lets it snap back. "See something you like?"

"I like the entire package, but the one inside those shorts wins all the awards."

He pulls the right side down, then the left, lower and lower until the head peeks out. I sigh when he's fully unveiled. Bancroft gives himself a slow stroke and I push up, thinking I might like to be the one who does that, but he puts a hand up to stop me. "I'll come to you."

He shoves his underwear the rest of the way down and steps out of them. Nudging my knees apart with his, he stretches out over me. My legs are still hanging off the bed and so are his.

"First, I'm going to fuck you, then I'm going to love you."

I shiver from the promise and his tone. And then I groan when the thick head of his erection slides over slick skin. Bancroft keeps his eyes on mine as he rocks forward, easing inside.

The first few strokes are slow, but it's been a long week of silence and uncertainty, so an undercurrent of desperation makes it hard to maintain the sweetness.

"I'm sorry," I whisper.

He strokes my cheek with warm fingers. "For what?"

"For thinking the worst."

"No need for apologies, but if you still feel bad about it later you can let me fuck your mouth."

"I was going to do that anyway."

He flashes a smirky grin. "I figured as much since you couldn't seem to get enough of it last time."

"You're losing points again."

"I guess I should do something to earn them back, then."

Bancroft starts with a slow grind that makes the bed rock a little, but when he picks up speed and starts fucking me in earnest, the creaking grows infinitely louder.

I'm getting close, but I'm worried we might actually break Amie's bed and it's distracting.

"Maybe we should move to the floor," I say somewhat breathlessly. It's hard to talk and be plundered at the same time.

Bancroft shoves a hand under me, grabs hold of my right butt cheek, claps my palm against the back of his neck, and lifts me up on the next thrust. Spinning around, he pins me against the wall, and keeps right on going.

Every muscle in his torso is straining and tight, his neck corded, biceps flexing. He really wasn't kidding about fucking me. It might be lovingly, but the impending orgasm promises to be nerve shattering.

I struggle to keep my eyes on him, on his dark, intense expression, on his gorgeous face, his parted lips.

"Come on, babe, I want to feel you come. Let me know how much you missed my cock."

I have no idea why that makes me so hot, but it does the trick. I come. Hard.

"There it is," he groans.

All I see is black, not because he's fucked me blind, but because I'm looking at the back of my lids. I pry them open with some effort. Bancroft's expression is complete male satisfaction. With one hand still gripping my ass cheek he brings the other one up, his index finger and thumb slide along the line of my jaw and he holds my face, his mouth an inch from mine.

"This is what I want. You. The way you're looking at me right now. This feeling right here. Don't take it away from me again."

It doesn't sound like an order so much as a plea. He kisses me hard and shudders as he comes. We're both sweaty and breathing heavily as he adjusts his grip and backs up until he hits the bed. He sits down on the edge and I unhook my legs, maneuvering us until he's lying with me on top of him, stretched out on the covers.

He slips a hand behind my neck and pulls me down, claiming my lips. After a few minutes he rolls us over, so he's on top.

"What are you doing?" It feels a lot like he's getting hard again.

He rolls his hips. "Exactly what I said I was going to."

"Which is?"

"I've already fucked you, so now it's time to love you, isn't it?"

And he does. All night. With actions and dirty words I can't get enough of.

CHAPTER 23
BREAK A LEG

RUBY

"You need to call your father."

The water is running in the sink, so I pretend not to hear Bancroft, making loud splashing noises while I drop pots into the water. Dishwashing is one of my preproduction stress relievers. I didn't realize it was my thing until this past week.

His arm slips around my waist, lips brushing the shell of my ear. "Are you ignoring me?"

I tilt my head to the side, encouraging him to put his lips there as well. He nips a slow path from my ear to my shoulder and then back up again.

"Opening night is a week away, you need to call him."

"He's not going to drop everything and fly down to see me play pretend on stage," I reply, distracted by his mouth and his hands.

Gently, Bancroft forces the pot I'm scrubbing out of my hands and turns me around. He's smart enough to pin me to the counter with his hips and barricade me in with his hands.

"First of all, do not belittle yourself like that. You are an incredible talent and calling it anything other than performing or acting is unacceptable. Secondly, you need to at least give him the opportunity, Ruby. This is a huge accomplishment and he should learn to appreciate how hard you've worked to get here." I hate how soft and logical he's being. And sweet. It makes it difficult to argue.

Two weeks ago I finally caved, at Bancroft's insistence—he enticed me with orgasms and Italian takeout, in that order—and called my father to inform him of my role in an Off-Broadway play.

His response: So I still wasn't done playing pretend yet.

It was painfully deflating. I had to beg Bancroft not to call him back and give him a piece of his mind. I didn't want their first introduction to consist of Bancroft calling my father names, such as *insensitive, dream-crushing dick*. However, I do appreciate how willing Bancroft is to come to my defense. It's rather sexy.

"I'll call later today. After rehearsal."

Bancroft sighs. "Call now so you're not thinking about it all day."

Getting it over with is a double-edged sword. "If he says he doesn't have time it's going to ruin my day, and I need to be on point. Dress rehearsal is later this week and I don't want anything compromising my performance today."

Bancroft sighs and strokes my cheek with a fingertip. "So tonight you'll call?"

I swallow past the lump in my throat and nod.

"Is there anything I can do to make today easier for you?"

I finger the buttons on his dress shirt. I'm wearing yellow rubber gloves, they're still sudsy, so I'm making a mess of his outfit. "You could love me–fuck me," I say softly.

"You want me to love you first?" He peels the soapy gloves off my hands.

"Please."

He takes my face in his palms and kisses me. It doesn't seem to matter that we've been dating now *officially* for a month—every kiss still makes my toes curl.

"I always love you, don't I?" he whispers against my lips.

"You do. And I love it when you do it slow and soft or hard and dirty."

Bancroft shoves my shorts down my legs and lifts me onto the counter. He drops to his knees and loves me with his mouth first, then with his fingers and his cock, still fully dressed.

It's an excellent distraction from the nerves. I also never get tired of being loved by him.

Later that evening I'm sitting in my lounger—my old, ugly one that still takes up space in Bancroft's condo— reviewing the script for the four-hundred-millionth time while he watches a DVR'd rugby match. I'd sit next to him, but then he'll want to touch me, and I won't be able to focus.

I know my lines. I can see the stage, my placement, the position of the male lead—I have to kiss him, which makes me a little nervous since Bancroft is going to see that happen. I'm not sure how he's going to react. He's said he's fine, and he knows it's acting, but I'm not so sure he'll be as okay with it as he says he's going to be once he actually sees it.

"Did you call?"

I look up and pretend I didn't hear the question. "Hmm?"

"Your father, did you call?"

"He was in a meeting. I left a message with his secretary and provided the necessary details."

"Has he called you back?"

"Not yet. He will. When he's not busy with work." Which could mean a few days from now, or even next week, which would be perfectly fine, because that's after opening night.

Bancroft sighs, but says nothing. He keeps pushing this, and I understand why. This truly is a huge accomplishment. I have a lead role in one of the best Off-Broadway productions in the city. And I managed to do it all on my own, without anyone making phone calls to get me an audition. My new agent, who I secured a week ago, was highly impressed.

I've managed to pay off my overdue rent, and my credit cards are no longer maxed out. It's still going to take time to get them all down to zero, but I feel like I have control of my life and that's the important part.

When I move into Bancroft's condo, which is an eventuality if things keep going the way they are, I want to come in as a positive contributor—maybe not with a huge bankroll, but at least I'll be stable and not a burden.

"Does he realize how important this is to you?"

It's my turn to sigh. "I know you just want to help, but you have to understand, my father's first priority has always been himself." It's why my mother is all the way in Alaska—she desperately wanted to make opening night, but she's in the middle of the ocean taking pictures of whales or something. It was a challenge to hear her over the crashing waves.

She's coming later this month and she's promised to

stay a week or so. I can't wait for her to meet Bancroft. She's going to love him.

Bancroft drops the conversation. I'm glad. I don't think my heart can take more of my father's disdain or his dismissal of my chosen career path.

Six days later I'm in full costume. Butterflies have taken over my stomach. I peek through the curtains. Somewhere out there in the crowd are Bancroft and Amie. He wanted to bring his parents, but I told him it would be better if we waited on that. I've been to their house for dinner. Bancroft warned me about his mother being uptight. He didn't have anything to worry about, though, she was nothing but sweet with me. And his brothers are a trip. He was right, they look nothing alike, but they're all huge.

Three days ago I spoke with my father. He informed me he had meetings and golf, but he'd see whether it would work later in the month.

I tried not to be disappointed. But I am. Bancroft knows it and so does Amie, but I'm done trying to prove myself to my father. He's not even a role model I want to look up to. He's made his millions on penis-inflating drugs. Our ideas on what counts as a successful career don't align.

I push aside all the worries and focus on the present. It's opening night, and I'm the lead in an Off-Broadway performance. It's a huge, positive step. It's an accomplishment. It's in that frame of mind that I step out onto the stage and wait for my cue.

It isn't until it's over and the house lights come up that I can finally see Bancroft and Amie in the audience. Armstrong had a thing so he couldn't be here, which is fine, since I'm still struggling to warm up to him even after all this time. To the right of Bancroft is my father. He's a good head shorter than Bane, lean and wiry rather than built. His hair is gray at the temples, receding at the crown. His typically serious face is cracked wide with a smile. He claps with vigor rather than with his usual golf-course propriety.

I shift my gaze to Bancroft as I link hands with the cast and step forward to take a bow. The cheers and applause grow louder, a thunderstorm of clapping that makes my heart soar and tears spring to my eyes.

The overwhelmingly positive response and the packed theater feed my pride. Someone hands me a massive bouquet of flowers so heavy it makes my arm ache. Backstage is a whirlwind of excitement. We're all buzzing from the adrenaline of a successful performance.

I rush to change and greet the people who have stayed to congratulate us on a successful first night. My stomach is a knotted mess as I make my way through the crowd in search of Bancroft, but I keep getting stopped, for introductions, shaking hands with new people who pay me compliments that make me blush.

I've just finished thanking someone when an arm slips around my waist. "How's my starlet?" Bancroft says in my ear. He politely excuses us and steers me away.

"Are you responsible for this?" I ask as we maneuver through the crowd, toward my father and Amie.

He doesn't need me to explain the question. "I may have called and had a conversation with him about the importance of being supportive. He seemed very receptive once I made it clear how hard you had worked to get here. And that carving our own path rather than blindly following the one that was laid for us takes infinitely more courage. That seemed to resonate with him."

I stop walking and grab the lapels of his suit jacket.

He seemed shocked at first, but then he smiles and bends to kiss me. "I have so much love for you."

"You were stunning up there tonight. Perfect."

"You're a little biased, what with you being my boy-friend."

"I think the reaction of the audience should indicate that, despite my bias, I'm correct. Also, I wanted to mur-der your costar when he kissed you. Later, when I get you home, I'm going to claim that mouth as mine again."

"I look forward to that."

Amie is the first to hug me, and then I turn to my father, bracing myself for whatever it is he's going to say. He's holding a massive bouquet of flowers. He looks al-most as nervous as I am. I haven't seen him since Christ-mas. He'd been too busy to attend my convocation.

"I'm so very proud of you, Ruby." And then he wraps me in a huge, warm hug, the kind I'd forgotten he could give. And that's all I need from him. Just his pride and his love.

EPILOGUE
SOCKS

BANCROFT

Four weeks later

Ruby's schedule is very much the opposite of mine, so text messages and brief phone calls are sometimes all we can manage for days on end.

Tonight is one of her rare nights off. She performs five days a week, often twice a day, especially on weekends. It's wonderful, but it means I've restructured my own schedule so I'm home on her days off.

She spends most of those days in my condo. Currently, she's lounging in her hideous recliner and I'm stretched out on the couch with Francesca curled up in my lap. She moved here about fifteen minutes ago, and before that she was snuggled up in Ruby's shirt with her head peeking out of the neckline. Ruby thinks she needs a friend to love. I'm inclined to try the stuffed variety first. I'm not sure why Ruby's sitting so far away—apart from her need to give that awful chair a reason to continue to take up space in my condo. Not that I would throw it away on her. Sometimes I threaten to, though.

In the time we've officially been dating, I've managed to convince my father to limit my business trips and to allow me to oversee the renovations on the New York hotels alongside Griffin.

Ruby has had a huge role in helping to facilitate this. My father adores her. It's not a surprise. She's easy to adore, and when I mentioned sending me out of the country would take me away from a new relationship I was trying to foster, he softened. Then I threw my brother Lexington under the bus, saying he was still unattached, so sending him instead wouldn't be a bad idea. I was hoping it would help rebuild my father's trust in him after the London hotel issue.

Beyond that, I've shown him that my strength lies in the renovation-management side of this business and that while knowing everything is important, having a core skill set will make me a stronger asset down the line.

I tuck an arm behind my head. "Are you going to sit in that chair all night?"

She glances over at me, then back at the TV. "You're watching rugby. You're not going to pay attention to me even if I do sit over there."

"I won't ignore you." I move Francesca so she's on my chest and spread my legs, patting the space between them.

"I'll come sit with you if you take those socks off." She gestures to my feet.

I look down. "What? Why?"

She glares at me.

Ruby has a thing about my socks. Apparently they drive her nuts, which is the exact reason I keep them on all the time when she's here. Also, I don't like it when my feet get cold.

I lift one leg, bend my knee, and lower my head to sniff. They smell fine to me.

"Ew. I can't believe you just did that."

"I was checking to see if odor was the problem."

"It's not the smell. They're ruining my view." Ruby rolls her eyes and takes a sip of her wine.

"Are you drunk? What're you talking about?"

"I've had one glass."

"So you are drunk."

"My tolerance is better than that now." This is somewhat true. Ruby has discovered a fondness for wine over martinis. The lower alcohol content and the fact that it takes her two hours to finish a single glass means that she rarely passes from tipsy territory to drunk off her ass. Although she has been that drunk a couple of times. I will say, she's very adventurous in the bedroom when she's imbibing, and that's saying something since she's already pretty damn open to trying new things.

She struggles to get the footrest of her ancient recliner to fold down. It rocks forward when it does and she almost ends up wearing her wine. It sloshes over the side and drips down her hand. She sets her glass on the coffee table, beside the coaster, not on it. There are rings all over it. It should drive me up the fucking wall, but I kind of don't care. Okay. I care, but the housekeeper will be here tomorrow to deal with that.

Ruby wipes her hands on her camisole, the one that doesn't require her to wear a bra. It's distracting me from the rings on the table. And the game on TV. And everything, really.

She rounds the coffee table, grabs the toe of my sock, and starts yanking.

"What're you doing?"

"Fixing the view." The sock comes free and she tosses it on the floor. Then she drops to her knees.

At first I think I'm about to get a Ruby Special. Especially when her tongue peeks out as she rolls my other sock down, forcing it over my ankle. Ruby's oral skills are fucking phenomenal.

She blows her hair out of her eyes and purses her lips, then wraps her hands around my ankle and rubs up and down my calf—kind of like a vigorous hand-job, except it's my leg.

She uses my thigh to push back to a standing position. She's wearing my favorite shorts. The ones that ride up on her right ass cheek all the time.

She props her fist on her hip. "Much better."

I drag my eyes back up to her face, pausing at her chest for a few short seconds. "You want to fill me in on the issue?"

"You know what the issue is."

"I don't understand why you hate socks so much."

Ruby huffs, annoyed. God she's hot when she's annoyed. I was so right about her and angry fucking. I was also accurate about her being a biter and a scratcher.

"Socks are not sexy. You ruin all the sexy with the socks."

"But without them?"

Her voice goes low. "So much sexier."

"Sexier?"

"Yes."

"What about sexiest?"

"Mmm, you'd have to up your game for that." Her grin is what sin is made of.

"What would take it from sexier to sexiest?"

Her smile grows wider as she grabs the hem of my

shirt. Francesca jumps up and scampers across the back of the couch, settling at the other end, away from all the commotion.

"What're you doing?"

"Making you the sexiest." She tugs it up, until I have no choice other than to raise my arms. It takes a little effort on her part to get it over my head. She tosses it on the floor beside my socks.

The way she looks me over has me flexing every damn muscle in my body, particularly the one below the waist.

"Perfect." She sighs and flops back down in her chair.

"So that's it?"

"Unless you want to lose the shorts, too, yeah." She grabs her wine and focuses on the TV again.

"What if I'm commando?"

"Even better," she mutters.

"You do realize this is objectification, right?"

She lifts her gaze briefly. "You asked how you could make the view better and I showed you. No one said you had to keep your shirt off."

I stretch an arm across the back of the couch and spread my legs. Her gaze drops.

"What about my view?"

She gestures to the TV. "You can always change the channel if it's a problem."

"I'm not talking about the TV."

She looks down at what she's wearing, stretches her legs and wiggles her toes. "I'm not wearing socks, so your view is fine."

"I don't think we're even here." I gesture to my chest and then motion to her.

Ruby fingers the strap of her tank. "You mean this?"

I quirk a brow and wait.

She doesn't look away as she lowers her hands to the

hem. I stop breathing. I stop moving. I stop everything. That camisole, the one that barely hides anything anyway, rises up, up, up, exposing her belly ring and she keeps going until it's over her head and on the floor. She's braless. We're totally even now.

I push up off the couch as she struggles to bring the footrest back up. I straddle the chair and her legs, forcing her to make space for my knees.

"I'm not sure this chair can handle both of us." She palms my erection through my shorts.

The tinkle of a bell draws our gazes away from each other for a second. Francesca has found one of her toys and seems to want to play. She'll have to wait her turn.

"I guess we're about to find out how much it can take." I put one hand on the backrest, pushing to make it recline. "Do you have any idea how long I've wanted to do this?"

"Do what?" She slides one hand up my chest.

"Fuck you in this chair. I wanted to do it that first night you were here."

"Is that right?" She hooks her feet around my waist.

"It is. I wanted to bend you over, yank these fucking shorts down, and find out exactly what it was like to be inside you." The backrest seems to be stuck. I push harder and all of a sudden it drops back with a huge crack and we land in a heap on the floor, with me on top of Ruby.

She looks around, startled. Francesca bounds past us, down the hall toward our bedroom.

"Huh. In my imagination we got a lot further than this though."

"You killed my chair!"

"Your chair was too fragile." I kiss her neck.

"I love this chair."

I lift my head. "More than me?"

She makes a noise and gives me a look. She's perfectly annoyed.

"If this chair can't even withstand my love for you it's worthless anyway. I'll get you a new one. Or we can use that one—" I motion to the one that's still intact. The huge chair we can both fit in. The one we can screw in comfortably.

"I think you broke my chair on purpose."

"Untrue. If you hadn't started taking off my clothes and then your clothes, your chair might very well still be in one piece." I drop my head and kiss the tip of her nipple.

Her hand goes into my hair, gripping tight to keep me there, her voice is breathy now. "I knew I should've moved it to my apartment."

I move to her other nipple. "What would be the point since you're not going to be there much longer."

"I still have"—she gasps when I bite gently—"some time on the sublet."

I push up on one arm so I can look at her. "You don't have to stay until the sublet is up. Besides, my place is closer to the theater."

"By all of five minutes."

"Why can't you make this easy for me? Does everything have to be hard?"

She smiles and tightens her legs around my waist, pulling me closer until my erection is pressed against her.

"I like hard things."

I ignore the comment, although it isn't easy. "I want you to move back in."

Her smile drops a little. "I thought we were waiting until the sublet is up."

"Do you want to wait until then?"

"Well, it's been the plan." She plays with the hair at

the nape of my neck. It's what she does when we're having conversations she's unsure of.

We're still lying sprawled out on the floor. I push up onto my knees, which causes another huge crack and the top and bottom of the chair separate completely. At least there's absolutely no way to fix it now.

"Are you committed to sticking to the plan?" I fold back on my knees and rearrange her until she's sitting in my lap.

She glances at the broken chair beside us on the floor and nudges the top with her toe. "I don't have to be."

"Then move back in. You've proven you can do this on your own and I know that's important to you. We both know you can. I want us to do this together."

"Are you sure? It hasn't been that long . . ."

"It's been months if you count all our video chat dates."

"You make it sound like bad Internet dating."

My stomach drops a little. Maybe I've read all the signs wrong and she's not as interested in taking this to next level like I am. "Is this you skirting an answer?"

"You're so cute when you're insecure." She wraps her arms around my neck. "I just wanted to give us enough time to make sure it's not all hormones driving us, and you know, that the sex wouldn't get boring or anything."

At my narrowed eyes she leans in and kisses me softly through a smile.

"Of course I want to move back in with you."

"We can clean out your apartment tomorrow."

She laughs. "No rush, though, right?"

"I want what I want, and I don't want to wait if I don't have to."

"It must've been hell for you to wait more than five weeks between first kisses."

"Exactly."

"Okay, tomorrow we move me back in."

"And tonight we celebrate."

"Oooh . . ." Ruby bites her lip. "What kind of celebration?"

I slide my hands down to cup her ass and pull her tight against me. "A naked one, with lots of orgasms. You in?"

"Will there be naughtiness to go with the nudity and the orgasms?"

"Isn't there always?"

She doesn't need to answer and I don't need to say anything else. She skims my lips with her fingertips, then replaces them with her mouth.

Every kiss is an echo of the first time. Accidental or not, some part of me recognized her as my future and now she's mine to love.

ACKNOWLEDGMENTS

To my partner and best friend, thank you for being my number-one supporter, and thank you to my family for always having my back. Debra, my soul sister, my girl-bestie, the pepper to my salt, I love you. Thank you for being with me all these years.

Kimberly, thank you for always being there to field questions, to be my cheerleader, my problem solver, and the most incredible agent. I'm so honored to work with you.

To my team at SMP, thank you for making this such an amazing experience. Rose, your belief in my words still makes me all sappy.

Jenn, Sarah, and Nina I couldn't do any of this without all of you. I'm constantly amazed by how incredible you all are, and I'm so very lucky to have such a phenomnenal team.

Hustlers, you are such an amazing and wonderful group of women. I'm so very fortunate to have you all on my side.

Beavers, you're my safe place and the best cheer-leaders. I love being able to share all my boys with you!

To my Backdoor Babes: Tara, Meghan, Deb, and Katherine, I'm so glad I have somewhere to talk about inappropriate things.

Pams, Filets, my Nap girls, 101'ers, my Holidays and Indies, Tijan, Susi, Deb, Erika, Katherine, Shalu, Kellie, Ruth, Melissa, Sarah, Kelly, Melanie, and J—thank you for being my friends, my colleagues, my supporters, my teachers, and my soft places to land.

Jessica—thank you for kicking my butt so I can sit in a chair for a lot of hours every day.

To all the amazing bloggers and readers who have come on this journey with me: Thank you for believing in happily ever afters.

Read on for an excerpt from another great book by
Helena Hunting!

I FLIPPING LOVE YOU

CHAPTER 1

ANGRY HOT GUY

RIAN

I flip through my stack of flyers, checking for a sale on the jumbo box of Cinnamon Toast Crunch cereal so I can price match it. I'm a conscientious price matcher. I mark the sale with a big circle before tucking the red Sharpie into the front of my shirt. If I'm going to wheel and deal at the cash register, I want to make it as easy as possible for the cashier and the people in line behind me. Nothing is worse than getting stuck behind an unorganized price matcher.

I shimmy a little to the song playing over the store intercom as I toss boxes of my most favorite, unhealthy cereal in my cart. A prickly feeling climbs the back of my neck, and I shiver, glancing over my shoulder. A mom rushes past me down the aisle, her toddler leaning precariously out of the cart in an attempt to grab a box of Fruit Roll-Ups. I can't blame him. They are artificially delicious.

But the mom-toddler combo isn't the reason for the prickly feeling. Halfway down the aisle is a suit. A big suit. Well over six feet of man wrapped in expensive charcoal-gray fabric. He doesn't have a cart or a basket. And he's staring at me. Weird. I can't look at him long enough to decide if he's familiar or not without making it obvious that I'm staring back.

I have the urge to check my appearance, worried I have his attention because my hair is a mess, or there's a sweat stain down the center of my back. I'm not particularly appealing at the moment. I've just come from a boot camp class at this new gym my twin sister forced me to try out.

Marley bought an online two-for-one coupon for forty bucks, so now I have to attend six of these stupid classes with her. I managed to get out of last week's class, but she wouldn't let me escape two weeks in a row. My tank is still dewy, post-exertion, I have terrible under-boob sweat, and my thong is all wonky. If I were alone in this aisle, I'd for sure fix the last issue, but suit guy is here so I must leave the thong where it is for now, wedged uncomfortably between my vagina lips.

The suit quickly shifts his attention to the shelves and picks up the jar directly in front of him, which happens to contain prunes. He inspects it, then maybe realizes what it is, because he rushes to return it, exchanging it for another item. I bite back a smile, pleased that even in my disgusting state I'm being checked out.

As suit man gives the shelf in front of him his full attention, I return the checkout favor. His attire and his posture scream money and a twinge of something like longing combined with jealousy makes my throat momentarily tight. At one time, price matching was a practice I would've laughed at—like an entitled jerk—now it's a necessity.

Suit man must be warm, considering it's late April

and we're experiencing temperatures far above average for this time of year. Based on the tapered fit of his suit, I'm guessing it's a high-end brand. He's complemented it with black patent leather shoes. Very impractical for this weather and location. Does he realize he's in the Hamptons?

He's wearing a watch, and from his profile, he can't be much beyond his early thirties. I have to assume the only reason for the watch is because it's expensive and he wants to show it off. In my head, I've already profiled him as a pretentious, rich prick who probably commutes to NYC a few times a week where he bones his secretary and has a penthouse with the barest of furniture. The rest of the time he works from home.

I return to shopping and continue down the aisle, in the opposite direction of the suit—it's my way of finding out if he's actually creeping on me or not. I keep tabs on him in my peripheral vision as I scope out more sales and more delicious, unhealthy food items. My job is to balance out all the fruit and vegetables my sister, Marley, is currently picking out in the produce section.

I grab a jar of the no-name peanut butter since we're out and the good stuff isn't on sale, dropping it in the cart. My phone keeps buzzing in my purse. It's distracting, so I give up ignoring it and check my messages.

It's my sister.

We're in the same store. It's not particularly huge, so I don't know what could be so pressing that she needs to text four thousand times instead of finding me.

ABORT SHOPPING
LEAVE NOW
Meet me in parking lot
RIAN??????

Jeez. What the heck is going on? Maybe the grocery store is being robbed. *Holy Hot Pockets*. What if there *is* a grocery store heist going down? I'm about to abandon my cart in a bid to find Marley and escape the mayhem I've created in my head. It's all very dramatic. As I turn, I come face-to-face with the suit.

I suck in a breath and slap my hand over my chest. The tank is still damp, and my skin's a little gritty with salt-sweat, so I drop it quickly, because *ew*.

"Hi." His expression is hard to read. He seems . . . smug.

"Hi, hey. Uh . . ." I wave a hand around in the air, a little flustered, and conflicted, because it's not often I get approached by a guy this hot—and in a grocery store of all places. Maybe he'll be here again next week. "I'm sorry, I'd like to stare at your pretty face, I mean . . ." Crap, why are words so hard? "I have to go."

I try to step around him, but he mirrors the movement, taking a linebacker stance, as if he's considering tackling me. Which is an odd way to stage an introduction.

"Recognize me?" he asks, one perfect eyebrow arched.

As I take him in, I wrack my brain for a time or place I might've run into him before. I don't think so, though. His light brown hair is neatly styled, and the cut of his suit highlights all of his assets. Well, the visible PG ones, anyway.

He widens his stance and crosses his arms over his chest. His very broad chest. The sleeves of his suit jacket pull tight, biceps bulging and flexing. He's a bit intimidating based on his size alone, but we're in a public grocery store, so I feel relatively safe. And he's just so gorgeous. Which is a silly reason not to be concerned, some of the most notorious serial killers are attractive men. Also, I need to find my sister, in case the grocery store is really under attack—although maybe this suit could save us.

I adopt his crossed arm pose, but I don't think I look intimidating. All I succeed in doing is awkwardly squeezing my boobs together inside my damp sports bra and jabbing the right one with the Sharpie. "Should I?"

He looks me over, a slight smirk tipping his mouth. His gaze gets stuck on the Sharpie for a few seconds before they come back up to my eyes.

It's possible I met him in a bar, but I swear I'd remember his face if I did. The bar scene is also more my sister's speed than it is mine. Oh God. It's also possible he's mistaking me for her. It's happened before.

While we look nearly identical at first to most people, we're actually fraternal twins. After a few interactions, most people can tell us apart. I have a distinctive Marilyn Monroe mole on the right side above my lip, and my eyes are amber, where Marley's are closer to green. My mouth is too big for my face, my lips a little too full and my nose too small. At least that's my perception. Marley's also the more outgoing of the two of us and an inch taller. And about ten pounds lighter.

Marley is a little less cautious than I am with men, so there have been a few uncomfortable occasions where her previous hookups have approached me, asking why I haven't returned their calls. It's too bad if this is the case, because this guy is inordinately attractive and it would be nice if he wasn't one of my sister's castoffs.

His face is a masterpiece of masculine perfection; straight nose, high cheekbones, an angular jawline that could cut glass, full lips. Especially the bottom one. The kind of full that makes me think of kissing, with tongue, of course. He's all-American handsome with a shot of alpha hotness. It's a lethal combination for the state of my already damp panties.

"I recognize *you*." He has a low, rough voice, like the delicious scrape of fine grit sandpaper.

He breaks me out of my ogle daze. He must think I'm Marley. I'm actually rather disappointed. "I think maybe you've mistaken me for someone else."

"Oh no, sweetheart." His gaze rakes over me again. I feel very naked all of a sudden. And hot. It's really hot in here. "You drive a powder-blue Buick."

"How the heck—"

"I knew it!" he shouts, eyes alight with some kind of weird, victorious satisfaction as he points a long finger with a blue-black nail at me. Maybe he slammed it in a door or something. Or based on the way he's rudely pointing, maybe someone slammed it for him. "I fucking knew it! You hit my car."

I definitely would've remembered hitting someone's car, especially if a guy this good looking was driving it. He should probably come with a warning, like: Panties may combust if you get too close, or something. I take a step back since he's all up in my grill and clearly he's not looking to flirt like I originally thought. "I have absolutely no idea what you're talking about."

"Don't play dumb with me! You think you can flip your ponytail"—he reaches out and flicks the end, which is rather startling—"flash a smile and some cleavage, and it's going to get you out of this. Well, think again, sweetheart. I guarantee my paint is still all over your bumper." He's leaning over me, face way too close to mine. So close I can see tiny gold flecks in his deep green eyes. They're an unusual shade. Dark like pine tree needles.

And he's chewing gum. Juicy Fruit. I can smell it when he breathes in my face. I would've expected a man like him to chew something more along the lines of Polar Ice, or Arctic Ice—strong mint.

I put a hand on his chest and take one deliberate step backward as he opens his mouth to resume his tangent. It's a solid chest. Extremely hard. His gaze darts down, brows furrowed. I use his distracted state to my advantage. "First of all . . ." I point my finger in his face, like he did to me. "Don't 'sweetheart' me. That's condescending. Secondly, I'm sure I would've noticed if I'd hit another car. Thirdly, there are literally hundreds of powder-blue Buicks in this stupid city. It's not an uncommon car. And I'd like to point out, that the cleavage comment was completely unnecessary and unwarranted and actually, pretty damn sexist."

He blinks a couple of times, possibly taken aback. That expression doesn't last long. His lip curls in a sneer and that pretty all-American handsomeness morphs into downright malevolent hotness. "Nice try, *sweetheart*. But there's no way I'd forget you." His gaze sweeps over me—it's not in an unappreciative way either.

I poke his hard chest. "Stop leering at me, you pervert. I don't know what kind of drugs you've been snorting, but I assure you, you've got the wrong person."

"Oh shit!" my sister's voice comes from behind me.

I turn to find Marley doing an about-face, and then she breaks into a little grapevine step as she moves back toward me. Her eyes are wide, mouth contorted into some kind of grimace as she grabs my wrist.

"What the fuck? There are two of you?" hot-crazy guy asks, eyes bouncing between us.

"We gotta go." Marley latches onto my hand and drags me down the aisle, away from crazy-hot suit.

"Whoa! Wait a damn second!"

Hot suit makes a grab for me, but Marley yanks me out of the way and shoves my shopping cart at him—hard. He's not quite quick enough to get out of the way, and the corner of the cart slams right into his crotch. He doubles over with a groan and aggressively pushes the cart aside. It ricochets into a display of canned peaches, which spill into the aisle with a deafening crash.

"What the heck, Mar?"

"Come the fuck on!" She sprints down the aisle, dragging me behind her. I'd protest, but I don't think I have much choice in the matter, considering the death grip she has on my hand, or the fact that she's assaulted the sexy-crazy suit with my shopping cart.

Marley fast-walks to the exit, glancing over her shoulder. "Act natural."

"Will you tell me what's going on? Who is that guy?"

She flips her hair over her shoulder and smiles as we pass the cashiers and the automatic doors open. Marley fast-walks down the sidewalk toward our car. "I may have tapped that guy's car last Saturday when I was shopping."

I stop walking, which brings her to a jarring halt. She yanks on my arm. "Seriously, come on. I'll explain when we're in the car."

"Nope. No way. You explain now."

Her eyes are bouncing all over the place. "It's not a big deal. I just grazed his bumper." Marley spin and tries to push me forward from behind. "Now let's get out of here before he finds us again. We should probably shop somewhere else for a while."

I stumble forward a step and then spin away from her. "You *hit* that guy's car?"

"It was more of a graze. At least I think it was." She wrings her hands and makes her *oh crap* face.

Now crazy-hot suit guy seems a lot less crazy and much more justified in his reaction. Except for the cleavage comment. That was still unnecessary. "It sure didn't seem like nothing with the way he freaked out in there."

"He's probably overreacting. Where are your keys?" She's still wringing her hands.

I pat my hip with the intention of keeping my purse safe and away from my sister. Except all I end up patting is my actual hip. I look down, running my hands over my stomach, searching for the cheap, faux-leather knockoff. "Oh fudge."

"What?"

"My purse. It's in the cart. I have to go back and get it."

Marley grabs the back of my tank. "You can't! What if he's still in there?"

"It has my identification in it, Marley. And my bank-cards, and my money, and keys to the car and the apartment. I can't leave it in there!"

Marley flails and paces around in a circle. "What if he's waiting for us to come back and get it?"

"You can stay here if you want, but I'm going back for it. I'm not leaving my purse behind because you hit some guy's car in a parking lot. I can't believe you just drove away!"

"I thought I tapped it, and then I panicked." Her fingers are at her mouth now. "I didn't want to drive up our insurance premiums over some guy and his Tesla."

"You hit a Tesla?" This keeps getting worse.

"Anyone who has the money to buy a Tesla has the money to fix it, right?" Marley says.

"So you drove off! Jeez, Marley. What were you thinking?" I shake my head. I'd like to say I'm surprised by this, but sadly I'm not. Marley doesn't always use common sense in day-to-day life.

"I don't know. I wasn't thinking. That's the problem, I guess."

I'm about to go back into the store, but stop short at the sight of the suit leaning against the side of my car, one ankle crossed over the other, all calm like. Dangling from a single finger is my knockoff, hot-pink Coach purse. "Forget something?"

CHAPTER 2

DOUBLE TROUBLE

PIERCE

Getting hit in the nuts with a full grocery cart hurts like hell. But I keep the smug smile in place as one of the twins walks toward me. The one who apparently *didn't* hit my car. The other one—who *did* hit my car—stands about twenty feet away, nervously twisting her hands.

The twin making her way closer seems fairly embarrassed. Her cheeks are a fiery shade of pink as she approaches, full lips pressed into a line that almost looks like a pout. Her eyes are on her purse, which is hanging from the end of my finger. Since she's not looking at me, I have the opportunity to check her out. Again.

Last week, I stopped at this grocery store on the way to my brother's after a meeting I had in Manhattan. It hadn't been a fun meeting, so I'd already been in a salty mood as a result. I've never been to this store before—but it's not too far from his place on the beach, and I was in a bit of a rush at the time and in need of a bathroom. I figured while I was there, I could pick up some steaks for the barbeque and a whole lot of beer. As I was standing in line, waiting to check out, I noticed a woman with a belt full of vegetables and a box of Cinnamon Toast Crunch—one of my favorite juvenile indulgences.

Once I cashed out, I headed to the parking lot, where I noticed the same woman slip into the driver's seat of her car—parked beside mine. And then I proceeded to watch her scrape the front of her car across my rear quarter panel when she pulled out of her parking spot. I stood frozen in horror as she ruined the paint job on my two-hundred-thousand-dollar car. I was expecting her to jump out of her car to check on the damage, or even to leave a note, because that's what a decent human being would do. But no, she stopped for a moment, looked around, saw me standing all the way by the entrance of the grocery store, and drove off.

And now here she is again, except there are two of her. I hadn't notice her then—she was just a woman who liked Cinnamon Toast Crunch and hit my car. But when I saw her in the cereal aisle and really got a good look at her, I noted how gorgeous she was. The kind of beautiful that numbs your tongue and jacks up your heart rate. It's odd, but despite them being nearly identical, I'm only attracted to the one approaching me. It's also good to know that I'm not into women who pull hit-and-runs.

She stops when she's about three feet away and motions behind her, to her sister. "Mar told me what she did. I'm really sorry about that. And about"—she gestures to my crotch and her nose wrinkles in a grimace—"getting hit with the cart. But in all honesty, I thought you were some weirdo who was stalking me through a grocery store, and you knew what kind of car I drive. You have to admit it's kind of creepy, plus you made that inappropriate comment about my cleavage, which was completely uncalled for." What begins as an apology quickly turns into righteous indignation. She snaps her fingers and crosses her arms over her chest. "You're looking at my boobs."

I lift my gaze to her face. "You were talking about them." She does have a legitimate point about the cleavage comment, but I'm not admitting to that yet, not when her sister pulled a hit-and-run.

She plants her fists on her hips, eyes narrowed. They're a pretty honey color, framed with long, thick lashes. She's not wearing makeup, clearly the exercise wear is authentic, and she's not one of those women who walks around in spandex all the time pretending she's been to the gym. Based on the curve of her backside, which I'd been checking out in the grocery store, she definitely puts some work into it.

"Can I have my purse back, please?" she snaps.

"Sure." When she takes a halting step toward me, I hold it out of reach. "As soon as I have your insurance and contact information."

She blows out a breath and her eyes fall closed for a few seconds. When she opens them again, she plasters on a sweet smile and holds out her hand. "It's in my purse."

"Nice try, sweetheart, but that's not going to work."

She purses her lips and her nose wrinkles. "Would you stop calling me sweetheart?"

"Give me a name I can use if it bothers you so much." Antagonizing her is ridiculously fun. I recognize I'm being an asshole, but then, I feel justified considering the three thousand dollars in damage that's been done to my Tesla. I've had to resort to driving my truck most of the week, which is not as easy to park.

She sighs. "Rian. It's Rian, and you are?"

"Ryan?" I try to fit the name with the woman standing in front of me.

"Like the boy's name, except it's spelled with an 'i' instead of a 'y,' in case you'd like to write that down somewhere." She shoots me an annoyed smile. "And you are?"

"Pierce."

"Of course." She rolls her eyes. I don't know what that's all about, and I don't get a chance to ask because she barrels on, "Well, I'd like to say it's nice to meet you, *Pierce*, but under the circumstances that'd be a lie, so . . ." She gives her head a shake and mutters something else under her breath.

Beyond my ability to appreciate her appearance, I think I might be even more attracted to how prickly she's being. "Not big on tact, are you?"

"Not really, no. Surprising I'm single, huh?" She looks up at the clear blue sky. "So, Pierce, why don't you take down my contact information so we can deal with the scratch on your steel baby, or whatever, and we can all be on our way."

"It's a three-thousand-dollar scratch."

She blinks a few times, mouth dropping open. She shoots a glare over her shoulder. "For the love of Golden Grahams. She couldn't have parked beside a Civic or something. Had to be an expensive car that's expensive to fix."

I dig my phone out of my pocket, pull up my contact list, and add her name. "Your number?" I consider how differently this might've played out if I'd approached her under alternative circumstances.

Rian rattles off a number, and as soon as it's added to my phone I call it. Muffled lyrics come from inside the purse dangling from my finger.

She arches a brow. "Satisfied?"

"I will be when I have your sister's license and insurance information."

"Mar, get over here," she calls over her shoulder.

Her sister trudges our way, looking more than a little cagey, and angry. Which is ironic since she's the one who hit my car, not the other way around. "What?"

Rian motions to me. "He needs a picture of your license and insurance information."

"My license is at home. You drove." She's still doing that hand-twisting thing. "I really thought I tapped it."

"Tapped? Feel free to check out the missing paint." I motion to the side of my car.

Rian's eyes go wide as she takes in the long scratch gouged out of the side. "Oh, for frack's sake. Look at this!" She drags her sister over to see the damage.

"That could've been there before. Maybe I really did bump his car and someone else did that and he's using us so he can get our insurance to pay for it."

"My paint is still on your car." I point to the streak of black marring the front bumper.

"Maybe you put it there," Mar says.

"Seriously? Well, if you had bothered to stop and get out of your car to look at what you did instead of driving off, you would know. You fled the scene. That's a crime," I point out. "Punishable by law."

That gets her back up. "I panicked! And obviously you can afford to have it fixed. Look at you." She motions to my suit. "What is this, an Armani?"

"It's a Tom Ford, actually, and I could've called the cops and reported it. Do you have any idea what the fine is for that?"

Rian holds a hand up in front of her sister's face. "Can you stop talking and get the insurance card out of the glove box? This is so embarrassing." She directs her next comment at me. "I appreciate you not calling the police on my sister."

"Especially since it was an accident," her sister chimes in.

Rian grabs her sister by the arm and hauls her about fifteen feet away. They have a brief whispered, but heated, conversation. When they return, Rian passes the keys to her sister. "Get in the car, please."

"What? Why?"

"Because I'd like to avoid making this situation worse." Rian has a stare down with her sister that lasts all of four seconds. She heads for the driver's side until Rian stops her. "Passenger side." There's a lot of huffing and muttering of profanity as she rounds the hood and throws herself into the passenger seat.

I feel a little bad for Rian as she rummages around in the glove compartment and produces the insurance card and her license since her sister doesn't have hers, especially considering how stressed she seems to be over the cost of the repairs. I have her number now, which is nice, although it's come with quite the price tag.

Rian rubs her forehead with a sigh. "If you can forward me the quote and the bill for the repairs, we'll work something out. I don't know if it's possible to avoid going through insurance, but we'll manage it, however it suits you best, considering the circumstances."

"I'll get everything to you in the next couple of days." I hand her back her purse.

"Great." She gives me a smile that in no way matches that single affirmative word. "I'll just wait until you leave before I do, you know, to avoid further potential damage to your very pretty, very expensive car."

"Your thoughtfulness is much appreciated." I give her a wink, to which she responds with pursed lips, flushed cheeks, and a muttered *right*.

I motion for her to get in her car before I get in mine. I even go so far as to hold the door open for her, like the gentleman I can sometimes be. She gives me a strained, slightly frustrated smile as I close her door, then get into my own car.

Her windows aren't tinted the way mine are. So despite her best efforts, I can clearly see she and her sister are having some kind of tight-lipped argument. Her sister is also flailing her arms all over the place. Which is quite entertaining. I'm only half paying attention to what's behind me as I back out of my spot, and nearly end up getting hit by a little old lady, also driving a powder-blue Buick.

Rian's eyes are wide, one hand covering her mouth as I slam on the brakes and narrowly miss losing the back end of my car.

Once the old lady passes, and I'm sure I'm in the clear, I back the rest of the way out and give Rian a jaunty wave as I pass her car.

Her sister is right. I don't need the money. In fact, if I wanted to, I could replace this Tesla with a brand new one. But that's not really how I do things. Just because I have access to excessive funds, doesn't mean I want to fritter them away on unnecessary toys. Well, more than the ones I already have. I secured three quotes for the repair to make sure my dealership wasn't trying to scam me.

Regardless, it's the principle that matters. Hitting someone else's car in a parking lot and driving away is a shitty thing to do. And while I feel bad that Rian seems to be the one taking the heat for it, someone needs to assume ownership for the mistake.

Besides, it'll give me an opportunity to talk to her again. And despite her prickly demeanor, or maybe because of it, I'm hoping it's going to be her I deal with.